ALSO BY GILES TIPPETTE . . .

Unforgettable novels of the Williams clan and the old West:

BAD NEWS . . . They wanted to hang him for a murder he didn't commit. That was their first mistake.

CROSS FIRE . . . He worked long and hard for what he had. And he'd fight to the death to keep it.

JAILBREAK . . . When a man's got his back against the wall, there's only one thing to do. Break it down.

HARD ROCK . . . Rough country breeds a rougher breed of man . . .

SIXKILLER . . . No one fights harder than the man who fights for his kin.

GUNPOINT . . . There are two things more important than money: honor and survival . . .

AVAILABLE FROM JOVE BOOKS

Praise for Giles Tippette's novels:

"TIPPETTE CAN WRITE ROUGH AND TUMBLE ACTION SUPERBLY." —*Chattanooga Times*

"TOUGH, GUTSY, AND FASCINATING." —*New York Newsday*

"TIPPETTE CAN PLOT AWAY WITH THE BEST OF THEM." —*Dallas Morning News*

Books by Giles Tippette

Fiction

THE BANK ROBBER
THE TROJAN COW
THE SURVIVALIST
THE SUNSHINE KILLERS
AUSTIN DAVIS
WILSON'S WOMAN
WILSON YOUNG ON THE RUN
THE TEXAS BANK ROBBING COMPANY
WILSON'S GOLD
WILSON'S REVENGE
WILSON'S CHOICE
WILSON'S LUCK
HARD LUCK MONEY
CHINA BLUE
BAD NEWS
CROSS FIRE
JAILBREAK
HARD ROCK
SIXKILLER
GUNPOINT
DEAD MAN'S POKER

Nonfiction

THE BRAVE MEN
SATURDAY'S CHILDREN
DONKEY BASEBALL AND OTHER SPORTING DELIGHTS
I'LL TRY ANYTHING ONCE

DEAD MAN'S POKER

GILES TIPPETTE

JOVE BOOKS, NEW YORK

DEAD MAN'S POKER

A Jove Book / published by arrangement with
the author

PRINTING HISTORY
Jove edition / February 1993

ISBN: 0-515-11042-6

Jove Books are published by The Berkley Publishing Group,
200 Madison Avenue, New York, New York 10016.
The name "JOVE" and the "J" logo
are trademarks belonging to Jove Publications, Inc.

PRINTED IN THE UNITED STATES OF AMERICA

10 9 8 7 6 5 4 3 2 1

CHAPTER 1

I was hurt, though how badly I didn't know. Some three hours earlier I'd been shot, the ball taking me in the left side of the chest about midway up my rib cage. I didn't know if the slug had broken a rib or just passed between two of them as it exited my back. I'd been in Galveston, trying to collect a gambling debt, when, like a fool kid, I'd walked into a setup that I'd ordinarily have seen coming from the top of a tree stump. I was angry that I hadn't collected the debt, I was more than angry that I'd been shot, but I was furious at myself for having been suckered in such a fashion. I figured if it ever got around that Wilson Young had been gotten that easy, all of the old enemies I'd made through the years would start coming out of the woodwork to pick over the carcass.

But, in a way, I was lucky. By rights I should have been killed outright, facing three of them as I had and having nothing to put me on the alert. They'd had guns in their hands by the time I realized it wasn't money I was going to get, but lead.

Now I was rattling along on a train an hour out of Galveston, headed for San Antonio. It had been lucky, me catching that train just as it was pulling out. Except for that, there was an excellent chance that I would have been incarcerated in Galveston and looking at more trouble than I'd been in in a long time. After the shooting I'd managed to get away from the office where the trouble had happened and make my way toward the depot. I'd been wearing a frock coat of a good quality linen when I'd sat down with

1

Phil Sharp to discuss the money he owed me. Because it was a hot day, I took the coat off and laid it over the arm of the chair I was sitting in. When the shooting was over, I grabbed the coat and the little valise I was carrying and ducked and dodged my way through alleyways and side streets. I came up from the border on the train so, of course, I didn't have a horse with me.

But I did have a change of clothes, having expected to be overnight in Galveston. In an alley I took off my bloody shirt, inspected the wound in my chest, and then wrapped the shirt around me, hoping to keep the blood from showing. Then I put on a clean shirt that fortunately was dark and not white like the one I'd been shot in. After that I donned my frock coat, picked up my valise, and made my way to the train station. I did not know if the law was looking for me or not, but I waited until the train was ready to pull out before I boarded it. I had a round-trip ticket so there'd been no need for me to go inside the depot.

I knew I was bleeding, but I didn't know how long it would be before the blood seeped through my makeshift bandage and then through my shirt and finally showed on my coat.

All I knew was that I was hurting and hurting bad and that I was losing blood to the point where I was beginning to feel faint. It was a six-hour ride to San Antonio, and I was not at all sure I could last that long. Even if the blood didn't seep through enough to call it to someone's attention, I might well pass out. But I didn't have many options. There were few stops between Galveston and San Antonio, it being a kind of a spur line, and what there were would be small towns that most likely wouldn't even have a doctor. I could get off in one and lay up in a hotel until I got better, but that didn't much appeal to me. I wanted to know how bad I was hurt, and the only way I was going to know that was to hang on until I could get to some good medical attention in San Antone.

I was Wilson Young, and in that year of 1896, I was thirty-two years old. For fourteen of those years, beginning when I was not quite fifteen, I had been a robber. I'd robbed banks, I'd robbed money shipments, I'd robbed high-stakes poker games, I'd robbed rich people carrying more cash than they ought to have been, but mostly I'd robbed banks. But then, about four years past, I'd left the owlhoot trail and set out to become a citizen that did not constantly have to be on the lookout for the law. Through the years I'd lost a lot of friends and a lot of members of what the newspapers had chosen to call my "gang"—the Texas Bank Robbing Gang in one headline.

I'd even lost a wife, a woman I'd taken out of a whorehouse in the very same town I was now fleeing from. But Marianne hadn't been a whore at heart; she'd just been kind of briefly and unwillingly forced into it in much the same way I'd taken up robbing banks.

I had been making progress in my attempt to achieve a certain amount of respectability. At first I'd set up on the Mexican side of the border, making occasional forays into Texas to sort of test the waters. Then, as a few years passed and certain amounts of money found their way into the proper hands, I was slowly able to make my way around Texas. I had not been given a pardon by the governor, but emissaries of his had indicated that the state of Texas was happy to have no further trouble with Wilson Young and that the past could be forgotten so long as I did nothing to revive it.

And now had come this trouble. The right or wrong of my position would have nothing to do with it. I was still Wilson Young, and if I was in a place where guns were firing and men were being shot, the prevailing attitude was going to be that it was my doing.

So it wasn't only the wound that was troubling me greatly; it was also the worry about the aftermath of what had begun as a peaceful and lawful business trip. If I didn't die from my wound, there was every chance that I would become a wanted man again, and there would go the new life I had built for myself. And not only that life of peace and legality, but also a great deal of money that I had put into a business in Del Rio, Texas, right along the banks of the Rio Grande. Down there, a stone's throw from Mexico, I owned the most high-class saloon and gambling emporium and whorehouse as there was to be found in Texas. I had at first thought to put it on the Mexican side of the river, but the *mordida,* the bribes, that the officials would have

3

taken convinced me to build it in Texas, where the local law was not quite so greedy. But now, if trouble were to come from this shooting, I'd have to be in Mexico, and my business would be in Texas. It might have been only a stone's throw away, but for me, it might just as well have been a thousand miles. And I'd sunk damn near every cent I had in the place.

My side was beginning to hurt worse with every mile. I supposed it was my wound, but the train was rattling around and swaying back and forth like it was running on crooked rails. I was in the last car before the caboose, and every time we rounded a curve, the car would rock back and forth like it was fixing to quit the tracks and take off across the prairie. Fortunately, the train wasn't very crowded and I had a seat to myself. I was sort of sitting in the middle of the double cushion and leaning to my right against the wall of the car. It seemed to make my side rest easier to stretch it out like that. My valise was at my feet, and with a little effort, I bent down and fumbled it open with my right hand. Since my wound had begun to stiffen up, my left arm had become practically useless—to use it would almost put tears in my eyes.

I had a bottle of whiskey in my valise, and I fumbled it out, pulled the cork with my teeth and then had a hard pull. There was a spinsterish middle-aged lady sitting right across the aisle from me, and she give me such a look of disapproval that I thought for a second that she was going to call the conductor and make a commotion. As best I could, I got the cork back in the bottle and then hid it out of sight between my right side and the wall of the car.

Outside, the terrain was rolling past. It was the coastal prairie of south Texas, acres and acres of flat, rolling plains that grew the best grazing grass in the state. It would stay that way until the train switched tracks and turned west for San Antonio. But that was another two hours away. My plan was to get myself fixed up in San Antone and then head out for Del Rio and the Mexican side of the border just as fast as I could. From there I'd try and find out just what sort of trouble I was in.

That was, if I lived that long.

With my right hand I pulled back the left side of my coat, lifting it gently, and looked underneath. I could see just the beginning of a stain on the dark blue shirt I'd changed into. Soon it would soak through my coat and someone would notice it. I had a handkerchief in my pocket, and I got that out and slipped it inside my shirt, just under the stain. I had no way of holding it there, but so long as I kept still, it would stay in place.

Of course I didn't know what was happening at my back. For all I knew the blood had already seeped through and stained my coat. That was all right so long as my back was against the seat, but it would be obvious as soon as I got up. I just had to hope there would be no interested people once I got to San Antone and tried to find a doctor.

I knew the bullet had come out my back. I knew it because I'd felt around and located the exit hole while I'd been hiding in the alley, using one shirt for a bandage and the other for a sop. Of course the hole in my back was bigger than the entrance hole the bullet had made. It was always that way, especially if a bullet hit something hard like a bone and went to tumbling or flattened out. I could have stuck my thumb in the hole in my back.

About the only good thing I could find to feel hopeful about was the angle of the shot. The bullet had gone in very near the bottom of my ribs and about six inches from my left side. But it had come out about only three or four inches from my side. That meant there was a pretty good chance that it had missed most of the vital stuff and such that a body has got inside itself. I knew it hadn't nicked my lungs because I was breathing fine. But there is a whole bunch of other stuff inside a man that a bullet ain't going to do a bit of good. I figured it had cracked a rib for sure because it hurt to breathe deep, but that didn't even necessarily have to be so. It was hurting so bad anyway that I near about couldn't separate the different kinds of hurt.

A more unlikely man than Phil Sharp to give me my seventh gunshot wound I could not have imagined. I had ended my career on the owlhoot trail with my body having lived through six gunshots. That, as far as I was concerned, had been aplenty. By rights I should have been dead, and there had been times when I had been given up for dead.

But once off the outlaw path I'd thought my days of having my blood spilt were over. Six was enough.

And then Phil Sharp had given me my seventh. As a gambler I didn't like the number. There was nothing lucky about it that I could see, and I figured that anything that wasn't lucky had to be unlucky.

Part of my bad luck was because I *was* Wilson Young. Even though I'd been retired for several years, I was still, strictly speaking, a wanted man. And if anybody had cause to take interest in my condition, it might mean law—and law would mean trouble.

For that matter Phil Sharp and the three men he'd had with him might have thought they could shoot me without fear of a murder charge because of the very fact of my past and my uncertain position with regard to the law, both local and through the state. Hell, for all I knew some of those rewards that had been posted on my head might still be lying around waiting for someone to claim them. It hadn't been so many years past that my name and my likeness had been on Wanted posters in every sheriff's office in every county in Texas.

I had gone to see Phil Sharp because he'd left my gambling house owing me better than twenty thousand dollars. I didn't, as an ordinary matter, advance credit at the gambling tables, but Sharp had been a good customer in the past and I knew him to be a well-to-do man. He owned a string of warehouses along the docks in Galveston, which was the biggest port in Texas. The debt had been about a month old when I decided to go and see him. When he'd left Del Rio, he'd promised to wire me the money as soon as he was home, but it had never come. Letters and telegrams jogging his memory had done no good, so I'd decided to call on him in person. It wasn't just the twenty thousand; there was also the matter that it ain't good policy for a man running a casino and cathouse to let word get around that he's careless about money owed him. And in that respect I was still the Wilson Young it was best not to get too chancy with. Sharp knew my reputation, and I did not figure to have any trouble with him. If he didn't have the twenty thousand handy, I figured we could come to some sort of agreement as to how he could pay it off. I had wired him before I left

Del Rio that I was planning a trip to Houston and was going to look in on him in Galveston. He'd wired back that he'd be expecting me.

I saw him in his office in the front of one of the warehouses he owned down along the waterfront. He was behind his desk when I was shown in, getting up to shake hands with me. He was dressed like he usually was, in an expensive suit with a shiny vest and a big silk tie. Sharp himself was a little round man in his forties with a kind of baby face and a look that promised you could trust him with your virgin sister. Except I'd seen him without the suit and vest, chasing one of my girls down the hall at four o'clock in the morning with a bottle of whiskey in one hand and the handle to his hoe in the other. I'd also seen him at the poker table with sweat pouring off his face as he tried to make a straight beat a full house. It hadn't then and it probably never would.

He acted all surprised that I hadn't gotten my money, claiming he'd mailed it to me no less than a week ago. He said, "I got to apologize for the delay, but I had to use most of my ready cash on some shipments to England. Just let me step in the next room and look at my canceled checks. I'd almost swear I saw it just the other day. Endorsed by you."

Like I said, he looked like a man that might shoot you full of holes in a business deal, but not the sort of man who could use or would use a gun.

He got up from his desk and went to a door at the back, just to my right. I took off my coat and laid it over the arm of the chair, it being warm in the office. I was sitting kind of forward on the chair, feeling a little uneasy for some reason. It was that, but it was mainly the way Sharp opened the back door that probably saved my life. When you're going through a door, you pull it to you and step to your left, toward the opening, so as to pass through. But Sharp pulled open the door and then stepped back. In that instant, I slid out of the chair I was sitting in and down to my knees. As I did, three men with hoods pulled over their heads came through the door with pistols in their hands. Their first volley would have killed me if I'd still been sitting in the chair. But they fired at where I'd been, and by the time they could cock their pistols for another round, I had my revolver in my hand and was firing. They never got off another shot; all three went down under my rapid-fire volley.

Then I became aware that Phil Sharp was still in the room, just by the open door. I was about to swing my revolver around on him when I saw a little gun in his hand. He fired, once, and hit me in the chest. I knew it was a low-caliber gun because the blow of the slug just twitched at my side, not even knocking me off balance.

But it surprised me so that it gave Sharp time to cut through the open door and disappear into the blackness of the warehouse. I fired one shot after him, knowing it was in vain, and then pulled the trigger on an empty chamber.

I had not brought any extra cartridges with me. In the second I stood there with an empty gun, I couldn't remember why I hadn't brought any extras, but the fact was that I was standing there, wounded, with what amounted to a useless piece of iron in my fist. As quick as I could, expecting people to suddenly come bursting in the door, I got over to where the three men were laying on the floor and began to check their pistols to see if they fired the same caliber ammunition I did. But I was out of luck. My revolver took a .40-caliber shell; all three of the hooded men were carrying .44-caliber pistols.

Two of the men were dead, but one of them was still alive. I didn't have time to mess with him, but I turned him over so he could hear me good and said, "Tell Phil Sharp I ain't through with him. Nor your bunch either."

Then I got out of there and started making my way for the train depot. At first the wound bothered me hardly at all. In fact at first I thought I'd just been grazed. But then, once outside, I saw the blood spreading all over the front of my shirt and I knew that I was indeed hit. I figured I'd been shot by nothing heavier than a .32-caliber revolver but a .32 can kill you just as quick as a cannon if it hits you in the right place.

The men I'd shot were members of the Galveston Citizen's Vigilante Committee. I knew that because Phil Sharp had been bragging about it the last time he'd been in Del Rio. He'd bragged that he'd organized it and was the leader and that the committee was more powerful than any other form of law in all of Galveston. He'd even told me about the hoods they wore. Said his was black because he was the head honcho.

So I hadn't just shot three men; I'd shot three members of a law and order organization that might or might not have been legal. And if the men were, indeed, considered law, it wasn't going to make a hairpin's worth of difference that I'd shot them in self-defense. Galveston, it seemed, was a rough town on account of all the sailors from different countries and different ports. Sharp had said most of the sailors were rough trade and that they'd caused so many killings and holdups and beatings and such that the local law couldn't handle them. He and other important men in the shipping business had decided that something had to be done so they organized the vigilante committee.

But it appeared to me that Mr. Sharp wasn't above using his committee for something other than good works for the city. I wondered if the man I'd only wounded would pass on my words to Mr. Sharp that our business wasn't concluded. I had gut-shot the man, and he might not live to pass on any messages.

As *I* might not live to do much of anything, if I didn't get some relief soon. My whole left side was now on fire and throbbing so that I figured anybody looking would be able to see the beat of the pounding pain. And I was starting to feel more and more weak, a sure sign I was losing too much blood and a sure sign I'd be a walking advertisement, as soon as I got off the train, of a man who'd been shot. That was going to cause just some little curiosity, people being what they were.

And I was armed with an empty revolver and no extra cartridges. The reason I had not brought along any extra ammunition was that I'd taken too long saying good-bye to Evita, the woman who ran the bordello part of my operation, and whom I thought of as my girlfriend—or at least my main girlfriend. As a consequence I'd rushed my packing, and the box of cartridges I'd meant to bring was still sitting on top of the bureau in the bedroom of my ranch house in Mexico, just across the river from Del Rio.

About then the conductor came walking through the car. He said, "Bay City, Bay City, next stop. Bay City, ten minutes. Bay City, ten minutes."

I thought, Only to Bay City. Only sixty miles. And God knew how much further to the junction where the train switched lines to head for San Antonio. Of course I could get off in Bay City and try and find some help. Maybe they had a whorehouse, and I could get one of the girls to fix me up. Give her a few dollars and at least get bandaged up so I wouldn't be showing blood through my clothes.

But I didn't know if they had a whorehouse in Bay City. Besides, all whores weren't good-hearted. In fact, some of the meanest women I'd ever met had been whores.

I wondered if I had any friends in Bay City. I couldn't remember any. It seemed like all my friends were as far away from me as I was from them.

I began to notice I was feeling a little feverish. I put my palm to my forehead and felt it clammy with sweat. It was becoming damn clear I was going to have to do something and in pretty short order.

I had lost weight since my outlaw days. I didn't know how that had worked out, but it had. Back a few years I'd been about six foot tall and weighed 190 pounds. I was still six foot tall, but now my weight had dropped to 175, and that had been muscle. I couldn't figure it. In my owlhoot days I'd never done no what you might call physical work. The heaviest thing I ever lifted was somebody else's money. But once I'd given it up and sort of settled down, I'd began to drop muscle. It was a thought to ponder on. My eyes were another. Sometimes they were gray and sometimes green. I could never be sure which color they'd be when I got up in the morning. A rich woman had once told me I was handsome in an unimportant way. I hadn't understood what she'd meant by that, but I'd figured that any woman who could get rich on her own without either stealing or going on her back must be pretty smart. I had taken to using it after that. The only surviving member of my gang was a black Mexican named Chulo. He was, without a doubt, the meanest-looking, ugliest Mexican outlaw you ever saw. I used to tell him he was ugly in an unimportant way. He didn't understand it either.

But I damn sure knew I wished I had him with me right then and there. But he was back in Del Rio watching the store. Chulo wasn't very smart, but he was hell for loyal.

The train began slowing and then slowed some more and finally jolted to a stop. The conductor come through again saying, "Bay City, Bay City, all out for Bay City."

The jolt hadn't done my side no good, but the stillness of the car after all the swaying and shifting was a relief. Across the aisle the spinsterish woman got up and got her little carpetbag valise off the overhead rack and went down the aisle. It was a temptation to get up and follow her, but I figured if her kind lived in the town, I wouldn't make it five steps before I got throwed in jail. Give a man a dirty look for taking a drink when his whole side was on fire. She reminded me of my old-maid aunt back in Corpus Christi who'd raised me after my parents had died. Or at least she'd *thought* she was raising me. In actual fact I'd been handling most of that job myself. But I was grateful to her for one thing: She'd been a schoolteacher, and one way or the other, she'd kept me in school through the tenth grade. I hadn't appreciated it at the time, but I'd come to later in life when I could see what benefit an education was to a man. Of course it hadn't helped much robbing banks, but it had put me a cut above most of the other riffraff I was running with and had consequently brought me some respect before I'd begun to earn it with a revolver.

I took advantage of the stillness of the train to have another pretty good pull off the whiskey bottle. It helped a little, but I was more worried about the way I was feeling feverish and faint. I didn't know how long it took for a gunshot wound to get infected, but I didn't reckon it was long. And then there was the matter of all the blood I was losing. The hole in the front of my chest had maybe clotted, but I doubted damn serious that the exit wound was going to close itself without some medical help. I moved a little against the seat, trying to see what would happen if I eased off the pressure I'd been holding against my back, holding it tight against the seat in hopes it would help stop the bleeding. All the movement did was make the wound start throbbing anew.

Pretty soon the train started up, and the first jolt, as the couplings between the cars took up slack, damn near fetched me. I sucked in air through my gritted teeth and just kind of steeled myself against the pain. I thought of the distance ahead to San Antonio and the time that would be involved. It was a long way and a lot of hours. And even after the train got there, there was going to be the problem of getting to a doctor or some kind of infirmary or a hotel or a friend's house.

And, all of a sudden, I knew I just wasn't going to last. I was either going to pass out before then or I was going to bleed to death. I was going to have to do something, and I was going to have to do it the next opportunity.

It all made me angry as hell. I reckoned a man couldn't remember pain, and I ought to know, but it seemed like this little old piddling gunshot was hurting worse and giving me more trouble than any of the others I'd experienced.

I kind of laid my head back against the seat rest and tried to think. It ain't as easy to think when you are hurting like hell and kind of light-headed, not as easy as it is when you are in first-class condition. I was hoping like hell the plug I'd tried to stick in the hole in my back was still in place and stopping some of the blood. If it wasn't, the blood was going to run down my leg and fill up my boot when I stood up.

I was trying to think what might be the best stop for me to get off at, a stop where I might have some hope of catching a doctor. But the hell of it was that I didn't know the line all that well. I'd come from Del Rio direct to San Antonio and then direct from San Antonio to Galveston. This little spur line I was on was really the route to the border at Laredo, and if I'd had time to catch it, there was an express that ran straight from Galveston to the border. But this little bucket I was on seemed to want to stop at every crossroads or where the last man watered a horse. I couldn't think what the next town after Bay City was likely to be or how big it would be.

The train had been going for about another twenty or twenty-five minutes. It was hard for me to really know because I was getting weaker and feeling more and more like I was fixing to fall over on my head or just plain slip out of the coach seat. Outside the window the country was getting lusher. It was all rolling pasture and prairie with green, green grass anywhere from a foot to a foot-and-a-half high. Here and there were little thickets of mesquite trees and some post oak and live oak and now and then a tall cottonwood. It was the kind of country does a cattleman's heart good to just look at, but since I wasn't no cattleman, what I wanted to see was some buildings and some people, at least one of which was a doctor. I didn't know much about infection, but I figured I was getting it judging from the way I felt. I reckoned I could put a mirror up in front of my face and I'd be pale. I felt the sweat on my forehead again, and I could damn near feel the fever running through my body. It was only late April and the weather was very mild, so I knew I wasn't sweating on account of any heat on the outside of my body. As best I could with one arm I cracked the window beside me and leaned my head down to the opening at the bottom and breathed some of the outside air. Generally the ladies riding in the coach didn't like the windows opened all the way on account of the danger of the wind blowing their hair or blowing their hats off or cinders from the engine's smokestack blowing in and burning holes in their clothes.

So I had just opened the window a little, but the fresh air wasn't doing me much good, mainly because fresh air wasn't what I needed. I was trying to figure out how I was going to get off the train without attracting attention. I figured I could maybe carry my hat and kind of hold it over my heart like the flag was passing, but even as faint as I was getting, I realized that would look sort of ridiculous. No, the thing to do was get up, get off, and go on about my business as if I'd never had a bloodstain on my clothes in my life. That was if I could get up and go about my business.

Just then I saw the conductor coming through our car. He said, "Blessing, Blessing. Ten minutes to Blessing."

Blessing!

My God, was a place ever better named? There was help in Blessing. I didn't know if they had a doctor, but I knew I had a friend there, a man named Justa Williams. He and his family were ranchers, big ranchers, and wealthy. I figured they owned about half the town also. I knew they owned the bank, because I'd had occassion to rob it some six or seven years past, when I was still in that line of work.

But that was done and forgotten. Not more than a year past I'd had occasion to do Justa a good turn when he'd been down in my part of the country. In the couple of weeks I'd known him then, we'd become what you might call friends. He was near about my age and of a like character and temperament, though he hadn't ever robbed any banks so far as I knew. But I'd helped him with a sort of tricky situation, and he'd said if he could ever help me, just to get him word. And I figured he was good for it or else I was a mighty poor judge of character. He just hadn't struck me as the kind of man who'd forget a turn in his favor.

So it was with some hope that I felt the train slowing as we started to come into Blessing. Out the window I could see a few outlying shacks and a big cattle auction barn and then some more houses, and then the train was beginning to brake as we headed into the depot. I took a quick, hard slug out of the bottle and shoved it back in my valise and got ready to see if I was capable of getting off a train. The whiskey hit the bottom of my stomach and commenced to spread, and I felt a little better. Whiskey will do that, give you a little boost right off the bat, but it don't last. I figured the long slug I'd taken down would give me strength for about ten minutes. I didn't reckon to waste any of it.

Then I could hear the wheels squealing as iron skidded on iron and the train slowly came to a halt. The conductor was coming back through saying, "Blessing, Blessing, all out for Blessing."

I got slowly to my feet, gripping the seat in front of me with my left hand and holding my valise in my right. I stood like that for a second or two, making sure I wasn't too light-headed. I was the only passenger for Blessing, at least in that car, and I made my way carefully back to the door, holding onto the backs of the seats as I passed. The door at the end was heavy and hard to open. I was trying to use my right hand only, having transferred my valise to my left, and I was having trouble. I couldn't believe I was so weak I couldn't handle a passenger car door, but that was the fact of the matter. About the time I got it half-open and

14

was trying to wedge it further back with the toe of my boot, it was suddenly taken out of my hand and swung wide. The conductor was behind me. He said, "There you go, sir."

I looked back at him. I said, "Thanks."

He give me a good, hard stare. He said, "Ain't you ticketed to San Antonio?"

I swallowed. I didn't have no time for an extended discussion of my travel plans. I said, "Friend here. Forgot about him. Stop off."

He looked at me even closer, but fortunately he was just looking me in the face. He said, "You all right, sir?"

I said, "Yeah, fine."

"You are mighty white. You sick?"

"Get train sick," I said. "Motion. Be all right on the ground." Actually, it wasn't that much of a lie. There had been a time when I got train sick. Once me and some friends of mine had tried to rob a train, and the barrage of fire we'd got from the guards in the mail car had made more than one of us sick.

But I didn't explain that to the conductor, and he helped me down the steps and onto the depot platform. He said, "Hope you get to feeling better, sir."

I nodded my head and set off walking toward what I reckoned to be the center of town. I was looking for a hotel. As I was about to leave the depot platform, I chanced to spot a railroad hired hand unloading some freight. I asked him about a hotel, and he pointed me toward town. He said, "Be right thar in the middle."

"What's the name?"

He shook his head. "Don't matter. Onliest one we got. Jest says hotel. Right thar on the front."

It was about a quarter of a mile to the hotel. It looked like about the longest quarter of a mile I'd ever seen. Just into the main part of the town a wooden boardwalk ran along in front of the stores. I couldn't tell how big Blessing was, but I figured it to be somewhere around a thousand folks. Surely a town of that size would have a doctor, but then a man never knew.

Walking along the wide boardwalk, I passed saloons and mercantile stores and a ladies store and a café and a smithy. I could feel the sweat pouring off me, and I was growing more and more faint with every step. If that hotel was much further, I didn't reckon I was going to make it.

And then I passed an office that said Sheriff Lew Vara on the door, and I picked up my step as best I could. As I walked, I was meeting people. They seemed to be giving me an exceptionally thorough going over, and I didn't know if it was because of the way I looked or because I was a stranger.

Then, finally, I crossed an open space between buildings, stepped back up on the boardwalk, and the door to the hotel was there. It was a light screen door, and I managed it without any trouble and stepped into the lobby. It was cool and dim inside, and I paused for a moment to gather my strength and then headed for the counter where the desk clerk was. He looked up as I come up to him. "Yes, sir?" he said. He was a youngish sort of man wearing a dandy's high collar and a necktie.

I set my valise down and leaned against the counter. I said, "Need a room. On the first floor."

He spun the register around for me. He said, "Will you be wanting that for just the one night?" I could see him glancing at my front where the stain was showing through.

I signed the register as best I could. I used my real name, but I doubted it made much difference, my script being what it was. I said, "Would you know a Mr. Justa Williams?"

He give me a kind of startled look. He said, "Why, yes. Of course I would. The Williams family is well known hereabouts."

I was holding myself together. I said, trying to sound like I was just fine, "I need to get message to Mr. Williams." I took my roll of bills out of my pocket and peeled off a ten. I put it on the desk counter. I said, "You reckon you could arrange to get a message taken out to him? It's mighty important. I need it done quick."

He looked at the ten dollars. He said, "Why, that could be handled, sir. But I don't know how fast. The Williams ranch is seven miles out of town, about, and it being the middle of the afternoon, he is most likely out on his ranch somewheres."

I was starting to have a little trouble breathing. I said, "Just give me a piece of paper so I can write a note." I put another ten dollars on the countertop. I said, "For that kind of money somebody ought to be found who will make an effort."

"Yes, sir!" he said. He whipped around and put a piece of paper and a pencil in front of me. I printed out

> JUSTA
> I APPEAR TO BE HERE IN YOUR TOWN AGAIN THOUGH I AIN'T NOWHERE NEAR YOUR BANK. I'D APPRECIATE YOU GETTING ON INTO TOWN AND PAYING ME A VISIT AT THE HOTEL. DON'T BOTHER TO LOOK FOR THE GUITAR PLAYER AS I DON'T FEEL MUCH LIKE DANCING. YOU MIGHT HURRY.

I just signed it "WILSON" and then folded it and handed it to the clerk. He'd read it, but I didn't much give a damn. It wouldn't tell him anything. The reference to the guitar player was a joke me and Justa had kept running while he was down in Del Rio. I wanted him to understand that the part about me not feeling like dancing meant I wasn't in too good of a shape. I said, as the clerk took the note, "I'll appreciate this."

"Yes, sir," he said.

I nodded my head at the two ten-dollar bills. "Pick up the money," I said.

The clerk was looking at me hard. He said, "Are you a friend of Mr. Williams?"

I nodded. Even if I wasn't swaying on my feet, I felt like I was. I said, "I think I am. I reckon he'd agree with me."

The clerk looked hesitant. He said, "Then I really shouldn't take this money, sir. You see, the Williams family owns this hotel and—"

I wiped at my brow. I said, "Look, fella, I don't give a damn about the money. Buy yourself a horse or something, but just get somebody started for Justa Williams. You got a doctor in this town?"

"Yes, sir, we got a fine doctor, Dr. Adams."

I leaned up against the desk. "Send for him. Right away. And point me at my room. I ain't feeling just real good."

He was looking at my shirt where the blood was. He said, "Are you hurt, sir?"

"Boy," I said a little unsteadily, "I can't talk much longer. I'm hurt. Fell on a railroad spike. Now will you get a doctor over here and get me to bed and get that note off to Justa!"

He finally moved. I didn't know if it was because he got scared I was going to pitch over on my head or because I was a friend of Justa's, but he finally come out from behind the desk and helped me to my room, which was on the first floor, just across the lobby. It was good that it was close because I wasn't going much further. I sat down on the bed and pitched my hat over on a little table. The desk clerk kept standing around looking worried. He asked me if he could give me any help with anything. I finally took pity on him and let him help me off with my boots and my coat. I figured if he got a look at all the blood on my shirt, it would speed him along. He just saw the front side, but he said, "Oh, my!" He really was younger than I'd thought. He said, "I think I'd better hurry for the doctor."

As he was going out of the room, I said, "Get that note off to Mr. Williams."

He said, "Yes, sir!" from the hall, and then I heard him yelling for somebody named Nathan. "Nathan!" he yelled. "Nathan! Damn you! Where are you?"

I took a drink of whiskey and then, as best I could, worked my shirt off, leaving just the other shirt that I'd wrapped around me as a bandage. Of course I was bloody as hell. The bandage-shirt hadn't held all the blood, and little runlets of it had trickled down my side and my belly. Fortunately they'd been light and had dried. I didn't bother taking off the shirt-bandage. The doctor would do that, and besides, I didn't want to see. I took another drink of whiskey, set the bottle on the bed stand, and then lay back sideways across the bed. I was very hopeful that Justa would get the message quick and then lose no time in getting into town. The doctor was not going to believe I'd fell on a railroad spike. He was going to know I'd been shot, and he might just mention it to the local law, and the law just might come around wondering how I'd managed to get myself shot. The local law might even have a telegram from Galveston to be on the lookout for a wounded man who'd killed at least two of Mr. Phil Sharp's Vigilante Committee. I figured if Sharp had gone to the law, they'd have sent out word to every lawman within reasonable reach of any escape route I'd take.

And if the law came and I was called upon to do some explaining, I wanted Justa there, because I figured he had influence in the town. I knew he couldn't bend the law, but I reckoned he could get me a fair hearing and maybe even see to my comfort. The only thing I knew that was worse than being in jail was being in jail with a gunshot wound. The last can be a mighty uncomfortable experience if the folks running the jail ain't especially disposed to worry about whether you are enjoying yourself or not.

While I waited for the doctor, I lay there and thought about Phil Sharp. There had been a time, in my younger days, when I'd been a very angry man. But, as the years had passed, I had done my fair share of mellowing and taking a different view of events. Not that I had ever been what you might call a vicious man or a vengeful man or even all that dangerous. I wasn't a good man to go to messing with, but I could honestly say that I had never shot nobody that wasn't trying to shoot me, and I had even walked away from situations where I knew the man or men lined up against me didn't have much of a chance. For whatever reason, I had been gifted with an extraordinary speed and reflexes and a sense of premonition that let me know of danger even before it presented itself.

I knew, from the two weeks that I'd spent with Justa Williams down at my place in Del Rio, that we shared many of those same characteristics and viewpoints. Not that he was as fast as I was or as good a shot; few were. In fact I had never met my equal in that respect. Most of the gun hands of reputation that I knew were either backshooters or men who always arranged to have the odds on their side in some manner or other. Without exception they were ruffians and thieves and murderers and scoundrels, mostly without a single redeeming quality to offer society. I had met a few of them in my time. Suffice it to say that they were dead and I wasn't.

But Justa Williams was a man I could respect. Even without the natural gifts that I had been given, he was not a man I would want to be at cross-purposes with. I figured that, like myself, he made a damn good friend and a mighty bad enemy. I was content that we just go on being friends. Justa Williams had a natural gift that I figured was more important than my hand speed or the way a bullet always went exactly where I wanted it to. His gift was his brains. He could out-think the devil and steal his pitchfork and tie a knot in his tail while he was doing it. I knew because I'd watched him do that very thing to a man named J. C. Flood down in Del Rio who was the closest thing to the devil we had to display.

So I wanted him in town as quick as he could get there in case there was to be trouble of any kind. Meanwhile I just lay there and wondered if the doctor was ever going to come.

He came bustling in, not even bothering to knock, about a year later. He had his little black bag with him and was wearing a vest with an open-collared shirt. He was a little sort of short man with quick movements and not a hell of a lot of hair, though I didn't figure him to be much over thirty years of age. He said, "Well, what have we got here? Heard you got yourself stuck with a railroad spike. How did you manage to do that? Here, turn around and lay lengthwise on the bed."

All the time he was talking, he was opening his bag and taking stuff out and laying it on the bed. I got turned around like he told me and got my head on the pillow. He leaned over and took off the makeshift bandage I'd made out of the shirt I'd got shot in. He looked at the wound. He said, "Hmmmmm." Then he had me roll over on my right side and looked at my back. He said, "Hmmmm" again.

When he had me back on my back, he got out of his bag a bottle of some kind of clear liquid and then took something that appeared to be a funnel of some kind and rammed the end of it in the hole in my side. I kind of sucked in my breath. He said, "Oh, you haven't felt anything yet. You like alcohol, don't you?"

I was kind of clenching my teeth. I said, "Yeah."

He said, "You can't drink this kind. Grain alcohol. Very strong." About then he poured some of that clear liquid into that funnel kind of thing, and it felt like someone had run a red-hot poker right clean through me. I let out just a little smothered moan and kind of shook all over.

The doctor said, "That hurt?"

My teeth were still clenched together. As best I could I said, "Seemed like it did. Might have just imagined it."

He said, "That's funny. I didn't feel a thing."

That was enough to make me want to shoot him. I reckoned he'd used that old saw about a thousand times. But I didn't say anything. I figured we was just getting started, and I didn't see no point in getting crossways with him.

He said, "That alcohol was just to kind of clean things out inside. That must have been a damn long railroad spike you fell on. Went completely through you."

"That so," I said. I was kind of panting a little.

He said, "Yeah. If Wayne, the desk clerk, hadn't told me different, I'd have swore somebody shot you."

He had a kind of dry way of speaking that I favored in a situation that was on the serious side. "That so," I said.

"Yeah," he said. He got some more gadgets out of his bag of tricks and said, "Now, *this* might hurt a little. I'm going to kind of probe around in there and see what kind of damage got done. How long since you got shot?"

I was still panting a little. I said, "What . . . what time is it?"

"Near four o'clock."

"Almost five hours ago. Doc, is it infected yet? I feel kind of feverish and I been sweating pretty good."

He said, "It would take a good deal longer than five hours for it to get infected. You're suffering from what we call shock."

I said, "You damn right I was shocked. Man like that is not supposed to be able to get a shot in at me. Not and hit me in the front."

He was leaning over. He said, "I meant shock in the medical sense."

I could see some long, shiny instruments in his hands. He said, "Lay as still as you can."

That was easy for him to say, but it was another proposition for me to do. Finally, after a couple of days had gone by and I'd come near passing out, he straightened up and said, "Now let me have a look from the back. That won't be so bad. It came out much bigger. How did you know to put a cloth plug in the holes to keep them from bleeding so much?"

I started to answer him, and then I reckoned he saw a few of the scars from some other gunshot wounds I'd suffered. He said, "Oh, I see you have experience in these matters."

I was very anxious to ask him how bad the damage was. I was considerably concerned that the bullet might have nicked something vital there in the inside of me. But he was busy with the damn instruments of his, and I didn't feel much like even opening my mouth, much less asking questions.

Finally it was over with, and he let me lay quietly while he got some bandages ready. He said, "You are a very lucky man."

That wasn't the way I would have described it, but I asked him how he figured such.

He said, "The angle you got shot at caused that slug to hit your lowest rib and then just follow it on around and come out the back. If it had gone on through between the ribs, it would have got your liver and your lungs and maybe a little of your spleen. If it had, you wouldn't be here in this hotel. You'd have been dead an hour after you got shot."

I kind of halfway raised up on my elbows. I said, "You say the slug just run along on top of my rib?"

"Yes. That lowest rib on that side is a floating rib. In other words it's not attached to what you call your chest bone. It gave with the slug. Fortunately it was a small-caliber bullet. A .45-caliber or .44 would have broken on through and made one hell of a mess."

I let out a long breath. I'd done considerable worrying about just how bad I'd been hit. I said, "So I'll be all right, Doc?"

He was still busy with the bandages. He said, "Yeah, if you don't get sepsis."

That startled me. I said, "Sepsis? What the hell is that?"

"Another name for infection."

"What happens then?"

He shrugged. "You die. Now I'm going to put some drain cloths in both of those holes so the outside of the wound won't heal over and leave the inside to supperate. Then I'm—"

"Tents," I said. "I always heard them called tents."

He gave me a look, a kind of half smile. He said, "Very good. I see you are a very experienced man in these matters. You might want to set up shop on your own. But I think we'll give you one more wash through with that alcohol and then bandage you up. After that you'll need some food and some rest."

When he was done, he let me sit up on the bed so I could take down a stiff drink of whiskey. He pointed at the bed. He said, "Looks like you've pretty well ruined those bed clothes."

I looked around. The bedspread was soaked with blood. I figured it had gone on through and got the sheets too. I said, "I reckon the hotel will allow me to pay for them." I was feeling considerably better, though there was no good reason for it. All the doctor had done was cleaned out the wound and bandaged it. I reckoned the biggest thing he'd done was relieved my mind that I really wasn't shot all that bad. I'd asked him how such a shallow wound—because that was really what it had been, on account of the bullet never getting more than half an inch deep in me as it had tracked along on my rib—could bleed so much, and he'd said superficial wounds always bled a great deal.

He said, as he was gathering up his gear, "I hear you are a friend of Justa Williams."

I said, kind of hesitantly, "Yeah, I reckon you could say that." I was hoping the doctor wouldn't have occasion to speak to Justa before I could see him. Me and Justa kind of rode each other pretty hard, given the opportunity, and I had been a kind of a baby while the doc was working on me. If Justa got ahold of that, he'd make it pretty warm for me. I said, "Uh, Dr. Adams, I know I kind of played the calf when you was digging around in them holes I got punched in me. But I was kind of hoping you wouldn't feel called upon to mention any of that to Mr. Williams.

He might not understand how serious matters was."

Dr. Adams give me a smile I didn't much like. He said, "Oh! You mean you wouldn't want me mentioning that you screamed out like a woman or got tears in your eyes?"

"Now, Dr. Adams . . . ," I said.

He shut his bag and put on his hat. He said, "You need rest and food, plenty of food. You've got a lot of blood to replace. Come by my office tomorrow afternoon and I'll see how you're getting along. We may not have to cauterize those wounds if we get lucky."

"Cauterize! Damn, Dr. Adams, I—"

"I'll tell them to send you some food. If we do have to cauterize, I'm sure we can get your friend Justa to help hold you."

I said, "Now, look here, Dr. Adams . . ." But it was too late; he was already closing the door behind him. I lay back down and reflected on my luck. If the bullet hadn't taken the path it had, Phil Sharp would have killed me. It made me angry as hell to think of some pipsqueak like him killing me.

My side was commencing to throb again. While the doctor had been working on me, the pain I'd endured on the train had been replaced by a whole new kind of hurt that the good doctor had brought with him in his little black bag. When he'd finally quit, I'd been so relieved that I hadn't felt like I was hurting at all.

But then he'd left and my old friend from the train had come back. I eyed the bottle of whiskey where it was setting on the little bedside table. It was nearly about gone and didn't seem to do that much good anyway. Besides, brandy was my drink of preference. I only had the whiskey because I'd had to buy what was handy in a low-class saloon near the depot as I was leaving San Antonio for Galveston. They hadn't had anything but whiskey and tequilla, so I'd made the best of a bad choice.

It kind of surprised me when I realized that it had only been that morning when I'd left San Antonio and gone to Galveston. The night before I'd come up late from Del Rio and spent the night in San Antone, taking an early train out the next morning to see Phil Sharp. The whole matter had left me kind of weary. Since I'd gotten into the casino and cathouse business, I'd taken to keeping late hours and then sleeping late. But I had to get up that morning earlier than I wanted, to catch that train to Galveston, a train that had not turned out to be very lucky. Well, I thought, if a thing ain't lucky, it's unlucky.

Of course getting shot will make you wearier than losing sleep, and *it* ain't a damn bit lucky.

CHAPTER 2

The doctor hadn't been gone very long when there came a knock at my door. I called out to come in, and the door opened, and the young desk clerk came in, balancing a tray on one hand. I was sitting on the side of the bed with a proper bandage around my chest, smoking a cigarillo. I had just been on the point of putting out the smoke and laying down for a little rest when the knock came.

The desk clerk, Wayne I thought his name was, came across the room and set the tray on the little bedside table. He had to remove some of my paraphernalia to get it all the way on, but he managed by setting the whiskey bottle on the floor, and the ashtray and a glass or two that had been there. There was a bowl of stew on the tray and a plate with some thick slices of bread. Wayne said, "Dr. Adams said you was to eat all of this." He set the table in front of me so I could help myself and eat while I was sitting on the bed. I noticed a little brown bottle with a tablespoon beside it. I said, "What's that?"

Wayne said, "That's laudanum. For the pain. Dr. Adams said he didn't have any when he was here so he fetched some back. He said you might want to save it for tonight. Said he expects that's when you will really be hurting."

I looked at the little bottle. I said, "Did he mention why he didn't give me some of that when he was digging around in me with them running irons he carries in that little bag of tricks?"

Wayne said, "I don't know, sir. Reckon he forgot it."

I just nodded and put the cigarillo out and tasted the stew. It was good, good and hearty. Wayne was standing, looking at me. He said, "I'm mighty glad to see you lookin' better, Mr. Young. When you was at the desk, I declare I was a-feared you was going to swoon."

I looked up at him. I said, "Wayne— Your name is Wayne, ain't it?"

"Yes, sir."

I said, "Well, Wayne, you want to get along with me, don't you?"

"Yes, sir."

I said, "Well, Wayne, if we are to get along, I am going to have to straighten you out about something. Ladies *swoon*. Men pass out. Or fall over on their heads. Or drop over like a dead horse. They *don't* swoon. You understand?"

"Yes, sir!"

"So if you should have occasion to tell anybody about how I looked when I was checking in, especially if that anybody happens to be Justa Williams, you'll be careful and not say swoon, won't you?"

"No, sir! I mean, yes, sir."

I said, "Now you did get that note off?"

"Nathan taken it. He's a colored boy works here. Got a good fast mule."

"A mule? Shit! Hell, he'll be till Sunday getting that message out there."

"That's a mighty fast mule. I reckon he's at the Half-Moon by now. That's the Williams ranch."

With a little effort I got out my roll and pulled off two twenty-dollar notes. I said, "Wayne, I wonder if they's anybody can go out and gather me up a few things."

Wayne said, "Well, I reckon I could. Things is kind of quiet right now. If I wouldn't be gone too long."

I said, "Ain't much. I'd appreciate it if you'd buy me a couple of good-quality shirts. White, Western cut if they got it. Either good-quality cotton or linen."

"Yes, sir."

I looked at him, figuring him at about a slim 150 pounds. I said, "Get the shirts about two sizes bigger than what you take." I give him another look. He was pretty young, but he looked like he'd be a dandy if he had the money for the clothes. He was wearing that high, starched collar and a cutaway coat that might have looked good on him except it didn't fit. I figured it had been cut down from one of his daddy's or some other relative's. I said, "Don't get nothing fancy. Just plain shirts, but good ones." I nodded my head to where I'd pitched the two shirts I'd been bandaged with and wearing. I said, "Like them. And you might want to throw them out when you leave."

"Yes, sir," he said.

I said, "And get me a couple of bottles of the best brandy you can find. Is there a saloon here in the hotel?"

"No, sir. Just the dining room. Don't serve no liquor. Good saloon just down the street. Crook's."

I said, "All right. And get me a box of .40-caliber cartridges. Rim fire. Make damn sure they are rim fire. Now, can you tend to that for me? I don't feel like going out just right yet." I held the two twenties out.

He said, "That's too much money, Mr. Young."

I said, "You can bring me the change. Or put it on my bill. I know it seems puzzling, but it generally works out better if you have more money than you need 'stead of less. Like having an extra girlfriend."

He suddenly blushed like I'd struck home. He said, "Beggin' your pardon, sir, but that ain't always for the best."

"Well, take too much money, anyway, and figure it out later. I'll help you." If I hadn't been hurting and not feeling just all that well, the kid would have been tickling my funny bone. He was trying to act so serious and grown-up.

Now he said, "Mr. Young, Dr. Adams told me I was to tell you you couldn't have no whiskey with that laudanum. He said you could take the laudanum and not hurt or you could get drunk. But you couldn't do both."

I said, "Brandy ain't whiskey, son."

"Brandy ain't strong spirits?"

I shook my head. "Naw. Why they give it to little babies and ol' folks."

He give me a little frown. I didn't think he exactly believed me. I reached out and picked up the little brown bottle with my right hand. My left arm still didn't care to be used over much. I said, "How much this stuff can I take?"

Wayne said, "Dr. Adams said you could have two table-spoonfuls if you got to hurtin' real bad. But he said to tell you he'd never known Mr. Justa Williams to ever take more than one."

I looked up at him. I said, "Where did this doctor come from, a circus or some such?"

"No, sir. He's from up east. Some high-class school. Mr. Norris, that's Mr. Justa's brother, was the one got him to come to Blessing. We ain't supposed to have no such high-class doctor in this here kind of town. You better eat that stew, Mr. Young. I'll see to them things you want." He picked up my bloody shirts and started toward the open door. Before he left he said, "About meals, Mr. Young— hotel runs a boardinghouse style of dining room, meals at regular times. If you ain't going to feel like coming out to eat, I reckon I can fix it up so you get yours brought to you till you're back on your feet."

Before I could answer, a big, hard-looking man with a tin star on his chest suddenly filled the door. I was about half-afraid he was going to tell Wayne for me that he could just plan to deliver my eats over to the jail.

But he said, "Wayne, yore patient feeling all right?"

Wayne said, "Sheriff Vara. Howdy."

"Wayne," he said. Wayne passed by him, and I took note that he was taking a good look at the bloody white shirt I'd been shot in, Wayne not having had enough sense to try and conceal it.

I sat still and just went on eating my stew. There wasn't much else I could do. I was hurt and my revolver was empty. And even if I hadn't been hurt, there didn't seem to be much I could do against the sheriff. He was near six foot tall, but he had heavy shoulders and big, muscled-up arms. From one direction his face looked Mexican; from another it looked Indian. Straight on it didn't look either one. He came into the room, his hat pushed back on his head, a big Colt revolver in a very handy position on his hip. He said, "You'd be Wilson Young. Least that's what Dr. Adams said."

I nodded. I said, "I would."

He said, "My name is Lew Vara. I'm the sheriff in this county."

"Howdy," I said. I took another spoonful of stew and just sat there.

Vara pulled up a chair and sat down opposite me. He said, "Would you be the Wilson Young from Del Rio?"

There didn't seem to be much point in denying it. The fact was easy enough to check. I was surprised he hadn't recognized my name already. I said, "I would."

He pointed at my bandage. He said, "You get that around here?"

I shook my head. I said, "No. Didn't happen in your county."

He looked at me for a long moment. Finally he said, "I've heard considerable about you."

That didn't come as much of a surprise. I figured he had a Wanted poster on me somewheres in his desk if he just looked far enough back. I said, "Is that a fact?"

"Yeah," he said. "We got a friend in common. Justa Williams. He come back here from Del Rio and told me you helped him out of a pretty good spot of trouble."

I shrugged. It hurt my side. I said, "Man was slightly outnumbered. And I didn't much care for the folks as was giving him trouble."

Vara said, "Justa says you went a little further out of yore way than most Christians would have. Like I say, Justa is a friend of mine. He's the man put me in this office, and he's helped out more folks around here than I'd care to name. Including me. I hear you sent word out to him you was in town."

I was still not certain where I stood with this sheriff. I said, "They sent a boy on a mule. He might get there this month."

Vara nodded. He said, "Yeah, that would be Nathan. He's a good boy, but he ain't real fast-moving. You ought to have come by my office. I'd've got word to Justa in a hurry."

I didn't mention that I was still a kind of wanted outlaw and he was the sheriff. I just nodded my chin down toward my bandaged chest and said, "Well, there was this. I figured on a doctor as a first thing."

"Doc Adams says you ain't hurt too bad."

I said, "Doc Adams ain't got a bullet hole in him."

Vara laughed. He got up. He said, "Maybe me and you and Justa can have a drink together when you get up and around."

I said, "Sheriff . . ."

He was about to start for the door. He stopped. I put the spoon in the bowl of stew. I said, "Do you know who I am other than a friend of Justa's?"

"Oh, yes," he said. "You're Wilson Young. You've robbed just about everything in the state. Hell, I been hearing about you for ten years. Never thought I'd meet you. Heard you got off the owlhoot trail and went to helping the poor and needy."

I said, "What about me being here?" I said it carefully, letting nothing get in my voice.

He said, "What about it?"

I said, "Might still be some paper out on me."

He shrugged. He said, "I ain't got any. I don't care what you do so long as it ain't illegal and don't scare the horses."

"I'll be careful about the horses," I said.

He pointed at my bandage again. He said, "Anybody else involved that come off the worse for it?"

"Yes," I said.

"Close around here?"

"Not real close."

"You figure they'll be looking for you?"

"I don't know," I said. I looked up at him. I said, "I acted in self-defense, but with the folks that was involved, I don't think that fact will help much."

He nodded. He said, "Sometimes it's like that. If I hear anything, I'll let you know first thing. You better eat that stew and get well as quick as you can."

I watched him go out, shutting the door behind him. It appeared that Justa Williams pulled considerable weight in his part of the world. Well, I wasn't going to complain about that so long as it didn't scare the horses, as the sheriff had said.

I set in to finish the big bowl of stew. I wasn't all that hungry, but I figured I needed it, even if that meant agreeing with that doctor. I ate some of the bread and then downed a short pull of whiskey. The laudanum was still sitting in front of me, but I was damned if I was going to take any, even though my side was doing its best to make certain I knew it had been shot. I had every intention of returning the bottle to the good doctor unopened and unused. Which, I'd expect him to note, was a tablespoonful less than Justa.

Wayne came back with my purchases. I had him just pitch it all on the bed. He said, "There's a little over twelve dollars in change."

"Hang on to it, boy," I said. "We'll get it spent yet."

He went out with the tray and I opened one of the bottles of brandy and had a good drink out of a glass. I didn't mind pulling on a whiskey bottle like some damn border ruffian, but I didn't drink brandy that way.

I started to light another cigarillo and then changed my mind. I was passing weary. Pain will do that to you. And then I'd had to get up damn early to catch that blasted train to Galveston. It wasn't a thing I ordinarily did, but I wheeled around on the bed and lay back. I figured I'd sleep a minute or two and then load my revolver. It had been empty a little longer than it was used to.

Sometime later I come half awake, conscious that there was someone in the room. My revolver was in my holster at the foot of the bed, but it wasn't going to do me any good on account of I'd never got around to loading it. Little by little I come full awake. I was laying on my back, but I didn't betray my waking by either opening my eyes or changing the pattern of my slow breathing. It wasn't that I'd heard a noise or anything else that would have caused me to suddenly come alert; it was just that I could *feel* someone in the room. They weren't moving around, and I couldn't hear whoever it was fumbling with anything or breathing. Whoever it was was being mighty still. I let my eyelids just flutter open a slit, to where I could just barely see through my eyelashes. I could tell I must have slept longer than I'd thought because the room was dim. I figured it must be dark outside. But that wouldn't tell me what time it was. It being April, it got dark a little after six, so it could be anywhere from that time to six the next morning.

I nearly jumped because a voice suddenly said, "Why don't you quit playing possum? I know you're awake, you faker."

I opened my eyes and looked to my left. There, sitting in a chair that he'd turned backwards so he could rest his arms on the top of the back and straddle it, was Justa Williams. I could just barely make him out in the dimness.

I said, "What are you doing in here? I didn't hear you knock. This is a sickroom, you know."

He said, "Hell, it's my hotel. I don't have to knock." He got up off the chair and struck a match and lit the kerosene lamp that hung from the ceiling. The light ran most of the dimness out of the room, and I could get a good look at Justa. He hadn't changed much since I'd seen him last. He was a little over six foot tall with big shoulders and hands and not much waist to speak of. He'd told me in Del Rio that his weight generally come in at around 190 pounds, and I didn't see much change. His face was like that of most men who made their living out of doors—tanned and weathered with wrinkles around the eyes. I guessed there were women who'd figure his face might not scare small children, but he wasn't nowhere near as handsome as I was—a fact I'd reminded him of several times.

He shook out the match after he got the lamp lit and came back to straddle the chair. I said, "If I owned a hotel that was still using coal-oil lamps, I wouldn't be going around bragging about it. Every hick-town hotel I've been in for the last five years has had gaslights."

He said, "I thought you was partial to jails, not hotels. They got gaslights in them? Who shot you anyway, the guitar player?"

"One of the dancing girls," I said. "Or I shot myself on purpose. I forget. What the hell you doing here? Lose a horse race because you couldn't find a good jockey?"

He said, "Naw, I got some whining, moaning message from somebody sounded like he needed help. This would have been the *last* place I'd come looking for a man to ride a horse for me."

That was the way of it between me and Justa. Wasn't either one of us about to let on we was glad to see the other.

I said, "You taken any trips lately that you didn't want to make?"

I was digging him about being herded out to Del Rio by the hired guns of a vicious little cripple named J. C. Flood. Flood had been trying to extort a good deal of money out of him by threatening his family and his ranch, but we'd finally settled the whole business with three horse races and a gunfight. I'd ridden two of the races for Justa, winning both of them, and, in the gunfight, he and I had taken on Flood and six of his hirelings. They had lost. I'd killed four and had given Justa credit for two and a half, counting Flood, on account of him being a cripple, as just a half. Justa had irately insisted that there wasn't nothing crippled about the shotgun Mr. Flood was carrying. As he was leaving Del Rio, he'd given me a black Thoroughbred racehorse that he'd come by as a present. The horse was the fastest thing I'd ever ridden and was, at that moment, stabled back at my ranch in Mexico just across from Del Rio. I hadn't wanted to take the horse because he was worth four or five thousand dollars, but Justa had given me the bill-of-sale transfer just as his train was pulling out of the station. It is damn hard to give a horse back to a man that is on a moving train.

He ignored my question about being herded and said, "What have you done with my Thoroughbred racehorse, lost him in a poker game?"

I said, "First off, he ain't your Thoroughbred racehorse, and if anybody was likely to lose him in a poker game, it would be you. I've seen you play poker. I reckon if I could get you in a poker game just once a week, I could retire from the cathouse and casino business."

He suddenly laughed and reached out and got a glass and what was left of the bottle of whiskey and poured himself out a drink. I swung around on the bed and sat up, and Justa poured me out a stiff belt of brandy and handed it to me. We clinked glasses, said, "Luck," and then knocked them back as befitted the toast. When we'd both had the benefit of the liquor, Justa said, "Well, I am glad to see you, though I'm damned if I know why. What kind of a mess you in?"

I told him what had happened. It didn't take long. I said, "Your sheriff has already been by. I think the doctor told him I'd been shot."

"Yeah," Justa said. He rubbed his chin. "You ain't got nothing to worry about from Lew. I run into him on the street coming here. He knows you're a friend of mine."

I was feeling stronger, but I was still weak. I didn't much feel like sitting up, but I didn't want to lay back down while Justa was there. I said, "He may be your friend, and he may know we're friends. But if Wanted notices start coming out on me, he's still the sheriff."

Justa said, "Don't worry about that. I kind of doubt that this here Phil Sharp is going to go to the regular law. They ain't, from what I've heard, all that fond of those vigilante groups. And he's going to have a hell of a time explaining how one man come to gun down three of them. Not to mention what they were doing there in the first place. But the thing I don't understand is how you come to let this Sharp fellow run up twenty thousand dollars in gambling debts. You gone into charity work?"

I started to shrug and then stopped myself. My side didn't want me shrugging. I said, "Hell, he'd been a damn good customer from almost the day the place opened. I figure he'd been through there five or six times and always lost a bundle of cash. He was a good customer and, from what I could gather, was a well-to-do man in the shipping business. He showed me a wad of cash but said he was going on into Mexico on business and needed the cash, and could he wire me the money when he got back to Galveston. I figured, why not."

Justa shook his head. He said, "That don't make no sense! All right, I ain't seen it, but let's just say you got a cathouse and saloon and casino that is the toast of Texas. Del Rio is still a hell of a long way from Galveston. And they got some pretty good cathouses in Galveston, though I don't know about gambling casinos."

"He always said he was on his way to Mexico. Shipping business."

Justa said, "Well, goddam, Will, there are quicker ways to Mexico from Galveston than going up north to Del Rio, which is at least three hundred miles from the damn ocean."

"I don't know." I said. "Man just told me his business took him to the ports in Mexico to grease matters, ports like

Tampico and Vera Cruz. I reckoned he was going down there to spread some money around amongst the different officials to speed matters up when he was shipping goods down there."

Justa said, "That still don't explain Del Rio. You must have a hell of an establishment to drag a man that far out of his way. Hell, he can take a train direct from Galveston to Laredo to Monterrey to Tampico. Del Rio is way out of his way. Even after he's there, he's got to take the train 150 miles south to Laredo just to get back to where he ought to have been in the first place."

I said, "I never asked the man. He usually come in with a couple of associates, and they spent a lot of money and didn't cause no trouble. Just because the man didn't have a good head for geography wasn't no reason for me to throw him out."

Justa sighed. He got out his watch. He said, "Hell, it's seven o'clock. You got to eat some supper. You feel like going down to the dining room, or you want me to have them bring it up here?"

I was thinking of just laying back. I said, "Tell you the truth I think I'd rather just take a little rest. I—"

Justa said, "Hell, no! Dr. Adams left word you was to eat and eat plenty. You are going to eat a steak if I got to cram it down you."

I said, "Me and Dr. Adams is going to have to have a little talk here pretty soon. I ain't sure he ain't done me more damage than the gunshot."

He reached out and picked up the little bottle of laudanum and held it up to the light to see how much was missing. When he seen it was still full he said, "You must not be hurting."

I said, "Oh, I don't reckon you want to trade places with me right now. I expect you'd have tears in your eyes."

He gestured with the little bottle. He said, "This is good stuff. You might ought to take a couple of tablespoonfuls. Give you some rest from the pain."

I said, "Oh, I've taken it. Used it once when I'd been shot three or four times. I forget how many."

He gave me just the slightest trace of a smile. He got up. He said, "I'll go get us a meal sent up. You want that iced tea you like or you want a cold beer with your steak?"

I said, "This town got a icehouse? Wooo ha!"

He said, "Hell, we even got a bank. Ain't got no money in it, though, since somebody robbed it a few years back."

I said, "Any man that would put his money in a bank is foolish in the first place. Why you reckon all them crooks rob banks? It's because they got the money gathered up there."

He went out, and I laid back so as to get what rest I could before I had to eat steak. Hell, I didn't even know how I was going to be able to cut the damn thing. If I moved my left arm, my side let me know about it, and I was already doing a pretty good job of hurting, though I hadn't wanted to let on to Justa about it. I glanced over at the little bottle of laudanum and considered it, but the idea that I'd give in to the pain would give Justa more ammunition than he needed.

He was back in about half an hour with three hired hands helping him. One was carrying a fair-sized table that I figured we were going to eat off of, and the other two were carrying trays with our supper on them. While they were getting us set up, Justa pulled the two straight-backed wooden chairs over to the table, setting them opposite each other. He said, to me, "You need help getting over here?"

I heaved myself off the bed, using my right leg and right side for most of the work. I said, "I reckon I can manage it."

I pulled my chair out with my right hand and sat down and looked at my plate. Somebody had already cut my steak up for me. I looked up at Justa. There was faint amusement in his eyes. He said, "I taken notice you weren't just all that spry with your left arm, so I asked the cook if he could help out an invalid."

I didn't say anything, just kind of stared back at him. I waited.

He looked puzzled. He said, "What?"

I said, "Ain't you going to ask grace? Man with your sense of humor ought to get in a little praying ever' chance he gets."

He laughed. He said, "Wasn't me that got shot by some tinhorn gambler with no little bitty pistol. Now you want to talk about who needs to pray?"

They'd brought me a pitcher of iced tea, but it wasn't right. I could see they didn't know the first thing about making iced tea, because there wasn't any lemons or sliced limes or even any sugar. But I made do with it without comment, not being one to complain.

We had the steak along with a pile of mashed potatoes and gravy and some sliced tomatoes. In that country, that far south, they could damn near grow crops all year round, especially with the warm sea breeze.

We finished up, and then had a drink and lit up cigarillos. Justa was studying me. He said, "You are looking a mite peaked. I reckon I better get out of here and let you get to bed."

"What time is it?" My watch was in my frock coat.

He said, "Going on for nine." He got up. "I'm going to stay here in the hotel tonight. I'll come around about eight in the morning to see if you feel up to making it for breakfast."

My side was throbbing like hell, and I was just wanting him to get out of there so I could lay down. But I said, "Oh, I reckon I'll be able to make it. Of course you might want to get there early and get the cook to cut up my eggs for me."

He said, "Way you're acting, I might have to. Hell, it ain't like you was actually *hurt*. You just got a little bitty hole in you. I've seen men hurt worse than that finish out the day's work and then go out dancin'."

I pulled on my cigarillo and said, "Say, am I going to have the honor of seeing Mrs. Williams while I'm stopping in your fair city?"

He said, "I don't see why not. Why?"

I looked at the glowing end of my little cigar. I said, "Oh, I just wanted to get it set in my mind not to mention anything about dancing girls. Didn't want to slip and mention a girl by the name of Lupita in front of the missus. Man had got to protect his friends." I give him a righteous look that would have done credit to a Baptist preacher.

For a second or so he just stared at me. I swear his face started getting red. He opened his mouth. He said, "Wilson Young, you better—You son of a bitch, you wouldn't do something like—" He stopped. After another few seconds he said, "You better not be threatening me like that."

"I wasn't threatening you. I didn't hear nobody in this room say anything about threatening you."

By now he was red in the face. He said, "Look here, you know as well as I do that nothing—*nothing*—ever happened between me and that girl. From the dead-level first I said I was a married man, and you know I said that. Now, didn't you hear me say that?"

I lifted the palm of my right hand upwards. I said, "I ain't trying to cause no trouble. I was just cautioning us to be careful what we said about that situation around your missus. After all, you did have your britches off in front of Lupita. And Evita, too, for that matter. And you don't favor underwear."

He had hold of the doorknob, and I thought he was going to squeeze it off. He said, "Goddammit, Wilson, you know that was innocent, you know the facts of that particular matter."

I said, "I know you had your pants off and you wasn't wearing no underwear and they was two young girls right there with you. Correct me if them ain't the facts."

"Aw, hell!" he said. He jerked open the door. Before he left, he said, "I ought to take that laudanum and your brandy and just leave you here to suffer tonight."

I said, "Go ahead, I won't need it. Won't hear no moaning from me like I heard from a certain party down in Del Rio over a little piddling nothing."

He went out without another word and slammed the door after him. I had to laugh. It was pretty hard to get under Justa's skin, but I'd got him pretty good. But, if the truth be told, he had a right to hurrah me about my wound on account of the way I'd treated him in Del Rio. In the gunfight we'd got in, he'd had a slug take all the flesh off his right hip and expose the hip bone. Then he'd had to sit in the saddle for an hour during the ride back to my ranch house. Then he'd had to put up with the indignity of having to let me help him out of the saddle and into the house. After that the girls had nearly had to fight him to get his pants down so they could look at his wound. Evita, my woman, was pretty good with them herb cures, and she was determined he was in for a little doctoring, even if it did mean his pants had to come down. He put up a pretty good fight, but he was weak from loss of blood and the shock of being shot. So he finally gave in. But, of course, there was all kinds of ways to tell a story.

Naturally I'd given him a hard time about the whole matter, claiming he was carrying on over nothing. I told him I'd seen men get hurt worse than that getting a haircut.

Wasn't no sense to it; this was just the way we carried on with one another.

After Justa was gone, I turned off the lamp and worked my pants off and then laid down. Only way I could rest was on my back, which ain't my natural way of sleeping, but I was just grateful to be able to stretch out. It was cool in the room but not cool enough to need any covers other than the sheet. As tired as I was, I figured to go right on off to sleep. It didn't, however, work that way. As soon as everything got still and quiet, my side got to throbbing so bad I could damn near hear it. All in all I spent a pretty bad night. On several occasions I took a good pull of brandy, but it didn't help all that much. I thought of the laudanum, but I was too stubborn to use it. I was going to return that bottle full to the doctor or die in the attempt. Besides, every time the temptation came on me, I just took some brandy, knowing I couldn't mix the two.

It seemed to me that I felt feverish even though the doctor had said it was too soon for sepsis, or whatever fancy name he gave infection. Why couldn't he just say infection instead of throwing in names that nobody knew unless they'd read the same book as him?

I did doze off and on, but it was still a pretty long night. I saw the light of dawn and was glad, but I didn't see it long, because it was about that time that my side decided to let up on me and I dropped into a heavy sleep.

I come awake to a pounding on the door. I opened my eyes just as it opened. It was Justa. He said, "Hell, we just rent these rooms by the day, not by the day and a half. It's nine o'clock. You planning on getting up? Dr. Adams needs to see you after breakfast. He's got to go out of town this afternoon and tend to a man that is really hurt."

I got up slowly. My side, bless its heart, was not throbbing, but I felt stiff from the waist up. I sat around on the side of the bed. My pants were on the floor. I went to bend over and get them, but had to straighten back up on account of how dizzy I got all of a sudden.

Justa walked over and picked them up and put them in my hands. He said, "Now look at who ain't got no britches on. And who don't favor underwear. You going to feel like going to the dining room or you want to be mollycoddled up here in bed?"

I said, "I been up since dawn. Waiting on you. I've dressed and undressed twice."

"You're a liar," he said. "I've checked on you three times since seven o'clock. Only banged on the door this time so you'd have to wake up. I've already had four cups of coffee, seen Dr. Adams, saw my brother Norris over at the bank, and arranged for a horse and buggy. How'd you sleep?"

"Just fine," I said. I had managed to get hold of my boots, but I wasn't in no hurry to try and pull them on.

Justa went over to the bedside table and picked up the bottle of laudanum and looked at it. Then he unscrewed the top and smelled it. He said, "What'd you fill this back up with?"

I said, "Huh! I ain't touched it. I don't moan and groan and take on over some little scratch like some people I could name. Hell, go ahead and taste it if you don't believe me."

And damned if the son of a bitch didn't. He tilted the bottle and got a little on the end of his finger and then touched it to his tongue. He looked all kinds of disappointed. But he said, "You need some help with those boots?"

I'd got the right one on, but it was difficult with the other because I didn't dare pull with my left arm. But I finally got it about half on and then stomped it on the rest of the way. I stood up and went over to the wash stand and poured some water in the bowl and washed off my face with my right hand and then did what I could about my teeth. I needed a shave, but I wasn't going to attempt it. My side still wasn't hurting all that bad, but I wasn't going to rile it up and get it started. I said, "I reckon I owe myself a barbershop shave."

Justa said, "Ha!"

I picked up one of the new shirts that Wayne had brought me and got it unbuttoned. In the mirror over the washstand I'd seen that no blood had seeped through the bandages that Dr. Adams had put on. Either all the blood in me had run out or my wounds had clotted.

I got my right arm through the proper arm of the shirt, but Justa had to come over and help me with the left. He didn't say anything, which was kind of surprising.

I picked up my gunbelt, contemplated it, and then dropped it back on the bed. Justa said, "I don't reckon you'll need that here."

When I had my hat on, we went on into the dining room. It was empty, of course, but I guess when you own the place, you can have breakfast anytime you want it. I drank some coffee, and then they brought us each a big plate of bacon and eggs. My side was loosening up some, but the going was still difficult. While we were eating, I asked Justa what he had the horse and buggy for.

He said, "To carry you out to the ranch. I know you can't sit a horse, and a buckboard would be too rough on you. Dr. Adams said you might as well be out there as bothering him here in town."

I said, "Hell, Justa, I never meant to fall in on you like some grubline rider. I can make it here in the hotel. I need to be getting on, anyway."

He said, firmly, "That ain't what Dr. Adams says, and I reckon he knows more about doctoring than you do. Though I figure you'll want to argue that point with him. He says you need to rest for at least a week. You did get shot, you know."

"So you're going to put me in a buggy just to shame me. That the idea?"

"No. In spite of the fact I'd like to drag you behind my horse for them remarks about them girls, I am going to carry you in a buggy with good springs so you don't start bleeding again. I hear you've already ruined one set of sheets at the hotel, and you do that to one of my wife's sheets, and she'll say to you, that's all right and don't think nothing about it, and then she'll kill me."

I hated to intrude on his hospitality, but I reckoned it was for the best. In spite of my brave talk, I knew I was going to be laid up somewhere for a time, and it might just as well be that much closer to my target. As soon as the doc was finished with me, I'd figured on going on back to Mexico and healing up at my own ranch house, but I wasn't averse to a little socializing with Justa and his family. We did not, after all, know each other that well, though a stranger, listening to us getting at each other, would figure we'd tumbled out of the same crib.

Of course we had sober moments. We never made light of serious matters.

We went directly from breakfast over to Dr. Adams' office. Fortunately it wasn't but a walk of a short block. The doctor showed us into his examining room and then helped me off with my shirt and told me to get up on a little bedlike table. He asked if the laudanum he'd brought over had helped.

Right then Justa said, "He never used it. Said he didn't need it."

I give him a look that should have fried his brains. Dr. Adams just said, pleasantly, "Oh, is that right? I guess that means the wound's not sore, and I won't have to be careful while I treat it."

I give Justa another look, but he was leaning up against the wall and looking as pleased with himself as a cat with cream on its whiskers.

Dr. Adams took the bandage off, and that part was all right. Then he pulled out the tents, and that didn't do much more than make me wince a little. But then he went to probing around again, and I had to start in to gritting my teeth. He said, "I hear you'll be going out to the Williams ranch. Well, that's just as well. This thing will either get infected or it won't. If it does, they got plenty of room out there to bury you. If it don't, you won't need me."

And all this time he's talking, he's digging around inside me until I near about want to weep like a baby. He said, "Closing up a little too fast on the outside. Need to debride that a little. That doesn't hurt, does it?"

Naturally I had to shake my head no. Behind me Justa let out a little laugh.

The doctor said, "You've clotted up nice. Was very little blood on that dressing I put on last night. You shouldn't bleed anymore unless you wrench it around. I'm going to put another drain in each wound. Justa, you can jerk them out in a couple of days. Then just put on a clean bandage."

I don't reckon he shoved those drains into me more than a foot and a half. If he'd gone any further, it might have hurt. But he finally got through just before I passed out. He wrapped another bandage around my chest, charged me ten dollars, and said I was free to go. I said, "Hell, Doc, I got to you on that one. I'd've given a hundred to get out of here."

Walking back, my side was still stiff and painful, but I was pleased to note that I no longer felt weak and light-headed. We went to my room, and I loaded my revolver and then put the box of cartridges in my valise, along with my other new shirt and the two bottles of brandy and the bottle of laudanum. Justa helped me to buckle on my gunbelt.

He said, "I noticed in Del Rio that you don't wear cartridge loops in your belt either. I don't because they make the damn rig too heavy."

I said, "That and because I don't see no use to them. The line I take is that if you've got a revolver in your hand, you are engaged in close work. And if you don't get matters settled with six shots, you ain't going to have time to reload anyway. And maybe ain't going to be in no condition to reload. Of course I like to have extra cartridges on hand, say a few in my pocket and a box in my saddlebags. But I'm like you. I don't want no four or five pounds of lead hanging around my waist I might never need or get to use."

We went out of the room, and I waited in the lobby while Justa went to get the buggy. Wayne gave me my change, a matter of some twenty-four dollars. He said, "Mr. Williams said not to charge you for nothin'."

"He did, huh? Likes to get me beholden to him." I gave Wayne five dollars for his help and then went out on the boardwalk. Justa pulled up a minute later, his riding horse, a nice-looking dun gelding, tied on behind the buggy. I got in and we set off.

We wound out of town and then hit a wagon track heading due east. As soon as we were rolling down the road, Justa turned to me. He said, "Well, Will, what are you going to do about this Phil Sharp business?"

CHAPTER 3

I thought a moment. I said, "Obviously I ain't going to do anything until I get healed up and in good shape. Then I calculate to go see him again. Only this time I ain't going to be so trusting, and if there's any surprises, they'll be on my side."

Justa was quiet for a moment. The buggy horse was trotting along nicely, raising little puffs of dust with his hooves. It was a pleasant spring day, not yet too warm, with just a hint of rain in the air. Justa said, "Why don't you just let it go?"

I shook my head. I said, "I can't do that."

Justa said, "Will, you're in an awkward position legally. I know that Phil Sharp, or a half dozen Phil Sharps, ain't no match for you. But the law is. The way I understood it from you, and from talking to Lew Vara, is that you are betwixt and between. You ain't exactly an outlaw or a wanted man, but you ain't quite what is considered an honest citizen. You stir up any trouble, and the law is going to come after you. They might already be so far as you know. Lew hasn't heard anything, but that don't mean nothing. Let it go, Will. Go on back to Del Rio after you've rested up and run your whorehouse and casino."

"I can't," I said.

"Is it the money? I know it's a lot of money, but it's not worth your freedom."

I shook my head. I said, "It was the money at first, but now it ain't got nothing to do with that. The son of a bitch set me up, Justa, planned on killing me. And then he shot

46

me. If I don't do something about it, every Phil Sharp in the country will think I'm easy pickings."

"Maybe it won't get out."

I looked over at him. "What?"

He smiled. "All right. I don't know the man, but I expect he will talk."

I said, "Won't take much for word to get around. It ain't all that big of a bunch that frequents my establishment. Besides, Justa, I'm not going to let Phil Sharp think he can get away with shooting me. Even if I knew he'd never tell another soul."

Justa nodded slowly. He reached out and flicked the reins at the buggy horse. The horse picked up his pace. Justa said, "Well, you ain't got to think on it now. For the next week you are supposed to concentrate on healing up."

I said, "I got to admit I am anxious to hear what your family has to say about you. All I know about you so far is what you've told me. I imagine that was kind of one-sided."

He said, "You never have told me what you did with my black Thoroughbred racing horse."

"Whose racing horse?"

"All right, the horse I let you keep for a while."

"You mean that packhorse you palmed off on me? Hell, animal wasn't worth his grain and hay. I give him to a Mexican just to get shut of him and get out of the expense of his upkeep."

"I'll bet," Justa said dryly. "You've probably won fifty thousand dollars running that horse and are scairt to tell me because I might claim my rightful share."

We hit a bump about then and I winced in spite of myself. Justa looked at me quickly. "You all right?"

It had given me a good pain, but I was trying not to let it show. I said, "Yeah."

Justa said, "What makes you so damn stubborn? Why don't you take some of that laudanum. Ain't no point in hurting if you don't have to. I broke my big toe here about six months ago. Horse stepped on it. And I guarantee you I drank that laudanum like it was water."

I stared at him. I said, "You did?"

"Hell yes."

"Dr. Adams know it?"

"He was the one give it to me."

"Why, that lying son of a bitch!" I said. I rummaged in my valise, which was on the floorboard between Justa and me, and came out with the laudanum.

Justa said, "What lying son of a bitch?"

"Never mind," I said. I didn't want to tell him what the doctor had told Wayne to tell me about Justa only having to take one tablespoonful, because it was already starting to sound damn silly in my own ears. I tipped up the bottle and had a good swallow and then screwed the top back on and put it in my valise.

"What lying son of a bitch?"

"I told you never mind."

Justa said, thoughtfully, "Dr. Adams, probably. He never could get me to use it. I told him such stuff was for little babies and old people." He said it straight-faced, having waited until after I'd taken the dose.

I finally said, "Well, now we know *who* the lying son of a bitch is."

We did that, went to ragging each other when we needed to turn the conversation away from serious matters. For the time being Phil Sharp would go to the back of the shelf. There was no use talking about him or the danger he represented until I was well enough to do something about it.

We traveled in silence for a time. That laudanum was pretty good stuff. My side had went to acting up from all the chousing around I'd been doing plus the buggy ride, but the laudanum was taking the edge right off the pain.

We started passing some herds of cattle. I could see, even though I didn't know a hell of a lot about cattle, that these animals had been upgraded by crossing them with blooded stock from up north. Justa had told me a good deal about his breeding program when he'd been in Del Rio, but I hadn't been very interested, so I hadn't paid much attention. I was all for the rancher making money. It just meant that much more he'd have that I could take away from him across a poker table, and that without the bother of fooling around with a bunch of cow brutes and having to see to the care and feeding of them. I had a thousand acres in Mexico, but I didn't bother with no cattle. I let my neighbors run theirs on the place in return for them clearing the land so the grass could grow without being choked out by huisache and cedar and mesquite and greasewood and bramble.

But I could see Justa didn't have that problem. As far as the eye could see the green grass was a foot high, waving in the light breeze. Justa said, "We're on Half-Moon property. These are Half-Moon cattle. Crossbreds. I got a herd of purebred Herefords, but they are grazing on the south range. You won't see them today."

I said, "Damn, and I was so-o-o looking forward to it."

He gave me a sideways look. He said, "We'll go straight on to my house. It's after lunch, but Nora will fix us something. Or the maid. You can meet the rest of the family tonight. My dad is probably napping, and my brother Norris is in town and won't be in until just before supper. My youngest brother, Ben, will be out with the horse herd."

We drove on for about a mile, and I could see, in the distance, riders working a large herd. I knew enough to know it was calving season, so I reckoned every hand on the place was trying to keep up with the mama cows that were dropping calves. A little further on, a big, rambling house rose out of the prairie. It was surrounded by a number of outbuildings and corrals, including a big barn. Justa said, "That's the main headquarters of the ranch. Dad and my two brothers live there. It started out as a one-room cabin a long, long time ago and just got built onto. Eight or ten rooms in it now. We keep twelve regular hired hands for the cattle, and Ben uses three or four *vaqueros* to help him with the horse herd. Seasons like now we'll put on extra help."

He left the wagon track and headed the buggy to his left, across the open prairie. He said, "My house is about a half a mile ahead. I built it when I married Nora."

We raised his house just after we came over a little hill. It was a lot like mine, being made out of stone and mortar and topped with red Mexican tiles. Behind it was a little barn and a small corral. Justa said, "Nora will see us coming. I don't know how she does it, but she always does."

Sure enough, as we approached the house, a woman in a light yellow frock came out the front door and stood on the front porch, waving. Justa waved back.

We pulled up in front, and I got out of the buggy on my side and Justa got out on his. Mrs. Williams came forward. She said, "Mr. Young, welcome. I've heard a good deal about you. Welcome to our house."

It didn't take much eyesight to see why Justa didn't have much trouble being true to her. She had wheat-colored hair and a trim waist and the kind of bosom a woman of her youth is supposed to have. She was not beautiful in a painted lady sort of way, but she was about as pretty as it was possible to get. And there was something in her face and eyes that couldn't be gotten out of any ladies paint box. She come toward me, her hand out, but I swept off my hat and made her a low bow. It nearly killed my side to do so, but I still managed to say, "Your servant, ma'am."

Justa laughed. He said, "Would you look at that tinhorn gentleman? Making them fancy manners. I bet he's sorry now."

Mrs. Williams said, "Justa, now you hush!"

Justa said, "Hell, he's been shot in the side, been whining the whole way about how bad he's hurting. Then he gets here and goes and makes a big bow to impress the womenfolk. I'm surprised it didn't near kill him."

The bad part of it was that he was right. Mrs. Williams came and took my arm and said, "Let's get you sat down, Mr. Young."

"Thank you, ma'am. Thank you." I looked over her shoulder at Justa. I said, "I don't let what he says bother me. I know he never learnt no manners, and if other folks uses them, it embarrasses him."

"That's right." she said. She gave Justa a look as we went inside.

It was cool and pleasant inside the house. Mrs. Williams led me into the parlor and got me set down in a big, comfortable chair. She said, "I just made some lemonade, Mr. Young. Of course we haven't got any ice out here, but we've got an artesian well and the water is passing cool."

"I'd favor some," I said gallantly. Though what I really wanted was a good hard drink of brandy.

Justa came in and saw me with the lemonade in my hand. His wife had gone back into the kitchen for something. He made a small smile. He said, "You know, I calculate I drank near on to a hundred gallons of that stuff while I was courting Nora. Of course I commenced to sweetening it up toward the last. She never caught on. Drink some out of that before she gets back."

I took a good swallow, and Justa dived his hand in my valise and came out with the opened bottle of brandy. He pulled the cork and then poured me a good slug in with my lemonade. It darkened it some, but I didn't care. Justa put the brandy away and sat down as his wife came in with a glass for him. He said, "Ah, boy, I can use that, dry as I am."

But then he immediately got up and went into a room just off the parlor. The door was half-closed. He was back in a minute, and his lemonade was considerably darker also. He sat back down and raised his glass to me. He said, "Luck."

I did likewise, and then we had a good long pull. The brandy and the lemonade mixed mighty well, though I generally favored it unblemished.

Mrs. Williams said, dryly, "I thought you only made that 'luck' toast with whiskey."

"Oh, no, no," Justa said. "You can do it with water."

She said, "So long as it's got whiskey in it?"

We had better sense than to say anything, and Mrs. Williams said she had lunch on the table whenever we were ready. She said, "It's not much. I didn't know when y'all would be getting here. It's just some cheese and cold roast beef, and I made some potato salad."

Justa said, "Did you cut Wilson's meat up for him?"

I give him a sour look, but Mrs. Williams said, "Oh, Mr. Young, I'm so sorry. I never thought. I'll go and do it right now."

I waved her back with my right hand. I said, "Thank you, Mrs. Williams, but it won't be necessary. That is just one of the thousand poor jokes your husband has made at my expense ever since he found me wounded. Had it not been for the pleasure of your acquaintance, I would have viewed this stop off on my trip as some sort of punishment for my past sins."

Justa whooped. He said, "Honey, do not let this man fool you! He used to be a snake oil salesman."

She looked at him. She said, "Hush, Justa. And leave our guest alone. Besides, I thought you told me he used to be a bank robber."

I said, still using my humble, sincere voice, "No use trying to defend me, Mrs. Williams. Mr. Williams is determined to pay me back for some imagined wrongs when he was in Del Rio."

She said, "Of course I knew you had been wounded, Mr. Young. Justa's brother, Norris, who works in town stopped by last night to tell me Justa would be staying in town with you. He told me you had been gunshot. I'm amazed to see you looking so well."

Justa said, "Hell, it's just a pinprick! Don't amount to a hill of beans."

She ignored him. She said, "How did it come to happen, Mr. Young? And don't be shy." She looked over at Justa and said, "I'm *used* to gunshot wounds in this family."

I said, kind of fumbling around, "Well, it was—"

But Justa broke in and said, "He was bowing to a lady and bent over too far and his gun went off and peeled off a little bit of skin."

We went in and ate lunch in the kitchen without Mrs. Williams being any the wiser about my situation. I had got the impression that Justa didn't want his wife to know too much about it. Fortunately, over lunch, we finally dropped the formality, and she started calling me Wilson and I called her Nora. She said she was ashamed of the way her husband was acting, especially as he'd come home with the wound in his hip and told her how I'd doctored it. When she said that, I just gave him a significant look and he was a defeated man.

They put me in a spare bedroom that had a good bed and some nice big windows that let in the sea breeze. It was about three o'clock in the afternoon, but I figured I ought to have a little rest. My side had gone to throbbing again, so I took a little of the laudanum and got my boots off and laid down for a rest. Justa said we'd eat supper there with Nora, but then he and I would go up to the main house to see his brothers and his father.

I reckoned it was the laudanum, but I dropped off right away and slept right through until Justa came and woke me up about six-thirty. The nap had done me good. I got out of bed and put on a fresh shirt without any help from Justa, and then washed up and brushed my hair, and we went into supper. We ate in the dining room, off a big, long, heavy table with those high-backed Mexican chairs. The maid had cooked supper, *arroz con pollo,* and it was near as good as Evita could have made. Justa had told me they might not have the best cook and maid in the county, but they damn sure had the fattest, and this Juanita didn't make no liar out of him.

When we were finished, me and Justa had a drink and then set out for the main house to see his brothers and father. He said he went up there every evening after supper, and they sat around and visited or talked business for an hour or so. The Half-Moon was what you called a corporation, and Justa was the head of the business. His brother Norris handled everything but the ranch itself, but he couldn't make any decisions without Justa's say-so. I figured Justa to be thirty-one or thirty-two, and he'd already told me that Norris was two years younger than him and that Ben was two years younger than Norris.

Justa had offered to hitch the buggy back up, but it only being a half mile, I thought the walk would do me good.

We went in the back of the house and passed down a hall with a door opening off to the right, into what I took to be the dining room and, beyond that, the kitchen, judging from the sounds and the smells. Then, a little further on, we turned left into a big, comfortable room that Justa said doubled as an office and a place to sit around. He said there was a parlor, but he said it hadn't got much use since their mother had died.

We came in, and I recognized them right off from Justa's description. His brother Ben was sitting against the far wall in a straight-backed chair he had tipped back against the wall. Norris was sitting in a swivel chair on one side of a huge double desk. He had his face buried in some papers and didn't look up right away. The old man, Howard, was sitting in a rocking chair right near the door to another room. That was the father of all three of them. He didn't quite fit his clothes anymore, but I could see from the framework of the man that he'd once been of a size not to take too lightly. Justa said he'd never been the same since he'd lost his wife, and then, some seven or eight years back, a bullet had nicked his lungs and his heart had been affected. He was on doctor's orders not to drink more than one watered whiskey a day, but Justa said he probably snuck about four or five straight ones and never even felt guilty about it.

They gave me a good welcome when we came in. Justa had been over while I was sleeping and told them we'd be coming up to visit. Ben and Norris got up to shake hands. The old man started to make a struggle with the rocking chair, but I got over to him and said, "Keep your seat, keep your seat," and we shook.

Justa said, "Ben, go look in the liquor closet and find Wilson a jug of brandy. He don't *drink* whiskey."

I waved away the idea. I said, "No, no. Whiskey is my regular drink. Justa seen me drinking brandy one time when I couldn't lay my hands on nothing else and got crosswise of the entire matter."

"Liar," Justa said. "You lie worse than Howard does about them drinks he sneaks."

The old man said, "Here! What kind of talk is that? Mr. Young, you'll pardon these rowdies. Their mother and I done our best, but you see what it's come to. Grown son callin' his father a liar."

Ben got me and Justa a glass, and then we poured out all around, the old man included, said, "Luck," and then knocked them back as befits the toast. After that Ben refilled our glasses, and me and Justa found seats along the back wall. Ben set the bottle of whiskey on a handy table, and we settled down for a visit.

It was easy to see that Ben and Justa were brothers. Except for Ben being closer to my size, they favored in nearly every way including both of them looking like there was some Indian blood in their past. And I could see they took their looks from their daddy, even though the flesh was starting to sag around his face. Norris must have took after the mother because he wasn't a thing like Ben and Justa. Where they were dark, he was fair; where they were muscled up and hard-looking, he sort of had a soft appearance. Of course it could have come from the clothes he was wearing. He had taken off his tie, but he was still dressed in a linen sack suit and was wearing shoes instead of boots.

The senior Mr. Williams said, "How is your wound coming along, Mr. Young?"

"It's fetching up right nicely," I said. "Course it wasn't much to start with."

Justa must have told them something of what had happened because Ben said, "How did this man in Galveston come to shoot you, Mr. Young?"

I said, "Well, I guess it was over a matter of some twenty thousand dollars."

Ben said, "That don't sound very smart to me. Not unless he set a hell of a store on money."

"Why not?"

He shrugged. He said, "Hell, Justa says he knew who you were. Unless he knew he was going to kill you, I'd think shooting you would be a mighty risky business."

I said, "Maybe he thinks he did kill me."

Justa said, "I thought you said he just took the one wild shot at you and run through the door back into the warehouse?"

"He did. I didn't have but one cartridge left in the wheel, and I kind of took a wild shot at him. But he was through the door by then."

Ben said, "He might not have even thought he hit you."

I took a drink of whiskey. "One thing for damn sure, he wasn't sticking around to find out. But he might have thought that one of them other three had hit me even though I was still shooting. I was just starting to raise up when he shot. But I'd been down on my knees."

Mr. Williams leaned forward in his rocking chair. He said, "Justa said there were three others, so-called vigilantes, with hoods over their heads. He said they came in with drawn pistols. Did they come firing?"

"Yes, sir. They come through the door Phil Sharp opened for them and let off a barrage the minute they were in the room. But I was on the floor by then."

Ben said, "Did you fan?"

I shook my head. I said, "No. I fan sometimes, but I couldn't then. The corner of the desk was in the way, and if I'd lowered my revolver to fan it, I couldn't have got at them. I was drawing when I went to the floor, and I had my revolver cocked. I shot the first one that way and then fired three shots double-action at the other two. There was one still standing, and I cocked my pistol and shot him in the chest because, even as close as they was, you know a man can't get no real accuracy pulling the trigger double-action. Too much barrel deviation."

Ben said, "I still think the man was a damn fool to try and kill you over money, even twenty thousand dollars. That's too big a risk."

Justa said, "Ben, there were four of them."

"Yeah, but it was Wilson Young they were planning to shoot. If Sharp had had any sense, he'd 've given you the money and then shot you in the back when you were leaving."

I half smiled. I said, "That wouldn't look too good for a vigilante committee. Besides, they might figure I still got friends."

Norris said, "He should have paid you. I have heard of Phil Sharp, and twenty thousand is not that much money to him."

I said, "He took on like it was."

Norris said, "Maybe it was because he considered you fair game."

Ben said, "What do you mean by that?"

I answered for Norris. I said, "Well, Ben, I ain't exactly clear of the law throughout the whole state. We got us a kind of Mexican standoff right now in certain areas. I don't do nothing illegal and they leave me alone. But I reckon Sharp figured I could still be considered a wanted man, especially that far off my range, and it wouldn't be no hardship on him to bring in three of his bully boys and gun me down. Give them a little practice, impress the sheriff with what a good outfit they were. And if he could save twenty thousand dollars in the bargain, why so much the better."

Ben said, "And get known as the man who brought Wilson Young down." He sipped at his whiskey. He said, "Wonder what he thinks of the idea right now."

I said, "If I get the chance, I intend to find out."

Norris said, "Would you expect him to go to the law on the matter? Make some claim that you broke in and were threatening him?"

I looked over at Justa. Neither one of us knew for certain, but I was curious as to what Justa thought. He said, "Well, Phil Sharp has already acted like a fool once. Nothing to keep him from doing it again. But he is going to have a hell of a time explaining how Will broke in on *four* of them and shot the three who *didn't* owe him money and let the least likely man with a gun get away."

Norris said, "Can't we get Lew Vara to look into this matter? Communicate with the Galveston sheriff in some way or go see him and find out what he knows?"

Mr. Williams said, "I reckon we better let Mr. Young do the deciding about what he wants to do. If we can help him, we will, just like he helped Justa. Until then we better just set back." He held out his glass to Ben. He said, "Son, if you'd fill me up here again, I'd like to make a toast to Mr. Young in appreciation for helping to get Justa out of that mess he got himself in down there in Del Rio."

Ben started to pick up the whiskey bottle, but Justa said, right quick, "Hold on there, Ben. Howard, you slippery devil, that was a mighty nice effort, but if you want to toast Wilson, you'll be doing it with water."

The old man said, "Now, Justa—"

Justa said, "Listen, old man, you might can fool Ben with that tomfoolery, but you ain't going to catch me out that easy. Now, you want to toast with some water?"

The old man frowned and rocked back in his chair. He said, "Well, them things is always getting overdone, toasts and such."

The old man really was a pistol. If Justa hadn't jumped in, Ben, without thinking, would have poured him out a tumblerful of whiskey. It near made me laugh.

Justa said, to me, "You can see now how this ranch got started. With stolen cattle. Forty years ago Howard showed up out here with nothing more than a running iron and a chaw of tobacco. I think he wore the running iron out before he did the chaw."

We had another drink and then left. Walking back, Justa said, "Norris is right. This matter ought to be looked into as quick as possible. We can't go on operating in the dark."

I said, quickly, "There ain't no 'we' to it, Justa. There was killings involved in this. Two at least. I ain't letting you get mixed up in that."

Justa said, "There was more killings in my trouble in Del Rio."

"Yes, but that was my home ground. This is different. Galveston is as much off your range as it is mine."

Justa said, "Well, we'll talk about it tomorrow. How's your side?"

"It's doing better. But we ain't going to have any more to talk about tomorrow than we do tonight."

Justa said, kind of to himself, "You know, now that I think about it, I wonder why Phil Sharp would try and have you killed. Pretty goddam dumb play when you think about it."

I said, "Have you folks all gone deaf? It was twenty thousand dollars."

"Norris said that wasn't big money for him."

I said, "If it wasn't big money, how come he didn't pay me in Del Rio? Write me out a bank draft? He said he needed his cash for some business inside Mexico, but a big operator like him would have his checkbook with him. Or why didn't he wire the money when he got back home? Hell, if I'm recollecting correctly, was a man named Justa Williams almost went to war over a matter of thirty-two thousand dollars. Which ain't a hell of a lot more than the twenty Sharp owed me."

Justa said, "That was different."

"Oh. I see. It was you and now it's me. Yeah, that is different. All right, why do *you* think he tried to kill me?"

It was a well-lit night and I could see him shrug. He said, "Hell, maybe he wanted your whorehouse."

In the dark and over the uneven ground I stumbled. Justa put out a hand to steady me. I said, "It ain't no whorehouse. I mean I don't run it like a whorehouse. It is mainly for the use of the big gamblers, to keep them playing. Just like the saloon part. Hell, if a man is betting enough, win or lose, I seldom charge for the girls or the whiskey. It's a cathouse. I keep telling you."

"He have anybody with him this last time?"

"He always come with a couple of what looked to be hired hands. I couldn't say if they was *pistoleros,* but they looked capable. But you'd expect that of a man that was going into Mexico with cash, a lot of cash."

"Did they gamble?"

"Not so you'd notice. Mostly they just stood around and watched Sharp."

"Even when he went upstairs with the girls?"

I gave him a disgusted look. I said, "Now, don't talk like you've got a stick of peppermint candy in your mouth. Besides, the cathouse wouldn't have done him no good. Evita and Lupita run that part, and they got the girls. They wouldn't have worked for Sharp. And they damn sure wouldn't have worked for him if he'd shot me."

We had got to the back of Justa's house. I could see a dim light burning inside. We let ourselves in through the kitchen door and then went into Justa's office, the little room off the parlor where he'd disappeared to sweeten up his lemonade. The office was where he kept his drinking material. I got myself a tumbler of brandy, and Justa poured himself some whiskey. We went into the parlor, where the lamp was burning. Nora had already gone to bed, it being about half past ten. I was feeling a little wore out myself in spite of the long nap I'd had. Losing blood will do that to a man. Takes him a while to get it all back.

When we'd got settled, Justa said, "How was your business doing?"

I said, "Hell, I couldn't believe it. I thought I'd discovered a money tree. I was way ahead of my loan."

"Then maybe he wanted your casino. He was a gambler. He could see the business you were doing."

"Killing me wouldn't have got him my place," I said. "Not unless the bank took him in as a partner."

Justa said, "Banks ain't naturally in the casino business. Kill you and all the bank has got is an empty building. Maybe Sharp figured to get you out of the way and open a place of his own."

I said, "You're throwing a long rope now. With a little loop."

He said, "Whatever possessed you to think of such a thing in the first place?"

I said, "Hell, Justa, you know Del Rio. There's a lot of money around that place, loose money what with the outlaws and the illegal cattle being brought across from Mexico. You couldn't find a better place than Del Rio to put up that kind of joint. Hell, you saw the turnout for the horse racing. Tell you the truth it was the horse racing put the idea in my mind. First time I saw one of those race meets and saw all that money changing hands, the idea come to me that there ought to be better ways to gamble than on something as chancy as a racehorse. I got to thinking a man would want to lose his money in elegant surroundings while he was sitting in a plush chair with a good glass of whiskey and a pretty woman to console him later when he lost. So the idea just kept on growing until it seemed like the thing to do."

Justa drained his glass and got up. He said, "Well, I better get to bed. You know where your room is. Can I trust you to put the lamp out?"

"If you'll show me how to work it first."

He said, "I'll be gone when you get up. You sleep late, you hear? Juanita or Nora will fix you some breakfast. I'll be in around noon, but you take it easy. You still ain't as strong as you think you are."

I'd throwed out most of what Justa had said but, laying in bed that night, I got to thinking about Phil Sharp and my casino and about Del Rio. Del Rio was a kind of odd place, even for the border, which was pretty strange country in a state, Texas, that wasn't exactly known for being normal. Del Rio's commerce was based on the smuggling of illegal cattle across the Rio Grande and then holding them on the lush ranches around the area, to fatten them up before shipping them on up north as regular Texas beef. The cattle were illegal because they hadn't been held in quarantine for the ninety days or whatever the time was, while they were checked to see if they were carrying infectious diseases. Of course there was no profit in that. Even if the cattle were stolen, the price of feeding them while they were being held by border customs officials would eat up all the profits. Nearly all Mexican cattle were poor on account of the condition of the land in northern Mexico. The Mexican ranch owners, with all the cheap labor they

could need available, could just never get on to the idea
that they had to clear the land of the mesquite and huisache
and greasewood and whatnot if they wanted to grow good
grass and hay. And, hell, they didn't have to look very
far for proof of the fact. A man could stand on a bluff
on the south side of the Rio Grande and look over his
shoulder back into Mexico and see barren, hardscrabble
grazing land. Then he could look north and, not a half a
mile away, see pastures with foot-high grass and fat cattle.
It wasn't no accident, and it wasn't because God just didn't
like Mexicans; it was because they didn't understand that
you had to feed cattle if you wanted them to get fat. So
because there was so little grass in northern Mexico, there
were too many cattle. Half as many would have been too
many. Hell, a man didn't even have to steal them. Hiring
the men to rustle the cattle probably cost more than what
it took to just outright buy them.

I never knew what the workings of the bribery was that
allowed the rich ranchers around Del Rio to bring the
cattle over without benefit of official papers or stamps
or approval or whatever was necessary. I figured a lot
of money changed hands. But there was big money to
be made. The ranchers around Del Rio just brought them
poor little old Mexican cattle across, stuck a brand on them,
fattened them up for about six months, and then sold them
to the northern market for about ten times what they'd had
to invest in them. Was nearly as good a game as playing
poker with a trusting blind man.

That's loose money, money that's too easily made, and
there's nothing a gambler likes better than to get the chance
at a bunch of folks with loose money. The folks that have
it don't seem to think as much of it because it come so
easy. And as a consequence they don't seem to mind taking
chances with it. Not, of course, that there's much chance
involved when you play against a professional gambler.
In fact a man can generally save himself some time if he
just goes ahead and hands over his money and don't even
bother to play.

And of course it was all that loose, easy money around
that had caused me to make Del Rio my headquarters when
I'd changed professions. It really wasn't much different

than robbing banks except you used a gun less and the customers were usually more satisfied.

But I still couldn't see Phil Sharp wanting to kill me so as to get me out of the way so he could set up his own casino. It ain't all that easy to learn the ins and outs of gambling. Oh, it's easy to learn how to gamble; the hard part is to learn how to win more money than you lose. I'd been lucky in running across an old riverboat gambler who'd cut a deck or rolled dice for fifty years and knew every trick and every set of odds there was to know. I'd met him when I was laying up in Mexico recuperating from my last bad wound and deciding I was through with the owlhoot trail. I'd paid him, and he'd taught me that gambling didn't have a thing to do with luck; it had to do with skill. The old man didn't cheat, but he knew how and he knew how to spot a cheater. I worked with him for a year, and when I was through, I had me a whole new profession.

Maybe Phil Sharp did want to get into the casino business. Maybe there was something wrong with his shipping operation. Maybe he'd found him a man that could run a casino like I could, and he figured there was some heavy money in it. God knows, there wasn't no letup in the stream of Mexican cattle coming across the Rio Grande.

But laying in Justa's house and speculating wasn't going to fill a straight. I had to get well and go and find Phil Sharp and have a conversation with him. That was the only way I was going to get any answers, or any answers I would be ready to believe.

I didn't get up until going on nine. When I come out of my bedroom, Nora showed me where I could wash up and shave. They had a regular bathroom there, just like the hotel. Of course the main facilities were out back, but there was a built-in washbasin and a bathtub and a big mirror and nearly everything you wanted including running water, even though it was cold. Nora offered to heat me up some hot water to shave with, but I thanked her and said it had never made that much difference to me and I could just make do with the cold.

Except I'd forgotten how cold that artesian well water was. She said that Justa had rigged up a shower bath outside in a stall with a cistern over the top, but she couldn't take it except in the hottest months of the year, preferring to heat water on the stove and then have a proper bath. She said that Justa used the outside shower winter and summer, and she just couldn't see how he stood it in the cold months, but that was Justa for you. She was just grateful to have water piped into the house even if it was cold.

She cooked me ham and eggs, Juanita being occupied washing floors, and then sat down with a cup of coffee to keep me company at the kitchen table. She said, "How did you sleep, Mr. Young?"

"Just fine, Mrs. Williams." I flexed my left arm. "This little inconvenience is coming along mighty nicely."

With Justa out of the house it seemed fitting that we go back to formal names.

"Are your eggs all right?"

I nodded. "Couldn't be better."

"I'm sorry about the biscuits. I should have whipped up a fresh batch. My mother would have a hissy fit if she knew I'd served a guest warmed-over biscuits."

I shook my head, chewing as fast as I could. I said, "Uh-huh. I wouldn't have these biscuits any other way. No, ma'am! Mrs. Williams, you are talking to a man who only got biscuits on Christmas morning for a good many years of his life. Why, I'd rather have these biscuits than cake."

She laughed. Lord, she was a looker. She was wearing a little lightweight robin's-egg-blue frock that did nothing to hide that figure that I reckoned Justa was generally anxious to get alone with. She had her hair pulled back and tied off so that it just kind of hung down in one bunch. I asked about their son, going on two if I recollected right, but I hadn't seen him about the place.

Nora said, "Oh, he's in town staying with grandma and granddaddy. I may have to take a shotgun to go in and get him back. And then they just spoil him something rotten. He's starting to talk, and he's just ever so sassy when he comes back from grandma and granddaddy's. Wants sweets all the time. I tell Mother not to let Daddy bring him all that candy home from the store, but it does no good." She sighed. "They will be grandparents, and I suppose there is nothing can be done about it."

"No, ma'am," I said, though I didn't have much idea what she was talking about. I'd barely had parents, much less grandparents. I knew she'd been a schoolteacher, so I asked if she missed it.

She said, "Oh, not as much as I'd thought. I do miss town, though. I wish we'd get in more, but Justa's work keeps him so close."

I said, "I don't know if you could call it that in my case, but I was mostly raised by a schoolteacher. My old-maid aunt. Used to crack my head with her thimble if I didn't get my lessons up."

Nora said, "I could tell by your speech, Mr. Young, that you have been exposed to education to quite an extent. Or at least for this part of the country." She all of a sudden cocked her head to one side and stared at me for a few seconds. She said, "You know, Mr. Young, you don't favor yourself."

I was a little startled. Near as I could figure, I'd favored myself the last time I'd looked in a mirror. I said, "What?"

She laughed as she realized what she'd said. She said, "No, I don't mean that of course. I mean you don't look like I'd pictured you. Of course I'd heard of you for a number of years. Wilson Young, outlaw! Wilson Young, bank robber! It hasn't been that many years ago when my sister and I used to hear my parents talking about you. Then they'd hush up when we came into the room."

"Not fit conversation for a young girl's ears," I said dryly.

She said, hastily, "Oh, I'm not trying to make it sound like you're going on ninety. I'm younger than you and Justa, and my father is a storekeeper, and I think my mother has the key to the front door of the church. So my sister and I were rather protected. But I had heard of you for some time, even before Justa came home from Del Rio to tell me how you'd helped him."

I said, "Well, now you've got my curiosity up. Just how did you see me, Mrs. Williams? With a gray beard?"

She laughed, but she said, "No, not with a beard, but with a mustache. A great big black, drooping mustache. And I thought you'd be bigger and much meaner-looking, and just bristling with guns and knives. Maybe even with a knife cut on your face or something."

I said, "Well, you've done a pretty good job of describing Chulo. I got to say I'm glad I don't look like him."

"Chulo?"

I said, "I guess you could have called him one of my gang, though I never thought of us as a gang, just a bunch of people in the same line of work. Chulo is the biggest, meanest-looking, ugliest Mexican you ever saw. He's got the mustache and the scar on his face and a big, hooked nose, and he just fairly bristles with guns and knives, as you say. He's the only one left out of my old bunch."

"Where is he now?"

I said, "He's at my establishment in Del Rio, works there. Sort of helps folks to remember their manners."

"Ah," she said. "Tell me, Mr. Young, exactly what sort of establishment do you have? I've never quite got the straight of that yet."

I had finished my breakfast and pushed my plate back. I got out a cigarillo and lit it. I said, "Uh, it's kind of like a saloon. Little, uh, gambling."

"You mean it's a casino?"

I cleared my throat. I said, "Well, uh, yes, yes, we do have gambling. Yes, you might call it a saloon."

"Justa says you have a whorehouse."

That give me a fit of coughing. It carried on so long that Mrs. Williams got up and got me a glass of water. I drank it down, trying to think what to say. I said, "Well, uh, no, uh, not really, Mrs. Williams. That was, uh, a kind of little joke I told Justa."

She looked at me, smiling slightly. She said, "I see."

"Yes . . . ," I said, "them jokes will backfire on you sometimes." I tried desperately to change the subject. I said, "Well, I'm sorry to disappoint you, Mrs. Williams, about my looks. I'd have looked meaner if I could have."

"No, no," she said, "I didn't say I didn't like your appearance; I do. Very much. It's just that you are so gentle-acting and so pleasant. It's hard to believe you are this feared outlaw who makes men tremble in their boots."

I raised a finger in contradiction. "Ex-outlaw, Mrs. Williams, if you don't mind."

"Oh, of course."

I stood up. I said, "Well, I reckon I ought to go out and walk around a bit. Try and work some of the stiffness out."

I was about half out of the kitchen when she said, "Mr. Young?"

I turned back. "Yes ma'am?"

She said, "I want you to know that I am very much beholden to you for helping Justa in Del Rio. I was away on a family reunion when it all took place. I've gotten a few of the details from Justa and a little of the story from his brothers. I know I'll never know it all because that's Justa's way of protecting me from some of the things he has to do. But I know that it was very bad and very serious, and I know from Justa that if it hadn't been for you . . . Well, let's just say that you have my gratitude and I am in your debt. As we all are."

I shook my head and gave a self-deprecating look. I said, "Mrs. Williams, I appreciate praise as well as the next fellow, but it ain't due me. Justa was in a little bit of a tight place, but he could have got out without no interference from me. All I did was hold the horses, so to speak."

She said, steadily, "In a gunfight against seven men, you were holding the horses?"

I opened my mouth. I said, "Uh, well . . ."

She said, "Mr. Young, I'm sure my husband has sworn you to secrecy. He goes off and gets himself shot and then tries to tell me that he's been looking at ranches. Or cattle. Or something. It usually takes me a day or so, but between him and his brothers, I catch them out in enough lies, so that I finally get most of the truth. I know what happened, Mr. Young, and you were not holding the horses. Now, what would please you for lunch? Chili and tamales?"

"Be fine."

"With lemonade?"

"Oh, yes!"

"With brandy in it?"

I got out of there before she picked me clean.

I walked out on a fine spring day. I knew that Justa's house was at least three miles from the gulf, but with the breeze blowing in off the water, it seemed as if I could hear the waves breaking onto the shore. It had been a long time since I'd seen a beach with breakers rolling in, and I determined to borrow a horse and ride down to the nearest point before I left.

I just walked aimlessly, heading, more or less, in the direction of the headquarters house. My strength was returning rapidly, and my side, other than an occasional twinge when I caught it wrong, seemed almost back to normal.

After a while I began seeing cattle. I figured they were steers that weren't involved in the calving operation going on on the south side of the range and had drifted toward the north. But as little as I knew about cattle it was obvious, even to my ignorant eye, that Justa's cattle were a world and gone from the Mexican beef we had down in Del Rio, even after it had been fattened up. These cattle had been improved and it was easy to see.

I hadn't been walking far when I saw a rider coming my way, loping his horse. I figured he was about to ask what a stranger was doing on Half-Moon land, so I stopped and waited for him to come up. He skidded his horse to a stop and said, "I'll jest bet you are Wilson Young, ain't you?"

I nodded and said I was. He leaned out of the saddle and put out his hand. He said, "My name is Ray Hays. Me and Ben run the remuda."

I smiled. Hays was a man of about my age with sandy hair and a light build and a friendly face. Justa had told me about him. Some years back he'd been instrumental in getting Justa out of a tight scrape, and Justa had brought him back to work at the ranch. Or at least, Justa had said, that had been his intention. But, as it turned out, Hays had taken up a position as a member of the family and Ben's best friend, and Justa wasn't sure exactly what it was he drew wages for. But Justa said he was a mighty good man to have on your side in a fight and that, next to Ben, he was the best with a gun on the place.

Hays said, "Say, you don't look like you been shot."

I half smiled. I said, "Well, for a while there I did."

"Taking a little air this mornin'?"

"Getting out."

"Ought to walk up to the big house. Mr. Howard Williams is settin' out on the front porch in his rockin' chair. Reckon he'd welcome some company. Ain't but a quarter mile up there."

"Sounds like a good idea," I said.

Hays said, "I'd show you the way, but I got to turn these here steers back. Some of 'em is startin' to drift down towards the salt grass, and they ain't got no better sense than to eat it."

"Mighty glad to have made your acquaintance," I said.

He was about to rein his horse around when he suddenly said, "Say, lemme see you draw."

I didn't know what he was talking about for a second. I said, "What?"

He made a motion toward his own holster. He said, "You know, draw yore weapon like you do. I always heared you was the fastest thing alive. I jest wanted to see it."

Justa had told me that, aside from his usefulness in a fight, Hays was a lot like owning a good pet dog with fleas. You liked the dog, but you wished the fleas would go away. Asking me to show him my draw was his fleas. I said, "Well, Ray, I'd like to accomodate you, but I'm still a little stiff and sore. You understand."

"Aw, yeah," he said. He touched his hat. "Well, I better git."

I walked on toward the main house shaking my head. Justa said Hays was funny as a pet raccoon except he was too easy to kid. He said, "Ain't no sport in it. He takes everything I say seriously."

The old man acted like he was glad for the company. I dragged me up a wicker chair beside him and lit a cigarillo, and we set out to have a visit. Mr. Williams looked out over the rolling plains and said, "You know, Mr. Young, won't be long before this country won't be ours anymore. It's getting civilized. Won't be room in it for men like me and you. Pretty soon the most important people will be the schoolteacher and the preacher. And maybe the lawyers. Yes, the lawyers. They'll do our fighting for us with papers and writs and such instead of guns."

I reckoned he was still thinking of me as a desperado and was doing me the honor of fitting me into the rough life he must have led while he was founding the ranch in the early days. I figured he could tell some tales if he was so inclined.

But, besides that, he was talking about how civilized matters were becoming, and I was sitting there with a bullet hole in me. I said, "I don't know, Mr. Williams, that all these here modern improvements like gaslights and piped-in water and icehouses and that kind of truck are really ever going to civilize this country. Men are still going to be men. Some are going to cause trouble one way or the other."

Mr. Williams worked his mouth and then put his nose up like he was scenting the air. He said, "Mr. Young, what I think we need on a fine morning like this is something to work us up a spit with. Now, if you was to just step through the front door there and go on down the hall and into the office where we was last night, you'd find a bottle of whiskey and some glasses. If you was to fetch them out here, why I think we'd be set for the morning."

I didn't say anything for a second and I didn't move. Finally I said, "Mr. Williams, are you trying to get me in trouble?"

He give me the innocent look of a horse thief about to be hung. He said, "Why, whatever do you mean, Mr. Young?"

I said, "Justa told me about you not being allowed but one drink a day."

"And this is it."

"In the *morning?*"

"That's when I prefer it."

I got up slowly. I said, "If I catch hell from Justa about this I'm going to tell him you out-and-out lied to me."

He gave me that same look. He said, "Ain't a man's word good no more?"

I went, but reluctantly. I poured myself a small one because I really wasn't in a drinking mood. And I watered Mr. Williams's. I knew he was expecting it straight, but I also knew he wasn't supposed to have it that way.

When I brought him his drink, he looked pleased at the size of it, but then he took a big swallow and said, disgustedly, "You watered it."

"Yes, sir," I said. "I did. I don't want them sons of yours on my back."

"Damn doctors," he said. "Worse than old women."

But after a few minutes he brightened up and said, "By God, sir, I know what this house needs tonight! A poker game. Damn right! We'll have a good game of cutthroat poker tonight." He looked sideways at me. He said, "Justa tells me that's your line of work now."

"Yes, sir," I said.

He said, "Well, we'll have to see about that."

I got away when I could and got back to the house just as Nora and the maid were commencing to fix lunch. I got myself a brandy and then sat down in the parlor to sort matters out. I was healing faster than I'd expected, and it was coming to the time to think about how and when to go and visit Mr. Philip Sharp. I was not planning on informing him of my visit this time.

Justa came in not too long later, and we all went in and sat down to a lunch of chili and tamales and onion-and-tomato salad. About halfway through the meal Justa put his fork down and said, "I been into town this morning. To see Lew Vara. Him and me are going to go to Galveston to see what's up with your Mr. Sharp."

CHAPTER 4

I said, "The hell you are! Mr. Sharp is my business."

Justa said, "Now, don't talk like a fool, Wilson. You ain't got the slightest idea what's up with Sharp or the law in Galveston. For all you know they'll arrest you the minute you get near the place. It ain't been four days since you shot three members of the vigilante committee, or have you forgot?"

I said, "Ain't got nothing to do with it. This is my trouble and I'll tend to it."

Then Nora surprised me by saying, "Just like you let Justa tend to his in Del Rio?"

I had been surprised by Justa speaking of going to Galveston on my behalf in front of Nora. I had been more surprised at him doing it after having told me her attitude about him involving himself in any uncivil program that could get him shot. He'd told me that he had to constantly be lying to her about his doings because she just couldn't stand that sort of thing. She wanted the country civilized, and she wanted the guns put away and all the differences settled by a show of hands. Justa had said that she'd once grown so tired of his involvement in dangerous practices that she'd refused to let him court her anymore and had nearly run off with a Kansas City drummer that traveled in yard goods.

And now here she was taking the position that Justa should involve himself in my trouble. I just stared at her for a second. Then I said, "Mrs. Williams—Nora—Justa is a family man. I'm not. He don't need to be getting himself in this particular horse race."

She said, "He's not going down there to shoot this Mr. Sharp. He and Lew are only going to get you some information."

It sounded to me like they'd already talked it over.

She said, "Of course I wouldn't want Justa going into a dangerous situation—not that what I want has ever stopped him." And she gave him a good, hard look. "But that's not the purpose of the trip, not according to the way he explained it to me. Sheriff Vara will see the Galveston sheriff and, without letting him know he knows anything about you, sound him out about the shooting. See if it was ever reported. And find out how he feels about the vigilantes. Many sheriffs don't like them, you know. And, of course, he'll try and find out if your name has come up. Meanwhile, Justa is going to go over and see Sharp, maybe on the pretext of shipping some cattle to New Orleans. Just talk business with him. Your name will never come up unless Sharp mentions it. So I don't see where that's so dangerous. And it's the least we can do."

I looked at Justa. He was slowly chewing a piece of flour tortilla. I said, "Well, hell, you certainly can make yourself clear when you want to."

He said, "I let Nora explain it so you wouldn't think I was doing it behind her back and object on her account. Not," he added right quick, "that I ever do anything behind her back."

Nora raised her eyes to the ceiling. She said, "We built a good strong roof on this place. Not so much to keep the rain out as to keep Justa's lies from rising up to heaven."

I said, "Only thing about your plan is I'm starting to get a little itchy. I'm feeling pretty good and I'd like to get kicking. When was you thinking of going to Galveston?"

Justa said, "Well, tomorrow's Sunday. Wouldn't be much point in going then. We'll go Monday. That's just two more days. Ought to make it up and back the same day. Besides," he said, "I got to take those tents out of your wounds this afternoon."

"Like hell," I said.

"You heard Dr. Adams. Got to jerk them out. You might not be so spry and ready time I get that done."

I'd forgotten all about removing those tents. My wound had been itching at both openings, which, from past experience, I knew was a good sign. It meant they were healing in a proper manner. I said, kind of resignedly, "All right. I guess it's got to be done. But you damn well better not act like you're enjoying it."

Justa said, to Nora, "Honey, will you find me some kind of bandages? They've got to be wrapped around his chest."

She said, "I know just the thing. I've got a clean sheet that's seen better days. I'll rip you some strips from that."

Justa said, "Better bring plenty. It'll probably start the bleeding again." He looked at me. He said, "Them tents are really stuck up in them holes a good ways."

I said, "Why don't you just go to hell?"

When lunch was over, I had a drink of brandy, and then Justa and I went into the bedroom I was occupying. Justa had the bandages his wife had given him. I took off my shirt and sat down in a chair. Justa unwrapped the old dressing that the doctor had put on. The tents, the cloth strips, were hanging out of the bullet holes. Of course I could only see the one in front, but it looked remarkably clean, like the wound hadn't drained much at all.

Justa said, "You want me to work these out or just jerk them out in one pull."

I said, "Just jerk them out."

"All right. Grit your teeth."

But, amazingly, they slid out with no more pain than a stubbed toe. Justa said, "This back one ain't even bleeding. Some little pink stuff kind of leaking out."

I looked down at the hole in my side in the front. I said, "Same here. I believe it is doing all right. I may live."

Nora came in then and pushed Justa out of the way and took over the job of wrapping the bandages around my chest. I think she'd known without me saying nothing that I hadn't wanted her in there when the tents came out in case I had to let out a yelp. But she could do the bandaging better than an old fumble fingers like Justa.

After I had my shirt back on, we went and sat in the parlor and had a drink, and I told Justa about my visit with his father. I said, "He wants to play poker and no mistake."

"He try to work you for a drink?"

I looked innocent. I wasn't going to tell on the man. I said, "Naw. What are you talking about?"

Justa shrugged. He said, "I'm just surprised. Howard has got a peculiar honor system when it comes to the whiskey. The bottle sits in there all day, and he could have half a dozen if he wanted, but he generally won't sneak one. But if he can get somebody to bring him one so that he's drinking with a guest, why then he figures that one don't count. Not that he don't sneak them anyway, but he don't count them others that he finagles his way into. Yeah, I reckon we ought to play some poker. Howard don't get all that much recreation. And he does love to play poker."

I didn't much want to play with friends. I said, "What we going to play for, two-bit, four-bit?"

Justa said, "With Howard? Hell, no! He'd tell you right quick that's just draw out. Howard can play, believe me. And he knows how to use a bet. He don't figure it's a bet unless it's going to hurt you to call and lose. I imagine we'll play dollar ante, pot limit."

That kind of poker could build some sizeable pots and also dig into a man's pocketbook. I said, "Justa, you reckon we ought to play for that much?"

He said, "Howard won't play for less. And we ought to have a sixth player. I guess I'll loan Ray Hays some money, five hundred or so."

"Five hundred?" I couldn't imagine loaning a cowhand that kind of money. I said, "He draw those kind of wages? Where you can loan him that much money?"

Justa said, "Hell, no!" He looked at me like I'd lost my mind. He said, "He draws what everybody else draws. We are just a good deal freer about loaning him money."

"How does he pay it back?"

"He don't. But we can't pay him more than the other hands. That would cause trouble. Besides, any money I give him won't leave the game. I'll see to that."

I said, "Well, if you're sure this is going to be all right. I guess I could play kind of bad."

He cut his eyes around at me. He said, "You think you're a better poker player than I am?"

I said, "No. I don't *think* I'm a better player. I *know* I am."

"We'll see," he said.

Out of respect for the old man's bedtime we started in playing early, about seven o'clock that evening. I didn't play too hard, kind of hiding my light under a bushel, except when I got a shot at Justa. Ben, as might have been figured, was a wild, plunging player, having no idea of managing his money or any of the strategies of the game. Norris was a very cautious better, throwing in his hand too early sometimes and then other times not betting enough when the odds were on his side. Ray Hays played like a man playing on borrowed money. On the few occasions when I found myself head up with him at the close of a hand, I threw my cards in just to make sure he won enough pots to stay about even.

Justa played a good, solid game. That evening he wasn't catching many good cards, but, over the course of time, he would take the money of most amateurs. I nearly had him sandbagged one time in a hand of five-card draw when I drew one card to a hand of three kings, a hand I'd normally have drawn two cards to. The one-card draw made him think I was holding two pair. He could have thought I was drawing to a straight or a flush, but I'd opened, so he knew I had at least jacks or better. I checked my three kings, and Ben bet twenty dollars. Justa raised him fifty dollars, making it seventy dollars to me. I called the seventy and then raised two hundred. Ben folded, and then Justa spent an awful long time looking at me and then at his cards. Finally he said, "I think I got the best hand," and he showed me three tens. He said, "But I'm going to throw them in. I don't think you made a full house. I think you got two pair."

I said, "What I got is two hundred dollars. How about you?"

He pitched his cards in. He said, "I'll bet you fifty dollars on the side you ain't got better than two pair."

I showed him the three kings, and he silently passed me over fifty dollars in chips. Ben said, "He make his full house?"

"I can't say," Justa said. But I could see he was broiling to make some sort of remark about people who disguised their hands by making a one-card draw to three of a kind.

But it was the old man who was the revelation. He, indeed, had done his fair share of shearing the sheep. I imagined that more than one nail that had gone into the roof over our heads had been paid for with poker winnings. I took special note during the early part of the game that he was careful to get caught bluffing, especially when the bet was small. Of course the purpose of that was to trap you, later on, when he was holding the real goods and the bet was much larger. Then you'd think the old man was just trying to buy another pot, only to discover, to the reduction of your pile of chips, that he had the best hand.

We had resolved to quit no later than ten o'clock so that Howard could get to bed. We were playing five-card stud, and my first four cards were all of a row—a four, five, six, with a seven in the hole. All I had to do was catch a three or an eight on the next card, and I'd have the straight. But Howard had been betting hard almost from the very first. Of course I didn't know what his hole card was, but before the last card, he had a pair of aces showing and a ten. His hard betting had driven out everyone but me and him, and I'd called a twenty-dollar bet to see the last card. Justa was dealing and he gave me an eight. I had my straight. Then he gave Howard a ten, and the old man had two pair showing, aces and tens.

He said, "Heh, heh, heh!" pracitally rubbing his hands in glee. He said, "Oh, I've got you now, Mr. Wilson Young. You have made your straight, an eight high I'll bet. And I've got a full house and you don't believe it! Yes, sir, I have got you now! With that straight which I am convinced you've got, you've got to call any bet I make. And I've got a full house!"

Of course he'd known I was drawing for a straight since I'd stayed through some stiff bets without any pairs showing, certainly nothing that could have beat his aces. He couldn't necessarily know I had the straight, though if he had the full house, he'd sure be hoping I did. The odds on drawing a straight in five-card stud are very long. The odds on drawing a full house are very, very long. The sad part about making a full house in stud is that usually no one can beat the two pair you've got showing, so everyone folds and you don't make any money off a superb hand. What you dream of is to have the full house and to have some poor sucker have a straight, or even a flush. Or even three of a kind. All of those beat two pair, and he can't fold without seeing your hole card.

So Howard had me over a barrel. He said, "Yessir! Yessir! I have got me one professional gambler and I've got him good. Tell you what, Mr. Young . . . I am going to make this mighty light on you. I am just going to bet a hunnert dollars into you. Now you can raise, you understand." And then he went, "Heh, heh, heh," again.

I said, to Justa, "That's some poker face your daddy has got there. What does he act like when he actually get a good hand?"

Howard said, "You'll think good hand, Mr. Young, if you pay to see this here hole card."

I looked down at my pile of chips and calculated that I was about three hundred ahead. I thought I'd give the old man a little fun for his money. I knew he didn't have the full house. The other players in the game were careless about throwing their hands back in the discard pile when they folded, and some of them had been thrown back faceup. I had already seen two aces and two tens, and unless the old man was playing with a different deck, there wasn't another ace or ten for him to have facedown as his hole card. I said, "All right, sir, tell you what I'm going to do." I picked up chips and threw them in the jackpot in the middle of the table. I said, "There's your hundred, and I'm just going to raise you back fifty dollars."

"Fifty dollars!" he said. "Is that all you be going to raise? My Lord, son, you are playing a child's game. I never heard of such a thing, man raising just fifty dollars with a wired straight. I'll show you what a raise is." He went to fumbling around in his chips with his old, gnarled hands and pushed two stacks forward. He said, "There! There's your fifty and two hunnert besides. Now, that's what we call a raise."

I looked at him for a moment and laughed. He was having a mighty good time. Finally I looked sour. I said, "What the hell. You convinced me. I guess you've got the full house."

I turned my cards over and threw them in.

Boy, that got a rise out of him. He raked in the chips, chortling all the while like a rooster in a henhouse. Then nothing would do but that he had to show me he'd bluffed me out of the pot. It ain't considered real good etiquette in a serious poker game to do so, but he turned his hole card over to show me it didn't match his aces or tens. It was a jack of diamonds. Naturally I had to swear around for a minute or two and call him some names for bluffing me out like that and generally just let him enjoy the moment.

That was one of the last hands. Walking through the night, Justa said, "You knew Howard didn't have a full house. How come you let him win?"

I yawned. I said, "What would you have done? Reckon how much fun that old man has from day to day?"

Justa said, "Well, you done good. Though I didn't know you could be a professional gambler and have a soft heart. I thought you was supposed to be willing to win the milk money off new mothers."

"Only the ugly ones," I said.

But my mind was really elsewhere. Now that I was nearly healed, I was itching to get the business settled with Phil Sharp and get back to the running of my establishment. I had no idea of how I was going to get at him because I expected that he would be wary for some time to come. But I just had to hope that I could manage to arrange matters to my advantage somehow. But of course I knew better than to put much faith in hope. Hope and four quarters make an even dollar.

I got up around eight o'clock, having lain awake studying on how I was going to approach Sharp, went into the bathroom and washed my face and tended to my teeth and then wandered into the kitchen. Justa was sitting at the table drinking coffee. I said, "Where's Nora?"

He said, "It's Sunday. She's gone in to church. Had to leave early on account of she teaches Sunday school."

I said, "How come you didn't go?"

He was measuring sugar into his cup. He said, without looking up, "I don't teach Sunday school."

I got myself a cup and went over to the stove and poured myself out some coffee from the pot. Justa said, "Juanita's around here somewhere. She'll fix you some breakfast. I already ate."

I wasn't particularly hungry, but Justa thought it was a good idea that I eat, so he hollered up Juanita and she fixed me some ham and eggs.

After breakfast we went out and Justa saddled up a couple of horses. He kept three in the little trap right behind his house. He rode the dun he'd been on when he'd come into town and saddled a little roan mare for me. I protested that I could saddle my own horse, but Justa said it was best not to risk tearing anything at this late date. He said, "I can't have you ruining all that careful doctoring I done for you just because you got to be bullheaded."

We mounted up, and then Justa took me on a circuit of parts of the ranch. Of course it was too big to cover in one day, being about two hundred thousand acres in grazing land. But we took a look at the purebred Hereford herd, which was Justa's pride and joy. They were little square-built cattle that Justa said were gentle and easy to work and pure beef from one end to another. He said they were worth, when the market was right, better than twice what a crossbred steer would bring and that there was no comparison between them and the old longhorns.

Every now and then we'd see a rider tending to a small herd of mama cows. Justa said the calving was just about over, so they'd given half the men the day off. The other half would get the next Sunday off.

We fooled around until just about noon and then rode up to the big house. We'd take lunch there, as Nora wouldn't be back until the afternoon and Juanita was given Sundays off as soon as she fixed breakfast.

The five of us ate around a great big old-fashioned round dining table that looked like it must have weighed a ton. Ben said, to me, "We're in luck. Buttercup's drunk."

I didn't quite get that until Justa explained that Buttercup was an old bronc buster who'd been with his daddy since Noah and the flood. Justa said, looking at his daddy, "He can't cook a lick. In fact he's going to kill somebody someday, but Howard insists on letting him cook for the family. We got two Mexican women that are good cooks,

and they cook for the crew. The hired hands would all quit
if they had to eat Buttercup's cooking, but Howard figures
it's all right if he poisons the family."

Howard said, "Now, Justa, you got to leave a man a
little pride. Tom Butterfield helped me settle this place—I
wish you boys would quit calling him that awful name—
and he's entitled to his dignity. He won't take a pension
without earning it. That's the way of the man."

Ben said, "But it's all right today. The Mexican women
will do us up fine."

Howard was looking to be in pretty good shape. Justa
said he didn't often get up to eat with the family, just
took a light meal back in the dayroom he stayed in right
off the office. Now he looked at me and said, "Well,
Mr. Young, run into any more bobtailed full houses lately?"

I said, "Next time we play with my deck."

He give a pretty good "Heh, heh, heh" at that one, but
I was just glad to see the old man feeling fine. Justa had
talked about him in Del Rio and had said he didn't know
what he was going to do when Howard finally crossed on
over. He said, "I know as much about ranching as any man
in the country. And I know how to direct Norris in his
business ventures and how to control Ben when he gets out
of hand. But there's something about knowing that Howard
is always there, that I can go to him for advice, that gives
me a sure feeling about matters. I don't go to him that
often, but I dread the day when he ain't going to be there
to go to." Justa had said he had his good days and his bad
days, but he'd said, "As time passes he's having more bad
days than good ones. One day a bad day is going to be his
last one."

For lunch we had a beef stew that was just about the
best I'd ever had. It was in a good thick gravy with big
chunks of tender beef and potatoes and carrots and onions.
To go with it the Mexican women brought in big platters
of thickly sliced light bread, and I just ate until I thought
I'd pop. We drank beer with the meal. The Williamses kept
a number of kegs down in the cellar, and the women kept
bringing up big pitchers of the cool beer. When we finally
finished, I wasn't sure I could walk.

We all went into the office and sat around. Ben passed the whiskey bottle, and everybody got himself a tumblerful and got comfortable.

Ben said, to me, "How you figure to go after this man?"

I shook my head. I said, "I don't know. I don't know enough yet. Justa is going to do some scouting for me, and then I'll have a little look myself if everything appears all right."

"Hell, I'd just call him out and blow a hole in him."

I said, "No, I want to talk to him first."

"Talk to him?" Ben looked at me in some amazement. "What the hell you want to talk to him about? Hell, the man bushwhacked you. He deserves the same. It's only a miracle and his bad aim you ain't dead right now."

I said, "I want to know why he did it. I want to make sure it was just the twenty thousand dollars. Justa has got me thinking." I took a drink of whiskey. I said, "Anyway, I want to talk to him, see what he has to say." I half smiled. "After all, he was a good customer. Maybe I did something that set him off. I need to find out so I don't make the same mistake again."

Norris said, "Excuse me, Mr. Young, but I find your manner of speech and your demeanor difficult to reconcile with your legend."

I was pretty sure what he meant, but I looked over at Justa just to be sure. Justa said, "He means you don't talk and act like the kill-crazy, gun-happy, bank-robbing son of a bitch that everybody always heard you were."

I said, dryly, "I appreciate you putting it so well, Mr. Justa Williams." I got out a cigarillo and lit it and looked at Norris with a kind of amused smile on my face. I said, "I can't tell from the way you put that, Mr. Williams, if you are disappointed or just surprised."

Ben laughed, but Norris barely smiled. He didn't appear to me to be a man who was ever likely to break anything from laughing too hard. He said, "I didn't mean it so much personal, Mr. Young, as an inquiry into the stuff of myths and how they begin and grow."

I was about to say something when Justa broke in. He said, quietly, "I'd be a little sparing with that word *myth*, Norris, was I you. You just ain't seen Wilson in the right situation and circumstances. I have."

I was getting a little tired of being talked about, so I got up and said I thought I'd go out and sit on the porch, it being such a fine day. Justa said, "Go ahead. I'll just hunt me up something to smoke and be right along."

I went out on the porch and sat down on the steps. I had the feeling I had just been high-hatted by Norris, but I couldn't be sure. The way he talked, you couldn't be sure of anything he said. But I had got the distinct impression that he was hinting that I might not be the real goods.

Down the row of buildings that led to the big barn I could see a group of men squatting around and talking and whittling and spitting tobacco juice. They would be the hired hands that had the day off. While I watched, one of them detached himself and came walking my way. I recognized him right off as Ray Hays. He came up and touched his hat brim and said, "Well, howdy, Mr. Young. You look like you be perkin' up more every day."

I said, "The undertaker has give up on me and gone back to town."

About then Justa came out and set down beside me. He said, to Hays, "Ray, what the hell are you doing here?"

Hays kind of jerked back. He said, "Why, Boss, I'm off. It's Sunday. Them boys down there in front of the bunkhouse is off too."

Justa said, "The *working* hands get the day off. What's that got to do with you?"

Hays said, "Why, I—"

Justa said, "Never mind. I want you to go hunt up two empty whiskey bottles. Might be some in the cellar under the kitchen."

"*Empty* whiskey bottles?"

"Empty. And be quick about it."

Hays said, "Boss, a empty whiskey bottle is about as much good as a dry cow."

Justa said, "Hays!"

"I'm goin', I'm goin'."

When he'd gone into the house, Justa looked around at me. He said, "Ben wants to draw against you."

I made a face. I said, "Aw, hell, Justa. You know I don't care for that kind of foolishness. It's silly."

Justa said, "He's been dying to do it ever since you got here. He's just barely been able to hold himself in until you got healed up some."

I said, "Oh, hell! What am I, some kind of prize pig at a fair?"

Justa said, "Indulge him. It ain't going to hurt you none. Besides, he might surprise you. He is damn fast, the fastest around here by a country mile."

I gave him a sour look.

Justa said, "Quit being a bastard. Hell, you're his hero."

He had the good grace to laugh when he said it.

Ben came out just then. He stepped off the porch and down to the ground. He said, "Did Justa ask you?"

I nodded.

"Will you? I know it sounds kind of childish, but I ain't ever likely to get this kind of opportunity again. I'd just kind of like to know how I stack up against the best."

I took my cigarillo out of my mouth. I said, "What makes you think I'm the best?"

"That's what they say," he said.

I glanced at the way he had his gun rig set up. He was wearing a cutaway holster, but I still couldn't make out the caliber of his gun. I thought he was wearing the holster rig set a little too far back. I said, "You get slower when you get older, Ben. I might not can give you a fair showing."

He said, "I sort of doubt that for some reason."

I said, "Well, it's something to do on a spring afternoon. Justa has sent Hays for a couple of whiskey bottles. I reckon that is their purpose. Where you want to do this?"

He looked around. Not too far from the front of the house there was a small catch pen with posts sticking up about four feet. He said, "How about over there? Nothing behind except the barn. We can't hit no cattle by mistake."

About then Hays came out with the empty whiskey bottles. I dropped my cigarillo, ground it out with my boot heel, and then started off toward the little pen with Ben and Justa and Hays. The posts were about ten feet apart. Justa had Hays put one bottle on top of each post. I said, to Ben, "What distance?"

He shrugged. He said, "I don't care."

I said, "Well, what are you after, speed or accuracy or both?"

"I guess a little of both."

I said, "Then I'd say about five paces. You won't get into many gunfights at a much longer range and them whiskey bottles is pretty small targets for a handgun. Ain't exactly the size of a man's chest."

I took the bottle on my right and stepped off the distance. Ben lined up to my left in front of the other bottle. Out of the corner of my left eye I could see Ben standing there, his right hand twitching toward his holster. That was a mistake. A man wanted his hand nice and calm, nice and relaxed as he drew. Twitching around just got the muscles confused. I said, "Justa?"

"I'll just say go."

"That suit you, Ben?"

"Yeah." His voice sounded tense. I could see the men from the bunkhouse starting to wander our way. We were kind of facing away from them at an angle, but they could see us and see the bottles on the fence, and they could figure out what was going on.

I don't have a trigger guard on my pistol. As I draw, I am cocking it with my thumb, and I'm using my trigger finger to point toward my target as I'm clearing the holster with my revolver. Just an instant before I come level with my target, my trigger finger comes back in a smooth pull and the gun fires as it bears on the target. It's all one motion. I've practiced it maybe a million times. Maybe more.

Justa said, "Go!" and my bottle exploded in time with the explosion of Justa's word and my revolver. I stood there, the smoke curling slowly out of the barrel of my revolver. Ben hadn't fired. I looked over at him. He was standing there with his gun clear of the holster, but not quite leveled on the target. He looked at me and said, "My gawd!"

Justa said, "Satisfied?"

I could hear the hired hands, who'd moved close enough to see, murmuring among themselves. Ray Hays said, "I think I saw that."

I put my revolver back in the holster. I said, to Ben, "Let's go talk. Maybe I can show you a few things."

DEAD MAN'S POKER

"Hell!" he said. He put his revolver away. "What's the point? Not after what I just seen."

I got him to walk on around the house with me. I said, "Let's get out back here where we don't have so damn much of a crowd."

He was still shaking his head. He said, "When Justa came back from Del Rio, he told a story about when you and him were sitting in a saloon in Del Rio and some man on the prod come up looking for trouble. Justa said that one second your hand was just laying on the table and the next instant it had a revolver in it. He said it just kind of appeared there. I didn't believe him then, but I do now. Hell! I been thinking all this time I was fast! Son of a bitch!"

"Just let me show you a few things," I said. "You ain't all that far off. The main thing you are doing is making too many moves. Just needs to be that one."

Nora cooked supper for us that night. She fixed us pork chops and fried potatoes and sliced tomatoes. Justa said, poking at a slice of tomato, "Nora has got a garden full of tomatoes and such truck, and she is determined we are going to eat them up if we have to have tomatoes for breakfast. How'd you like to get up to a breakfast of tomatoes and peas?"

Nora turned to me. She said, "My husband contents himself with the *Stockman's Journal* and other publications that specialize in the price of cattle. If he'd ever read a newspaper—and I don't mean that rag they put out in Blessing—but a good newspaper, like the *Houston Post* or the *Galveston Gazette,* that comes in every day on the train, or even a good magazine, he'd know that medical science is discovering that vitamins are very important and can affect our health. And fresh vegetables are very heavy in vitamins."

Justa said, "Show me a vitamin. Just point out a vitamin on this here tomato."

Nora gave him a look. She said, "Well, of course, you can't see a vitamin."

He said, "I don't see how something I can't see can affect me."

She put her fork down. She said, "Oh, really? Can you see a bushwhacker?"

He said, "Awww, that ain't the same thing."

"Just answer me. Can you see a bushwhacker?"

I laughed. I could see that she had him.

He said, "Well, hell no, you can't see a bushwhacker. He wouldn't be a bushwhacker if you could see him."

"But he can affect you?"

He threw up his hands. He said, "Don't ever argue with a woman, Wilson. Just eat your damn vegetables and don't argue. You can't win."

It was a treat for me to eat fresh produce. Them Mexican girls of mine were in the habit of throwing every kind of hot sauce on hand at anything that even looked like a vegetable. When they were done, the poor little onion or whatever didn't look a thing like it had when it started out. My girls figured if a meal didn't have grease and chili powder on it, it wasn't fit to eat.

After supper we sat around the parlor for a time. Me and Justa were having a drink, and Nora was doing a little fancy sewing. Out of the blue Nora asked me practically the same question Norris had. Well, Norris's hadn't been exactly a question, more like a bald statement. But it amounted to the same thing. Nora said, "Wilson, I confess I am more than consumed by how your feet found the outlaw trail. Was it an accident? Was it forced upon you? It seems so alien to your nature, at least what I've seen of it these few days."

Justa laughed and shook his head. He said, "Boy howdy, must be something wrong with my eyes. Ain't never crossed my mind to wonder about your 'nature,' Wilson."

Mindful that Nora had been to church services that day, I kind of tempered the truth enough in my favor to reach a sympathetic ear, but not so much that the roof of the house might fall in. I said, "Well, Miss Nora, it was some of both. I know that when I ran away from home at the age of fourteen, having just completed the tenth grade in school, I never done so with the express purpose of being a outlaw. I won't go into the circumstances that forced me to leave my home with my old-maid aunt in Corpus Christi, but I felt they were sufficient."

Nora said, "That's a very tender age for one to set out on his own. Especially if he has come from a genteel background."

Justa made some kind of a sound, putting his hand over his face so as to cover his mouth. I never let it bother me. I said, "But once set on that course, I left that comfortable home with scarcely more than the clothes on my back. I was riding an old nag that had once carried me back and forth from the school I had attended with such pleasure. Other than that, all I had to my name was the legacy my daddy had left me: a U.S. Army issue .44-caliber revolver. Well, as fate would have it, I wasn't but five miles from home, already hungry, when I chanced upon a rancher driving a buggy down the little road into Corpus. I knew this man by sight, though I didn't know his name. But I knew he was a man of means. Miss Nora, I do not know how it happened or why it happened, but the next thing I knew I had stopped that man on the road and was pointing that big revolver at him and demanding money. I remember as if it was yesterday. I can still see the surprise on that poor man's face. He said, 'Boy, are you crazy? You're nothing but a kid!' I recall replying, 'Yes, but this here revolver don't know it. Now I'll have your money!' "

Nora said, "Oh, my!"

Justa made that sound again like he was suffocating.

I said, "Yes, ma'am. I am sorry to tell you, but I taken nine dollars and change off that rancher and, to add to that, took his buggy horse as well."

Justa said, "I guess that was a surprise to you too, stealing his horse so as to get a better getaway time."

I ignored him. I said, "So, Miss Nora, that was my first step on the outlaw trail. I don't know if you could call it an accident or the devil working through a young, bewildered boy."

Justa said, loudly, "Most people call it robbery."

Nora said, "Hush, Justa. Can't you see it's painful for Wilson to talk about it?"

Justa said, "Oh, my aching—"

I said, "After that, try as I would, I couldn't find a place to stop for many long years."

Nora said, "Well, you're all right now. You've found the right path now."

Justa muttered something. Nora turned on him. She said, "What?"

He said, "Nothing, honey. I was just wondering when Wilson was going to be called to the ministry. I know for a fact he's already got a place in Del Rio he can hold services."

She gave him a severe look. She said, "You just must be sacrilegious. One of these days, Justa, it's all going to catch up to you."

I just sat there looking pious and going, "tsk, tsk, tsk."

It wasn't long before Nora retired for the night. I knew Justa wasn't going to be long behind her because he'd have to be up really early. He and Lew Vara were taking the eight o'clock train next morning for Galveston, and it was a good hour and a half ride into Blessing. I got a piece of paper and a pencil from Justa. I wanted him to send a telegram for me when he got into town. I addressed it to Evita Obregon care of the Border Palace in Del Rio. The message instructed her to put Chulo on the first train to Blessing, as I wanted him here as soon as possible. I instructed her to have him go to the sheriff's office as soon as he got to town and wait for me to show up. I sent the message to Evita because Chulo couldn't read. I knew the idea of going to a sheriff's office on purpose was going to be a little strange to him, but I told Evita to be sure that Chulo went there and stayed there and that word would be brought to me of his arrival. I especially instructed her to instruct Chulo to behave himself and to speak to no one but the sheriff and not to drink any whiskey.

Justa looked at the message. He said, "Border *Palace!* Is that what you call that honky-tonk and whorehouse you got down there? Palace?"

"Send the telegram."

He said, "Did you listen to yourself telling that story to Nora about how you come to be an outlaw?"

I said, "It's the way it happened."

He said, "A little of it might be true. But you make it sound like they was six men holding shotguns on you forcing you to stick that rancher up. My word, I never heard such a line of bull. Don't shoot Phil Sharp, talk him to death. It will be a much crueler fate."

I said, "I wouldn't say too much was I you. Remember what Nora said, it's all going to catch up with you some sweet day."

He tapped the piece of paper. "This Chulo. What are you sending for him for?"

"Little help," I said.

"We got plenty around here."

I said, "Let's play it out as the cards get dealt. You be careful in Galveston."

He said, "They ain't looking for me. I'm just going to be a rancher looking to ship some cattle."

I said, "You will ask Sheriff Vara to keep an eye out for Chulo in the next couple of days? He ought to get to Blessing the day after tomorrow if he ain't off somewhere."

"What does he look like?"

I said, "Oh, he'll know him. Just tell the sheriff that Chulo will look like someone that *ought* to be in jail if anyone does."

CHAPTER 5

It was a long day spent waiting on Justa to return. He thought they'd be back on the four o'clock train, which would put him back at the ranch sometime after five in the afternoon. I killed as much of the day as I could by saddling the little roan I'd ridden the day before and wandering over the ranch. Whenever I'd come upon a cowboy working a bunch of cattle, I'd wave and he'd touch his hat and then watch me like I was going to suddenly draw on him. One of them gave me directions for the closest route down to the coast. It was a distance of about three miles, the grass changing to the coarser salt grass the nearer I got to the coast. I finally ended up on a shallow bluff about five feet high and looked down and out at the blue water. There was a little sandy strip of beach, not much like what I'd seen in my days in Corpus Christi, but the breakers came rolling in and toppled over in a froth of white water and then gentled out to wash in on the wet sand. I sat my horse there for the better part of a half an hour, just smelling the salt air and remembering younger days. I didn't exactly wonder what I would have turned out as if I'd finished school and stayed in Corpus, but the thoughts flittered across my mind of me as a merchant or a storekeeper or maybe even a banker. But they just flittered, none of them staying for very long. I couldn't see myself as being anything but what I was.

Finally I turned the horse and headed back for Justa's house. It was going on for five o'clock. I might already be a wanted man again.

We didn't talk at supper. Justa said it would be better to go on over and counsel with his brothers and Howard, that one of them might have an idea. I didn't make mention of my thought that I hadn't understood it was a family affair. After all, Justa had gone well out of his way to do me a turn, and I figured I'd let him lead for a time.

We went up after supper, and as usual, everybody got settled down with a drink. The old man wasn't there. He was laying down in his little bedroom, the day having been a bad one for him. But Ben was tipped back against the wall in his straight-backed chair, and Norris was at his desk, and Justa and I were sitting in chairs against the back wall.

I said, "Well, Justa? I sent you to Galveston to fetch back Phil Sharp so I could shoot him. You ain't even got part of him."

Justa said, "Sharp ain't in Galveston."

That brought me up short. I said, "Where in hell is he?"

He shook his head. "I don't know."

"Who does?"

"I don't know that either." He killed his drink and then got up and got the bottle of whiskey that always sat on the little table by Ben, filled his glass, and went back to his chair. He said, "I went to his office. I imagine that same office in that warehouse where you run into trouble. There was some clerks there and one man who said he was kind of Sharp's partner. He's a big, tall drink of water that can't weigh over 140 pounds. About in his forties. Pretty bald on top. Name is Patterson."

I nodded. I said, "Yes. I saw him. He was in the outside part of the office. Sharp's office is more back in the warehouse."

Justa said, "Yes, but now Patterson is there."

"What did he mean he was 'kind of' Sharp's partner?"

Justa said, "Hell, Wilson, I couldn't just go in there asking any-which-way kind of questions. My pretense for seeing Sharp in the first place was to discuss getting some cattle shipped to New Orleans. Then when Sharp wasn't there, I couldn't say to Patterson, 'Look here, where's Phil Sharp? I got a friend wants to shoot him.'"

I said, "Well, when he said Sharp wasn't there, did he make it sound like Sharp would be back in a day or two?"

Justa shook his head. He said, "The man kind of had a hangdog way about him. I asked him, naturally, when Sharp would be back, and he said, 'Damned if I know,' like he'd like to know himself."

Norris said, "Did you get the feeling that the place was a going concern or that they were in trouble?"

Justa said, "Trouble. This guy Patterson had lately put some money in the business. He volunteered that part to me, why I don't know, but he did. In fact, he went so far as to say that if I found Sharp, would I let him know. I got the impression he was trying to hang on by the skin of his teeth."

Norris said, "He have a title?"

Justa nodded. He said, "When I asked for Sharp, one of the clerks said he wasn't there but that their bookkeeper and manager was. Patterson. I went in and sat down with Patterson like I'd come to do business with Sharp and I was considerably put out by coming so far only to have the man I was to see be absent. I made it sound like we had had an appointment."

I said, "When did Sharp leave?"

Justa smiled around at me. "Sounds like the day after you and him had the disagreement."

Norris said, "I still don't understand this disintegration in their business. As I mentioned the other evening, Sharp had a going concern."

Justa said, "Well, it ain't going no more. Except down. I put it to Patterson that I wanted to ship some cattle to New Orleans, that I'd practically had a deal made with Sharp. Patterson said I couldn't have. He said they'd lost their only oceangoing vessels to the bank about six months past. Two steamboats with sail. He said all they had left were three sail-driven coasters capable of handling only about three hundred head of cattle each." He looked over at me. He said, "A coaster is a shallow draft vessel that sails along the coast. It ain't built for big seas, but you can land at little harbors and bays you couldn't get a big boat in."

Norris said, "I wasn't aware Sharp was in the business of shipping cattle. There's been very little shipping of cattle by water in a long time. Too much cheaper by rail."

Justa said, "Patterson asked me if these were Mexican cattle."

"Ooooh," Norris said. He nodded.

I said, "What the hell does that mean?"

Justa said, "It probably means why Sharp is going broke. It probably means that he did shoot you over twenty thousand dollars. Isn't the biggest business around Del Rio fattening up illegal cattle swum over from Mexico?"

"Swum?" I laughed. "Crooked as that place is you can march them across the International Bridge if you've paid off the right people."

"Was it always that way?"

I shook my head. "No. For a good while the officials on the Mexican side kept the lid clamped on tight. And, of course, the ranchers on the Texas side damn sure didn't want any Mexican cattle crossing over. So damn few was getting through."

Norris said, "Except by way of Mr. Sharp. Isn't there a small port at the mouth of the Rio Grande where it flows into the gulf?"

I said, "Yeah. Bodega. But it's only a hundred or so miles up the coast to Tampico."

Justa said, "But then the border loosened up and the cattle could be walked across and fattened up around Del Rio. Which didn't do Mr. Sharp's business one damn bit of good." He turned to me. He said, "That's what Sharp was doing in Del Rio so much, trying to buy cattle to ship to New Orleans and maybe Cuba or Florida or even Galveston or Houston. Only he couldn't compete with the ranchers around Del Rio or Eagle Pass or maybe even Brownsville."

Ben said, "How come them Mexicans suddenly started letting the cattle through? The pay get high enough?"

I said, "That and the fact that they just flat don't like gringos. When they were stopping the cattle, they thought they were hurting us. But then one of them bright son of a bitches figured out that the way to really hurt us was to flood our market with cheap beef."

"Which knocked Mr. Sharp and his shipping business in the head. No wonder he had vigilantes along the docks. He didn't want people to see him unloading illegal cattle."

I said, "I wonder where he's gone."

Justa said, "I don't know. But Patterson said he left in one of the coasting vessels. So he could be anywhere from here to Vera Cruz. He just left Patterson a note that he was gone on business. Nothing more than that. Boat carries six crewmen."

Norris said, "Did he clean out their assets?"

Justa gave him a look. He said, "Of course, Norris, I asked Mr. Patterson if Sharp had emptied the safe. As it was the man was getting damn curious about all my questions."

Ben brought me over the bottle of whiskey and poured me out a fresh drink. I thanked him. I said, to Justa, "Did your sheriff find out anything?"

Justa said, "Lew sounded him out as best he could without giving away all he knew. The Galveston sheriff knew about the shooting but not the way you described it. The bodies were just found on the docks."

"Three of them?"

He nodded. He said, "So either the one you gut-shot died or Sharp finished him off later so he wouldn't say anything."

"What else did the Galveston sheriff have to say?"

"He for sure does not care for vigilante committees. As far as he's concerned it's the vigilantes who have been doing most of the dirty work down on the docks. If he had his way, he'd disband them by putting them all in jail. But he says the docks are such a rough and dirty place that it would take ten sheriffs to do the job."

"Sheriff Vara mention me?"

Justa shook his head. "Not that I know of."

I took a drink of whiskey. I said, "Well, partner, I am much obliged to you. You've told me a lot I couldn't have found out on my own."

Ben said, "What are you going to do now, go back to Del Rio?"

"No," I said. "I reckon I'll go on up to Galveston as soon as Chulo gets here."

Justa said, "What the hell for?"

I was fumbling in my pocket for a cigarillo so I was a second in answering. I struck a match and got it lit and drawing and then said, "To bring charges against Sharp."

Norris said, "What!"

I looked at him. "Man tried to kill me. That's against the law. Might bring civil action against him in a Galveston court over the twenty thousand dollars. I got his promissory note."

Justa started laughing. He said, "Why don't you do that? Why don't you just march into that sheriff's office and tell him you're Wilson Young and you want to bring charges against a leading citizen for attempted murder."

They were all laughing. I said, "That's what I intend to do." I tapped off the ashes of my cigarillo into a little saucerlike thing. "I plan to get it on record that I got a right to be seeking the man."

They stopped laughing. They could see that I was serious. Justa said, "Will, you might want to think about that a little."

"Already have," I said.

After a time they appeared to accept that my next move would be to go after Phil Sharp. They began talking about it, each in his own way. I found it a curiosity to note the difference in the brothers by what they found the most interesting in my plans. Ben was mainly interested in speculating how and what I'd do to Sharp and the men he had with him when I ran them to ground. Justa was concerned about the risk. Norris found the financial end of the matter the most worthy of note. He said, "Well, it is clear that Sharp's business got badly undermined when they began crossing the illegal cattle by land. Obviously he couldn't compete with that arrangement and lost the biggest part of his trade." He said, to me, "I'll warrant you that when Sharp was gambling in your casino and losing twenty thousand dollars on credit, he was gambling to win cash. He may have told you he had plenty of cash with him but that he needed it to keep for business in Mexico, but I'd wager his intent was to win a large stake."

I said, "I don't generally run the place on those principles. Very few gambling houses plan to lose much money. It's in the nature of the business not to let that happen."

Norris said, "So we have a man left with the shell of a business. He's lost his two biggest assets, his steamships.

And he's lost his supply of trade goods, illegal cattle. I would imagine that Mr. Sharp has run up considerable debts in Galveston and thereabouts. I think he was planning on fleeing anyway. Your arrival demanding money he couldn't spare only speeded up the process."

I said, "Well, now I'm going to process him. If I can catch him."

Justa said, "The man could have done otherwise than what he did. There's plenty of cargo along the coast and even to Florida and Cuba and other islands. He could have hauled rum or sugar or lumber or cotton."

Ben said, "Probably wouldn't have been crooked enough for him."

"You have a point," Norris said. "But not so much crooked as not as big a margin of profit as shipping illegal cattle that could be bought for a song. A hundred years ago Mr. Sharp would have been a slave trader. I wonder if this Patterson has realized the boat has sunk beneath his feet."

Justa said, "He didn't look none too chipper."

I said, "But if he was the bookkeeper, he'd have known what was going on."

"Not necessarily," Norris said. "Not necessarily."

Me and Justa walked back to his house after another drink. On the way he asked me what my plans were. I told him I wanted to get away as soon as possible, all I was waiting for was Chulo. From Del Rio his train would have to go through San Antonio to get to Blessing. I asked Justa what times trains got in from San Antone. He said there was one at noon and one at eight at night. He said, "They both go on to Galveston and Houston?"

I calculated. "Well, if Chulo was to hump himself, he could make that morning train out of Del Rio tomorrow and be in here by noon. Eight tomorrow night at the latest. I guess the best thing for me to do is to leave out of here in the morning early enough to meet that noon train."

Justa said, "I ain't quite sure I understand what you want with a big, mean *pistolero*. This here errand you're on sounds like it might take some maneuvering."

I said, "I figure some folks might need some scaring, and Chulo is just about the scariest-looking thing on two legs. Besides, he don't argue. He'd charge a Gatling gun with an empty pistol if I told him to."

Justa said, "Well, here you are running all over the country to settle up a debt. What's happening to your business meanwhile?"

I said, "I got an old New Orleans gambler looking after the casino part."

"Who's looking after him?"

I said, "Evita. And she knows where every dollar is."

We went on in the house and got us a drink and sat down in the parlor. Justa said, "Will, I think I ought to come with you. Some sheriff might decide to lock you up."

I shook my head. I said, "Can't let you do that. Don't know what I'm liable to run into. Maybe I would have before, but now I've met Nora and your brothers and your daddy, and I know you got a small son with his grandparents. I appreciate it, though."

After a moment Justa said, "I been thinking. Sharp may not be running from you. He may be running from debts or trouble we know nothing about. If that be the case, he ain't going to do what you think he'd do if it was just you."

I said, "Somebody knows where the man has gone to. There is somebody in Galveston knows where that man has gone and why. I'm going to find that somebody and he's going to tell me where I can find Sharp."

Justa said, "He took a coaster, Paterson said. Maybe he just run for Bodega or Tampico to try to pick up a load of cattle and sell them somewhere up the Texas coast or even beyond. But at least we now know what he was doing in Del Rio so often: trying to get those Mexican ranchers to keep on doing business with him. Seems clear it didn't do him no good. But the man should have seen what was coming before it got too late."

I said, "Maybe he was spreading around a lot of money trying to plug the gap so he could get the business back." I laughed. "Maybe he was bribing the officials to stop the smuggling so he could do it. Crazy as that sounds."

Justa said, "If he was, it would have been like pouring water in a bucket didn't have no bottom. I doubt the man understood Mexico, especially the border."

About that time we both heard the sound of hoofbeats. I looked up, but Justa just kept on tending to his glass of whiskey. The sound got nearer. I said, "Now, I wonder who that could be this time of night? You reckon you got cow trouble?"

Justa shook his head. He said, "No, that would be young Ben."

"Ben?"

"Yes. Coming to tell me that the calving season is nearly over and that the remuda is in good shape and that Ray Hays can handle it anyway and can he have a few days off to go with you to Galveston if you'll have him."

I said, "Pshaw! You don't know that."

Justa said, "Just keep right still and listen."

He must have seen us through the window because he came in without knocking. He said, "I figured y'all would be having a last drink."

Justa said, "You know where it is."

He went into Justa's office and come back with a half a tumbler of whiskey. He sat down on what Nora had told me was a Morris chair. After a little polite conversation on his part and a kind of waiting silence on ours, he said, "Say, Justa, I had me a idea. Calving season is nearly over and the horse herd is in pretty good shape. What little work still needs doing on them new colts we got in here won't be no chore for Ray and the two *vaqueros*. I was wondering if I couldn't have a little time off. I thought I might string along with Wilson and give him a hand if he'll have me."

Justa looked over at me, laying it on me. I cleared my throat. I said, "Ben, it won't do. I've already asked Justa if I could have the use of you, but he's said no. And no argument I've given him has changed his mind."

Then I smiled ever so nicely at Justa. In return he gave me a look that would have killed young corn. He said, "Ben, I can't spare you. Wilson is most likely going to be on a long trail and I need you around here. You ain't half through going into the herd books, and if you're ever going to take a bigger hand in the cattle end of this ranch, you are going to have to learn the breeding."

Ben said, "Aw, hell, Justa, I can get that stuff by heart any old time. If it looks like Wilson is going to be out too long, I can break off and come home."

Justa said, "Oh, that'd be a nice way to do. Offer a man help and then decide to go home just about the time he needs you. The answer is no, Ben, and you might as well take it for that."

Ben looked at me. I just shrugged and held my palms up as if to say, "See? What'd I tell you?"

After a little he took it with good grace. I said, "Justa, one thing you can do for me is loan me a couple of horses. I don't want to be afoot in Galveston in case I have to leave in a hurry. Last time I got lucky. The train wanted to leave at the same time I did. Might not work out that way this time."

Justa said, "Ben?"

Ben said, "What kind of horses you want, Wilson? Trail horses?"

I shook my head. I said, "I don't figure to track Phil Sharp overland. He don't strike me as the kind to spend all day in a saddle. No, I just want something with some damn quick speed and some staying power."

Justa said, "Why don't you take that little bay mare of mine that you've been riding. She's plumb full of quarter horse and is dependable as hell."

I said, "She'd suit me fine. But I need another horse that can carry a big man. Chulo has got to weigh at least a hundred pounds more than a big stump. He's the biggest Meskin I ever saw."

Ben said, "I got just the horse. A piebald gelding. Least he's piebald in the face. Rest of him is mostly black. He's nearly seventeen hands high and must weigh a little over a thousand pounds."

"Is he steady?"

"He'd stand in the middle of a lightning storm and never flinch. He ain't as fast as some, but he's pretty quick. Looks mean as hell, but is gentle as that bay mare of Justa's."

I said, "Well, I am much obliged. I'll get them back to you quick as I can."

Ben said, "Keep 'em as long as you need 'em. Ain't no shortage of horses around here."

I said, "Well, I'm going to bed. I'm going to make an early start for town tomorrow. Or early for me I guess I ought to say."

Ben said, "I'll bring that piebald over in the morning all saddled and ready."

I gave them a good-night and then turned in. For all practical purposes I was healed up. I was still wearing a bandage, but that was more to keep me from picking at the scab of the front wound than anything else. I'd come out of a near miss with luck on my side. Now I was going to go and see how Phil Sharp's luck was. I was hoping that Chulo would be on the noon train, but if he wasn't, I was going on without him. I'd been laying around too long, and the steam that Mr. Sharp had started up in my boiler with his ambush was about to blow over the top.

In spite of my protests Justa rode into town with me the next day. We left about nine of the morning. Nora fixed me a good breakfast and then put me up some cheese and cold roast beef and biscuits for the train trip. I thanked her for her hospitality and promised to send Justa right on back to the ranch and not let him get into any poker games with anybody over twelve years old. She surprised me by giving me a light kiss on the cheek and saying that I was welcome back anytime. Riding away from the house, Justa said that there was no accounting for women's judgment. He said, "Here you are, a notorious sinner, bank robber, gunslinger, horse thief, cattle thief, and ain't seen the inside of a church since yore mama and daddy was married, and Nora still likes you. And she generally don't like nobody except schoolteachers or lawyers or federal judges or what not. Likes a man like *you*. Beats anything I have ever seen. How do you account for that?"

I said, "Your dear wife is a good judge of character. So far as I've seen it has only failed her once."

We took it slow, just ambling along. The piebald wasn't used to being led, and he nearly jerked me out of the saddle a few times, but then I gave him some of his medicine back and he found it to be a good idea to trot up alongside the rest of us.

It was just before eleven o'clock when we got into town. We rode down to the depot, and Justa helped me arrange for a stock car for the two horses. Normally you had to pay for the whole car on an arrangement like that, a stock car usually carrying eight horses, but the Half-Moon ranch did so much business with the railroad that the agent let me have a car to myself for just the two horses and me and Chulo.

After that we rode down to visit with Lew Vara for a few minutes. He was in his office but thought that Justa looked like he needed a beer, so we went down to Crook's Saloon and Café and had a couple of rounds. I was a good deal interested in anything that Lew could tell me about the Galveston sheriff.

Lew said, "He's an older man. Been in the law business a good long time, I'd reckon. Might not be sixty, but he ain't lacking it far. Name of Mills, Ben Mills. He was mighty sociable to me. I don't know how he's gonna act toward *you*."

Justa said, "What do you think of him just walking in there and announcing he wants to bring charges against Sharp?"

Lew shrugged. "He might just surprise the old man so bad he won't know what to do. But I don't think Mr. Young will have any trouble about who he is. There is enough outlaw trade running loose right now to keep ten times the sheriffs busy. Mills'll know that Wilson is a different case. But I don't think he's going to do a damn thing about Sharp. Course he don't like them damn vigilantes."

I said, "I don't want him to do anything about Sharp. I just want it on the record that I'm going after the man in a legal manner. I've got the right of self-defense."

Lew smiled. "You going to put a gun in his hand?"

"If I have to," I said. And I didn't smile.

About a quarter of noon Justa and I took leave of the sheriff and rode on back to the depot. I got down off the bay mare and tied the stirrups over her saddle so they wouldn't be swinging around and agitating her on the trip to Galveston. Justa did the same with the piebald. Off in the distance I heard the train blowing, announcing its coming.

Justa said, "Wilson, now you keep me posted. You get in a bind somewhere, you get off a wire to me. You hear?"

I nodded. "All right. You do the same. Of course I don't know where I'll be."

"You figure to come back through here when you get your business tended to?"

"I might," I said.

Then the train came hurtling in, brakes screeching, bell ringing, whistle blowing, gasping out great clouds of steam. It was a combination freight and passenger train about twenty cars long. The engine ran on past us and stopped the other side of the depot. Justa and I were a good ways back, back with the cattle cars that were hitched into the train just in front of the caboose. One of the railroad hired hands came and took the piebald and the bay from me to load them into a cattle car. Up toward the depot the passenger cars were letting out a few people who had come to their destination. They was about fifty yards off, but Chulo wasn't hard to recognize at that distance. I said, "Well, there's my Meskin. Guess I better gather him up before he scares some of the women and horses."

Justa put out his hand. He said, "Be careful, Will. This Phil Sharp sounds like a slippery customer. You get a loop on him, don't give him no slack."

We shook, and then he got on his horse and rode away, and I went up toward the head of the train to collect Chulo.

CHAPTER 6

It had always been my custom, when taking a horse along with me on the train, to ride in the stock car with the animal. I found it more comfortable than the chair cars, cooler, and a hell of a lot more private. But Chulo didn't care for it on this occasion. He'd worn a new pair of brown gabardine pants and a good-quality white linen shirt, and he was afraid he was going to get his new clothes dirty in the stock car. It made me laugh. I had known Chulo when it would have taken a whole river to wash him clean. He was just about the last candidate for fastidiousness that I would have picked out. But since we had gone "honess'," as he called it, he'd become mighty particular.

I was wearing one of the new shirts that Wayne, the clerk at the hotel, had bought for me, and a pair of lightweight corduroy riding britches. I'd abandoned the frock coat I'd been wearing when I was shot. Juanita and Nora had tried their best to get the bloodstains out, but it had been a lost cause, and I had sent it home with Juanita for use by one of her male relatives. But the weather was turning unseasonably warm, and a coat would have been just a decoration. I was content to be dressed as we were, and what little straw and dust and hay we picked up on the train ride could easily be brushed away in a barbershop.

I asked Chulo how things were going back at the Palace. He said, "The besiness is not so good, but et es not so bad. The wheesky besiness is good. The girl besiness es good.

The besiness with the cards an' the leetle dice es not so good."

I said, severely, "You been leaving those girls alone?"

Chulo was terribly addicted to that secret that girls had between their legs. He was convinced that if he could get between enough of them, he'd finally figure out what the secret was. I had been convinced for many years that he would screw a wildcat if he could get somebody to hold it.

He said, "Oh, chure."

I said, "Don't you 'oh, chure' me. I know you, you son of a bitch. I have enough trouble making you leave those girls alone when I'm there. God knows what you tried with me gone."

He looked a little guilty. He said, "The Señora Evita she say no. I leesen."

I said, "She ain't a senora. We ain't married. But you better 'leesen' when she talks. That woman would cut your balls off in your sleep. Do you know that?"

One of the horses snorted and stamped his hoof. The train was rushing through the landscape, the terrain just flying by. I calculated we were doing upwards of thirty miles an hour. I'd never, if I lived to be a thousand, figure out how they got something as heavy as a railroad train to run as fast as it did.

Chulo said, "I doan geeve Señora Evita no troubles, *jefe*. Che pretty bad, that woman."

"Damn right she's pretty bad. So you better leave her girls alone or she'll shoot your *pistola* off."

We'd been traveling better than half an hour, and so far, Chulo hadn't asked me where we were going or why, or why I'd sent for him. But then that was the way it was between Chulo and me. In the seven or eight years he and I had rode together, it was understood I was the boss, the *jefe,* and he wasn't. That meant he did what I told him and didn't ask a lot of questions. But then Chulo had never been much of a hand about the why of a thing. If there was something needed doing, you just went and did it. I had to occasionally take him in hand about women or when he occasionally got too much whiskey in him. But most times he was easy to herd. Chulo, for reasons I had never known, was afraid of me. At least that was the impression he gave. Well, if he was, then I was the only man breathing that he was afraid of.

I said, "Chulo, you got any idea why I sent for you?"

He shrugged. Somebody had left some empty wooden boxes in the car, and he was sitting on one. The box was little and Chulo was big, so he wasn't far off the floor. In fact he looked like he was kind of doubled up. I was standing up, leaning against the slatted side of the car. Chulo shrugged. He said, "*Yo no sabe.* I doan know."

I said, "We are going to Galveston to look for a man, a man that shot me."

He'd been kind of lazing around until then. Now he sat up straight. He said, "Some mans chot you?"

I nodded and raised my shirt to show him the bandage. I said, "It was about an inch from being real bad. I got real lucky."

Chulo mulled that over for a moment, and then he said, "I doan thenk thees mans he gets so lucky. Maybe hees lucky es real bad. We see heem en Galveston?"

"I hope so," I said.

A lot of folks made a mistake about Chulo by thinking he wasn't very smart. Now, I ain't going to say that he was a candidate for the university up at Austin, but there weren't no flys on Chulo when it came to being smart in the matters that were of concern to him. He was smart like a hog; he wasn't going to waste time rooting around under a pine tree looking for acorns. And his English was better than he let on. He wanted folks to think he was just a big, dumb Mexican who didn't speak the lingo so good and who was an easy mark. He heard everything he wanted to hear, either in Spanish or English. Sometimes he'd slip up around me and speak pretty good English, but most times he'd stick to that stumbling gait he used just to keep his hand in. I didn't object because it served him well and I generally could understand him anyway.

He could be lazy, when I'd let him get away with it, but most folks just thought of him as some big, shiftless, shambling low-class Mexican. But Chulo could move as fast as he needed to move, and he was strong enough that when he took hold of something or someone, that something or someone wasn't going anywhere until Chulo decided that something or someone could get loose. I reckoned he would have weighed over two hundred pounds except he was missing half of the little finger on his right hand. He'd lost that on the occasion of our first meeting. He'd come into my camp outside of the town of Uvalde, where I'd planned on robbing a bank as soon as it had got open. I was cooking up some breakfast, and he reached out for some of my bacon without asking me first. To teach him some manners I shot the end of his little finger off. Actually it was a bad shot, because I'd been aiming for the middle of his hand. But it impressed Chulo so that I'd never got around to telling him that just taking off the tip of his smallest finger had been an accident. He'd joined up on the spot, and it was a certain fact that without his presence through the years, I might not have been in a position to go searching for Mr. Philip Sharp.

He'd brought along his saddlebags, containing, I reckoned, a change of clothes and some other odds and ends. Now he opened a flap and got out a bottle of rum. I never could understand how anyone, Meskin or not, could actually drink that stuff and claim to like it. He offered me the bottle even though he knew better. I just shook my head and moved over to the bay mare and got out a bottle of brandy that Justa had thoughtfully provided me with. I pulled the cork, and then me and Chulo clinked bottles and said, "Luck," and each took a good hearty swig. Then I pointed at the rum and said, "Now you go light on that, señor, or I'll throw you off this train. You got to be on your best behavior in Galveston."

He looked at me in some amazement. "En Galveston es thees man that chouts you. We going to be nice?"

I said, "He ain't going to be easy to find. I'm going to have to ask some people some questions."

Chulo said, "That es berry good. You ask thees mens the questions and I will get the answers."

I said, "That's about the way I had it figured."

Chulo said, "What we do *primero?*"

I said, "First I got to get you settled someplace where I can find you when I want you and you can't get in no trouble. I guess we'll take a room in a hotel, even though we may not stay the night. Then I'm going to go see the sheriff."

He pulled his head back. He stuck a finger out at me. He said, "*Chou* are going to see *el* shereef?"

"Yeah," I said. "Train is supposed to get into Galveston by four o'clock. If I get done with the sheriff in time, we may be going to see a Mr. Patterson who is a worker for the man that shot me."

I didn't want to try and explain who Patterson was. There was never any point in overloading Chulo with needless information. He did better with a light cargo.

He said, "Why doan we chust go see thees Patterson? He tell us plenty queeck about theese other mans. I doan theen you want to see thees shereef. Es no *bueno por nada.*"

"Yeah, it is," I said. "We ain't outlaws no more, remember? I got to do this legal."

"Oh, chure," he said, and looked up at the ceiling of the car.

We pulled into the Galveston depot just about on time. We had a few minutes' wait until a couple of trainmen came along and opened the door on our car and put up a ramp we could lead the horses down. After that we untied the stirrups, tightened up the girths, and swung aboard the two horses. I could see without looking very hard that the piebald was just about a fit for Chulo. I could also see he was well mannered and calm. A man who is in a business where guns are liable to be going off around his horse's head wants an animal that don't spook too easy. Justa said there wasn't an animal on the Half-Moon that hadn't been trained to the sound of gunfire.

From the depot we rode on down toward the docks and then turned onto what I calculated to be the main street. It was a good, wide affair, but it wasn't too wide by much. The thoroughfare was just thronged with the buggies and carriages of the gentry, some of the gentlemen even wearing plug hats and nearly all of the ladies turned out in their finest. And then there were wagons hauling every possible commodity, from squealing pigs to lumber to sacks of corn. And working their way through that crowd were solitary horsemen, or here and there a bunch of them, having to go single file to make their way through. Some daring souls were venturing to leave the wooden boardwalks in front of the stores and risking their lives by trying to cross through that stampede of vehicles and animals. Somebody had told me there were twenty thousand people in Galveston, but I didn't believe it. There might be twenty thousand passing *through* at some given time, but there couldn't have been no amount like that actually sleeping over at the same time.

We took rooms at the Galvez Hotel which was right in the middle of town but still pretty close to the docks. Galveston was an up-to-date town, and they had gaslights in the rooms and running water. They even had some boys that wanted to carry our saddlebags up for us. I'd seen them before in my travels, but Chulo thought the boy was trying to steal his and drew his arm back to give him a cuff. I got the matter straightened out and gave the boys a dollar to mollify their feelings. We had two rooms side by side, which they got four dollars apiece for. But then, the Galvez was a first-rate hotel, and a man had to figure to pay such prices if he wanted to stay in that kind of place.

We had rooms right next to each other on the second floor. We could have got by with just one room, but times being what they were and in a place as fancy as the Galvez, it wouldn't have looked proper for a white man to be rooming with a Mexican. But I got Chulo settled, strongly recommended to him that he stay in the room until I got back and not get drunk, and then I set out to find the sheriff. As luck would have it his office was just down the street, right next to the biggest post office I'd ever seen. I'd have reckoned there weren't that many people in Galveston could read and write to require such an edifice to handle their daily mail.

The sheriff's office was in a two-story brick affair. From the outside I could see bars over all the upstairs windows, and I figured that the jail took up a whole story by itself. I went into a big office kind of place with several young men sitting around wearing guns and badges. They didn't any of them look to be the Sheriff Mills that Lew Vara had described, so I asked after him. He had a little office in the back, an office within an office and one all to himself. One of the deputies, as I figured him to be, took me back. The office door was open and the young man said, "Feller to see you, Sheriff." He hadn't asked my name or my business. But I figured they didn't expect anyone would be fool enough to come walking into a nest of lawmen with the intention of starting trouble.

Sheriff Mills was slouched back in a swivel chair turned half sideways to his desk. I couldn't tell his age for sure, but from his lined face and the gray hair I could see under his pushed-back hat, I figured he'd been around for a time. Without looking up at me, he said, "Yep?"

I said, "Sheriff Mills, my name is Wilson Young."

He was a man that chewed tobacco, and he took a second to lean over and spit in a cuspidor before saying anything. He said, "Wilson Young. I've heard that name off and on. Come to Galveston to rob one of our banks, have you?"

He didn't invite me to sit, so I stayed standing. I said, "Not this trip. I've come in to see you and make you acquainted with my presence in town and tell you my business."

"Take a chair," he said, nodding his head toward a heavy wooden affair across from his desk. I sat down.

I said, "Sheriff, a man shot me in this town five days ago. I'm here to press charges against that man for attempted murder."

That caused him to straighten in his chair and swing around to his desk. He looked faintly amused. He said, "I'm to understand that you, Wilson Young, are here to press charges against a man for attempted murder?"

I said, "Sheriff, think what you will of me, of my past, of the stories you've maybe heard about me. But I can say I never shot nobody that wasn't either trying to shoot me or fixing to try and shoot me. Every man that has died at my hand has done so in a fair fight. And some of them was more than fair." I said, "This man was attempting to cheat me out of a fair-sized amount of money. I can also say that I never cheated nobody for a nickel."

The sheriff spit again. He said, "And I guess you never took money from folks that didn't want to give it up. Banks and such."

I said, "I won't argue that point. What I done I done. But I've reached an agreement with the state law officials, and I'm trying to live up to my part of the bargain."

He said, "Oh, I know all about your parole. So do most other lawmen around. They even say you're supposed to be trying to pay restitution, or whatever that word is, to some of them places come out on the short end of your count when you left their bank."

I said, "Well, that is not generally known. And ain't supposed to be. If it was, I'd have every bank in three or four states claiming I robbed them and lining up for their cut of the pie. I'm doing what I can in what little way I can."

And it was true that part of my agreement with the governor was that I would make an honest attempt to return some of the money I'd stolen. But it had to be kept secret for the reason I'd just given the sheriff. I'd never told anyone, not even Justa or Chulo or Evita. No one. But secrets are like silver dollars; they have a way of getting passed from hand to hand.

Not that it really made any difference. I was doing what I could, but I wasn't exactly busting a gut in the process. All the state law wanted me to do was not cause any more trouble than I already had. They had a state they were trying to get civilized enough to attract desirable settlers from other states, and outlaws like I'd been weren't the best advertisement.

I said, "But whatever the situation is between me and the state law ain't got nothing to do with how you might feel about me being in your town. That's why I figured to walk in here and let you know I was here and what my plans were."

He made a kind of dry chuckle. He said, "Well, I can see you've got enough crust for a young man. But then I reckon it takes a fair amount of that commodity to rob as many banks as you did." He spit again. "Since you are goin' to the expense and risk of making so bold as to walk into my office, I'll tell you exactly what my position is. I ain't got no quarrel with you being in this town so long as you don't cause me no trouble. I got all the trouble, and then some, that I can handle. For thirty-five years I've been in the law business and I have worked some tough towns, all the way from Abilene, Kansas, to Tascosa, New Mexico, to Fort Worth in its day. But I never been in such a place as this. Yard for yard they is more crooks, cheats, killers, ruffians, thieves, whores, and just plain riffraff of any place I ever seen. I got me and eight deputies to try and keep the peace in this place, and if I wanted to, I could fill a jail ten times as big as the one I got upstairs. I'll be wearing this tin badge for about another year and then I intend to retire with all my arms and legs and fingers and toes and no more holes in me than I already got. You get my drift? I don't care what you done before, what mischief you been up to, just don't do none in Galveston."

I said, "Well, I can't say you ain't made yourself clear, Sheriff. But I want to make it clear that I'm here to get some business done against a man who done his best to kill me. And if he'd have been a better shot, he'd have succeeded. If you want me to pull up my shirt, I can show you the bullet wound in my side that I'm still getting healed up from. I want to swear out a warrant against this man. That's legal, ain't it?"

The sheriff sort of sighed. He said, "You expect me to thank you for bringing me more work?" He picked up a pencil. "Who is this man?"

"Philip Sharp. I want to bring charges against him and three other unknown parties who tried to kill me in Sharp's office."

The sheriff threw his pencil down. He said, "What condition did you leave these three other 'parties' in?"

I said, "Two was dead and one was gut-shot. Sharp had fired at me and then run out the back of his office. He hit me in the side."

"How did these three come to get shot?"

I said, "Sharp got up and opened a door to the back of his office, and the three come in with drawn pistols. They fired at me, but I'd hit the floor first sight I got of them. They was wearing hoods over their heads with holes cut out for their eyes. I shot them in self-defense."

The sheriff sighed. He said, "Was three of them all you could get?"

"What?"

The sheriff said, "We found them three—I reckon it was *them* three—down on the docks about four days ago. So that was your work."

"They fired at me first. I had come to collect a gambling debt from Phil Sharp, and I reckon he didn't want to pay."

The sheriff spit again. He said, "Pity you didn't get more of them. Those three was some of these so-called vigilantes that Sharp organized. Give me a choice, I'd rather have the crooks. Least they don't cover their heads."

"Who are these vigilantes?"

The sheriff yawned. He said, "Mostly riffraff. Some of them work—or worked—for Sharp or some of the other shippers. They are mostly trash of one kind or another, some of them off the ships that dock here. Hell, some of 'em are furriners that can't speak no lingo I ever heard."

I got up out of my chair. I said, "Well, I just wanted to make this matter legal. I'm accusing Sharp of trying to kill me."

The sheriff said, "Sharp ain't here."

"I already know that," I said. "I understand he cleared out the next day after the shooting."

"Near as we can tell. How'd you know that?"

I said, "You had a visitor, the sheriff from Matagorda County. Lew Vara."

Sheriff Mills said, "So that was what that was all about. I hear he had Justa Williams with him. You a friend of Mr. Williams also?"

"Yes, sir."

The sheriff gave me a steady eye. He said, "Don't get the idea that changes anything. If you catch Sharp outside of my jurisdiction, you can do anything you want to him. But don't start no trouble here."

I said, "I'll be going around town asking a lot of questions. Somebody knows where Sharp has gone. I'm going to get them to tell me."

The sheriff looked at me for a long second or two. He said, "You stay off those docks. Don't be going into any of those dives down there. You may be Wilson Young and you may be one hell of an hombre with a pistol, but yore back can get a knife stuck in it just like everybody else's."

I said, "I got my back taken care of. Was Sharp married?"

The sheriff shook his head and spit. "Don't know."

"Where did he live?"

"Don't know."

"Is this man Patterson in on the dirty end of his business?"

"Don't know. Like I said, I got too much trouble with out-and-out scalawags to watch the businessmen. They may steal more than the whole bunch of thugs down on them docks put together, but they don't generally do it with a gun or a knife."

I put on my hat. I said, "I'm much obliged to you for your trouble, Sheriff Mills. I hope you'll remember that I've made my intentions known legally."

He said, "You better stay away from those docks, Mr. Young."

"Good day, Sheriff."

I stood for a good half an hour across the road from the building that had SHARP SHIPPING COMPANY across the top of it. It was a little after five-thirty, and I was letting the place sort of clear out. I'd seen three or four young clerks come out of the front door, put on their derbies, and then stride off up the street. I hadn't seen anyone answering the description of Mr. Patterson.

Finally I decided I might as well have a few words with him in his office. I'd meant to catch him on the street because a man doesn't feel so secure under such conditions as he would in the friendly confines of where he works. But it didn't look like he was going to come out anytime soon, and I knew Chulo was probably getting restless back at the hotel, and one thing I didn't want was Chulo getting restless.

I crossed the street and opened the door. There was a big outer office with three desks on one side of the room and three on the other. At one a young man in tie and high collar and sleeve guards was working at a ledger. I asked after Mr. Patterson, and he pointed at a door at the back without much looking up. I figured if they were going to be that informal, I'd just go along with it, so I opened Mr. Patterson's door without bothering to knock. Behind a desk that had a bunch of cabinets in it, where I reckoned they stored papers, was a tired-looking man that pretty well fit the description Justa had given me of Patterson. He looked up when I came into the office. He said, "If you're a bill collector, you're wasting your time."

I said, "In a way I am. But I'm looking for Philip Sharp."

He leaned back in his chair and rubbed his hand over his face. He said, "You and a lot of other folks."

I said, "Do you know where I can find him?"

"Nope," he said.

"No idea where he went?"

"Nope."

I went forward until I was right up against Patterson's desk. I said, "Mr. Patterson, my name is Wilson Young. I aim to find Phil Sharp. He owes me twenty thousand dollars and a fair fight."

Mr. Patterson laughed slightly. He said, "I wish you luck, but I don't reckon you'll have it on either count."

I said, "I find it hard to believe that a man will just pull out and not tell his partner where he's bound for. I don't want to give you no trouble, but I will if you don't help me."

Patterson took his hand away from his face. He said, "Mister, you couldn't give me any more trouble than I've already got. You could shoot me, but I'd take that as a relief. Right now I'm trying to figure out who to pay with what little money we got and who not to. I am sitting here trying to clean up a mess that don't seem to have no bottom. I am trying to figure out how I ever got in the shipping business and why in hell it had to be with a man like Philip Sharp. But most of all I'm trying to figure out how my name ever got on company papers saying I'm part owner of this disaster and partly responsible for its debts. Sharp owes you twenty thousand, you say? Fine. What would you say to me signing over the whole mess to you in return for that debt?"

I said, "It's Sharp owes me. Besides, I got the feeling that might be a losing proposition."

"You have that precise, sir."

I studied him a minute. I felt like he was telling me the truth. I said, "All right, who's the ring leader of this bunch of vigilantes?"

Patterson said, "Now that was a part of Sharp's business

I had nothing to do with. And don't want nothing to do with it."

"Who knows about it?"

He studied me for a moment. He said, "Mister, I don't think you'll kill me. But if I go to talking about that vigilante bunch, one of *them* will. So I think I'll keep my mouth shut."

I said, "How long y'all been shipping illegal Mexican cattle? Or how long *was* you shipping them?"

He looked at me and then laughed shortly. He said, "Well, if you know so much, why do you need to ask questions?"

I said, "I know your supply ran out in the north here not too long ago. Where was Sharp getting the cattle before then?"

Patterson's sleeves were rolled up. He took a moment to roll them down and button the cuffs. He said, "I don't suppose it matters anymore. Besides, I had nothing to do with that part. I was just the bookkeeper before I signed some papers I shouldn't have."

"Where?"

"Originally Sharp was loading cattle out of Tampico, Mexico, for shipment to New Orleans and Cuba and Florida and even some to Houston and other ports. That's when we had the two big oceangoing steamboats. We could carry fifteen hundred head a boat. But then I heard him complaining that he was having to look further and further inland to get decent cattle and they were costing more. I think he was paying around two or three dollars a head delivered to the docks in Tampico at first."

"What were you selling them for?"

"Twenty, twenty-five dollars a head. Sometimes thirty. Of course those big ships cost money to run."

I said, "And then he run out of that supply and had to keep going further north. Up toward the border."

Patterson raised his eyebrows. "You are informed."

"And loading them at Bodega."

"No. We couldn't load the big steamboats at the harbor in Bodega. It was too shallow. We had to take them on the coasters and try and transfer them to the steamboats. It just didn't work very well."

"So Sharp was getting in trouble."

"Yes. The price of the cattle kept going up and up. It seems that all of a sudden these cattle could be driven overland. You see, Sharp's whole scheme had been based on the fact that the only way to get these illegal cattle into the country was by ship. Then something happened. I don't know what."

Of course I did and I told him. I said, "The drovers paid the right people more money to let the cattle through overland than Sharp and the other shippers were paying to keep them out so they'd have to go by water." I said, dryly, "It's considerably cheaper to drive cattle over good grass than it is to give them a boat ride."

"I would suppose," Patterson said. "You seem to know more about this than I do. Mr. Sharp never told me more than he thought I needed to know."

I said, "But came a day and things went bad. That about it?"

"If you mean we lost the steamboats, yes. Sharp said we simply couldn't get enough cattle to keep up the payments. I asked him why we didn't ship legal cattle, U.S. cattle."

"I bet that gave him a good laugh."

"No, that's when he sold me a share of the company for a very small amount of money. I should have realized . . ." He shrugged his shoulders. "It doesn't matter. I'm a ruined man. By law I'm an owner of this firm and responsible for its debts just as Sharp is. But I can't run. I've got a wife and children to think of. I've got a home here."

I said, "How could the debts be that big? Don't you still have three ships? Coasters I believe you call them."

"Those ships wouldn't cover a tenth of what this company owes, Mr.— Uh, what did you say your name was?"

"Young, Wilson Young. I own a gambling casino in Del Rio. Your Mr. Sharp left me with a promissory note for twenty grand. He also gave me a hole in my side that I didn't particularly want."

A light was dawning in Mr. Patterson's eyes. He said, "Were you here by any chance about five days ago? I was out when you visited, but I heard about it."

I nodded.

Patterson smiled, grimly. He said, "I see now why you're

interested in the vigilantes. I understand you met three of them. They were with Mr. Sharp for your benefit."

"You help move the bodies?"

He put up his hands, quickly. "Not me, sir. I have nothing to do with that crowd. But I saw them getting moved."

I said, "But I'm still trying to get at your finances. And I ain't doing it to pry. I'm trying to figure out if there's enough left of this business to fetch Mr. Sharp back."

Mr. Patterson leaned back in his chair. He said, "I can give you a solemn no to that one. I'd imagine criminal charges will shortly be pressed against Sharp. As well as every kind of civil suit imaginable."

"Well, what did he do, take off with the cash?"

"He took off with a lot of people's cash," he said. "You ever heard of a shipping contract, Mr. Young?"

"I suppose so. A contract is a contract."

"Not quite the same as a shipping contract. Let's say you're a cattle broker and you want to buy or have Mr. Sharp furnish you two thousand head of cattle at fifteen dollars a head. You give Mr. Sharp half of that or fifteen thousand dollars to go and buy the cattle and defray his other costs. Then you pay the balance when you get the cattle. Now that's square and aboveboard, right?"

"Yeah."

"Well, Mr. Sharp made about six of those contracts for varying amounts right before he disappeared. With the money, naturally. Quite a considerable sum, as I well know, because the brokers never got any cattle and now they want their money back. I'm in the process of what we call liquidation, Mr. Young. I doubt I'll be able to pay back ten cents on the dollar."

I shrugged. I said, "Well, Mr. Patterson, I have no choice but to believe you. I guess I'll have to find Sharp some way else. I'm obliged for your time."

As I was moving to the door, Mr. Patterson said, "You heard this on the street, not from me. The man who helped Philip start the vigilantes and the man who was also in the illegal cattle business is named Ross Bennet."

"Where do I find him?"

Patterson poked the air with his finger. He said, "His business is the next one down the docks. Bennet and Sons.

Except the old man is dead and the other brother has long since pulled out. It's just Ross. He didn't get hurt like we did because a great deal of his shipping was legal. The next three warehouses after ours are his."

"Where does he live?"

"Do you know Broad Street?"

"Yes." Broad was the main street, the street the Galvez Hotel was on.

Patterson said, "He lives down at the south end. House is blue, kind of reminds you of a river steamboat."

I thanked him and left.

About eight o'clock that night Chulo and I got our horses out of the livery stable and rode slowly south on Broad Street until we'd located the house of Ross Bennet. It wasn't hard to find since it was nearly out of town and was the only house painted a light blue. And it did look something like a steam riverboat with half a second story set back from the front porch. It was long and it was big. I figured it had cost a power of money to build.

We rode on past the place and then tied our horses to a cottonwood tree about a hundred yards past. After that we walked slowly back to the house. We went through the front gate of the picket fence that surrounded it and then crept softly up on the front porch. The house had a high front porch, not like the patios we had along the border. I put Chulo back in the shadows and then went and knocked on the door. There were lights on in the house, but they looked dim, like they were on in the back part of the place.

Nobody came, so after a minute I knocked again, louder this time. The door was one of those that had a big glass oval in the middle of it done up with all sorts of fancy scroll-work. After another half a minute I saw a light brighten, and I could see that the door opened on a long entry hall. I could see a slight young man coming to the door. He was dressed like a dandy, in a gray frock coat and waistcoat and tie. I took him to be no more than thirty. When he got to the door, he opened it and peered out. He was in the light and I was in the dark and there was a screen door in between, so I knew he couldn't see out too well. I said, "Mr. Bennet?"

"Yes?"

"Mr. Ross Bennet?"

"Yes. What is it?" He sounded impatient, like all important men are supposed to.

I said, "I hate to be disturbing you, sir, but I need to talk to you a minute."

He said, "Well talk. I'm listening. And I haven't got all night."

I said, "Could you maybe step out here on the porch, sir. What I need to tell you is kind of private. Wouldn't want it overheard."

He said, "What is all this? Why can't you tell me here?"

I leaned forward and kind of whispered. I said, "I got a message, sir. It's from Mr. Sharp."

"Sharp!" And he didn't put much affection in the word.

I said, "Ssssh, sir. Please, if you'd just step out here a little ways I can give you this message and get out of town. I'm taking a risk as it is."

"Sharp," he said grimly. "Well, it had better be about money."

"It is, it is," I said.

He pushed through the screen door, pulling the inner door closed behind him. He said, "Where is that son of a bitch?"

But I was leading him toward the edge of the porch where the steps were. I said, "Well, the fact of the matter is—"

But I got no further because Chulo, who, in spite of his size, could move like a cat, had come up behind and clamped one arm around Bennet's head and mouth and twisted an arm up behind his back with the other. Bennet immediately went to struggling and trying to make noise, but it wouldn't have done him any good if he'd been twice as big.

We went down the porch steps and out to the road and turned down toward where we had our horses tied. After about twenty yards I pulled out my revolver and stuck it in his ribs. I said, "Now, Mr. Bennet, we are going down here a little piece and have a quiet talk. If you don't give us no trouble, nothing will happen to you and you'll be back in your house in ten minutes. Now, my friend is going to let go of you, but if you go to yell or make a sound, I'll put a hole in you. You understand?"

He was still trying to struggle and making muffled noises under Chulo's big hand.

I said, "If you understand and agree, nod your head."

As best he could, against the iron grip of Chulo, he made a kind of nod. I said, "Just keep in mind I mean what I say. You'll never finish any yell you start. Let him go, Chulo."

Chulo gradually released him. Bennet worked his shoulders around and then rotated his head. I imagined he was trying to get it back in place after the twisting Chulo had given him. He said, a little too loudly for my tastes, "What is all this? A robbery? Take what I've got and be gone!"

I jabbed him with the pistol. I said, "It ain't a robbery, Mr. Bennet. I probably got more money than you do. Just keep walking and keep quiet. It ain't time to talk yet."

He said, "I demand to know what this is all about!"

I stopped him and got around where my face was in his. I said, "You want me to get my friend to help you walk along quiet? Or you want to do it on your own?"

"I resent this," he said, but he said it in a quieter tone.

I didn't blame him. Hell, I'd have resented it too. But then that was the price he was paying for being friends with Phil Sharp.

We walked on down to where the horses were tied and got in behind them as protection against detection by some chance passerby. I pushed Bennet up against the piebald. I wanted him facing both me and Chulo, especially Chulo. I've had Chulo come upon me when I wasn't expecting him, and for just an instant, it's given me a turn. So I could figure what he must have looked like to Ross Bennet out there helpless in that dark night.

He said, still rankled, "All right, what is this? By God, we have law in this town."

I said, "That's some of what I wanted to talk to you about. But first I want you to tell me where Philip Sharp is."

He said, "I don't know where the bastard is. I wish I did."

I said, "Don't sound like he left many friends in town."

He said, "The bastard owes me money. He lied to me on a deal."

"Illegal cattle, I reckon," I said. "Well, he owes me money too. I want to collect that and then I'm going to shoot him."

"Good luck," he said.

"How do I know you ain't lying? You and him was partners in some deals. And you did start them vigilantes together."

He just gave me a steady look and said, "I don't know what you're talking about."

I holstered my pistol. He wasn't going anywhere. I said, "Oh, I think you do. Reason I'm going to shoot Mr. Sharp is that he shot me. With some help from three of your vigilantes."

Bennet looked me over like he was inspecting something he didn't particularly care for. He said, "So you're that one. You're that Wilson Young."

I said, "I'm that Wilson Young my mama named. I don't know about no others. Now where's Sharp?"

"I told you I don't know. He came to me after your little incident and said he'd wounded a famous gunman and had to get out of town for a while. But it's become clear from some business matters that he's not coming back."

I started to say something about shipping contracts, but that would have been giving Mr. Patterson away. Instead I said, "All right. Then maybe you can tell me who the head honcho of these here vigilantes is."

"Sharp was."

I shook my head. I said, "I don't want to know about you pantywaists or dandies. I mean who's the head shitkicker, the one directs the dirty work?"

He said, "I don't know."

I sighed and looked away. I said, "Mr. Bennet, I am getting plumb sick of hearing you say you don't know to every question I ask you. Just to break the monotony I'm gonna ask you something I bet you do know the answer to. Do you use your hands?"

"What?"

I said, "Hell, it's a simple question. Intelligent-looking fellow like you ought to be able to take it in. Do you use your hands?"

He tossed his head. He had a nice set of blond locks. He

said, "Of course I use my hands. What a superbly stupid question."

I said, "How many fingers you reckon a man needs on a hand to make that hand useful to him? Two? Three?"

Now he saw where I was going and he suddenly got very wary. He said, "I'm going to smoke a cigar," and his hand started for the side pocket in his vest.

My hand got there just before his did. Chulo had grabbed him around the neck and jerked him backwards until his back was arched. I slowly came out of the pocket with a little pearl-handled derringer. I said, "Well, well. Funny-looking cigar."

Then I cocked it and shoved it up to his mouth. I said, "You want to smoke this, Mr. Bennet?"

In a choked voice he said, "For God's sake, man, be careful! That's loaded!"

I said, "Of course it's loaded. Man would be a damn fool to carry around an unloaded gun. Now about this vigilante foreman. Want to give me his name?"

"I don't know," he said, still sounding strangled on account of the way Chulo had him around the neck.

I sighed again. I said, "All right, Chulo, break the little finger on his right hand. We'll just keep going until he remembers."

Chulo suddenly whirled him around and took his right arm under his and grabbed Bennet's hand with both of his. Bennet tried to make a fist, but that was useless. Chulo just unclenched it. Then he held Bennet's hand with his left and took hold of Bennet's little finger with his other hand and looked at me. I said, to Bennet, "This is your last chance. I promise you we will break them one at a time, and when we're out of fingers, we'll move on to arms and legs. But you will tell me because I know that you know."

"Hull!" he said. "Mike Hull!"

"You're not lying?"

"I swear it."

"Where might we find Mike Hull this time of night?"

I could see how white his face was even as dark as it was, with the moon behind some clouds. I could even see sweat glistening on his forehead. The man was scared and I didn't blame him. I wouldn't want Chulo about to break my fingers. He said, "There's a saloon down on the docks. Very small place. It's called the Main Brace. He stays at some rooming house when he's in port. I don't know the name of it. I swear I don't."

I looked at the little derringer in my hand. Chulo always carried a derringer in his boot as a hideout gun. It was in odd contrast to the huge Colt .44-caliber revolver with the nine-inch barrel that he carried on his hip. I said, "Chulo, you want this little trinket for your other boot?"

He said, "Ah doan steal. Ees not right."

"I'm glad to hear that, Chulo." I pitched the little gun off into the brush. Then I turned back on Bennet. I said, "Now listen, *señor*, you better not have lied to us. If you have, we'll be back. And we will make your life right lively."

Then Chulo shoved him out of the way, and we mounted up and road back the way we'd come, back toward town, toward the docks.

CHAPTER 7

We took the horses back to the livery stable. It wasn't but a short walk to the docks, though I had no idea where this saloon that Bennet had talked about, this Main Brace, was. But I figured it would be better to have the horses safe in the stables and not hitched in amongst the dark buildings and warehouses of the waterfront. Some of the folks I'd seen in Galveston thus far didn't look like they needed much in the way of temptation to lead them from the path of the righteous, and I didn't want that temptation to be a couple of Justa's horses.

It was about half past nine of a nice spring night. As we walked the few blocks toward the docks, the wind from the Gulf was in our faces, bringing a not so pleasant smell of fish and decay and a few other things I couldn't identify. The area all along the docks was lined with warehouses. The only lights we could see were those coming from the windows and doors of various saloons and eating places. We walked to the end of the line of warehouses and then turned right and started along the waterfront. Just to our left was ship after ship. Some of them were tall masted schooners; some of them had the funnels that meant they were steamboats. A few had masts *and* funnels. They all lay right alongside the wooden dock, tied with heavy ropes. In the moonlight I could see them rocking back and forth with the motion of the water and hear the creaking of their planks and their rigging. I didn't know a hell of a lot about boats and didn't much care if I ever learned.

DEAD MAN'S POKER

The first place we came upon was a hellhole named The Cove. We looked in. It was smoky and dim. Some of the customers were drinking and some of them were eating and some of them were doing both. As we looked in, a man came staggering by us. I grabbed his arm and asked him if he could tell us where the Main Brace was. He just jerked his arm away and waved on down the docks in the direction we'd been headed. He mumbled something that sounded like "Further on," but I wasn't sure because he looked drunk and his accent wasn't like anything I'd ever heard before.

Chulo said, "These place steenk."

I agreed with him on that, but it wasn't the smell of the place that struck me so much as what an ideal area it was for an ambush. There were nooks and crannies everywhere and alleys between each of the wide and long warehouses. Occasionally there was the light of a watchman on some of the bigger boats or the lights from their cabins, but other than the saloons, if that's what you called such places on a dock, there weren't any lights to speak of at all. Occasionally we passed a man either going or coming. They went by us without a word of greeting. I heard more than one muttering to himself. I figured they were sailors who went out on those big boats. I figured if a man spent enough time out there in all that water, the result would be he'd just naturally have to end up talking to himself. The thought of being shut up in one of them boats for long months at a time, talking to the same faces day after day, just gave me a bad case of the shudders.

We finally found the Main Brace about three drinking joints down the way. We nearly missed it because all it was was an open front door with no windows and a little hand-painted sign over the door announcing who it was.

I took a cautious look inside. It was a small room. At a quick glance I saw about six or seven men sitting around, with a bartender behind a rough bar. The place didn't even have proper batwing doors like a saloon ought to have, but a big heavy door that was propped open with a small anchor. I stationed Chulo right by the front door. I said, "Don't let anybody come out while I'm in there. Especially if they act like they're in a hurry."

He had a big Bowie knife in his boot. He pulled it out. "They doan come by me."

I said, "Put that damn thing away. I don't want to kill this Mike Hull if we can help it. The idea is to talk to him."

He stuck the Bowie in his belt. He said, "I heet them hard."

"Not too hard," I said. "And if you hear me in trouble, come in there and don't be too selective about who you shoot."

Before I went through the door, I looked up at the building the joint was in. It was a big, two-storied clapboard affair. I could see a line of windows along the top story, but there was only a light, very dim, in one. All the windows looked like they had the shades drawn.

With another word to Chulo, I stepped through the door and went up to the corner of the bar. The barkeep, a fat, slovenly man in a dirty apron, gave me a look and slowly eased over my way. It wasn't a long trip because the main part of the bar was no more than ten or twelve feet long. I flipped a silver dollar on the rough surface of the bar and said, "Brandy."

He eyed me. "Ain't got none."

Turning slightly so I could see the rest of the room, I said, "I'm looking for a man named Mike Hull. He here?"

The barkeep picked up a piece of rag and acted like the was polishing the bar. He said, "Never heered of him."

There was no one else at the bar. I turned full sideways, but not so much so that I couldn't still see the bartender out of the corner of my eye. The room was small, surprisingly so considering the size of the building it was in. There was another door off to my left and a narrow flight of stairs in the direction I was looking. I was wondering if maybe the place doubled as a rooming house for the men who worked on the docks—stevedores I'd heard them called— and maybe the sailors off the ships.

The ceiling of the bar was low, and there was a haze of smoke hovering just at the ceiling. There were six or seven men sitting at tables, with drinks in front of them. There were two bunches of three and then one man sitting off by himself toward the front door. To a man they were staring at me. They were a rough-looking lot, dressed in work clothes, some of them wearing a kind of cap I'd never seen before. There wasn't a spur or a Western hat in the bunch of them. Most of them were wearing brogans like farmers wore or else waterproof boots made out of india rubber. Some of them had knives in their belts, and one or two had pistols shoved down in the waistbands of their pants. The man to my right, I took careful notice, was carrying a pretty good-looking Colt with a pearl handle. I couldn't tell the caliber, but I figured it was ample.

I said, to the bunch, "I'm looking for Mike Hull. Anybody tell me where he is?"

To a man they were smoking pipes. I didn't know I'd ever seen that many men in one group smoking pipes. They just stared back at me in answer to my question.

I said, in a reasonable voice, "Don't you folks speak English? I done asked you if you knew where Mike Hull was. Somebody answer me."

A man in one of the groups of three said, "Never heered of him."

I reached in my pocket and took out a gold ten-dollar piece, spun it in the air, caught it, and laid it on the bar. I said, "There's ten dollars for the man can tell me how to find Mike Hull."

The bartender said, "Feller, you don't b'long in this place. You better git out whilst you still can."

I ignored him. I nodded at the ten-dollar gold piece on the bar. I said, "I'll double that. Now who can tell me where I can find Mike Hull?"

One of the men at the tables, a dried-up man smoking a clay pipe, said, "Ye be some kind of law?"

I said, "Nope. Just about the opposite. I don't mean this Hull fellow no harm. I just want a few words with him. I think he knows where an acquaintance of mine might be. A man that owes me money. Now, would one of you in here be Mike Hull? If you are, you got nothing to fear from me. Speak up."

The man sitting by himself said, "I'll speak up." The words kind of rumbled out of him. He was a heavyset kind of man, though it was difficult to tell how tall he was with him sitting in a chair. He had a layer of fat on him that gave me a pretty sure idea he wasn't no working man.

I swung most of my gaze to him, though I could still see the bartender out of the corner of my eye, as well as the rest of the crowd. I said, "You Mike Hull?" I noticed that he had let his right hand come up on the tabletop. The move brought it temptingly close to the butt of the big Colt revolver he had in his belt.

He said, "Naw, I ain't Mike Hull. But I'll tell you what you're a-gonna be. You gonna be damn sorry if you don't git out of here like you been told."

I shifted my weight to my left foot. It makes a right-hand draw just that much faster. I said, softly, "Make me."

His hand started for the butt of the revolver. He had it half out when the barrel of my gun came to bear on him. I didn't say anything, just stood there pointing the gun at him. He slowly let his hand slide off the butt of his revolver and fall in his lap. Everyone else was still. Out of the corner of my left eye I saw the bartender bend over under the bar. I said, "Barkeep, you better be coming out of there with a jug of whiskey or a rag or something that ain't a gun or a club."

He suddenly straightened up.

I said, "Move on down the bar where I can see you better. You look like you might get up to mischief." He kind of scuttled the length of the bar and then edged around the end until he was out from behind it.

I kept my gun on the man that had tried to draw on me. I figured he did his work with a gun or a crowbar or a knife. I also figured I was looking at one of the so-called vigilantes.

I said, "Well, Mister, looks like you have elected yourself spokesman. So I reckon it's you going to tell me what I want to know."

He was starting to sweat. He said, "Goddammit, take that pistol off cock! You got it aimed right at me. It might go off."

"It damn well might," I said. "And on purpose. This here revolver never goes off by accident. I am going to count to three and then I'm going to shoot your ear off. At least I'm going to try and shoot your ear off, but you're a good twelve, fifteen feet away from me. That's a tough shot with a revolver at such a small thing as a ear. I reckon you better hope that I miss to the outside if I miss at all."

Hell, I didn't know if I was going to shoot his ear off or not. It had just kind of popped out of my mouth. I didn't much want to, because I didn't figure it would be good politics to be letting off firearms in Sheriff Mills's jurisdiction. But I'd waded in and now I was going to have to get wet. I said, "You got any preference which one?"

The man was starting to shake a little and sweat a little more. He licked his lips. He said, "I don't know any Mike Hull."

I said, "Was I you, I'd quit that trembling. An ear shot is hard enough without no handicaps. I—"

And then I got saved the trouble. Out of the corner of my right eye I saw a man appear in the doorway of the joint. He'd taken a step inside when someone yelled, "Mike! Avast!"

I swung my gun toward the door, but the man was already almost out. I yelled, "Chulo!" and brought my aim back to bear on the room. The fat man had stood up and had his pistol clear of his belt and was bringing it up to level on me. I shot him in the chest. The shot boomed and echoed in the small room. The slug must have hit bone because the fat man kind of skidded a few inches backwards before he fell back over his chair and sprawled to the floor. I whipped my revolver around on the others. They were frozen. Not a man was so much as moving a finger. I started backing toward the door. Outside I could hear grunts and thuds and the sounds of a struggle. When I got to the door, I said, "If you come out this door anytime soon, you're going to need help getting back in—like a hearse."

I turned quickly and went out into the dark by the docks. Just to my left the two figures were struggling. Ain't many can match strength with Chulo, but this Mike Hull was giving it a try. Chulo had him from the back, trying to pin both arms at his sides, but Chulo's high-heeled boots were giving him trouble on the slick planks of the dock. I could see Hull wasn't as tall as Chulo, but he had big, thick shoulders and big arms and hands. Of course I wasn't going to rush over and grab hold of Hull and help Chulo wrestle him around. I had given up scuffling around in the dirt when I was a schoolboy. There's a whole lot of folks that are bigger and stronger than I am but damn few that can use a gun like me. And I am a man who is just naturally inclined to make use of the gifts he's been given. Without much ceremony I uncocked my gun so the jar wouldn't set it off, stepped forward, and cracked Mike Hull over the head with the heavy barrel of my revolver. I hit him just hard enough to stun him, not knock him out, and he all of a sudden just kind of collapsed in Chulo's arms. Chulo said, "These sumbetch es strong! *Muy fuente.*"

I said, "Get his arms jerked up behind his shoulders and let's get out of here. I had to shoot a son of a bitch in there. The law might be coming." I looked around. There was a narrow, dark alley running between the Main Brace and a warehouse next door to it. It led back toward town. I hadn't thought where we'd take Hull to talk to him; I'd just figured to find him first. I pointed down the alley. I said, "Let's go that way."

Hull was still groggy, but with Chulo supporting him and me walking beside him with my pistol in his ribs, we made our way slowly down the alley. It was dark as the ace of spades and long, but we finally came out at the end onto a little dirt street that was kind of the front of the docks. Broad Street, I knew, was two streets over. I said, "Chulo, let's take him to the hotel room."

Chulo said, not believing, "En the hotel? Chou *loco?*"

I said, "There's an outside stairway up to the second floor. On the stable side. I noticed it earlier. If we can get in that way, won't nobody notice."

Hull was groaning and trying to get an arm loose from Chulo so he could feel his head where I'd hit him. But Chulo had both his arms shoved up behind his back.

I said, "Quit jerking around, Hull, or the man that has got you will break an arm for you."

He said, groggily, "What the hell is all this? Eh? What the hell is goin' on? You crazy, fool with me."

I said, "Shut up. And stay shut up. Chulo, every time he says anything, just lift one of his arms a little higher."

Hull said, "You'll be one sorry—"

Chulo had nearly lifted him off his feet when he'd shoved his arms up. I got in his face. I said, "Hull, unless you like to hurt, you better keep your damn mouth shut. You ain't getting away from the man that's got you, and even if you could, I'd put a bullet through you so fast it wouldn't bleed until your soul was in hell."

I stepped out into the little street and looked left and right. It appeared to be empty, but anybody could come along at any time. I wasn't all that anxious to take Hull back to the hotel, but we needed someplace private to talk to him in. I didn't figure he was going to be an easy nut to crack, and I didn't want to try him in the alley, but it would have to do.

I stepped back in the alley where Chulo was holding Hull. I got up close to Hull's face. He was looking mighty sullen. He said, but he said it lowly, mindful of those powerful hands that had his arms rammed up his back, "Who are you, mate?"

"Never mind that," I said. "I'm going to ask you a question, and you better think about it before you answer. I'm looking for Philip Sharp. Where is he?"

He turned his head and spit. He done it like he had considered spitting in my face and then changed his mind. He said, "Never heered the name."

I said, "Hull, you can save us a lot of trouble and yourself a lot of pain if you tell me right now where Sharp is. I know you know him. I know you're his right arm in the vigilantes. Ross Bennet told me that much. And I know you know where he is."

He spit again, wider this time. I knew he wanted to spit in my face, but I was glad to see that he was sane enough not to. He was about six inches shorter than Chulo and weighed, I figured, about 180 pounds. And he was strong. He looked around at me and made some kind of lopsided grin, so that I could see he was missing several teeth. He said, "Gone, you bloody bastard."

I jabbed him in the belly with the barrel of my pistol hard enough to force an "Uuufh" out of him. I said, "I'll ask you one more time. Where's Sharp?"

"In England. Gone to see the Queen."

I sighed. I said, "He wants it hard, Chulo. Bring him along."

We were able to go down an alley between two more warehouses to reach the next street. This one was a little more lighted. I could see a few open cafés and saloons. The next street over was Broad. Fortunately we were nearly at the north end of town, so there were more residences than businesses and there was very little traffic out on the street. Nevertheless we hurried Hull across it and then down a dark side street. Leaving Chulo and Hull in the shadows, I stepped out for a look. The Galvez was nearly across from us, just a little to the left. I could even see the stairs on the outside running up to the second floor. But Broad Street was plenty busy, with any number of saloons and eating places doing a thriving business and men on horseback and afoot passing up and down the street. Also, Broad Street was just that, broad. It was at least twenty to twenty-five yards across, and if Hull got to cutting up, he'd surely catch someone's attention, most likely a deputy sheriff's. I came back to stand in front of Hull, biting my lip, trying to think of a way to get him across that street without attracting attention. The only thing I could think of was to make him look like a drunk that a couple of friends were helping get to bed. But I'd have to hit him just right—not too easy and not too long. And I didn't know how hard his head was.

I said, "Chulo, get ready."

In one motion I swung my arm up and then hit him hard over the head with the barrel of my revolver. He slumped immediately, nothing holding him up except the grip Chulo had on him. I holstered my pistol swiftly and then took his left arm and got it over my shoulder. When Chulo saw what I was doing, he did likewise with Hull's right arm. For a moment, the way he was sagged down, I was scared I'd hit the man too hard. I wanted him to look drunk, not dead. I said, "Let's go."

We stepped out of the shadows, Hull between us, hanging limp off our shoulders, his feet dragging in the dust of the road. Looking up and down the street I saw one or two passersby turn their heads briefly and look our way. About halfway across the street Hull started groaning and trying to shake his head. I felt him take a little weight on his feet, and then he was sort of stumbling along with our help. Fortunately I had stunned him just about the right amount.

We moved along briskly, crossed the street, and then stepped up on the boardwalk at the end of the hotel and right in front of the stairs.

It was still hard going. Hull didn't give us no help getting him up on the boardwalk, and he sure didn't give us no help climbing that flight of stairs, which was damn near too narrow for three men climbing abreast. But we finally made it to the top, and I was some relieved to find that the outside door was open. We got inside and then went along the hall, looking for Chulo's room, which was right next to mine. Hull was starting to groan louder and was rapidly coming awake. We were going to have to get him someplace and someplace quick. Finally we found Chulo's room. It had confused us coming at the matter from the opposite direction. I held Hull up while Chulo got the door opened, and then we carried him inside and flung him on the floor. I lit the overhead gaslight and looked down at Hull. His face was nearly covered with blood. I knew he hadn't been cut deep, but a scalp wound will bleed like a stuck pig. I told Chulo we were going to have to find something to tie him up with and gag him. I looked around. Not a thing in sight that I figured we could use. I was just about to say we'd have to make do with the belts that held our pants up when Chulo went to the bed, ripped back the spread, and jerked off the top sheet. With his knife he started cutting it into strips.

I said, "That's going on your bill. Destroying hotel property."

He didn't laugh. Chulo ain't got much of what you'd call a sense of humor.

I squatted down by Hull. He was starting to come around in spite of the way he looked with blood all over his face. Some of the vacant look was going out of his eyes, and once or twice, he put his hand to his head and grimaced. If you can feel pain, you ain't too far from being fully conscious. I said, "Hurry up, Chulo. The man is coming to."

Chulo went down to Hull's feet and jerked off his waterproof boots. The man wasn't wearing no stockings, which didn't surprise me at all. Working quickly, Chulo jerked Hull's ankles together and then wound a strip of bed sheet around and around the small part of his legs and tied it off tight. After that he grabbed Hull by the shoulders and flung him on his belly, jerked his arms behind him and tied his wrists together so tight I could see the strips of cloth cutting into his flesh. I said, "Not so hard, Chulo. You're going to cut the man's circulation off and he's gonna get gangrene."

Chulo said, "I doan geeve a chit."

Then he flipped Hull back over and stuffed a wad of cloth in his mouth, which he bound with a few strips around his head and over his mouth. Hull was staring up at me, and from the look in his eyes, I could tell he had all his faculties back. I got out my watch and looked at it. It was going on twelve midnight, and neither me nor Chulo had had a bite to eat or a drink since right about six o'clock. Chulo had a bottle of rum, and I went through the connecting door between our two rooms and came back with a bottle of brandy and a glass. I pulled up a chair by Hull's feet and poured myself out a drink. Chulo just sat on the bed and took his pulls straight out of the bottle. I sipped at my brandy, looking at Hull. I said, "Chulo, we could probably find some eatery still open, but I don't think we got the time. Wouldn't you rather just get to work and get it over with? I got a feeling we ought not to stay around Galveston too much longer. Remember, I shot that man in that place we were at. And I don't think he's going to get well. I don't know if them are the kind of folks, in that place, that will go to the law, but there's also that Bennet feller. What do you think?"

"Chure," he said, and took a swig of rum.

I got up. I said, "All right. There's a ten o'clock southbound train out of here in the morning. Hell, that's barely ten hours away, so you'll have to work fast."

"Chure," he said. He took the Bowie out of his belt and began honing it on the leather of his boot. I took a step and stood over Hull. I said, "Partner, you know where Sharp is and you will tell us before all this is over. Or maybe you won't. Maybe you like pain. Chulo is going to go to work on you. I'm going to go in the other room because I got a weak stomach. Whenever you feel like telling us everything we ask you, including where the birthmark is on the girl of your dreams, why you just nod your head to Chulo. But

I'd do it real vigorously because he ain't going to want to stop what he's doing. He likes it."

Chulo got up, testing the edge of his knife with his finger. I could see Hull staring at him, round-eyed and worried. All the bully-boy bluster was gone.

I said, "All right, Chulo, skin the bottoms of his feet."

Then I went out of the room, into mine, and closed the door behind me. Even with a gag in his mouth, a man can make some heartrending moans when he's getting the skin peeled off his feet.

But on a thought I stuck my head back into the other room. Chulo was on his knees down by Hull's feet, his left hand clamped around Hull's ankles so he couldn't move, the knife ready in his right. I said, "Chulo, I know the dining room is closed downstairs, so I doubt if I can get any salt. But a little of that rum of yours ought to do as well on the raw flesh."

"Chure," he said.

I went in my room, sat down in a chair, and looked out at the street. I got out my watch. It was half past midnight. I lit a cigarillo. I didn't know how long the matter was going to take. That was up to Hull. I just sat there staring out at the street below, which appeared to still be going strong, and thinking. Then, all of a sudden, I said, out loud, "Damn!" I'd just remembered I'd left that ten-dollar gold piece on the bar at that sleazy joint. Ten dollars wasn't shucks to me, but I didn't want them mongrel hooligans having ten dollars of anybody's money, especially mine. I was of about half a mind to go back and get it, but then I got to thinking that might not be such a good idea. Besides, I wanted to be handy when Hull broke. And he *would* break. It was only a question of time and pain. If he didn't break down by the time Chulo was through with the soles of his feet, then Chulo would start somewhere else tender and just keep on going until he skinned him alive. I'd lied to Hull when I'd said Chulo liked doing such things. That wasn't true. He just didn't give a damn one way or the other.

It was over a good deal quicker than I'd expected. It was barely one o'clock when Chulo came into my room wiping his knife on a piece of the bed sheet. He said, "Chit. He ees eezy. Some beeg tough *pachucho*. I theenk he want to talk to you now."

I went into Chulo's room. Hull was white-faced and shaking. Sweat was running off his face. His eyes had a kind of wild, crazy look in them. I looked at his feet. Hell, Chulo had only skinned the ball of one foot and not even all of that. Little strips of skin were still hanging down where Chulo had worked his way toward the heel.

I stood over Hull. I said, "You ready to talk now?"

He nodded his head, up and down, rapidly. He was making little sounds against the gag in his mouth.

I said, "You all done seeing how close you can spit at my face without hitting me?"

He nodded again, the same way.

I said, "I want to make one thing clear. If you don't answer every question I ask you, if you don't tell me everything you know, then we'll start over again. Only this time Chulo won't stop. You understand?"

More of the same nodding.

I motioned to Chulo. I said, "Take the gag out of his mouth. But put your knife against his throat. First thing that comes out of him that sounds like a yell, why just cut his throat."

Chulo knelt and cut the bandages that were wound around his head to hold the gag in place. Then he plucked the wad of cloth out of Hull's mouth. The man, for a moment, just lay there panting and gasping for air. "I—" he said. "I—" He gasped some more. "I can't, can't— My God! Are you crazy!"

I said, "I don't like that kind of talk. You want me to leave you alone with Chulo some more?"

Fright jumped straight up in his eyes. He said, "My God, man, no! Ain't you civilized? The bastard is skinnin' me! Is he a goddam Injun?"

All of a sudden Chulo stuck the point of his knife up Hull's nose. He said, "I cut hees *pinche* nose off."

I said, "Hold on, Chulo." Then to Hull I said, "I'd watch that line of talk if I was you. He will cut your nose off. And certain other parts as well."

Hull said, "For God's sake, give me a drink! I'm dyin'. I'm hurtin' like hell!"

I got Chulo's bottle of rum off the table and knelt down and held it to Hull's mouth. A good part of it ran down his face, but he did manage to suck down about a half a glassful. I took it away. A little of the color was starting to come back into his face, but he was breathing hard. Pain will do that to you, just flat wear a body out. While I was waiting for him to get his breath, I took a look at Hull. He was a little younger than I'd thought, at least ten years. I put his age at somewhere around thirty-five. He was dressed pretty much like the men I'd seen in the Main Brace, but his clothes were of a better quality and he seemed better spoke. He didn't seem to have much of an accent, so I couldn't tell if he was a Texan or a Southerner or from the North. I reckoned he'd knocked about in so many parts of the country, sailing around as he did, that whatever pattern of lingo he'd started out with had got all jumbled up with the rest. And I figured that all the weathering he'd taken from all them seas he'd been on was what made him look older. But whatever his age was, he was old enough to know he'd better answer my questions and damn quick. I was near out of patience.

I said, "Are you the pusher or the ramrod or the head honcho or whatever you want to call it of these here vigilantes along the waterfront?"

He shifted his eyes ever so slightly. He said, "Naw. That's Sharp."

I said, "You know what I mean. You in charge of the arm breaking and the shooting and the stabbing department?"

He said, "I'm a sailor, dammit! I've got my first mate's papers."

I didn't know what that meant and I didn't give a damn. I said, "You want some more rum?"

He looked eager. "Yessir, I do."

I handed the bottle to Chulo. I said, "Put some of that on the bottom of his foot where it will do the most good." Then I clamped my hand over his mouth because I knew he was going to scream. Chulo gave him a little dose and then held his legs down while he writhed around. After I saw a little of the pain beginning to leave him, I took my hand off his mouth. He gasped, "Oh, gawd! Oh, my gawd!" His face was just all clenched up.

I said, "Now then, you want to try that question again?"

He was still panting, but he managed to gasp out, "Who are you? You the law?"

"Who am I? That ain't the question. Question is, are you the one been seeing that Sharp and Bennet's errands get carried out? You want to answer or you want some more rum?"

He turned his face away. He said, grudgingly, "All right, all right. So what? Sharp said it was legal. Said it was a good thing. Said it kept order."

I said, "You remember about six days ago, maybe a week, when Sharp told you to have three men in his office? Told you he had somebody he wanted taken care of? Only them three got taken care of. It was right before Sharp cut and run. You remember that?"

He blinked. His eyes got a little bigger. He said, "Was that you?"

"That was me," I said. "And Mr. Sharp not only robbed me of money he owed me, he shot me. I don't generally take getting shot too lightly."

"Son of a bitch," he said. "Sharp told me was a man coming to collect some money from him he didn't have to spare. Said it would interfere with our plans if he paid the man the money. Said the man was dangerous and I'd better get three good men for the job."

"Doesn't look like you did," I said.

He licked his lips. He said, "I told him sailors and dockhands wadn't no good with guns. Told him knives or clubs was the thing. He said the man was too fast, that he'd kill them before they could get close enough. Can I have another drink? Hard to talk way I'm hurting."

I took the bottle from Chulo and let some more gurgle down his throat. He drank until he started coughing. When the fit passed, he said, "Can't I sit up? Fer gawd's sake, I'll tell you anythin' you want to know if you'll sit me up and untie my hands. I cain't take much more of this."

Chulo got one shoulder and I got the other, and we pulled Hull across the floor and set him up against the wall.

He said, "What about my hands? They tied so tight I cain't feel 'em no more."

I said, "Pretty soon. Now . . . Where is Mr. Sharp?"

He hesitated. First he looked one way and then the other. He licked his lips. He cleared his throat.

I said, "You can stall all you want to, but you'll tell me. And pretty quick. Me and Chulo ain't et, and we're tired and want some sleep and are just generally getting out of sorts. I'm going to ask you this once more. Where is Sharp?"

He looked sullen. He said, "He's probably in Bodega. That's a little port at the mouth of the Rio Grande river about—"

I said, "I know where it is. You said 'probably.' Where else could he be?"

He was still acting all sullen. He said, "If he didn't get what he wanted in Bodega, he was going on to Tampico. I was to try him first at Bodega and then follow on down the coast until I run him down."

The way he said it kind of puzzled me. I said, "What do you mean you was supposed to have followed him? Followed him how?"

He looked away. He was clearly a man didn't want to talk. I said, "Chulo, make a fresh place on his foot and give him some more rum. He seems to like it at that end better."

But before Chulo could move he almost shouted, "Wait! Dammit, wait! I'll tell you. It's just hard because it's going to mess up the first good proposition I ever had come across my bow in my life."

I had been wondering why he'd been protecting Sharp to the extent he had. Now, just guessing at what he'd said, it made a little sense. If he was tied in with Sharp on some matter, he'd want to protect Sharp to protect his own interests. I said, "What?"

He got that sullen look on his face again. He said, "I never had no chance to make some good money before in my life. Now I get that chance and you two fellers come along."

I said, "How are you supposed to follow him?"

He looked at me like I ought to already know. He said, "Why, in the *Polly Ann*. At least me in the *Polly Ann* with the *Galveston Queen* in my wake. Course we was gonna be sailin' shorthanded on account of Sharp took the best of the crews with him."

I said, "Wait a minute. What the hell you talking about? What is this Polly Anna stuff? This crew and all that?"

He furrowed his brow. "Ships," he said. "Two-masted cargo sloops. Course Sharp has already got away with the best of them, the *Dolphin*. Hunnert and forty feet at the waterline, can carry four hundred head of cattle or a thousand bales of cotton or tons of lumber and don't draw enough water to drown in."

"I see," I said. "So your plan was to steal all the boats Sharp's company had left. I guess you was gonna sell them and take off with the proceeds, leaving the creditors back here holding the bag."

He looked puzzled. He said, "Steal 'em? How can a man steal something that belongs to him? Them's Sharp's ships. Hell, he can do with 'em what he wants. No, Sharp has got a plan. A hell of a plan."

I squatted down so we were eye to eye. I said, "Tell me about this plan."

He said, "Well, it's been workin' for quite some time, right after we lost the two big steamboats. Sharp is down in Mexico buying sick cattle. Then we're gonna—"

"Sick cattle? What are you talking about?"

He said, "Hell, I don't know nothin' 'bout cattle. But these cattle get around other cattle, they make them sick too, and pretty soon all the cattle die. See, as a general thing we take a load of Mexican cattle to Cuba, they get slaughtered right away and never get a chance to get the other cattle sick. Only this time we ain't going to do that. We're going to haul nine hundred head of sick cattle to a little port on the Mexican side of Cuba and mix them in with the Cuban cattle. And as few cattle as Mr. Sharp says they got in Cuba, won't be long before all the cattle are dead, and then we're going to clean up."

I stared at him. That was the damndest idea I'd ever heard of. But I reckoned there must be some sense in it, though I was damned if I could see it. I said, "How are you planning on cleaning up?"

He said, "Why, when they ain't no more meat in Cuba, we come sailing in with three boatloads of cattle, all ready to be butchered. We'll be able to name our own price. Mr. Sharp already has some Cuban head honchos in with him, and they'll keep out other cattle shippers until we load up our sack. We was all ready to go on this when you come along."

So there was some sense in it. And a lot of money, it sounded like.

I said, "But look here, what kind of sickness are these cattle supposed to have, Mexican tick fever?"

He shook his head. "Naw, it ain't that. Somethin' longer. Kills 'em in about two or three weeks."

"Brucelosis?" I'd heard the word, but I was damned if I knew what it was. Now was when I needed Justa, though I didn't know what business it was of mine what happened to the cattle industry in Cuba.

"Naw."

I thought for a moment. "Hoof-and-mouth disease?"

He nodded his head. "Yeah, that's the one. Gawd, gimme another drink. An' my hands is killin' me."

I poured some more rum down him. It was easier with him sitting up. I said, "Just a few more questions." I was thinking of Justa mentioning that Patterson had said they couldn't ship to New Orleans on account of all they had left were coasting vessels. I asked Hull how he was going to get such ships across deep water to Cuba.

He said, "Way the currents and the weather run in the gulf, you can take a coaster loaded to Cuba, but you can't bring one back loaded. All different. But then we'll be coming back empty. Hell, I could sail a rowboat around the north pole with the right crew. I nearly got my master's papers."

I stood up. I said, "Well, this is some piece of work. It ain't none of my affair, though. Sharp is all I'm after. You boys can cheat them Cubans all you want. When was you planning on leaving?"

He said, "Was going tomorrow night, but— No, I guess it's tonight now. It's after midnight, ain't it?"

"Oh, yes," I said. I looked at my watch. "Going on for two o'clock." I said, "What was the real business of this vigilante bunch?"

He shrugged. He said, "Aw, it wasn't much. Sharp an' Bennet had a scheme goin' where they'd declare so much cargo sea-damaged, cotton and rum and sugar and such. They'd claim on their insurance an' then turn around and sell it to some outfit of thieves out of Houston. Us vigilantes was supposed to see that ever'body on the docks kept their mouths shut. It was just piddlin' stuff compared to this scheme Mr. Sharp has about making himself a market in cattle in Cuba. An' them was his exact words. He said, 'By gawd, if they're a-gonna cheat me here in Texas, I'll just *make* me a market in Cuba. By gawd, let me see them herd cattle overland to a goddam *island!*' Them was his very words."

I just shook my head. I said, "What a bunch, you and Bennet and Sharp."

He said, "You got to do something 'bout my hands."

I looked around. I said, "Chulo, there's a good, heavy wooden chair. Tie him to that. Try not to tie his hands too tight, but I don't want him getting away, neither. Even if he is a sorry example of human flesh, I don't want his hands to rot off."

While Chulo was getting Hull secured to the chair, I went over and tried the door to the closet. It was a good, heavy affair and locked with the same key as the room door did. It was plenty big enough to set Hull in, chair and all. I said, "Chulo, when you get him good and tied, pick him up and put him in this closet."

I had the rest of my glass of brandy while Chulo was finishing up the job. As he was shoving him in the closet, Hull said, "What about me? What are you going to do to me?"

I said, "Well, one thing we ain't going to do is turn you loose tonight so you can show back up here with about a dozen of them hooligans off the docks. I figure we'll cut you loose just before we leave. After that we'll have us a little race."

"Race?"

"Yeah. First one to Philip Sharp. You get there first, you get to make a lot of money off his little scheme. I get there first, I shoot him. *Sabe?* Gag him, Chulo, and then lock the door."

We had one last drink together before bed. Chulo said, "Why chou don't let me cut thees sumbeetch's throat?"

"Too messy." I said. "And I got a sheriff just waiting for me to put a foot wrong." I got up and went into my room, leaving the connecting door open. I said, "Sleep light, *compadre*. Wake me up if you go early for coffee."

CHAPTER 8

About eight o'clock the next morning I was sitting in my room, in a big overstuffed chair, drinking a pot of coffee a boy had brought me up, when there came a knock at my door. I wasn't wearing anything but a pair of twill trousers. I hadn't even put on my boots. But my gunbelt was hanging over the back of the chair, in easy reach, and I had a bottle of brandy at my feet that I'd been sweetening the coffee with. Strictly speaking I was on guard. Hull was in the closet, and Chulo had gone down to eat some breakfast. The knock came again.

I figured it might be one of the maids coming in to make up the beds. It was either that or it was some friend of Hull's who had scented us out. I couldn't think who else it might be. Finally I yelled out, "Come in!"

The door opened and Sheriff Mills strolled in. Maybe it was a holdover from my outlaw days, but the sight of a lawman coming on me unexpected always gave me a start.

But I kind of recovered my composure and said, "Sheriff Mills. Come in, come in. Take a chair."

He stopped about two steps into the room and took a look around, noticing the open door connecting to Chulo's room. Finally he took a straight-backed wooden chair away from the wall and sat down facing me about six or seven feet away. He leaned forward, resting his elbows on his knees. He said, "Good morning, Mr. Young."

I said, "Sheriff, I'd offer you some coffee, but I ain't got but the one cup."

He said, "I've had a-plenty, thanks just the same."

I pointed at the bottle of brandy. "Care for something a little stronger?"

He smiled slightly. He said, "I don't reckon so. Was a day I could have handled that in the morning, but no more."

I took a sip of my coffee. I said, "Well, I know you ain't gone to the trouble to run me down just for no social visit. What can I do for you?"

Before he said anything, the sheriff took off his hat, set it crown-downward on the floor beside him, and then smoothed his gray hair with a careless hand. He said, "Mr. Young, a Ross Bennet come to see me this morning. Damn near got to the office before I did. Do you know a Ross Bennet?"

"I sure as hell do!" I said. I straightened up in my chair, trying to look indignant. I said, "I called on that gentleman last night in the most polite fashion. Wanted to ask him some questions about Philip Sharp's whereabouts because I knew they'd had business dealings. Well, the upshot of the matter was he pulled a gun on me and ordered me away from him if I valued my life. The gun was a derringer and he had it in his vest pocket. He was acting so careless with it I took it away from him for his own safety and flung it away. I suppose he come and told you some quite different story. I wouldn't put it past his like."

The sheriff looked tired. "Yes, there was a difference in what he had to say."

"I notice he come running first thing so as to get his licks in early. That ought to tell you something."

The sheriff looked around again. He said, "Bennet said you had a big Mexican with you was going to break his fingers. You got a big Mexican with you?"

I tried to look as innocent as I could. I said, "A man don't see a lot of big Mexicans, Sheriff. You seen any real big Mexicans lately? They are mostly a small people."

He smiled slightly. He said, "You ain't going to call that an answer are you, Mr. Young?"

I said, "I just think Ross Bennet ought to be a little more careful before he goes charging around accusing folks of God only knows what. Bennet might be answering some charges himself before he knows it."

The sheriff said, "There was one other matter. A man named Oliver was found floating in the water down by the docks. Had a bullet hole square in his chest. Kind of shot a man was real handy with a gun would make. Now Oliver ain't no big loss. Fact of the business is I've had my eye on him for a long time. His business was buying damaged goods from some of these shippers down here. Mostly took them to Houston. We knowed something was wrong, but we never could catch him at anything crooked."

I said, dryly, "I bet the shippers he was buying the so-called damaged cargo from was either Bennet or Sharp. And I bet you was gettin' some inquiries from the insurance companies involved."

The sheriff looked at me. Then he took a pouch of tobacco out of his pocket and put a chew in his mouth. He looked around the room, and I got up and found a cuspidor over by the bed and took it over and set it by his chair. He nodded his thanks.

When he had his chaw worked down, he said, "You seem to have gotten hold of some information in a pretty short time."

I said, "I can tell you the main business of that vigilante committee was to make sure everybody on the docks kept his mouth shut about them *damaged* goods that Bennet and Sharp was collecting insurance money on and then selling. I hear it's right hard to tell sea-damaged goods if the insurance inspector ain't real thorough."

The sheriff spat. He said, "They was some talk around the docks concerning the demise of this here Oliver feller. They said something about some cowboy being around. That wouldn't have been you, would it?"

I poured a little brandy in my empty coffee cup and sipped it. I said, "Hell, Sheriff, I run a casino and a cat-house. Do I look like a cowboy?"

The sheriff said, "Oh, I wasn't thinking of you so much. Just kind of unusual fer them folks down at the docks to talk much about their business. They generally keep it to theyselves, handle it theyselves. But they seemed a little— what would you call it?—impressed by this, uh, cowboy. I don't guess you was down at the docks last night?"

I said, "Sheriff, I believe you warned me about going down there, didn't you? Said you didn't even let your own deputies go around the place after dark. Ain't that a fact?"

The sheriff spit and then chuckled. He said, "I can't seem to think up any questions will get an answer out of you. I'll just say I ain't concerned about what Bennet claims and I don't give a damn about this Oliver. But, Mr. Young, I wouldn't let this business of yours go on much further."

I said, "I'm leaving on the ten o'clock train. But I'll be back."

The sheriff picked up his hat and put it on his head. He said, "Yeah?"

"I'm going down to Mexico and gather up Philip Sharp. I'm going to bring him back here and give him to Mr. Patterson, who is having considerable trouble with the books and creditors that Sharp left."

"He gonna have any holes in him when you fetch him back?"

"That's up to him," I said. "But I will tell you one thing: You get Sharp and Bennet in jail and your troubles with these here vigilantes will stop. And so will all these sea-damaged goods and cargoes."

"You don't say."

I nodded toward Chulo's room. I said, "I got the chief ringleader of the vigilantes right in that there next room. Got him tied to a chair in the closet. He talked his head off last night."

"I see," the sheriff said. He didn't even so much as glance at the connecting door.

I said, "But right now ain't the time to arrest him. Either tonight or tomorrow night him and a bunch of them other vigilantes is going to try and steal them last two ships that Sharp's company has tied up at the dock. This head honcho, name of Mike Hull, is going to sail them two ships down to Mexico to join Sharp. I plan to get word to Mr. Patterson before we leave town."

"We?"

I kept my face straight. "Yeah, me and my horse."

Sheriff Mills said, "Well, can't say I'll be sorry to see you go. Have a good trip, Mr. Young."

I stood up. "Glad you dropped by, Sheriff."

He opened the door and then stepped out in the hall. Before he closed it, he stuck his head back in. He said, "You might want to take a look out here, Mr. Young. Yonder comes the biggest Mexican you ever saw. Thought you said they was all little."

Then he closed the door.

Chulo entered his room off the hall and then came through the connecting door. He said, "Eres the shereef."

"Yeah."

He motioned toward the closet in the other room. "What about thees sumbeetch in *la chiquita aparatada?*"

I said, "I told him he was in there, but he didn't seem much interested. Listen, you go and unlock the door and pull him out in the middle of the room. I got to get dressed and we got to get moving. It's past eight-thirty, and we got to arrange to get a stock car for the horses and check out of the hotel and three or four other things. I got to see Patterson for one. We got to hurry."

"But thees shereef. . . ."

I said, "Dammit, Chulo, get a move on."

Just before we left the rooms I stepped in to see Hull. He was still gagged and I intended to leave him that way. I said, "You're going to say it's cheating, but we're going to get us a little head start in our little race. I don't know how long it will take you to sail to Bodega and then maybe on to Tampico, but we're going by train and then by horse. So you better hurry as soon as you get loose. If I beat you down there, they won't be no Philip Sharp waiting."

He want to bobbing his head and moaning and groaning as best he could with the gag in his mouth, but I just gave him a little wave and said, "Nice to have met you, Mr. Hull. I wish you luck. All bad."

Time was so short that I sent Chulo to fetch Mr. Patterson while I bought the tickets and arranged for a stock car for us and our horses. Not having the influence of the Williams family, I had to pay the same price for the car as if I'd been shipping eight horses instead of just the two. We were taking the express train to Laredo. In Laredo we'd change and get shuttled on to the line to Brownsville.

Matamoras was right across from Brownsville, and Bodega was just a twenty-five-mile ride down to the gulf. If Sharp was in Bodega and if the railroads kept up their end of the bargain, I figured to have Mr. Sharp in hand within forty-eight hours.

I was standing on the far end of the depot platform, near where our horses were waiting to be loaded, when Chulo came up dragging a thoroughly bewildered and about half-frightened Mr. Patterson. I sent Chulo on down to watch the railroad hands load our horses and make sure they had plenty of hay and fresh water, and then I turned to Mr. Patterson. As briefly as I could I explained about my meeting with Bennet and then about my extended interview with Mike Hull.

I said, "You know Mike Hull?"

"Of course, of course! He was first mate on the biggest of our steamboats. I can't believe he's in this."

I said, "You better believe it, and you better either chain up them last two ships you got or get to the sheriff and get some help, because Hull is going to steal them and join Sharp. If not tonight, then tomorrow night."

Mr. Patterson looked even more nervous and tired than the first time I'd seen him. He said, "I'm just amazed he'd tell you all this, not only about the ships and Sharp but about the thefts and the insurance fraud."

I said, "Get him to take his boot off and show you the bottom of his right foot."

Mr. Patterson looked at me questioningly. He said, "Show me the bottom of his foot?"

I said, gently, "We skinned the sole off his right foot. To encourage him to talk."

He stared at me, his mouth open. No words came out.

I said, "He'll be the one limping when they go to stealing your boats."

"Ships."

"Ships, boats, what difference does it make?"

The whistle of the train blew, announcing it would be starting pretty quick.

Patterson said, "And he's still tied up in a room in the Galvez Hotel?"

I shrugged. "Unless somebody has let him out."

"Oh, my," Mr. Patterson said. He put his hand to his cheek. "I should go to the sheriff."

"That's what I'd do," I said. Behind me, Chulo whistled. I looked around. I could see the horses were loaded. I said, "Mr. Patterson, what is that ship worth that Sharp stole, the *Dolphin?*"

It took him a second to change directions in his brain. "The *Dolphin?* I think we carry her on our books for sixty thousand dollars."

I said, "Would it be worth twenty thousand dollars to you if I brought it back?"

"Her. Ships are feminine."

I was getting impatient. I said, "All right, *her,* dammit. Would it be worth twenty thousand dollars to your company if I returned her to this dock?"

He said, "I should think so. I don't know what Mr. Sharp would say, but— Oh, that's right. Mr. Sharp has her."

I said, "I'm planning on bringing back Sharp too. Will you give me twenty thousand dollars for the pair of them? Sharp would then be here to answer for most of the debt. If he gets away, it's all on your shoulders."

"I see," he said, nodding. "I see."

The train whistled again, a long, urgent blast.

I said, "Have we got a deal?"

He finally come to a decision. "Yes," he said. "Yes. I don't know how I'm going to juggle the books to keep that much money free, but I think I can do it. Yes, we have an agreement."

I turned around, ran down the platform, jumped to the ground, and ran to the door of our stock car. The train was beginning to move even as Chulo helped me aboard.

I scrambled in. From somewhere Chulo had found a couple of chairs. They weren't much, just old cane-bottomed wooden chairs, but they were something to sit on. I figured Chulo had stolen then out of the depot waiting room, but I didn't care, not after the price they'd charged me for the stock car. I looked at Chulo. I said, "Well, we're heading for the border. Back to Mexico."

Chulo raised a finger. He said, "I like to rob one Mesican bank."

DEAD MAN'S POKER

We laughed. Back when we were in the outlaw trade, Chulo was always wanting to rob a bank in Mexico. I never could get him to understand that we couldn't rob banks on both sides of the border because that wouldn't leave us anyplace to flee. I looked at him, seeing what Hull must have seen when he was getting skinned alive. He had a knife scar that ran down one cheek nearly to the corner of his mouth. This morning he had his black eye patch on. He'd been blinded when a splinter of hot lead had bounced off a strongbox padlock and hit him in the eye. He was blind as a bat in his left eye. The giveaway was that it never turned, just kept staring, unseeing, straight ahead. Sometimes Chulo wore the patch and sometimes he didn't. I think it was more a question of style than anything else. But this morning he had it on and he looked even fiercer than usual.

The train was gathering speed as we left Galveston and started on our southbound journey. The trip would take us through Blessing, although I didn't know if the train would stop or not. If it did, I planned to leave a note for Justa telling him of our plans and destination.

We had the loading door open, and the wind was whistling through the cracks pretty good and blowing around the straw and hay and dust. I said, "Break out the drinking material, Chulo, and let's have a swallow or two for luck."

But an hour into the trip I could tell it was going to be a long journey. Chulo had curled up on the floor of the car and gone to sleep. Apparently his concern over the condition of his new clothes had evaporated. But who could blame him? He'd worn them better than a day, so they were no longer new, so what was the sense of worrying about their appearance? I didn't mind him sleeping. He was about as good a conversationalist asleep as he was awake, maybe better asleep, because then he couldn't say anything that irritated me.

So I just sat there and watched the scenery go by, a chore that didn't require a whole lot of concentration since it never changed from mile to mile.

I thought of Evita. I'd been away from her for going on a week so it was necessary to think very carefully and purely

about her. I was in no situation to go to getting myself
aroused. Evita had been my woman for going on two years
and, other than Marianne, the woman I'd married, she was
as close to me as anybody ever had been in my life. I'd
come by her in a way that some might have thought odd.
She'd been a flamenco dancer in a cabaret in Monterrey,
a member of a dancing troupe that included six girls. The
owner of that troupe was a man who knew more about dancing than he did about poker. When I'd won all his money,
he threw Evita in the pot against a five-hundred-dollar bet.
Well, I didn't quite know how to take that. I asked him
what the girl was supposed to do for me, seeing as how I
didn't have no openings for a dancer right then. The man
said simply that she'd do anything I wanted. I looked at her,
and I got her aside and talked to her. I couldn't believe she
was a *puta,* a whore, but her father had sold her to the man
when she was fifteen, and he'd set out to make a dancer out
of her, a practice that was not too uncommon. Not meaning
that all the girls that got sold turned into dancers; it was just
the way it happened to Evita.

But I talked to her and asked her how she'd felt about
it. She was quite content with the arrangement. Her only
wish was that her cousin, Lupita, be able to come also.

So I worked it that way. I won them both. According to
the bet I was only supposed to keep them for a month, but
they didn't wanted to go back. On one occasion the man
came looking for them, but I convinced him they were
happier with me and he went away. When I'd won her,
Evita had been not quite twenty years of age. She was now
going on twenty-two. Lupita was two years younger, and
the two girls were more like sisters than cousins. They even
looked something alike. Both of them had shining black hair
and dancing eyes and olive complexions and skin so smooth
it felt like satin.

I had slept in the same bed with each of them, but all I'd
ever done with Lupita was sleep. I could have done more
with her if I'd wanted to wake up some morning with a
knife between my ribs. But not being crazy, I never gave
Evita no reason to feel jealous.

Not that it was easy. On hot days both of them would
sometimes walk around my *hacienda* without a stitch on.

A sight like that could very often test a man's character, and where a beautiful woman was concerned, I didn't have much.

But Evita was more than beautiful; she was smart as hell and was maybe a better businessman than I was. I had no fears about leaving my establishment in her hands while I went off on errands. I knew the casino part would suffer, but every dollar would be accounted for.

I had another man besides Chulo to handle the heavy work. He had been a *vaquero* on my ranch, Seveano, until I opened the Palace. After that I'd brought him in and showed him the ropes about keeping order, and with Evita to direct him, he was making a good hand. Besides, Evita was the last one I'd want to come up against. The woman was tough. She could shoot and she could use a knife.

And she could do other things, also, extremely well, things that I didn't have any business thinking about. Especially about her breasts or the shape of her small body.

I was commencing to get hungry. Naturally we'd got away in such a hurry that we'd forgot to buy any provisions. It wasn't bothering Chulo, him being asleep, but it was gnawing at my belly.

And, the train being an express, we weren't going to stop at many towns, and what few we did stop at, we weren't going to be there long. I tried to think of all the towns of enough size we might stop at between where we were and Laredo, but I just couldn't visualize the route. The map in my head was all turned around. And, naturally, back in the stock cars, there wasn't any conductor to come through calling out the next town.

After about a half an hour we slowed up a little to go through a town I thought was Bay City. We didn't stop, but if I remembered correctly, the next town ought to be Blessing. I wouldn't know if we were going to stop there until we actually did. If we did, maybe Chulo could run and find us something to eat while I left a message for Justa.

I got out of my chair and sat in the open door watching the range country go by, trying not to think of Evita. She had a kind of fine-boned body that was soft and round, and yet she was lithe and strong too. She was one of those small girls who had breasts just a touch larger than a man might expect. Someday they might begin to sag, but now they were erect and full with large nipples.

I turned around and woke Chulo up. I said, "Get up, man. We have plans to make, matters to study. You can't lay there sleeping like some lazy *peon*. Wake up, you *pendejo!*"

He didn't want to wake up, but he did. I gave him no choice. Having him for company was better than thinking about Evita when there was no chance I could get at her for at least a week. How I was going to hold out that long I had no idea.

How I was going to keep from starving to death in the next hour was something I also had no idea about. I took a swallow of brandy and told Chulo the plan if we stopped at Blessing.

Something was nagging at the back of my mind, worrying me. I didn't want to bring it out and examine it, but it had been going around in my head ever since I talked with Patterson. It had to do with having my cake and eating it too, only, in this case, the cake was Philip Sharp.

All along I'd gone looking for Philip Sharp to let him have a little taste of his own medicine, a bullet in the belly. But that had bothered me. All my life I'd lived by a code that I never took on anyone that didn't have a chance with me; even when I was a kid I'd been that way. And now here was this problem of Sharp. The only way he'd have a chance with me was if I turned my back, gave him a ten-second head start, and had Chulo help him to aim the gun. So I was reckoning that was what had caused me to have the talk with Mr. Patterson about the ship Sharp had taken and what he'd give me for it and about returning Mr. Sharp to Galveston to help stand up to the creditors with Patterson, and also, maybe, the sheriff, about them goods and cargo that had been making their way off the dock by foul means.

But I couldn't shoot Sharp and still fetch him and his ship back, not, at least, in any condition to be of any benefit to Mr. Patterson or to be worth putting in jail.

Chulo was leaning so far out the car door I thought he was going to fall out. He said, "I see thees *chaquita puebla.*"

I looked at my watch. It was a quarter to one. The only little town we could be coming up on was Blessing. I leaned a little further out the door, pushing Chulo back so I could see, and, sure enough, I saw the auction barn and then some other buildings I was familiar with. The train was already slowing more than it would have slowed if it was just going to pass on through, so I figured we'd be stopping. Which actually wasn't no great surprise. For some reason the little town of Blessing was where the line out of Galveston switched, one line going on to Laredo, the other on up to San Antonio. So the train had to stop to let off the San Antonio–bound passengers.

When Chulo and I jumped out of the stock car, I saw a brakeman just getting down from the caboose. I yelled and asked him how long we'd be stopped. He yelled back ten minutes and it might be a short ten minutes on account of we were behind schedule. I told Chulo to run like hell to the first place he figured to get any kind of grub and then hustle back as fast as he could.

After that I went in the depot and into the telegraph office. I asked the telegrapher if he could get a message to Justa Williams. He said, "Shore. You don't mean a telegram, because he's at the ranch."

I said, "No, I just want to write out a message and get it to him. I'm a friend of his."

He said, "Get you one of them blanks. There's a pencil. Mr. Norris, that's Justa's brother, stops by ever' evenin' on his way back to the ranch to pick up any wires they might have got. I'll give it to him."

I just wrote out a little note about having located the guitar player down in Mexico, probably Tampico, and that I was going down there to see if I could get him to play for a little dance I was trying to arrange. I handed it to the telegrapher. I said, "Tell Norris that Wilson Young said hello."

The train blew its whistle. There was an "I ain't kidding" sound about it.

The telegrapher said, "If you're off that train, you better get back on. That engineer hates to be late."

I went out the door and back to the stock car and jumped up into the door. Chulo wasn't there. I craned my neck and looked down the train, toward the engine, looking for him. Not a sign. The track ran behind the east side of the town, the side toward Justa's ranch. I kept looking and there was still no sign of him. I was commencing to get nervous when the train whistle blew again and I felt the cars start to creak. Hell, we were leaving! I didn't know what to do. I could jump off and we could catch a later train, but I didn't know when that would be. The next day maybe, and I was already worrying about the time, hoping to catch Sharp in Bodega so we wouldn't have to go so far inland, all the way down to Tampico. It was going to take Sharp time to find and gather a bunch of sick cattle in just the first stages of hoof-and-mouth and then to load them. But he'd already had a pretty good start. The one thing I didn't know was how long it took to sail from Galveston to Bodega.

The train was no longer just creaking, it was moving. My car was already coming opposite of the depot, and it had been a hundred yards back of it when we'd stopped. In another minute or so the train would be going so fast I wouldn't be able to jump off.

And then I remembered the horses. Hell, I couldn't leave Justa's horses to the mercy of the railroad. I'd just have to get along without that dumb Meskin.

And then I saw him running across the main street of the town with a flour sack slung over his shoulders. He was running awkwardly in his high-heeled boots, but he was covering some ground. The only question was would the train be going too fast by the time he intercepted it.

I leaned out the door and waved at him so he'd know where to aim. The train was still just going at walking speed, but it was gathering momentum. It appeared that Chulo was about forty yards away, quartering toward the train from the southwest. I could see it was going to be close. It appeared to me that the flour sack he had over his shoulder was impeding his progress, and I yelled for him to throw it away, but he never made no sign that he'd heard, just kept running.

I figured he and the train were making about the same speed when he arrived at the door. He heaved the sack inside and then grabbed onto the side of the door and tried to pull himself aboard. I leaned out as far as I could and got hold of the back of his belt and tried to pull him up. Lord, the son of a bitch was heavy. Finally he got in the worst position he could get in. He was nearly on the train, but not quite, and he was completely off the ground. If he fell now, he'd more than likely fall under the wheels, and the train was now really starting to roll. Cussing him at the top of my voice, I pulled on his belt, and he pulled with his arms, and finally, inch by inch, we worked him back in the car.

For a good long few minutes we just sat there, across from each other, both of us with our heads down, panting. Finally I said, "You dumb Meskin, how come you didn't come when they blew the damn whistle? Ain't you never rode on no train before?" Of course I knew he had; he'd been on at least a hundred with me.

He said, looking guilty, "I doan hear the first wheesel."

I said, "Then how did you know it was the first one? When are you going to quit trying to lie to me?"

I reached over and got his flour sack. There was a big chunk of cheese and some bread and two bottles of rum. I held up one of the bottles. I said, "This here is why you nearly missed the train, ain't it?"

He looked down. He'd been caught all right and he knew it. He said, "They don't sell thees rum in *la comida* estore."

I said, "So, since they didn't sell rum in the food store, you went and found a saloon. Didn't you?"

"Et es possible," he said.

I said, "You dumb Meskin, I ought to throw you off this train for that stunt. By God, I'm going to cut your pay! You make ten dollars a week less now."

He reached in his saddlebag and came out with a nearly empty bottle of rum. He said, "Señor Weelson, this is all Chulo have. Es very leetle."

"Shit!" I said. I give him a hard look, but my heart wasn't in it. He was just being Chulo. I said, "Well, dammit, break out the grub and let's eat something."

He'd also bought a long, tough sausage. We made a meal out of that and bread and the cheese. As hungry as we both were, it went down mighty easy. I finished my meal with a drink of brandy, noticing, for the first time, that I was getting a little low on drinking material. I said, to Chulo, "You damn *peon,* how come you got *two* bottles of that rotgut rum and didn't get me no brandy? Hell, I ought to stop your salary altogether."

He shrugged. He said, "Next time we stop, I go for the brandy. Thees time I listen for the wheesel."

The next time we stopped was in Victoria, a town about three times the size of Blessing. We got in there at right around six o'clock in the evening and left, by my watch, at eight-thirty-five. Two hours and thirty-five minutes. We had what the brakeman told me was a burnt-out journal, which is a kind of bearing, on one of the cars. He started out saying it wouldn't take more than a half an hour to fix but that they couldn't go on until the problem was corrected.

Every thirty minutes he was certain it would be fixed in the next ten or fifteen minutes. In that two hours and thirty-five minutes me and Chulo could have gone into town and had a seven-course meal at the finest resturant in town, taken in a stage show if one had been playing, and still got back in time to have that brakeman tell us it would be only another "ten or fifteen minutes."

About all the good that came out of the matter was that I got a couple of bottles of brandy and we replenished our supply of grub with some more bread and cheese. I figured the sausage was going to last us about six months.

We rolled along through the night. Sometime after we'd got started again Chulo and I made what passed for supper and then he bunched up some straw and went back to sleep. I sat in the doorway of the car, feeling the cool breeze, and watching the country start to take on that hard look it got the closer to the border you went.

I was still troubled about what I was going to do about Philip Sharp, assuming I actually did find him. It was strange to tell, but even during my outlaw days I'd never considered myself a wrong one. Certainly not mean or vicious or apt to cut up more ugly than I had to. I'd shot people, yes, but it had always been fair. And I'd robbed banks and other places where money was likely to accumulate. But I'd never thought of myself as robbing people, but robbing buildings and institutions and companies. Other than that first time when, as a kid, I'd robbed that rancher on the road into Corpus, I'd never robbed another individual. And even the robbery of that rancher had not been to my profit. I had later been so ashamed that I'd buried the few dollars I'd got off him (obviously to hide it from the eyes of God in hopes he'd think it was some other fourteen-year-old had done the deed) and turned his horse loose, knowing it would probably find its way home.

But I was angry as hell at Sharp. I'd trusted him, given him credit in my casino, gone to him in good faith—and run into an ambush. And on top of that the son of a bitch was just no good in a lot of other ways besides. There was all that thievery and murder on the docks, the vigilantes. There was the crookedness of him making contracts with folks he had no intention of keeping. And now there was this business of running a bunch of sick cattle in on a island full of poor folks who damn sure didn't need no more trouble.

Thinking of the cattle made me reflect for a moment on how it was I'd come to meet Justa Williams. He'd gotten crossways with a man who was intent on driving a herd of Mexican cattle across his range. Justa hadn't cared for the idea because the cattle hadn't been quarantined to make sure they didn't have tick fever, and as a consequence, he'd stopped the man and his illegal Mexican cattle. Unfortunately the man had borne a grudge, and three years later, he'd managed to get Justa to Del Rio, where I was living. We'd met and that had been that.

And now here was Sharp and his sick Mexican cattle. I liked Mexico. I liked Mexicans, even Chulo. I especially liked Mexican women, especially ones that looked like Evita and Lupita. But it looked like they ought to do a better job of taking care of their livestock. I wouldn't have been a rancher if they'd given me the whole state of Texas for grazing land, but I still figured I could do a better job of keeping cattle from getting sick than them Mexican *rancheros* did.

The horses were stamping around and plainly showing they'd had enough of riding the train for the time being. I didn't blame them. There are better ways to pass the time.

I looked at my watch and noted it was after ten. We were originally supposed to have been in Laredo at a quarter after midnight, but I reckoned, what with the delay in Victoria, that we wouldn't arrive until the smaller hours of the morning. One good thing was that we wouldn't have to go to the trouble of moving the horses. They'd shunt our car and any other cars that were headed for Brownsville off on a siding and then hook them up to the Brownsville train when it got made up. I wasn't exactly sure what time the train left Laredo for Brownsville, but it kind of stuck in my mind that it was somewhere around nine or ten o'clock. We'd been so rushed getting away from Galveston that I hadn't gotten straight about all the answers the ticket agent had given me.

After a while I took one last drink of brandy and then flipped the glowing butt of the cigarillo I'd been smoking out into the fast-moving darkness and closed and locked the door of the car. Might be we'd be asleep when we got shunted off onto the siding in Laredo, and I didn't want to make it too easy for somebody to just enter and relieve us of our belongings. I was carrying about a thousand dollars in my pockets, and I wanted to keep it. There were thieves everywhere, but there was a bunch more along the border.

CHAPTER 9

I came awake to the banging and jolting of our car and the clanging of steel against steel. For a second I couldn't think where I was, and then I thought we were in a train wreck. But after I got awake, I realized it was just our car being spotted on the siding and joined in with the rest of the cars there.

It was still plenty dark. The noise had woke the horses up, and they were moving around nervously and whinnying kind of quietly. I looked over at Chulo. If I hadn't known better, I'd have figured he was dead. He could sleep through an earthquake if it didn't have anything to do with him, but you'd better not try and slip up on him with intent to do him harm. He'd hear you if you didn't make any noise at all. That was one of the reasons he'd lived as long as he had. That and the fact that he was a hell of a lot smarter than most people gave him credit for. He could play the dumb Meskin with a rare style and fool just about everybody. He even tried it with me, for practice I figured, because he knew that I knew better.

I reached over and gave him a hard nudge. He was sleeping with his sombrero over his face, though God only knew why, because it was as dark as the inside of a cow. He made a noise, but it didn't sound like the kind of a noise somebody makes that is awake. I give him a harder nudge.

He said, "Hey, what chou bother me for?"

I said, "Wake up, you lazy son of a bitch. I'm the boss, remember? Anybody sleeps it's supposed to be me. *Comprende?*"

He sat up and his hat fell off. He yawned and looked around. He said, "The *ferrocarrilas* don't go no more."

I said, "No. We're in Laredo." I got out my watch and a match and struck the match. It was exactly four-thirty in the morning. I said, "You awake?"

He shook his head and blinked his eyes. "Chure."

"Chure," I said. "What's your name?"

He said, "Et es not Weelson Jung because nobody choot me like the leetle *nino.*"

I said, "All right, you smart-mouth *pendejo,* you're awake. Now stay that way. I'm going to send a telegram to Evita to let her know where we're going, and I want to find the horses here when I get back. There are thieves in Laredo, you know."

I unlocked the car door and pulled it back enough to jump to the ground. Then I took the time to pull it back to. Chulo might be suddenly struck down by sleep again.

I could see the lights of the depot about fifty yards away, but I had to pick my way over what seemed to be about a hundred railroad tracks to reach it. The waiting room was bare, and the only people that were around were a couple of yardmen and the ticket agent and the telegrapher. I got hold of a telegraph blank and wrote out a message to Evita telling her where we were and where we were going. I ended by saying that I was hoping to wrap up the business in a hurry. Until then she was to continue to manage my affairs and not to smile until I returned.

The telegrapher looked at the last a little funny, but he just shrugged and sent it. I reckoned he could tell some stories if he was of a mind to.

The ticket agent said the train for Brownsville was due to leave at eight o'clock, but it might be a little late on account of a connecting train due in from San Antonio that was running late.

I was beginning to wonder why the railroad even bothered to print up timetables. I said, "Has a train *ever* run on time?"

He just give me a cold look, and I let it go and wandered over and sat down on a bench. I got out a cigarillo and lit it. I wasn't in no hurry. The waiting room was a lot more comfortable than the stock car and smelled better too. And, even though it was late April, there was just the touch of a nip in the air. I figured to let it get a little later and then go fetch Chulo and go downtown somewheres and have breakfast. Laredo was an old stomping grounds for both of us, and there was always the good chance we'd run into an old acquaintance, friendly or not.

But my mind kept playing with the problem of what to do about Philip Sharp. Killing him would be a lot easier and safer than trying to subdue him and however many waterlogged hooligans he had with him and getting them to sail the boat back to Galveston. That in itself was a problem. I might get them all under gun and they might say they'd sail us back to Galveston, but how would I know they were doing it? I didn't know any more about sailing than a bull does about giving milk. I wondered if we would be able to find some sailors in Tampico or Bodega or wherever Sharp was that could do the job for us. It could also be that I might not have any choice in the matter. When I first confronted Sharp and his crew, they might not give me no selection; I might have to kill them all right then and there. And then there'd be no chance of getting the boat back to Galveston and getting my twenty thousand dollars.

Though, strange be it to say, the money was the least of it. I wanted the money, but I wanted to settle up with Sharp, one way or the other, more. Thinking about it was making me weary. Besides, I knew I'd better catch my rabbit before I decided how I wanted to cook him.

I went on outside and managed to make it across the rows of tracks without killing myself or falling on my head. It was still dark, but I could see the faint promise of light in the east. I got to the car and slid back the door. Chulo was sitting there smoking a cigarillo. He'd put his sombrero back on, but I couldn't see if he was wearing his eye patch. I said, "You trying to set this car on fire? Let's go get some breakfast. Be light pretty quick and I've seen plenty of trainmen around. The horses will be all right."

He got down, and we closed and latched the sliding door. The horses whinnied at us like they were being forgotten. I reckoned they were getting damn tired of standing around in a barn that sometimes banged and rattled and then other times didn't do nothing at all. Horses are sensitive about such matters.

Town was jammed right up next to the depot, but we walked toward the main plaza, where we both knew a good café was located, a place called La Cocina, the kitchen. I reckoned I'd been eating and drinking there for better than fifteen years. It wasn't nothing fancy; they just gave you your money's worth without trouble or fanfare. It was half saloon and half café. It was the first place open in the morning and the last to close at night. I'd never tried to figure it out exactly, but as best I could tell they were open about twenty-two hours a day. I think they only closed to sweep the floor and lay in supplies. La Cocina was where you could get your first drink of the morning or your last of the night, whatever time your night ended. The clientele was as mixed as the menu. You were likely to see elegantly dressed Mexican dons eating next to down-at-the-heels cowboys, or gamblers who'd just finished a night of fleecing the suckers, or a scattering of gunmen who were either drinking to get up for a fight or drinking to get down from one.

We went in and got a table, and a pretty little Mexican girl came over with a slate and a piece of chalk. We both ordered beer and eggs with chili and flour tortillas with plenty of butter. We were ordering Mexican, but we could just as easily have ordered steak and potatoes, and they'd have had that just as quick.

I looked around. The place was already about half-full. There were about twenty tables in what they called the eating area, not that you couldn't drink there, but it was kind of separated from the bar and the few tables around it by a little aisle that led to the door. Most people who came in just to do some drinking stayed up at the bar end and left the other end for them as wanted to eat. But it wasn't no hard-and-fast rule, not unless the place got packed.

There was the usual amount of noise you'd find in such a place, the low rumble of talk, the *ching-ching* of spurs, the sound of crockery being rattled around, waitresses calling out orders. But over that I heard a voice say, "Melvin, you know what're the two low-downest words they is? It ain't cow shit an' it ain't pig sucker. It's Wilson Young."

It was said just loud enough that those around us must have heard, the tables being packed in as tight as they were. I heard the level of the conversations drop down a notch, and I could feel men turning to look at the man who'd made the remark. Maybe some of them were looking at me. I was well enough known along the border that there would be plenty in the place who recognized the name if not the face.

I glanced at Chulo. The words had come from directly behind me, and Chulo was facing that way. He said, lowly, "*El Caballo.*"

The horse. It was the name given by the Mexicans to a man who made his living stealing good, blooded stock on the American side and then smuggling them into Mexico to sell inland, to the rich dons who owned big *rancheros*. His last name was Thorton. I never had known his first name. Everybody just called him Hoss. I hadn't seen him in two or three years, but that occasion had been just like this one looked like it was going to be. He'd tried to pick a fight with me in a cantina in Villa Acuna, and I'd walked away from him. He'd been so drunk he could barely stand up. And now, listening to him, I could tell he was in just about the same shape. He'd probably been drinking all night. I'd seen him a few times when he was sober, and he'd taken extra care not to cross my path. But when he got liquored up enough, he figured he could fight anyone.

I said, raising my voice a little so those around me could hear I wasn't the one causing the trouble, "Thorton, I ain't looking for any trouble and you don't sound like you could handle any. I'm here for some breakfast and then I'm leaving."

He came back at me, in a louder voice. "Big man Wilson Young talkin'. Ever'body s'pose to be 'fraid of him. Well, I ain't, by gawd. This here is one hoss ain't scairt of no high and mighty *Mister* Wilson Young."

I said, "Take it easy, Thorton. They don't want no trouble in this place."

Voices around me said, "Yeah, take it out in the street. Folks is trying to eat in here."

I didn't want to take it out in the street. We had horses on a train to catch in less than two hours, and no matter how fast and fairly I killed Thorton, there would have to be an inquiry, and by the time that was over the train would have gone.

Thorton said, still in a loud voice, "Well, I run you oncet, *Mister* Wilson Young an' I reckon I kin do it agin. Turn 'round here when I'm talkin' to you, boy!"

I saw Chulo inch his chair back just enough to clear his draw. At that instant the little girl brought our food, all oblivious to the fact that a fight was about to break out. She set the warm plates in front of us and I picked up my fork.

Behind me Thorton said, "By gawd, Young, what does it take, you son of a bitch? I'm callin' you out. You deaf?"

I looked up at Chulo again. He said, softly, "Only the two. The other one is talking to hem quiet. He doan leesen."

I could hear Melvin, or whatever his name was, saying, "Let it go, Hoss. You scairt him. They'll chuck us out of here you don't take it easy."

Thorton's voice was still as loud. "Don't give a by gawd! Look at that son of a bitch! An' him eatin' with a nigger Meskin, too."

Those were nearly his last words. Chulo's head came up and I saw him start to rise. I shook my head. He sank back down. I said, "Thorton, I come in here to eat breakfast and I'm going to do it. When I'm finished, I'll take you out in the street and give you all you want. In the meantime keep your mouth shut or wait out in the street."

Thorton said, "Not damn likely. Wait in the street so's you can slip out the back. I'll be on yore tail when you go through that thar door."

I looked at Chulo. I said, "Man is insisting on getting himself killed." I shook my head. "And he ain't leaving me no way out. And us with that damn train to catch. What about the other one?"

Chulo leaned forward. He said, "He es not en et. He es tryin' to talk to hes freen."

And, listening close, I could hear this Melvin saying, "Hoss, it ain't worth it. That thar is Wilson Young, an' them ain't jest stories you hear 'bout him. I've seen him with a gun."

Thorton said, "Don't give a shit. Kill his ass."

He was starting to slur his words pretty badly. There was the hope that he might pass out. I just kept on eating.

Melvin said, "Hoss, you've had a pretty good many dranks. Don't you reckon you ought to git him some other time? You been drankin' all night."

"Don' give no shit," Thorton said.

I wasn't all that surprised about what was happening. If his name hadn't been Thorton, it would have been something else. It was just another of the reasons I was glad to be out of the outlaw trail. Now, at least, the only saloon I generally went into was my own. And nobody started any trouble in there.

We were getting damn close to the end of our meal. I called the little girl over and asked her for another round of beer for me and Chulo.

Behind me, Thorton said, "Dawdlin' ain't gonna save yore worthless hide, Young. By gawd, you'll lick dirt 'er I'll kill ya. Goddam smart aleck!"

We took our time. After we'd finished our food but before we'd finished our beer, I leaned forward to Chulo. I said, "I'm going to arrange it so I go out first. Thorton will sure as hell come out right behind me. You be right behind him. Once we're outside the café, I'm going to turn and put a gun on him and his friend. As I do, you draw that big pistol of yours and hit Thorton over the head. Hit him hard. This Melvin won't do nothing because I'm going to have a gun on him. Maybe by the time Thorton wakes up he'll be sober enough to realize he's been a damn fool."

Chulo looked troubled. He said, "Et don' look right, you don't keel thees man."

I frowned at him. I said, "Chulo, a killing means the sheriff. Right or wrong it will cause us to miss our train. Can you understand that?"

"Chess," he said slowly.

I said, "And do I really need to kill some damn drunk?"

"I doan theenk so."

"All right," I said.

He said, "Hokay. But et steel doan look so good."

I give him a glare. I said, "You just hit the son of a bitch. Hokay?"

"Hokay," he said.

I called the waitress for our score, paid her, and then stood up. I looked around at Thorton. I said, "I'm going out now, Thorton. You can stay in that chair and save yourself a lot of trouble."

The whole dining room had got quiet, watching and listening to us.

Thorton stood up, a little unsteadily. He was a squat, ugly man with a broken nose and about a week's growth of beard on his face. I'd heard he was bad in a brawl, but I didn't know of any reputation he had for being good with a gun. Maybe he figured that a good horse thief was just naturally a deadeye. His friend stood up. He didn't look anywhere near the kind of a hard case Thorton was, though he wasn't much prettier. He said, "Hoss, let it go. Hell with it. Let's get another drink."

Thorton shook him off. He said, stumbling over the words a little, "Goan kilt tha bastard. Think he kin get the best of me. Shi-i-it!"

I turned and walked to the door and pushed it open. I walked through, crossed the wooden boardwalk, and then stepped out into the street. I took three paces and then turned. I could see the people inside the café lined up at the windows, waiting to see what happened.

I said, "Thorton . . ."

He made a motion, and I had my revolver in my hand while he was still struggling to find the butt of his. I could have shot him a half a dozen times. But as he finally got hold of his pistol and made as if to draw, I nodded at Chulo, who was standing just behind and to the left of him. Chulo drew his big revolver and slammed Thorton over the head. He dropped like he'd been clubbed with a sledgehammer. I returned my gun to its holster and walked over to Melvin. I said, "You seen I could have killed him and I didn't. When he comes to, remind him of that. I've got a train to catch and no time to be talking to the sheriff. Tell him to stay away from me in future."

Melvin was staring at me with round eyes. He kind of stuttered out, "Th-Thanks. He was dr-drunk an' din't know what he was a-doing."

Chulo and I turned and walked toward the depot. Chulo glanced back and said that Melvin was dragging Thorton off the street. I said, "That's good. Laying there he might scare the horses."

We got back to the stock car and found everything in order. The train crew had been by and given the horses fresh water and hay. But they were still restless. If there'd been a ramp handy, I'd have unloaded them and then ridden them around for a little exercise. As it was they just had to be content to stamp their feet and shift around and eat hay. We had an hour to go if the train did leave on time. Of course I doubted that it would.

Chulo had a deck of cards, and we killed a little time by playing some two-handed Acey-Deucey, but it wasn't a hell of a lot of diversion. Chulo was such a bad player that it didn't take me long to win all his money, and then I'd have to give it back to him so we could keep on playing.

Finally we got out of the car and went wandering up and down the train. While we'd been gone, the whole thing had been made up, including the engine. All they had to do now was crank up, pull into the depot to collect the passengers, and then be off for Brownsville. If they ever got around to it.

Most of the freight was stock cars filled with young steers. I figured they were headed to somebody's range for restocking, since they were too young for slaughter. They were bawling and slipping around and just generally acting like they didn't care for the accomodations. I looked at my watch. It was eight-thirty, time for us to be starting. We started walking back toward our car. About that time Chulo said, "I doan theenk thees es so good." He pointed.

I looked. Coming toward us from town were two horsemen. One was kind of lagging back. They were still a good three or four hundred yards away, but as they neared, I could see that the rider in front was Thorton. "Goddammit!" I swore. "Won't that bastard ever learn?"

I started walking toward him, moving away from the cars. Chulo was right behind me. Thorton was yelling something, but I couldn't quite make it out. Then he got close enough, and I heard him say, "Wilson Young, you pigsuckin' shit eater, I'm gonna kill yore ass!"

It was clear the blow to the head hadn't knocked any sense in him.

Chulo said, "Thees time he ain't goan geeve you no selecion."

He meant "selection," which he'd heard me say, but he could never get it right. I sighed. I said, "If this damn train would just start up, we could be out of here."

Thorton had ridden his horse to within thirty yards of where we stood. Melvin was back about another ten. Thorton dismounted and started walking toward us. His gait was none too steady. The man had got the idea fixed in his mind that he was going to have a fight with me and nothing else would do. If I drew and shot him, I would kill him. I'd heard of people shooting to wound, but I wasn't one of those people. As far as I was concerned it was a bad habit to get into, plus it was a risky shot. A man's chest was the biggest target, and that was what you aimed at.

Thorton kept coming, cussing me with every breath. "You'll lick dirt, by gawd, Young. Or I'll kill you where you stand."

At twenty yards, which was far too great a distance, even for a shot such as myself, he jerked out his revolver and let fly a wild shot. My only thought was that he was liable to hit one of Justa's horses. I saw him cock his revolver again and, waveringly, try to aim at me.

There was a sudden explosion by my left ear, and Thorton went over backwards like he'd been roped out of the saddle. I looked around. Chulo was standing there with that cannon of his with the nine-inch barrel. I said, "What the hell did you do that for?"

He shrugged. He said, "Chou let thees *hombre del mar* choot chou. I theenk chou es going to let thees *loco hombre* choot chou *tambien*."

"Damn!" I said. "Now we got trouble. Sheriff trouble."

We walked over to where Thorton was laying on his back. Melvin had dismounted and was standing over his friend. Thorton was laying there with his eyes wide open, his mouth sucking for air. The wound was bad, but it didn't look like it was going to kill him. Chulo's shot had taken him under the right collarbone. There was a lot of blood, and I reckoned the collarbone was broken and probably his shoulder blade, but if he didn't bleed to death, he ought to be all right.

Melvin said, "I tried to stop him. Folks in town will witness I tried to talk him outta comin' out here. But nuthin' would do him but that he done it."

I said, "You seen him shoot first."

"Oh, hell yes," Melvin said. "Ain't no question about that. He's jest crazy drunk."

I said, "You better get him in to a doctor as fast as you can."

Me and Chulo got Thorton to his feet while Melvin led his horse up. It took all three of us to get him in the saddle, and then Chulo and I held him there while Melvin mounted. Thorton was white-faced and sweating. Getting hit by a heavy-caliber slug ain't near as much fun as it's made out to be.

Melvin rode up alongside of Thorton and got an arm around his shoulders to support him. Thorton was still groggy, but he was coming around enough to help himself a little. Melvin said, hesitantly, "Say, I know I ain't got no right to ast somethin' like this, but me and Hoss is plumb out of money. That was one thang he was so het up about. I wonder if you could let me take ten dollars for the doctor. I'll get it back to you when I can."

"Sure," I said. I got out a twenty-dollar bill and handed it to him. I said, "You might need a little more."

"I'm much obliged."

I said, "Just don't be in no big hurry to visit with the sheriff."

Melvin said, "He'll have to find us."

We watched them ride slowly off. After a moment we walked back to our car. Up at the front I heard the engine give a little toot like the engineer was testing his whistle. That at least meant they were getting steam up in their boiler. It shouldn't be long before we left. At least we'd had a good breakfast.

We climbed in and sat down in the chairs Chulo had stolen. I said, "That was some stunt you just pulled."

He said, "I din theenk chou was going to keel the man."

I said, "Of course I wasn't going to kill him. He was falling down drunk. He couldn't have hit this train with a rifle. Now you'll have the sheriff on us."

He said, "I choust choot to wound hem."

I mocked him. I said, "I choust choot to wound hem. My foot! At twenty paces? Hell, you damn near missed him. You got mighty lucky is what you got."

He said, "Ef the cheeref come, he come for Chulo. Chou don't got to worry."

"Oh, shut up, you dumb Meskin. He comes for you, he comes for me, and I'm chasing a man owes me twenty thousand dollars and a bullet hole. I ought to cut your ears off."

Chulo said, "Leesen, chou heer what thees man calls me in La Cocina?"

I said, "Of course I heard him. So did everybody else. You are a nigger Meskin. So what?"

He kind of reared back. He said, "Et's hokay you call me such a theng. Et es no *bueno por nada* for that gringo sumbeetch call me that."

All of a sudden the train began to move, with a great jolting and yanking that got the horses all nervous again. We'd been watching Melvin taking Thorton back to town, half-expecting to see lawmen come riding out to meet them. But they'd disappeared into town without incident. There were several doctors in Laredo, most of them plenty experienced in gunshot wounds, and they'd done a bunch of business in that trade. I figured Melvin would take Thorton to a doctor first, but I was just holding my breath he didn't run right on over to the sheriff's office.

We still had a ways to go before we left town. The train backed and switched and finally got on the main track and pulled the passenger cars up next to the depot. We were a good ways behind in the freight section of the train, and the way the track ran and the way the depot set, we couldn't see the town to tell if anyone was riding our way.

I said, "If we get delayed, I am going to be mighty upset with you."

Chalo just kind of hung his head. Wasn't anyone could look more remorseful than Chulo, not until he done something else to be remorseful over.

And then the train finally moved. It was five after nine by my watch when we at last began pulling out of the station. I could see the town after we passed the depot, and I didn't see anyone who looked like a sheriff or deputy. I said to

Chulo, "You are a very lucky Meskin."

We settled down for the trip to Brownsville, first having a drink. I pulled my chair over close to the door. It was hotter along the border, and the incoming breeze felt good. I lit a cigarillo and went to thinking ahead. Counting back, I figured Sharp had been gone from Galveston about six days. But that didn't tell me much about whether he would be at Bodega or gone on ahead to Tampico, because I didn't know how long it took to sail a boat such a distance. For all I knew a boat was faster than a train. I also didn't know how long it would take him to gather up his sick cattle. I didn't know if he was going to wait until he got to Bodega or Tampico and then go to buying the cattle, or if he had some agent already on the job for him and he was just going to sail down, pick them up, and head for Cuba.

But, of course, that part wasn't right. He didn't know that I'd taken his man Mike Hull in hand, and he'd be waiting, wherever he was, with enough cattle to fill three boats, or ships as Mr. Patterson had told me to call them.

I was also wondering if he'd found a way to establish telegraphic communication with Hull, where he could have kept Hull abreast of his progress. But Hull hadn't said anything about it, and the telegraph, in Mexico, was a chancy proposition.

I turned around to Chulo. I said, "Hey!"

"*Sí,* señor?"

"The word is sailor. Understand? Sailor. Not *hombre del mar.* Man of the sea. And Sharp ain't a sailor, anyway; he owns ships and handles cargo. That don't make him a sailor."

"*Sí,*" Chulo said. He took a delicate sip of rum. "But he steel choot chou, no?"

It was supposed to be a four-hour trip to Brownsville, and I couldn't see how they wouldn't make it, not unless they burned out another journal or something. But there were no stops along the way, mainly because there wasn't a damn thing between Laredo and Brownsville except some of the ugliest, driest, most inhospitable country around. It was even worse than the sand and cactus and huisache country a little further north, because it got plenty of water and it looked like it ought to amount to something. But it didn't.

You'd see stretches of sandy, rocky wasteland and then acre after acre of solid cedar and mesquite trees in groves so thick a snake would have trouble wiggling through them. Here and there I could see a few poor, half-starved longhorn cattle who were either too stupid or too stubborn to seek pastures where there was something to eat.

As the sun got up, it became hotter and hotter. April in that part of the country was like June or July in more northern parts of Texas. We were out of food and, worse, we were out of water. The horses had plenty of water, but I was damned if I was going to drink after a horse no matter how thirsty I got, and I was getting pretty damn thirsty.

Finally I saw Chulo take an empty rum bottle and jam it down deep in the tin horse trough they had in the car. He was getting the bottle down below the slobber and bits of hay and whatnot that had come off the horses' mouths and was floating on top of the water. When his bottle was full, he took it out and had a good long drink, looking just as pleased with himself as if he had good sense.

I said, "That water is filthy. Ain't you got sense enough to know that? It's going to make you sick."

He said, "Pretty soon chou say, 'Chulo, geeve me some *agua*.' I gonna say, 'No, no, no, Señor Weelson Jung. It weel make you seek.' "

"Aw, go to hell, you dumb Meskin."

A nagging thought had begun working around in the back of my mind, more insistent than my dry throat. Talking to Chulo about complicated matters was better than talking to the horses, but not much. I said, "I'm worrying about something. I may not have made as certain about something as I should have."

"Sí?" Chulo said.

I said, "I told the sheriff that Mike Hull was going to steal those remaining two boats and sail down and join Sharp. And I told Patterson the same thing. What if neither one of them does anything about it?"

"Sí?" Chulo said. He was used to me talking things out to him. It didn't make any difference if he knew what I was talking about or not. He just sat there smoking a cigarillo and trying not to go to sleep. That was about the only rule for these discussions: that he not go to sleep.

I said, "Patterson told me that Sharp took six men on the boat he stole. If Hull was to do the same, that'd be twelve more men. That'd be eighteen in all not counting Sharp."

Chulo said, "He's a preety good chot."

I said, with a touch of heat, "Lay off the jokes. I'm serious. That sheriff didn't look all that impressed when I told him about Mike Hull. I think he just doesn't want anything to do with that waterfront. He acts like he don't give a damn what they do down there so long as they leave the rest of the town alone. And what the hell do we know about Mr. Patterson? Not a damn thing, that's what. He's sitting there at his desk acting like he's the one got left holding the bag and he can only pay the creditors ten cents on the dollar and he doesn't know what he's going to do and he doesn't even know how he got to be a part owner of the company and so on and so on. Hell, anybody could sit there and say that. How would I know if he's lying or not?"

"Chure," Chulo said.

I said, "And all the time he may be waiting for Sharp to get matters all set up in Mexico and then he's going to get on one of them two ships and sail down with Mike Hull. Not only not keep him from stealing them, but help him. How do we know that ain't the case?"

"Chure," Chulo said.

I said, "And then there we are in Mexico and we got eighteen men to deal with. I don't see how we can take on eighteen."

"Chure."

I gave him a glare. I said, "Hell, if we just knew how long it takes to sail a ship down to the border. I got to figure we're ahead of Hull right now. We ought to beat him to Bodega unless them damn boats are faster than I thought. If that's the case, all we'll have to deal with is Sharp and his six men. We can handle that."

"Chure."

I said, "How long you figure it takes to round up three or four hundred head of cattle with hoof-and-mouth disease? Hell, where do you go to find that many cattle with hoof-and-mouth disease?"

"One," Chulo said.

175

I looked at him. "Juan? What the hell are you talking about."

He held up a finger. "One."

"One what?"

"One cattles. Chou need choust one cattles with the hoof-an'-mouth. Chou put them in weeth t'ree, four hundred good cattles, en t'ree, four days all cattles got hoof-an'-mouth."

I was amazed. I said, "How'd you know that? You don't know any more about cattle than I do."

He said, "When I am *joven, yo soy un vaquero.*"

I said, "What a liar. You were not a cowboy when you were young. You were a thief. You've always been a thief. But you are right about the hoof-and-mouth."

He tapped his forehead. He said, "Chulo berry esmart."

"Bullshit," I said. "Chulo 'berry' estupid."

I turned around and looked back out the door, watching the sorry landscape go by. It was gaining on twelve noon and I was hungry and I was mighty thirsty. I was also plenty worried. All I could do was hope that Sharp was still in Bodega and hadn't sailed for Tampico and that Mike Hull was still a long way from joining him.

Chulo had laid back down on his pile of straw. When I thought he was asleep, I reached over and got the rum bottle he'd filled with water. I took a long, fast drink and then carefully set the bottle back in the same place. I was so thirsty I would have drunk muddy water out of the Rio Grande.

Chulo had his sombrero over his face. From underneath it he said, "That make you seek, Señor Weelson Jung."

I said, "Shut up, Chulo."

CHAPTER 10

Brownsville, like a lot of other Texas towns, had grown up around a fort, Fort Brown. Fort Brown was the southwesternmost fort in a chain of forts that had been established across Texas to try and control the Comanches back in the 1840s and '50s and '60s. But after the Civil War the Comanches had pretty well been rounded up and settled on reservations and the forts had been decommissioned and fallen into ruins. Fort Brown was no exception. It was mostly gone, but for some reason, the town of Brownsville lingered on. In fact, it not only lingered, it appeared, as Chulo and I rode into it, to be prospering.

Which was a strange matter indeed since there was not the slightest reason for its existence. It was at the very southern tip of the state, surrounded by land that you'd have had to pay somebody to take. You couldn't raise cattle there, you couldn't farm, you couldn't do anything. It was right on the Rio Grande, but the river was too shallow to use as a port even though the Gulf was only twenty or twenty-five miles away. Across the river, in Mexico, was the town of Matamoros, which didn't seem to have much reason for being either. But there they both stood, full of houses and stores and saloons and cafés and cathouses and even an occasional cathedral. You did see a lot of groves of oranges and limes and grapefruit, but I'd never seen no community founded on citrus fruit.

But it didn't mean a damn to me. Bodega was twenty some odd miles away down the Rio Grande, and I was anxious to get started. First me and Chulo hunted up a good café in Brownsville and had a big meal of steak and potatoes and light bread. Then we took the horses to a livery stable and had them grained good while he and I sought us out a general mercantile store. We wasn't exactly rigged out for the trail, and since I didn't know what the future might hold, I figured we'd better take along a few supplies, the country being as rough as it was. I bought us a ground sheet and a couple of blankets and two big gallon-and-a-half canteens, along with about thirty feet of soft rope in case we had to tie anything or anybody up. A lariat rope was no good for that; it was too hard, too stiff. After that we bought some canned goods, tomatoes and apricots and peaches and what not, along with a small wheel of goat cheese and some saltine crackers. We both had plenty of cartridges, and I didn't want to load the horses up too much, so we limited ourselves to those items. The man give us a big sack, and we stuffed our provender in it and then went around and picked up our horses.

We used the soft rope to tie the pack on the piebald that Chulo was riding and then mounted up and headed across the rickety bridge to Matamoros. We could just as easily have ridden down the river on the American side and found a shallow crossing, but it was better to not take a chance on the Rio Grande. It could be treacherous at times. A long time past I'd lost a partner and a good horse attempting what we'd thought would be a shallow crossing where the water wouldn't even be up to our horses' bellies. And then had come a sudden rise, and a friend and his horse were suddenly gone.

We had bought our supplies in Brownsville because I had never been to Bodega and, consequently, did not know what to expect there. We set out of Matamoros on a little road that ran along the river. The horses were good and rested. In fact they were so anxious to stretch their legs and so glad to get off the train, we had a little trouble holding them at first and getting them to settle down to a gait that would eat up the ground without wearing them out.

It was a little after three by the time we were well away from Matamoros. I figured we had about three and a half hours of traveling time before it commenced to get dark. In that country a careful man didn't want to travel after dark on account of the danger to his horse from rocks and thorny cactus and the broken terrain. And you couldn't ride right down next to the river on account of sudden soft spots. It didn't much matter, anyway. We could never make Bodega in one day, and I'd have to be content to see another day's sunrise before I knew if I'd cornered my quarry.

We stopped the day's journey with plenty of light left to make a good camp. We found a level place just back from the river and built a little fire of downed mesquite wood. While I got out our new coffeepot and filled it with water from a canteen to make coffee—not wanting to use water from the Rio Grande, which most folks considered too thick to drink and too thin to plow—Chulo took the horses back in the brush to find them what grazing he could and to picket them for the night. We hadn't brought any grain along with us because I'd figured we wouldn't be on the trail but one night and they'd been stocked up on corn at the livery stable in Brownsville.

We did the best with what provisions we had, eating cheese and saltine crackers and some canned beans and drinking coffee. It wasn't fancy, but it was filling and would take us through the night. Afterwards we sat around smoking cigarillos and drinking brandy and rum. The coffee had been pretty bad. A new pot never does make good coffee. It's something I've known and heard all my life, but I've never known the why of it. But, if we were lucky, except for breakfast, we'd never have to use it again. Not if I trapped my man aboard his ship in Bodega. If I didn't kill him, I'd let him make the coffee while we sailed back to Galveston.

Chulo said, "You theenk thees man es at Bodega?"

I said, "Damn you, you ignorant savage, keep your mouth off my luck. Don't ever say anything like that again. Ain't you got no better sense?"

He saw he'd done wrong and he kind of hung his head. He said, "I dun theenk we even get to Bodega. I theenk maybe we get lost."

"You're probably right," I said. I threw another limb on the fire. I said, "We'll probably get held up in the middle of the night by *bandidos* and roasted over this fire."

"Chure," he said.

179

We spread out the canvas ground sheet and then each took a blanket and, using our saddles for pillows, made ourselves ready for the night. The stars came out good, and I lay there a minute thinking about the chase I was on. Not often, but sometimes, I wondered if it was worth it. I'd probably lost more than twenty thousand dollars in the casino by just not being there, and the little wound Sharp had given me hadn't amounted to that much. In the meantime I'd been uncomfortable, lonesome, tired, and without the comfort of Evita and my place of business. Here I was, laying by the damn Rio Grande, riding a borrowed horse, with a hard ride ahead of me the next day just in the hope I might catch up with a man that I maybe wasn't even going to do anything to.

It didn't make a whole bunch of sense. But then, hell, a lot of things I'd done in my life hadn't either.

The morning stars were just disappearing when I woke up. I figured it was somewhere between four and five. I raised up. Chulo was just finishing adding wood to the fire. After that I saw him take the coffeepot down to the river to fill it with Rio Grande mud. I shrugged. It didn't make that much difference. The coffee was going to be lousy anyway. I just hated to drink water that so many bodies had been floating in.

We made a quick breakfast out of coffee and bread, and then I rolled the camp while Chulo brought in the horses. We got them bridled and saddled and were on the trail just as the false dawn was breaking. I figured we were no more than ten, maybe twelve, miles from Bodega. If we hurried along, we should make it in no more than three hours.

We stopped once to water the horses and liquor ourselves. An hour later we rode into Bodega. The place wasn't much. The town itself, if you could call it that, was set back about three or four hundred yards from the little waterfront. It consisted of ten or twelve dwellings, a chapel, and a place that was kind of a combination saloon, general merchandise store, café, and rooming house. All of the buildings were adobe except for the chief retail establishment, which had a wooden second story.

The waterfront wasn't a dock like the one in Galveston. Instead it was a wharf about ten yards wide sticking out into the bay about twenty paces or so. I figured they'd been trying to get it out as far as they could into water deep enough to handle bigger boats but just couldn't go no further. It had railings on both sides and a tilted-up chute at the end. The chute was obviously made for loading cattle, since it appeared it could be raised or lowered to suit the deck of the cattle boat they were loading.

If my luck had been good the *Dolphin* would have been moored right there at the end of the wharf with Mr. Philip Sharp on board. But my luck must not have been good because he wasn't there, and neither was the *Dolphin*. We rode up and down the waterfront, which wasn't much more than a few rickety piers sticking out into the bay, but there wasn't nothing that even faintly resembled a two-masted cargo schooner. There were a few single-masted boats with nets hanging on them. I figured they were fishing boats. What I didn't know was where Mr. Sharp was. He could have been here and gone, or have not arrived yet, or not be coming in the first place on account of Mike Hull.

But there were some cattle pens back from the waterfront about a hundred yards. Chulo and I rode over and had a look at them. They were holding what I calculated to be between two and three hundred cattle, most of them of slaughter size, meaning they were two or three years old. The cattle were jammed in pretty close, but here and there, we could detect a few of them limping. That is the first sign of hoof-and-mouth disease—sore feet. After about a week of that the cattle would begin to slobber, and about a week later they'd be dead. Sharp was going to have to work fast to get all his cattle gathered and loaded and make it to Cuba before the disease got too out of hand. Ideally, what he'd want would be a few sick cattle mixed in with healthy cattle right before he sailed. By the time they were landed, the healthy cattle would be sick, but they wouldn't be showing it.

I said to Chulo, "Let's go into the town and see what we can find out."

We tied up in front of the all-purpose establishment and went into the cantina part. They had Spanish brandy, which surprised me, and I bought a bottle and a bottle of rum for Chulo. Then we took a couple of glasses and sat down at one of the few tables in the place. We were the only customers, and there wasn't any real bartender because he kept going into the merchandise part to wait on customers there. There didn't actually seem to be that many people in town, and most of the ones we'd seen had been women. I figured the place was mainly a fishing village and most of the men were out fishing or maybe some of them were still rounding up cattle for Sharp. I let Chulo get about two drinks down and then told him to go hunt up the *jefe* and find out all he could about the *Dolphin* and about Sharp and about the cattle.

Chulo said, "Mabe they ain't got no *jefe?*"

I said, "Place like this has always got a *jefe*. He may not be an *alcalde,* elected, but he's still the boss. I bet it's the man that owns this place. Go on in there to the mercantile part and ask around. Find out everything you can."

"Why doan you go?"

I gave him a glare. I wasn't in a good mood. Even though I'd known it was a long shot, I'd hoped, in the back of my mind, that I was going to be able to make quick work of Sharp and get home. Instead, here I sat in a place that smelled like dead fish and was miles from anywhere, and no closer to my quarry. I said, "Because I told you to. Also, in case you ain't noticed, I'm a gringo and Meskins talk better to Meskins than they do to gringos. And you speak better Meskin than I do. Now get on."

I sat there drinking and waiting. Chulo was gone a good long half an hour. When he finally came back, he took the time to light a cigarillo and pour himself out a drink.

I said, "Well?"

"Chou was right. Es *el jefe* here. I talk weeth hem. A very esmart man. Every time I geeve him a dollar he remember a leetle more. That is esmart, no?"

"What'd he say?"

Chulo shrugged. "He leeeve this day before. We be here then, he be es here."

"He was here yesterday?"

"Sí."

"Damn!" I said. I slammed my hand on the tabletop, making the glasses jump. I said, "My luck has gone to hell. What else?"

"He has thees cattles in the corrals. He leeve the message that two more chips are coming. He tell *el jefe* theese chips are to take thees cattles. They bring in more of thees cattles. *El jefe* don't like thees cattles here because they are seeck. But thees Señor Charp pays hem moneys to not care."

I said, my pateince getting damn thin, "Where the hell is Sharp?"

Chulo said, "*El jefe* says he wait an' wait for thees other two chips, but they don't come. He says Señor Charp is nervous. He say he drink a lot and walk around in circles a lot. How you say?"

"Worried. Now where in hell is Sharp?"

"Chure. Worried. *El Jefe* say Charp is plenty worried to wait so long. So he geeves thees moneys to *el jefe* for more cattles and to tell the man named Hull to put thees cattles on hes chips and to come to Tampico. *El jefe* say the people don' like thees cattles here because they are seeck."

"He went to Tampico? Yesterday?"

"Chure. You din't heer me choust tell chou?"

"Goddammit!" I said. I slammed the tabletop again. I didn't know a hell of a lot more than I had before. I knew Sharp was on his way to Tampico, but I still didn't know if Hull was on the way with two more ships. And I couldn't afford to wait around and find out. I didn't know how long it was going to take Sharp to sail to Tampico and load up cattle. Or how long he'd wait for Hull, but I knew we didn't have a whole hell of a lot of time to waste. I tried to visualize the map in my head. I'd been all over this part of Mexico. I figured it had to be at least a hundred and fifty miles by land to Tampico, a hundred and fifty miles of rough, damn inhospitable terrain. Even pushing the horses as hard as we dared, we'd never make it there in less than three days, and more likely four. By that time Hull could join Sharp, if such was to be the case, they could have all three ships loaded and be on their way to Cuba.

We walked outside while I thought. We could go back to Matamoros and take the train from there. I knew there was one that ran to Tampico. But that would take us until the afternoon of the next day, and we might have missed the last train.

The railroad from Matamoros to Tampico ran mostly to the south. Where we were, in Bodega, was not much further from Ciudad Victoria than from Matamoros. I figured it to be about forty miles. We could start right away, and if there was no night train, we'd be sure to get out first thing in the morning. We walked on down toward the waterfront while I thought about it. You could see far out in the calm bay. Now and then I'd catch sight of a sail, its mast split by the horizon. The water was blue-green, and here and there were patches of sandy beach, Off to our left the Rio Grande came curling around a bend and then spread its brown waters out into the bay. There were no real waves to be seen, no breakers with white tops, just gentle swells that rode in and then lapped gently at the beach, at the docks, and made the fishing boats at anchor ride up and down.

I said to Chulo, "We got to go cross-country and try and hit Ciudad Victoria."

He shrugged. He said, "Preety bad country. Keel horses."

"We'll take it easy," I said. "I wonder if we can buy any corn to take with us."

"No mucho water," he said.

"Got to be some watering holes. Hell, I don't think it's but about forty miles. Why don't you go talk to your friend, *el jefe?* Find out what you can about the trip."

"Hokay."

He turned around and went back to the town. I stayed there staring out at the sea, looking at the boats. The biggest of them was anchored right next to a rickety little pier that was built out into the bay about seventy or eighty feet. The boat was painted blue with a little white stripe along her hull, right where it met the water. It looked like a big boat to me, but I didn't know much more about boats than I did about circuses, and I hadn't ever been to no circus. I figured the boat was about fifty or sixty feet long. It had one mast in the middle with another pole coming off it at a right angle. Up front a long pole stuck out from the bow. For some reason it seemed I'd heard it called a bowsprit, though I didn't know why.

I just kept studying that boat. It had a cabin of sorts. I couldn't judge how big it was, but it appeared big enough to hold four or five folks. I just kept looking at it and thinking.

But what I was thinking was so ridiculous that I turned my mind off it and started walking back up towards the huddle of buildings they called town.

I met Chulo coming back. He said that *el jefe* had told him that Ciudad Victoria was about eighty kilometers, but no one could be sure since there was no road. Chulo said that *el jefe* had said it was a very bad eighty kilometers and that water was very chancy, especially water enough for the horses.

I always had trouble figuring kilometers into miles, and I always wondered how come people couldn't just get one system and stick to it. I finally worked it out that eighty kilometers was around fifty miles. But I didn't need *el jefe* to tell me they were going to be a rough eighty kilometers. I knew the country. It was cut and slashed by barrancas and canyons and cliffs and arroyos. There was sand, there was big rocks, and there was every kind of plant known to man so long as it had big thorns growing out of it. Oh, yes, I knew that country. I'd killed horses crossing that kind of country with a chase party in hot pursuit. I sure as hell wasn't anxious to take two of Justa's horses across it, especially the little bay mare. The piebald might be able to handle it, but the bay just wasn't tough enough.

Chulo said, "*El jefe* will sell us a burro and two canvas bags which carry a lot of water. The burro will carry the water. He has the corn, *tambien*. He es a good mans, thees *el jefe*."

I said, "I am going in the cantina and drink some more brandy. Go ask *el jefe* who owns the big blue boat in the harbor."

He said, "Leesen, Señor Don Weelson Jung, *por que usted*—"

I said, "Go on and ask him. You always want to argue."

I went in the cantina and sat down. My bottle of brandy and glass were still where I'd left them. I poured myself out a drink and knocked it back. I was doing some hard thinking, and some of it was scaring me to death.

Chulo wasn't long. Pretty soon he came walking out of the mercantile part of the establishment followed by a dapper young man with long sideburns and shiny, slicked back hair. The man was well dressed and obviously of quality.

He came up to the table and gave me a short bow. He said, "Romando Reyes, at your service, sir."

I said, "You speak English."

He said, "Yes. I was born in Mexico, but I lived many years in your town of Corpus Christi. You know it?"

I smiled and nodded and thought, small world. I said, "Are you the *jefe?*"

He shrugged. "The office is purely honorary. We have no formal government here. I own this business, which is the only one in town, and most of the people come to me for advice. Some of them are like children. My father owned this place before me."

I looked around at Chulo. I said, "Why the hell didn't you tell me he spoke such good English?"

Chulo shrugged. He said, "You din' say nuthing about Ainglish. Chou said I speak better Espanish."

I gave him a hard look and then switched back to Señor Reyes. I said, "Sit down and have a drink with us."

He pulled out a chair. He said, "I will talk with you, but it is not my custom to drink until my day's work is finished."

I said, "If I followed that rule, I'd never get a drink because my work just seems to keep on going. Like right now. I want to talk to you about that blue boat out in the harbor. Is that your boat?"

He nodded. "Yes, that is my boat. She is a sixty-foot fishing sloop with a mainsail and a foresail. She is well founded."

I said, "Now you are speaking a foreign language. What I want to know is could you sail me to Tampico in that boat and how long would it take?"

"Oh, yes," he said. "I have sailed the boat to Tampico many times."

"How fast?"

He frowned. "It is not always the same. There is the will of God, the wind, the tide, the currents."

"Well, give me some idea."

He thought a moment. He said, "At the fastest, thirty hours. At the worst. . . ." He shrugged. "Maybe double that."

I said, "That's quicker than I thought. There was a big ship in here the other day, the——"

"The *Dolphin,* yes." He got a worried look on his face. "I think that ship has brought us trouble."

I said, "I know about your trouble. I've seen your trouble. What I want to know is how fast that ship could get to Tampico."

Señor Reyes shrugged. He said, "Not so much faster. It is bigger, but it is not the kind of ship, you understand, that is built to sail fast. It is a shallow draft ship for heavy cargo. It can no . . . how you say? It cannot sail close to the wind. It cannot tip . . . No, that is not right. Are you a sailor?"

I said, promptly, "Never been on a boat in my life. Whole idea scares the hell out of me."

He held his hand out and angled it. He said, "This ship, the *Dolphin,* cannot . . . heel over! Yes, that is it. She cannot sail close to the wind that makes her heel over so her cargo shifts. Do you understand?"

I said, "It don't matter if I understand. I just want to hire you and your boat to take us to Tampico."

He frowned. "When?"

"Right now," I said. "Quick as I can get enough of this brandy in me to get my nerve up."

He frowned and shook his head. He said, "I cannot do that now, señor. I have the problem of the cattle. You have seen them and I am sure you can see there is a problem."

I said, "You want to wait here for two more ships that are coming to pick up the cattle and probably pay you some more money. Is that about right?"

He nodded, trying not to show I'd surprised him a little. I said, "Well, you can forget that. Those ships won't be coming. They are all part of a plan of this man who sailed the *Dolphin* here. His name is Sharp, though I don't know what he called himself with you."

Señor Reyes was looking unhappy. He said, "Something like that. He gave me a little money to start rounding up cattle. And he said the ships that were coming would load the cattle and we would get the rest of the money. Now you say these ships are not coming. How do you know this?"

I said, "I have a matter to settle with this man Sharp. His business is in Galveston, but he does not own the business now. The ship he was sailing in doesn't belong to him anymore. I am going to Tampico to get that ship back and settle matters with Mr. Sharp. But before I left Galveston, I arranged it so those two ships would never sail and you better be glad of that."

He looked worried. "It does not sound like a thing I should be glad of. There are still those sick cattle. If we leave them there, they will lay down and die. Can you imagine, señor, what a mess two hundred and forty dead cattle will make? Right in the town."

I said, "If those two ships had got here, they would have taken the cattle all right, but they wouldn't have paid you any more money and they might well have robbed your town."

"Why would they do that?"

I laughed. "Because they are *bandidos,* señor. Very bad *bandidos.*"

Señor Reyes said, "Are you a sheriff?"

Chulo laughed.

I gave him a hard look and then said, to Señor Reyes, "No. I am involved because I have a personal matter with Sharp to settle. And he owes me money. I am going to take the *Dolphin* back to Galveston, and the company he used to own will give me my money in exchange for the ship. That's why I need to get to Tampico so quickly. You know yourself what a hard trip it would be to go overland and try to catch the train. And it would take so much longer."

Señor Reyes was looking worried. He said, "I don't know. These cattle . . ."

I said, "Tell me how these cattle came to be here. Did Mr. Sharp bring just a few cattle with him?"

"It was not exactly like that. One day a man, a Mexican, came down the river driving five cattle. He put them in our pens and said a ship would be along to load those cattle and any more we wanted to gather up. Well, naturally we were uncertain, but the *vaqueros* did bring in a few. And then this Sharp, as you call him, arrived in the ship and said he'd take six hundred head and would pay ten dollars a head. American! Señors, that is an amazing price! He gave me a sum of money, five hundred dollars, and said two more ships were coming and they would load the cattle, that he had other cattle to pick up in Tampico.

He stayed two, three, maybe four days waiting on the other ships. Then he sailed yesterday. And even now our *vaqueros* are out in the hills and the barrancas gathering more cattle."

I said, "You better get word to them to stop. Unless you want more sick cattle." I said, "I suppose you can see how it was done."

He nodded sadly. He said, "Yes, the cattle the man brought down the river were already sick. And now the healthy cattle we have penned in with them are sick also."

"And getting sicker every day." I said.

He wrinkled his brow and looked very unhappy. He said, "There is so much about this I don't understand. Why would a man want sick cattle?"

I didn't much want to, but I needed Señor Reyes's cooperation so I told him what Mike Hull had told me. I said, "So that apparently is the plan. The ships behind would gather up these cattle, and Sharp would go on ahead to Tampico to make up another load. But now you are stuck with these sick cattle."

He got excited and a little Mexican accent edged in. He said, "Thees man is *loco!* Thees man is going to hurt us verry bad! Do you know that sometimes ships come from Cuba and buy our cattle? Now they will not come no more. And what of these cattle that have been gathered? This is a very poor village. We all rejoiced when this man Sharp came. We thought of all the cattle at ten dollars American each. Six thousand dollars! Six thousand if we gather the six hundred he asked for."

I said, "You better stop your *vaqueros* from gathering any more. I don't think there are that many cattle around here. If you keep bringing them in and getting them infected by these sick cattle, you won't have any."

He sighed and put his head in both his hands. He said, "This village is too poor for a matter such as this. What am I to do?"

I poured myself out a drink and knocked it back. I said, "You get me to Tampico, and if I get my hands on Sharp, I'll make him pay you for the cattle you've already got gathered. That would be around twenty-four, twenty-five hundred dollars American."

But he was still looking overly worried. I figured the full extent of his trouble was just starting to sink in. He said, "But what are we to do with the sick cattle? We can't just turn them loose. They would infect every cow on our range. We would have no cattle. These people would starve."

I said, "You get me to Tampico, and when I get possesion of the *Dolphin*, I'll sail her back here and load those cattle and take them way out to sea and dump them overboard."

He raised his eyes to the ceiling and blew out a breath. He said, "I had thought that, for once, this village was going to have some luck."

"It still might," I said. "What about it?"

He put his fingers to his forehead, his head bent, his elbows on the table. He sat like that for a long time, thinking. I didn't rush him any. He was a man with a lot to consider, and the only information he was getting was from a stranger.

He said, "We have so little here. Just the fish in the sea and the cattle back in the hills. If we lose the cattle, it could be very serious for the people of this village. Some of the *campesinos* grow good corn, but that is not very much."

"Not a hell of a lot," I said.

"What is your name?"

"Wilson Young."

He stood up. He said, "Well, Señor Young, I will take you to Tampico and see if we can put this matter to rights. I seem to have no choice."

Chulo said, "Selecion."

Reyes looked at him. He said, "What?"

I said, "Don't mind him. He's correcting your English. You ready for that drink now?"

He shook his head. He said, "No, many thanks. I have much to do. I have to find Rodriquez; he helps me on the boat. Hermano helps me too when we fish, but this time we will not be fishing, so Rodriquez and I can handle the boat."

I said, "You better not forget to send somebody to head off them *vaqueros*. I don't know how many cattle you got back in those hills, but every one you bring into this town is a dead cow."

He said, "Yes, I will have to see to that immediately."

I said, "What about supplies for the trip? On the boat?"

"Those will be attended to."

I got out a hundred-dollar bill and held it out to him. He looked at it. "What is that for?"

I said, "The boat trip, I guess. You need more?"

He said, in that proud way that high-class Mexicans have, "It is not necessary. I am sailing you to Tampico to help with our situation. If you do as you say you can, that will be pay enough."

I said, "Then to help with the supplies. We need some extra cartridges, and we need our horses looked after while we're gone."

He said, "All that will be taken care of. We can have a reckoning when the matter is finally over. You should eat now. Go in the kitchen of the hotel and tell them to fix you what you want to eat. We are going to be sailing on the evening tide. That is no more than three hours from now."

I said, "I hope you understand that Chulo and I won't be a damn bit of help on that boat. In fact I'm scared as hell."

Reyes said, "Don't worry. You will be safe. I am as anxious as you to catch up with that Señor Sharp. Now I am angry." He started to walk away, and then he stopped and turned back and looked at me and Chulo for a second. He said, "You are *pistoleros,* yes?"

I smiled slightly. It had taken him long enough to notice. I said, "That's right."

"Good," he said. Then he turned around and walked out of the cantina.

I looked around at Chulo. He was about as white as a black Meskin could get. He said, shaking his head, "Chulo don't go on thees boat. Thees Chulo does not do. Sometime Chulo drink thees water. Sometime Chulo take thees leetle bath. But Chulo doan get in no leetle boat in thees beeg water."

I said, "Hell, Chulo, I'm scared myself. If you think I want to do this, you are crazy. But it's the only way. We can't ride back to Matamoros and take the train. Sharp is liable to be gone by then. And if we try and cut cross-country and intercept the train, we're liable to kill a couple of horses and still not make it."

Chulo said, "I walk. I walk en my bare feets."

"Now don't give me no trouble, Chulo."

"Hokay, I run. I run on my bare feets."

I said, "You are going to get on that boat whether you like it or not. I'm going to need you in Tampico. So you can just quit this whining and carrying on. You and I are going to get on that boat. You can put your head in a sack all the way or keep your eyes shut, but you *are* getting on that boat."

He looked away. He said, "Hokay, but I no can sweem, an' that boat is going to seenk because Chulo is on it. So I am going to die en thees water."

I poured myself out a drink of brandy. I wasn't feeling all that brave myself. I said, "You stop that line of talk. You hear me? I don't want to hear any more talk about boats sinking. You say one more word about that and I'm going to shoot half your goddam nose off."

To kill some time we walked down to the corrals and looked at the cattle. Even though it had been just a short time, it appeared that more of the cattle were limping. I said, "Remind me to tell Señor Reyes that they ought to cut out a few of the cattle that aren't showing the signs, so they can butcher them. I don't recognize any fat folks around here, so I don't reckon these people get over much to eat."

Chulo said, "I am standing on these ground for the last time."

I just gave him a look. Out on the rickety pier I could see that a couple of men had pulled the blue boat alongside and were on board working on her. Neither one of them was Señor Reyes, so I figured he was busy with other things. I said to Chulo, "Let's don't forget the rifles. Have they put our horses up yet? I didn't notice."

He said, "I doan see nothing but all thees water. Et look bad."

I had to kind of agree with him. When we'd first come, I'd thought the little fishing village was kind of pretty and I'd admired the blue of the water and enjoyed the lapping sound of the little waves. But now, realizing I was actually going out on the stuff, way the hell out, maybe so far out I wouldn't be able to see land, it didn't look at all pretty.

Well, this business had certainly taken a turn. I had set out to collect some money a man owed me and to pay him back for a hole he'd put in me, and now I was worrying about a bunch of sick cattle that didn't have any more to do with me than did the people that had them on their front porch. And I was fixing to get in a boat to go and try and get another boat and sail in it so I could get my money back, and I was either going to or not going to shoot the man who'd put the hole in me.

You talk about an hombre being off his range. I was that man.

CHAPTER 11

It was late at night, about eleven o'clock. We'd been sailing since around six, having left on what Romando had said was the evening tide. I was sitting with him in the back of the boat, on a bench that ran along each side of what he called the cockpit. He was steering the boat with a helm, which looked to me like a wheel with spokes sticking out of it. Chulo and Rodriquez were in the cabin. Rodriquez was in there on a bunk getting a little sleep before it came his turn to steer the boat. Chulo was in a bunk because he was so sick. Romando said it was *mal de mar,* seasickness. He said some people got it and some didn't. He said it was caused by the motion of the boat. I was privately convinced it was caused by all the rum Chulo had drunk just to get on the boat. The reason that I felt that was he had come near to crying when Romando made us take off our boots. High-heeled boots weren't the best footwear to wear on a boat that was pitching and rolling around. Even I could see that. But Chulo had taken on like he was being made to cut his last tie with the land and horses and shooting people and robbing banks and all them things he'd grown to love. I swear he got actual tears in his eyes when I had to finally order him to take off his boots. Right after that, maybe an hour, he got sick as a dog and spent considerable time leaning over the rail. Now all he was doing was laying on a bunk in the cabin and moaning. I'd been concerned at first, but Romando assured me it would pass and that Chulo really and truly would not die, even though he, right then, thought he was going to.

I went down into the cabin, walking carefully, and got a bottle of brandy. After Chulo's example I'd been a mite skittish about downing too much of the spirits. I didn't favor hanging over some railing and trying to throw up my toenails.

The cabin was lit with a small kerosene lantern. It was bigger than I'd expected. There was four bunks and even a kind of little kitchen with a stove and a supply of fresh water. I took the bottle of brandy and went back up into the cockpit and sat down by Romando. It was a nice night, pleasant and with a good breeze blowing that was causing both sails to stay bellied out and throwing out a nice wake at the back of the boat. It was a cloudless night with a three-quarter moon and a sky full of stars. I asked Romando if he steered by the stars or used a compass. He shrugged. He said, "For this trip the way is in my head." He tapped his temple. "We are sailing further out into the Gulf to avoid the little current that runs south to north along the coast. Coming back, I will sail close to the land so that the current will help me. But, yes, sometimes I look at the compass. But not often."

I was learning considerable about sailing and wasn't minding it near as much as I'd thought I would. I'd figured we were going to be rocking and splashing all over the place, but the boat gave a body a nice solid feel. We had them two sails up. The front one was connected to the pole that stuck out from the bow, the bowsprit. The other one was the mainsail, and Romando had told me that the big pole that came out perpendicular from the mast was the boom. It was secured by ropes, but it still swung back and forth over our heads as Romando changed directions, zigging and zagging to get a better handle on the wind.

I said, "This ain't bad at all. Hell, I almost feel like I could run one of these gadgets myself."

Romando laughed. He said, "You are very lucky. For your first voyage you have drawn an almost perfect sea."

I said, "Ain't it always like this?"

He laughed again and looked around like he was hoping somebody was there to share the joke with. He said, "I hope you don't get a chance to find out. I think you would join your friend very quickly."

I took a little drink of brandy and lit a cigarillo. When I had it drawing good, I said, "Romando, I taken note that you brought a sidearm along with you. A gunbelt. What is the purpose of that?"

Even with just the moonlight I could see his face get grim. He said, "I am very angry at this man you call Sharp."

I said, "Romando, let's get something straight. On this boat you are running the show. You tell me where to sit and I'll sit there. You tell me to jump up and down and I'll do that. But when it comes to this business with Sharp that's another story. There's going to be guns involved, and that's where me and Chulo take over. You ain't going to need that gun."

He said, stubbornly, "I have a sense of honor from my father. The people of the village look up to me. I am going to make the face-to-face with this Sharp myself."

I drew on my cigarillo. I said, "How old are you, Romando?"

"I have twenty-six years."

I said, "Well, if you want to have twenty-seven, you had better leave this business to me and Chulo."

He moved the wheel, and the boat heeled over and took a slightly different direction. Over my head the boom swung toward me on its short tether. He said, "They are too many for you. I saw myself when they came to Bodega that there were five or six others besides this Sharp."

I said, "Yes, and if you get mixed up in this, that will just be one more that I have to worry about. You asked me if Chulo and I were *pistoleros*. We are very good *pistoleros*. I have used a gun since I was fifteen years old. Against other men. That is many years now. Take my advice on this matter. Honor is a pretty expensive commodity. We get your village their money and get those cattle handled, that will be honor enough to go around for everyone."

He said, "We will see."

I could see he wasn't convinced. I was sure hoping I wasn't going to have to knock him in the head to keep him out of the way. But like all them high-quality Mexicans, he set a great deal of store by honor. It had killed many more of them than Sam Houston.

I let it lay. I knew what was eating him. He figured a gringo had come in and played him and all his village for fools. A Mexican will sometimes stand for being made a fool out of by another Mexican, but he won't put up with it from a gringo. There are some Mexicans who can actually like a gringo, Chulo being one in my case, but they are few and far between. The biggest mystery in their lives is how come the damn gringos have got so much more money and better horses and better cattle and just about better everything when a blind man can see that a Mexican is a much more superior human being to a damn gringo. Of course you wouldn't get one in a thousand to admit to the facts of the matter, but that's the way they think.

I said, "You get them *vaqueros* word to quit bringing in cattle?"

"That was seen to, yes."

"The people in the village ought to slaughter some of those steers that ain't got sick yet."

"Ten steers are being slaughtered. Most of the meat will be smoked and jerked. They are probably having a big feast right now. They are simple people."

I knew we were well fixed for provisions on the boat. Rodriquez had brought aboard a big batch of jerked beef and a wheel of cheese and a big pot of beans and a hell of a flock of corn tortillas. Romando had said, when I'd commented on the amount of food, that on a voyage you always planned on being gone twice as long. He said, "Very many bad things can happen on the water. It is best to be ready, to have more food and water than you need."

As we sailed along, I asked Romando how his little village managed to survive. I figured smuggling must have entered into it, but he said no. He said, "Our main income is from dried and salted fish that we take to inland markets by ox cart and sell. We sell some dried beef, we sell some corn, we sell whatever we can. Occasionally, as I have said, a boat comes from Cuba and buys some of our cattle. But you can see for yourself that they are very poor cattle."

I said, "As little as there is for a cow to eat back in those hills, I'm surprised you got any cattle at all. Yeah, I can see where y'all got plenty excited when this big man in his big boat come in there talking ten dollars a head. I bet y'all nearly made a fiesta."

"We thought it was a miracle," Romando said. His voice was tight. He said, "You may find this a strange thing, Señor Wilson, but I am not a poor man. My father did well in Corpus Christi in various businesses. But I chose to live in the village and help the people of that village."

"Not like Mr. Sharp," I said.

"No," he said.

"You got five hundred dollars, didn't you?"

"Yes. And then the other ships would have come if you had not stopped them. And they would have come with a lot of big gringos with guns, and they would have taken the cattle and what else they wanted. Now I think I will do a little taking."

I sighed and looked up at the moon. I had a dedicated zealot on my hands. I didn't know of anything much more dangerous except a drunk with a loaded pistol. Hell, I figured I was as fair as most folks, but this matter was my business. I didn't need no zealot or a village full of peons getting in the way. I'd see that they got a fair shake, but I was going to take care of the matter at hand first.

I looked down at my feet, noticing how white they were next to Romando's. We had all rolled our trousers up, except Chulo, on account of the amount of seawater that kept breaking over the bows and then swishing around in the bottom of the cockpit. Romando said it was supposed to run out the back through some kind of sea-cock, but it never did. But even though I was pretty damp, it wasn't all that unpleasant. It was one hell of a lot better, I thought, than taking two horses through thorn thickets, and getting them torn to ribbons, to catch a train that was coming when we didn't know. I figured, unless we drowned before we got to Tampico, that I had made the right choice. I knew Chulo was never going to agree.

About one o'clock in the morning Rodriquez came up out of the cabin without being called. He was a little, dark Mexican who never had much to say either in Spanish or English. He was wearing a torn shirt and tattered pants, cut off just below the knees. He had a knife in his belt. Romando got up from behind the helm, and Rodriquez

slipped into his place. Romando just said one word: "*Sud.*"
South. Then he started down the steps into the cabin. He
stopped and looked back at me. "You should sleep," he
said.

I shook my head. I said, "I ain't never slept on no boat.
I ain't sure I could sleep on a boat. Kind of scares me."

He gave me a funny look. "It scares you to sleep on a
boat?"

"Yeah. The son of a bitch could turn over in the middle
of the night, and I could drown to death without ever
waking up."

He laughed. He said, "If the boat turns over, you may
depend that I will wake you up. Look at the sea. It is calm,
no? Look at the sky. Do you see any clouds? Without clouds
there can be no weather."

I said, "I reckon I'll stay up here."

"Can you swim?"

"If I've got one hand on a horse, I can swim him across
a river."

"You have no horse here. You had better rest if you are
going to fight."

Well, he might have been a kid who thought honor was
some big shakes, but he made sense. A man don't want to
lose that split-second timing because he'd tired. I got up
and followed Romando down into the cabin. He flopped
on the forward bunk on the high side of the boat, and I
did likewise on the one nearest the door. Chulo was in
the forward bunk on the low side of the way the boat
was tilting. I didn't know if he was asleep, but he had at
least quit moaning, for which I was grateful. I lay there on
the bunk, on a rough blanket, and stared up at the ceiling,
watching the lantern swing gently back and forth. It had
been trimmed down so that it just put out a low glow.

Just about the time Romando said it, I had already reached
the same conclusion in the pit of my stomach. He said,
"Don't watch the lantern, Señor Wilson Young."

I turned over on my belly and listened to the boat creak
and slosh around. Romando had said the boat was well
founded. I didn't know what that meant, but I intended to
ask him sometime. But even as I was thinking the thought
I was drifting off to sleep.

I came awake with the feeling that somebody was pitching me all around a room. I felt like I was landing on the floor and the ceiling and the side walls. When I finally come fully conscious, I was half in and half out of the bunk and was banging my head against the side of the boat. I'd been on the high side when I'd gone to sleep, but now the boat had heeled over and I was on the down side of the hill. I come scrambling to my feet, grabbing hold of anything I could get my hands on. Chulo was on the floor, but I didn't pay him any attention; the boat was pitching and jumping and jolting like a monstrous bucking horse. As best I could, I made my way up the stairs to the cockpit. Romando was at the wheel, but he looked to be having a hell of a time holding it. The wind was shrieking and the boom was swinging back and forth wildly. I could hear the wind and I could hear the sails and the ropes and all the rest of the boat, but I could *see* the ocean. There were waves rising up at us that were taller than a tree. The boat would climb up one wave, get to the top, and then fall straight down on the other side with a thud you'd have thought would tear the bottom out of her. Where in hell had all those gentle breezes and calm little waves gone?

I could hear Romando yelling at me. It was just coming dawn. There was a kind of yellowish mist all around, with a blackness just hanging over it. I staggered across the cockpit and plopped down beside Romando. Spray was breaking over the bow and flying back on us. It came with such force that it actually stung when it hit my face. I could taste the salt of it.

Romando put his mouth close to my ear. He yelled, "You must steer!"

I said, "You're crazy! I can't drive this thing. I'll kill us all!"

He said, "You must only hold it into the wind! As it is now. I *have* to go forward and help Rodriquez get down the foresail! We could capsize if I don't!"

For the first time I looked toward the front of the boat. I could see the little figure of Rodriquez struggling with what looked to be about an acre of canvas. Just about the time it appeared he was making headway in gathering it in, a gust of wind would come along and jerk it out of his hands.

I said, "Hold it into the wind?"

"Yes!" he said, nodding. He took my hands and put them on the spokes of the wheel. "You must hold it just as it is. Into the wind. If we turn sideways to the wind we will capsize."

Hell, he couldn't have scared me any worse if he'd put a pistol to my head. I said, "Hold it just like it is."

"Into the wind."

I gripped the spokes. The wheel was like a live thing, wanting to twist first left and then right. It took more strength than I'd have thought Romando had to hold the damn thing.

He watched me for a second and then said, "I will be back quickly. You must hold it."

I watched him go forward and, with Rodriquez, wrestle with the damn foresail. I hadn't the slightest idea what they were doing, but they acted like it was mighty important, so I figured it was.

I just hung onto the damn wheel and tried to keep it positioned so the wind was blowing straight in my face. The damn boat was still climbing up waves and then falling over the other side. Sometimes I wasn't hanging onto the wheel so much to steer the damn boat as to have something to hold onto.

I had never seen such a mess in my life. The sun was up good, but that dark gray mist still hung in the air, and all around, big dark waves rolled up to us higher than our mast. I figured every one of them was going to sink us, but the little boat would climb up their side, somehow keeping her balance, and then point her nose straight down like she was going to dive to the bottom. Then, somehow, she'd rise and start back up the next wave. Hell, some of them waves were bigger than a hell of a lot of hills I'd seen.

It took Romando and Rodriquez about a year and a half to get that foresail down. When they finally had it all gathered up, they slid back some kind of wooden cover on the deck, dropped it through, and then slid the cover back.

Amazingly enough, once the foresail was down, the boat got a whole lot easier to handle. And the relief didn't come too soon, either. I was near about give out trying to hold that helm like I was supposed to.

Then Romando and Rodriquez came back and did something with some ropes around the mast, and the mainsail came down. However, they didn't let it all the way down, just partway. That left some loose canvas, and they tied that around the boom with some little ropes that were already hanging there. After that the steering got even easier.

Finally Romando came back and took over from me. When I let go of the spokes, my hands were so clenched it took me a moment or two to get them straightened out again.

Then the wind started to die down and some of the dark gray mist began to disappear. Before I knew it, we were riding along nearly as smoothly as a buckboard over a bumpy road. I let out a long breath. My hands were damn near trembling. I couldn't recall ever being much more scared in all of my life, and that included some pretty fearful scrapes. I said, to Romando, "So that was a hurricane. I'd heard of 'em, but that was the first one I've ever been in. Hell, I thought we was goners."

He looked at me with a strange expression on his face. "Hurricane?" he said. "You thought *that* was a hurricane? That little squall."

I stared back at him. I said, "That wasn't no big storm?"

He laughed. "If I'd had my regular crew on board, we would have had the sails down in five minutes and hardly noticed the wind. It came and went in half an hour."

The sun was out good now and the haze was gone. The water was calm and gentle and the breeze was steady. I said, "Well, hell." I didn't know what else to say.

Romando said, "You should go down and get some breakfast. Rodriquez is in the cabin. He will help you. As soon as we have had a little something to eat, we will put the sails back up. How is your freend?"

"I don't know," I said. I got up, not having any difficulty now, and made my way to the cabin and down the steps. Chulo was sitting on his bunk, his head in his hands. I said, "*Amigo, que paso?*"

He looked up and he looked awful. He wasn't pale no longer; he'd kind of turned a shade of green. He said, "I theenk I goan die."

I said, "You ought to get up on deck. Breathe some fresh air. The storm is over."

He said, "Storm? There es the storm?"

I said, "Maybe you ought to try and eat." Rodriquez was at the little place you would have called a tiny kitchen. He was slicing dried beef and cheese and getting out some tortillas. I said, to Chulo, "You want something to eat?"

He turned his head away and groaned. He said, "Chou crazy? I doan ever eat no more."

I got some bread and cheese and beef and went back up to the cockpit. Romando had a jug of fresh water, and we made a good meal and washed it down with the water while he steered us toward Tampico. I said, "We making pretty good time?"

He shrugged. "I don't know yet. How long have we been sailing?"

"About fourteen hours. It's a little past eight of the morning."

He said, "There is a little island about halfway. We could have already passed it, but I don't think so. The squall slowed us down because the wind was from the south. For a time it blew us backwards."

I was just about to ask Romando some questions concerning the harbor at Tampico when a hell of a squabble broke out from the inside of the cabin. "Now what?" I said.

Romando said, "What a noise!"

I rushed down the cabin steps. Chulo was backed up on one of the forward bunks. Rodriquez was on a bunk opposite him, looking dazed. He had a bottle of something in his hand. I said, to Chulo, "What the hell is going on here? You been fighting?"

Chulo said, "Thees man tries to keel me. I poush heem away."

I looked at Rodriquez. He was about half Chulo's size. He held up the little bottle. He said, *"Por mal de mar. Solo. Es bueno por mal de mar."*

I said, "Shit, you crazy Meskin. Chulo, he was only trying to help you. That stuff he's got is for seasickness."

Chulo said, indignantly, "Es benigar! He es tryin' to make me drink benigar."

"*Sí*," Rodriquez said, waving the bottle. "Es binegar. En Ainglish es benigar."

I said, "Chulo, it's only vinegar. Hell, a man would have thought he was trying to poison you."

Chulo said, "I am berry seek. Binegar make me seeker."

"Here," I said to Rodriquez. "Give me the bottle. I'll make him drink it."

The little man handed over the little bottle, and I pulled the cork out and held it out to Chulo. He shrank back on the bunk. I said, "Goddammit, I can't have you sick. Now this man is a sailor. He knows about this seasickness matter. Now you take a good swig of this or, so help me, I'll throw you over the side."

Romando had come to the top of the cabin stairs. He said, "The first he drinks will not stay with him. But then, if he drinks a little more, he will be all right very quickly." Then, in Spanish, he told Rodriquez to come on deck, that they had to get the sails back up.

That left me with Chulo. I said, shoving the bottle at him, "Now, goddammit, quit being such a baby. You're gonna throw up again, soon as this hits bottom. But then you drink a little more and you'll be all right. Now do it!"

He took the bottle, but he didn't want to. He took a drink, but he didn't want to. For a minute he sat there, looking worried, and then, all of a sudden, he shoved the bottle at me and went tearing up the stairs. Even down in the cabin I could hear him heaving over the side. While I waited for him to come back, I had a small drink of brandy. Then I tasted a little of the vinegar. I didn't much blame Chulo. It wasn't any stuff that I'd choose to drink.

Getting the second drink in him was easier than I thought. I guess because he was too give out to put up much of a fight. I left him laying on a bunk and went up on deck. Romando and Rodriquez had both sails back up, and it appeared to me that we were just flying along.

We passed the little island around eleven o'clock of the morning. That put us seventeen hours out from Bodega. If the island was halfway, we ought to be getting to Tampico at around five o'clock the next morning.

Romando said, "Perhaps later. We do not have such a favorable wind because we have to swing more to the southwest and we will not go so fast. I think maybe by daylight unless there is more trouble."

"Like squalls?"

He nodded. "The weather is very uncertain in the Gulf."

About an hour later Chulo came up and took a kind of shaky seat on the little bench that ran around the sides of the cockpit. His color had returned to normal, but he appeared to have lost about ten pounds. He looked at me with the eyes of a betrayed friend. I said, "Chulo, dammit, this was the only way I could figure to get there fast without going overland."

"Chure," he said. "Chou don't want to keel no horses so chou keel Chulo. Es hokay to keel Chulo. Chulo choust a dumb Meskin."

Romando said, "He ought to eat something."

Chulo got a look of horror in his eyes.

Romando said, "You will not be sick again. You have lost strength. Now you must eat to get it back."

I said, "Go take a swig of rum, Chulo."

He shook his head. "I neber goan drink rum again long es I leeve."

"Bullshit," I said. "Then go and eat something. I got a good feeling that Sharp is going to be there."

Chulo said, "Maybe thees time he choot me 'n' I doan feel so bad."

We sailed on through the evening and into the night. Somewhere around midnight Chulo and I went down into the cabin and lay down to get as much rest as we could. I slept fitfully, not so much because of the motion of the boat or because I was on a boat, but because I was getting ready for Philip Sharp.

If he was there.

Sometime in the gray dawn Romando called me up on deck. Chulo came with me. The sun was just struggling up from the horizon. There was a low mist on the water. Romando said, "We are very near Tampico. We are about to enter the harbor."

"Where?" I said. I couldn't see a damn thing for the fog.

He pointed in the direction we were sailing. "Straight ahead. In a moment you should be able to see the masts of the ships. It is a matter of only two or three more miles."

Chulo said to me, even while I was straining my eyes to see where Romando was pointing, "Say, how comes chou don't get thees seekness from the sea?"

I said, "Because I have been up and down on so many women. The motion is the same."

He said, "Awwww, chit!"

We kept coasting along in the still water. The sun was burning off some of the fog. I could see the land, low hills, and then, suddenly, I could see the tall masts of a lot of ships. I said, "Is that it?"

"Yes. What do we do now?"

I said, "I don't know. Just get up close and let's try and spot the *Dolphin*. But don't get too close to her. If Sharp sees me, he'll run like a rabbit."

Romando turned the wheel. He said, "I will go to one end of the docks and then sail down the other way. That way we will pass all of the vessels that are moored there."

I was getting excited. I said, "Just be damn careful. I can feel he's close. I don't want to spook him too soon."

CHAPTER 12

Rodriquez dropped the foresail, and we went cruising slowly down the line of ships tied up at the Tampico docks. There must have been at least twenty-five of them, but only about ten were of a size to match the *Dolphin*. A few were three-masters, but the majority of the big ships were two-masted like Sharp's boat. The smaller boats were tied up to piers and wharves, but the big ones were moored in a line along the dock, where you could just step down a gangplank and be right on shore.

The big wooden dock appeared to me to be about five or six hundred yards long. It reminded me of the Galveston dock with its forest of masts and then all the big warehouses set up close to where the boats would be unloaded. As we eased our way along, I noticed a big set of corrals shoved in between two warehouses. I couldn't see how many cattle were in the pens, but they had the corrals placed nice and handy for loading the ships.

But my heart was in my mouth looking for the *Dolphin*. We passed two, three, four, five, six big ships and no sign of her. Then we passed a couple more and there she was. No mistake. Her name was painted bold as brass on her bow. She was kind of worn and scruffy-looking like she hadn't had no good grooming in a while, but Romando said that was the look of all cargo boats, especially cattle boats.

But there she was. Romando got excited and let his accent creep into his nearly perfect English. He said, "Now we feex hem."

I said, instantly, "Don't say that, Romando. Don't mouth your luck. That's the boat, but we ain't after the boat. We're after Sharp and we ain't seen him yet."

We eased on down the line until we passed the last boat, and then Rodriquez dropped the main sail and Romando steered in for the dock. Rodriquez had gone up in the bow with an oar to fend us off from hitting too hard, but that wasn't going to be necessary. As we got closer, we started losing momentum and were just kind of drifting until a dockhand threw us a rope with a weight on the end. Rodriquez caught it, and he and Chulo pulled us in hand over hand. When we hit the dock, Rodriquez jumped out and tied our bow to a post that looked like it would have held a locomotive. Our stern drifted in, and the dockhand heaved Romando another line and pulled our stern in so that we were lined up like the big ships.

I was the first one off the boat. I wasn't more anxious than Chulo; I was just better situated, at the middle of the boat. I heaved a sigh of relief as I stepped on the solid planks of the dock, but then I discovered the damn thing was moving. Romando was just behind me. I said, "This damn dock is floating. I can feel it going up and down."

He said, "That is from the boat. You will feel the motion for several hours."

The dockhand came up to Romando and said something in rapid Spanish that I didn't get. I asked him what the man had said. Romando said, "He says we would be wiser to dock at one of the piers for boats of our size. He says it is much less expensive."

"What's the difference?"

"About a hundred pesos."

I said, "Screw the difference. This is the best place for us." I reached into my pocket and gave the dockhand a twenty-dollar bill. I said, to Romando, "Tell him when that runs out to let me know."

Romando just smiled. He said, "You have just paid the wrong man. But, never mind, I will get it straightened out. What is our plan now?"

All of a sudden I realized I was standing there in my bare feet with my pants rolled up. Chulo had just gotten off the boat, looking a little unsteady, and he was barefoot also. I was hoping I didn't look as silly as he did. I said, "Well, the first thing I'm going to do is go back on the boat and put on my boots and hat, and then, when this here dock quits bobbing around, I'll figure out something."

Chulo went back aboard with me. We sat in the cabin and pulled on our boots and put on our gunbelts. I'd been mighty careful to stay low as we'd passed the *Dolphin,* but I hadn't seen anybody on deck, certainly not Mr. Sharp. By my watch it was a little after eight o'clock. Could have been they were already up and about their business, except I didn't know what their business was. What I figured Sharp was mainly doing was waiting for Mike Hull and his other ships. Well, I was feeling much easier in my mind about that. Enough time had passed that they would have arrived if they'd managed to get away with the ships. But it appeared that Patterson and the sheriff had done their jobs.

I said, to Chulo, "You keep a close eye on little Mr. Reyes. He's liable to try and do something on his own, and I can't have that. He's got a little too much pride to suit me."

We went back to the dock. The damn thing was still rocking up and down, even after I'd put on my boots. I took a good look around. We were about a hundred and fifty yards down from the *Dolphin,* but as busy as the dock was, there wasn't much likelihood of us being spotted at long distance. The dock was working alive with hired hands busy at various jobs. Some of them were wheeling barrels of stuff on board one ship; others were trundling big heaps of sacked corn. I could even see cases of rum and tequila and brandy and other spirits. All that stuff was disappearing down into the bellies of the ships, ready to be shipped to God only knew where.

I said, to Romando, "Let's go get some breakfast. Do you know a little joint near here that wouldn't be high-class enough for Mr. Sharp? I ain't quite ready to run into him just yet."

We went to a little café about three blocks from the waterfront. It was small, but it was about as clean as could be expected. Chulo and I ordered eggs and tamales with chili gravy, and Rodriquez and Romando had chorizo sausages and eggs. Everybody but Romando had beer. He just drank water.

I could see he was itching to know what we were going to do, but I didn't say anything while we were eating. My first concern was going to be where Mr. Sharp was. I finally pushed my plate back and said, "Romando, is that ship big enough to live on? The *Dolphin*?"

He said, "But of course. What do you mean, señor?"

I said, "If you was on her, would you have a big enough cabin to be comfortable in or would you go to a hotel?"

He said, "On such a ship the captain's cabin would be quite large. And why pay for a room in a hotel if my business was on the docks?"

"I don't know," I said. "I don't care where Sharp is; I just want to get my hands on him. Let's go back to the docks."

I paid the score for the breakfast, and we wandered back toward Romando's boat. It sure as hell looked small lined up with all the big two- and three-masted ships. We went on board and sat around in the cockpit. At least me and Chulo and Romando did. Rodriquez went into the cabin and busied himself getting the place shipshape, as sailors said.

Romando said, "What do we do?"

I said, "First, we got to find out where Sharp is. I can't go up there because Sharp might see me and recognize me. I can't send Chulo because his English is awful and he looks too mean. So I reckon you have got to be the one to walk up there and ask after Mr. Sharp."

He was nodding, getting excited. He said, "And what will I say to him if he is on board?"

I said, sharply, "You won't say nothing to him. You'll get the hell back here as fast as you can and report to me."

A little disappointment showed in his face. He said, "We are the wronged ones. My village."

I said, "Now, listen, Romando, you sailed the boat. But the rest of it is my kind of business. You just go up there and ask whoever is on deck if Mr. Sharp is on board. If he himself is on deck, and you recognize him, you just keep walking."

"What do I say if they ask me what my business is with this Sharp?"

I said, "Tell whoever it is that you are from the village of Bodega and that you have some questions. If they ask you to come aboard, you suddenly remember some papers you forgot and you get on back here and tell me. If they say he's not there, you ask where you can find him or when he will be back. Get as much information as you can but *don't go on that ship!* I don't want to have to come get you off. Do you understand?"

"Yes," he said, but he said it stiffly. He wasn't much of a hand for taking orders. He said, "Do you think that this Mr. Sharp is trying to buy sick cattle here? In Tampico? Because I don't think he will find them. The *rancheros* kill such cattle before they can spread the disease."

Now I had my chance to laugh at him. He'd laughed at me all the way down the coast on that damn boat. I said, "Romando, see, he's got all the sick cattle he needs. He's still expecting one of his other ships to pick up the cattle at Bodega. Once it gets here, all he's got to do is put three or four head in with the healthy cattle he'll put on board the *Dolphin,* and they'll all be sick by the time he gets them to Cuba."

"Aaaah," Romando said.

I said, "Now go on down there and find out what you can." I looked him over. He was kind of sea-worn. I said, "I wish you looked a little better. You didn't bring no other clothes, did you?"

He shook his head. "I did not think of it."

I said, "You look like one of these waterfront rats. I need you to look more like a well-to-do Mexican businessman." I took out my roll and peeled off a damp twenty-dollar bill. He didn't want to take it, but I insisted. I said, "You can pay me back when we come to the reckoning. Now go buy yourself some better clothes. And get a shave. But make it fast."

He said, "What of yourself?"

I smiled slowly. I said, "Mr. Sharp ain't going to be concerned with my appearance so much as the fact that I have appeared."

He said, "But what is the plan?"

I said, "Goddammit, if you ask me that again, I'm going to shoot your ears off. I can't figure out a plan until I know where Sharp is. Now get going."

He started to leave the boat, but I suddenly called him back. I said, "Give me that gunbelt. It looks silly on you."

"But I must have protection."

I said, "From the way you are wearing that rig, it don't look like no protection to me. Now take it off and hand it to Chulo."

For a minute he thought he was going to refuse. Then he looked at Chulo. Chulo nodded and held out his hand. Chulo said, "Es the best *por usted.* Leeve the guns *por mi* an' Señor Weelson. We choot them like chou sail de boat."

He took off the gunbelt, if it could be called that, and handed it to Chulo. Then he said, "I will be as fast as I can."

We watched him go off down the waterfront. Chulo said, "How come chou call heem a Mexican an' you call me a Meskin?"

I said, "Because he gave me some medicine before we got on the boat so I wouldn't get sick like you. And he didn't give you any."

Chulo reared his head back and stared at me for a moment. Finally he decided that I was joshing him. He said, "Awwww, chit!"

We waited through the long morning. Rodriquez, like a sensible man, went into the cabin and took a siesta. Chulo and I just sat in the sun like we didn't have any better sense.

Chulo said, "Have chou made up chou mind?"

"What?"

"Are chou goan to choot thees Meester Charps?"

I shook my head. I said, "I don't know. It is a quandary."

"What es thees quan— What chou say?"

"Quandary. That is when you have two women you can screw. One of them is very beautiful, but she has three brothers who will surely kill you if you touch her. The other one has no brothers, but she is very ugly."

Chulo shrugged. He said, "That es no quontree. Chou wait unteel et es dark an' then chou make the satisfaccion weeth the ugly one. Or maybe chou geeve the brothers some moneys."

I looked at him. I said, "Chulo, sometimes you ain't as dumb as I think you are."

"Chure. Chou make thees Charps geeve you thees money he owes chou an' then chou choot heem."

That seemed like a simple enough solution to me. If I were Chulo.

But we still weren't on that boat, and we still didn't have Philip Sharp under our guns. We were closer than I'd been in eight or nine days, but there was still a ways to go.

I sat there thinking about what to do. Finally I said, "Chulo, we ain't got a deck of cards, do we?"

"Chure," he said.

"Where?"

"En the saddlebaga."

I gave him a sour look. I said, "The goddam saddlebags are on the horses, and the horses are a hundred and fifty miles from here. Go find me a deck of cards and be damn quick about it. Do not stop in any cantinas or whorehouses. Just go get the cards and get right back here. We could be going to see Mr. Sharp at any minute. Whenever Romando gets back."

I would have bet money that Chulo would be a half an hour behind Romando, knowing his habit of hurrying as well as I did. But Chulo was back within the quarter hour with a new deck of cards, and there was still no sign of Romando. I got out my watch. It was going on for eleven o'clock. He'd been gone nearly two hours. I said, "Where the hell can that boy be?"

Chulo sat down in the cockpit with me. He said, "We goan to play cards?"

I gave him a look. I said, "Hell, no. Why would I want to play cards with you? I win all your money and then I just have to give it back. What the hell good is that?"

He said, "I let chou ween sometimes."

I just looked at him. There wasn't anything to say to such a remark.

Noon came and went and there was still no sign of Romando. Rodriquez brought us up some bread and cheese for lunch. While we ate, I began to be convinced that he had been fool enough to go aboard the *Dolphin,* and now Sharp and his seagoing villains had him and were beating the truth out of him. If that were the case, there would be no surprising Philip Sharp now. We were going to have to assault the goddam ship. "Damn that boy!" I said. I took a nip of brandy. "That dumb little son of a bitch! I told that dumb Mexican not to go on that ship."

Chulo said, "What es thees talk?"

I told him what I was afraid of.

He furrowed his brow. He said, "He es not that estupid. Thees Charp will know heem an' he will ask heem what he es doin' en Tampico. He doan be that estupid I doan theenk, to go on that chip."

"Then where in hell is he? It's nearly one o'clock."

Chulo shrugged. "*Quien sabe?*" he said. Who knows?

Finally, just about the time I figured I was going to have to go out looking for him, Romando came hurrying down the dock and then jumped into the cockpit of the boat. He looked considerably better with a shave and new clothes, but I was mad as hell. I said, "Where the devil have you been? You should have been back here three hours ago. Did you go on board the *Dolphin?*"

"No, no, no," he said. He was very excited. "I have been watching the *Dolphin* to see how many crew we will have to deal with. I hid very carefully and watched for a long time so I would not count the same men twice. I watched so that I could recognize each man."

I said, somewhat mollified, "How many?"

"Six. The six that I see on board. Of course I am not counting this Señor Sharp."

My anger started back up. I said, "What about him? That was what you were sent to find out."

"He is in the town. I presented myself to a man at the gangplank just as you said. I told him I was there to see Señor Sharp about some cattle business. He said that the señor was in the town. I asked him when he would return, and he was not sure. He thought late in the afternoon, *las tardes,* but he wasn't sure. He asked me if I had some cattle for sale and were they near here. I said I had two hundred head of steers and they were just outside of town. He said I should come back. He said I should come back about seven or eight o'clock. That Señor Sharp would surely be back by then."

"You didn't tell him you were from Bodega?"

He shook his head. "No, no. I think if I do that, he is going to ask me about the other ships. If I have seen them. I think I just act like I am a *ranchero* from Tampico."

I nodded slowly. "Six, huh?"

"Yes. And there is always one guarding the gangplank. And they all have either pistols or knives in their belts."

I was thinking of how many we might have to deal with. Patterson said Sharp had sailed off with six helpers or sailors or whatever you called them, but that might not have been an exact count. Sharp was off somewhere for the day. I would have bet money to marbles he was meeting in some hotel with a bunch of local *rancheros,* arranging for a few hundred cattle for this trip to Cuba, and a whole lot more in future, once he got Cuba in the midst of a severe cow shortage. More than likely he had a man with him. Sharp just struck me as the kind of pantywaist that would go knocking around a rough town like Tampico with some help by his side. I decided to figure on seven more besides him. And it might be smart, I thought, not to set a figure at all, but just expect more than had been counted.

I was still thinking about what I was going to do with Sharp. I had promised I'd help clean up the mess the sick cattle posed, and there wasn't much could be done about that except to take the *Dolphin* back to Bodega, load the cattle on board, sail out to sea, and pitch them overboard and let the sharks eat them. They couldn't turn the cattle loose, and they sure as hell couldn't let them die where they were. The place would smell bad into the next century. And they couldn't drive them into the Gulf; they'd just wash ashore. So it looked like the *Dolphin* and I were going back to Bodega no matter what I did about Sharp. I said, to Romando, "Can you sail that big boat?"

"Of course," he said. "It is not very different than mine except it is bigger and square-rigged."

I wasn't going to ask him what "square-rigged" meant because I didn't care. But I said, "That ship ain't exactly facing the right way to sail out of here. How do you get the damn thing out of the harbor?"

He said, "You drift it out with the tide. Then when you are clear of the harbor and you have a breeze, you put the sails up and off you go."

I said, "What time is the tide?"

He pursed his lips. He said, "High tide here will be a little later than Bodega. I can ask, but I think it will be about seven o'clock."

"How long does it last?"

He shrugged. "That depends on the depth of the harbor. Two hours maybe."

It would be enough time, I calculated. I said, "But look here, how are you going to sail the *Dolphin* and your boat at the same time? Can Rodriquez sail your boat?"

He said, "Oh, no. I will need Rodriquez. We will tie my boat on behind the *Dolphin,* and the big ship will pull my boat."

I said, "Will you need any of Sharp's crew to help?"

He looked at me. He said, "Are you thinking of not taking them back?"

I shrugged. I said, "Might be they won't be real happy to see us. I can't tell you for certain what is going to happen. They might get to cutting up ugly, and we might have to calm them down some."

"You mean there will be shooting?"

I shrugged again. I said, "Man don't want to go to predicting them kinds of things in advance. What time do you reckon it'll start getting dark around here?"

He looked up at the angle of the sun. He said, "Perhaps six, six-thirty. Mexican time."

There was an hour's difference between Mexico and the United States. Or at least Texas. It was an hour later in Mexico. I said, "Good dark?"

"For sure by seven. Perhaps a little earlier."

I said, "Then I reckon we'll start their way a little before seven. Maybe they'll just be sitting down to supper and will invite us to eat with them."

Chulo said, "Maybe I chould go up to the cantina an' ask some questions."

I said, "Maybe you better go down in that cabin and take a siesta. You ain't getting off this boat until I do. I know you. Just about the time I need you you'll be laying up in some crib with a *puta* about half-drunk. And don't go to whining. It ain't going to do you a damn bit of good. It's already after two o'clock and ain't that much longer to wait."

Romando said, "Does this make you nerbous?"

I smiled. It didn't make me "nerbous," but it sounded like it was making him that way. I said, "Listen, while we got time, I need you to give me the layout of that boat. Do you know anything about it?"

"Oh, yes," he said. "When it was in Bodega, I boarded it and was shown around. This man that you call Mr. Sharp showed it to me like I was a peon who knew nothing of boats. He wanted me to understand how they could carry cattle on a ship."

I said, "Well, tell me about it. I got to know where they can be hid, where the nooks and crannies are."

He pulled a face. He said, "It is a very simple ship because it is not intended for long voyages and it carries cattle. So it does not need much for the crew, and most of its space is for the cargo." He leaned over and sort of sketched out on the wood of the cockpit, with a wet finger, the general outline of the ship. He said, "At the back is the main cabin. It is all of the way across the stern of the ship. Half of it is a big cabin for the captain. The other half is for the meals."

"It's the kitchen?"

"No, no," he said. He pointed to the middle of his little drawing. "Just here, right at the second mast, is a little shack. That is the galley, what you call the kitchen. If they cook meals, they do it there and then take them into the little salon for the eating."

I said, "Where does the crew sleep?"

He pointed at the bow. He said, "Forward. There is a little cabin under the top deck. In the hold, if you understand. That is also where most of the cattle will be kept."

"Not on top?"

"Some of them, yes. But some go below."

"How they get them down there?"

He said, "There is a big hatch almost at the rail. Then there is a big ramp. They are driven down that and then back up it at the destination. If some of the cattle are down, they are hoisted out." He pointed down the dock. "Like that."

I looked down to where a big pole-like affair, with a cable running from it, was hovering over a ship. While I watched, a team of horses, with a man whipping them, strained forward, and the line rose out of the hold of the vessel, pulling up some big crates that were too large for men to handle.

But I could tell it was getting close to siesta because much of the furious activity that had been going on along the dock was slowing down as men quit their chores and went off to either nap or take a visit to the nearest cantina.

Chulo said, "I theenk I chould go get some cigarillos."

I said, "I think you should get down in that cabin and get some sleep. You may have to be awake all night. Now go on!"

He got up, grumbling and cussing softly under his breath, but I knew, in five minutes, he'd be asleep and would sleep for six hours if somebody didn't fire a cannon by his head. He'd been sitting out in the sun for about three hours, and there ain't never been a day in his life when he could do that without going to sleep.

Romando watched him as he stumbled down the cabin stairs. He said, "Does he work for you?"

"Chulo?" I laughed. "Work for me? Chulo doesn't work for nobody."

"But he obeys you."

"Well, he does that for three reasons. He's my friend, he knows I'm smarter than he is, and he's afraid of me."

"Afraid of you?" His voice seemed to be saying, "That big, ugly, mean-looking Mexican is afraid of a little gringo like you?"

"Yeah," I said.

"But why?"

I said, "I dunno. You'd have to ask him. All I know is that he is."

"Are you so good with the pistol?"

I shrugged. I said, "Well, I'm still alive. And I've led a kind of hazardous life."

He said, "You have never told me . . . What is your work?"

I told him that I owned a casino and saloon in Del Rio. I left out the part about the whorehouse.

His eyes lit up. He said, "So you are a gambler. I love to gamble."

I yawned in spite of myself. The hot sun was getting to me also. I said, "I never saw a Mexican that didn't. Seems to run in the blood." I pulled out the deck of cards that Chulo had brought. "Want to while away some time for a little money?"

He said, rubbing his hands together, "Oh, yes. But I must warn you that I am very lucky."

I said, "Well, that's good because you'll need all the luck you got. I'm very skillful and that is better than luck."

He said, "We will see."

We played three-card monte, which is a sucker's game at best unless you happen to be the dealer. In three-card monte the player is shown two queens and an ace. Then the dealer throws them back and forth in a line on the table, his hands moving so fast the eye can barely follow, and then the player is asked to pick the ace. If he succeeds, he is paid even money, which, right there, is stupid because even if the game is honest—which it most often is not—his chance of picking the ace is only one in three. So he is being paid even money when the odds against his winning are really three to one.

But we played, for something to do, and I won a hundred dollars off of Romando. We started off for small stakes, but I let him win at first, and he got excited and kept edging the bet upwards. When I got him up to where I wanted him, I cleaned him out in about four hands.

Of course I gave him his money back, because I had cheated. When I told him this, he looked astounded. "You cheated! Why did you cheat?"

"To win," I said.

"You know how to cheat at cards?"

"Of course," I said. "I run a gambling casino. I have to know every way there is to cheat, so that when someone comes in and tries to cheat me, I can spot it."

He said, "Show me how you cheated at monte."

So I showed him how the dealer could palm an extra card in one hand, another queen, so that sometimes when he threw the three cards face downward on the table, the ace wouldn't be there, just three queens. He was amazed. I said, "So you see, you can't pick the ace if I have it in my hand. And before you can examine all three cards, I'll have them all back up in my hands, and if you ask to see the ace, I can show it to you."

"You have very fast hands," he said.

"I better," I said.

The time was passing. About five-thirty I woke Chulo up and we had a supper of dried beef and cheese and bread. I washed mine down with watered-down brandy and cautioned Chulo about the rum. Not that it was necessary. He could drink a half a gallon of rum before going into a fight and then be just as sober as a preacher's daughter when the trouble started.

By six dusk had a good start on night and the activity around the dock had pretty well come to a standstill. Up toward town I could see lights coming on in cantinas and cafés. I gathered us all up in the cockpit to lay out a sort of plan. All I wanted was to get on that ship and get a pistol leveled down on Sharp. But what I didn't want was any kind of commotion that might summon the *policia* before I got my business done and we were clear of the harbor. I said, to Chulo, "We got to get on that boat and we got to get by any watchmen without firing a gun. I know there's going to be one at the gate or door or whatever you call that thing that opens in the railing of the ship. We got to get close enough to him so you can shut him up without no bother or noise. *Sabe?*"

"Chure," he said.

I said to Romando, "Listen, I hate to involve you, but it might be that same watchman and he'll know you. I want you to go with us and get his interest, I don't care how you do it, until Chulo can get close enough to grab him. Are you willing to do that?"

"But of course," he said. "I will wear my gunbelt."

I said, "No, you ain't going to wear a gun. And as soon as we've got by that guard, you are going to come back here until I send Chulo for you and tell you to move this boat up and tie it to the *Dolphin*. How do we get it loose, anyway, to let it float off on the tide?"

He shrugged. He said, "The best way is to cut the hawsers, the big ropes, with an axe. If you are in a rush."

I said, grimly, "I reckon we are going to be in a rush."

It was good dark. There was no longer much reason to wait. I said to Romando, "Listen, you better explain to Rodriquez kind of what is going on. Tell him to stay here and be ready for anything."

I listened while Romando jabbered away to the little man in Spanish much too rapid for me to follow. It must have been to Rodriquez's liking because he kept nodding and saying, *"Sí, sí."*

Romando stopped and nodded and said, to me, "He understands. He is very excited that we have the chance to sail on the big ship."

I said, "It better be more than a chance." I looked at my watch. It was nearly seven. I said, to Romando, "Try and get the guard to come a little way down the gangway so Chulo can get at him. Wave a five-dollar bill at him or something. Speak Spanish. Act like it is important."

He looked at me. He said, "It is, is it not?"

"Damn right," I said. I stepped off the little boat and onto the dock. I said, "Let's go. Chulo, you stay on the side close to the big ship. Romando will walk a step or two behind us. You checked your revolver?"

"Chess."

So had I. It was full, and I had about another half dozen cartridges in my pocket.

CHAPTER 13

I wasn't two steps away from the boat when I remembered
something. I had left a half-full bottle of brandy sitting in
the cockpit. I halted the other two while I stepped back
to get it. Chulo said, "Chou 'fraid somebody steels chour
wheesky?"

I said, "You're going to act like a drunk. And you're
going to offer the guard or watchman or whatever a drink."
I shoved the bottle into his hand.

He said, "I doan like brandee."

"You do now," I said.

We set off up the dock, Romando trailing just behind
us. Chulo and I were laughing and talking. As we got
inside fifty yards of the *Dolphin,* we stopped, just inside
the light coming from a warehouse, and made a big show
out of passing the bottle back and forth and laughing like
we were having the best time anybody ever had. Romando
kept carefully behind us and out of the light.

About fifteen yards from the *Dolphin* we could see a
man leaning over the railing right near the gate at the end
of the ramp. He was leaning there, both arms and hands in
sight, watching us. We staggered just a little and laughed
and laughed.

As we got almost to the gangway I said, lowly, to Chulo,
"Notice the watchman."

We stopped. Chulo pointed up at the man. He said,
sounding drunk, "Hey, that es my freen'. I ain't seen hem
en a long times! I geeve heem a drink."

We both went lurching toward the bottom of the gangway. Chulo was holding up the bottle. He said, "Hey, my freen'. Chou come geet thees drink."

About then Romando came quietly up and stood at the bottom of the ramp talking quietly up at the watchman. The watchman put his hand to his ear. He said, "What? I can't hear fer these two drunks. Whatcha say?"

Romando was waving a greenback. I couldn't see the denomination, but I could hear him saying, "Mr. Sharp. Señor Sharp. About the cattle."

"What?" the watchman said. He had his eyes all over the bill Romando was waving.

Chulo and I took a step up the gangway. Only five or six feet separated us from the guard. Romando was coming right behind us, still talking in a low voice.

I said, "Whyn't you give that feller a drank? Hell, he looks like a good feller."

The guard was waving his hand at us, but looking at Romando. He said, "You damn drunks git on outten here! Dammit! What was you sayin' thar', mister?"

He had come halfway down the ramp. It was close enough. Chulo stuck the bottle out with his right arm like he was offering the guard a drink. The watchman turned an angry face at him and started to push the bottle away. He never got no further. Chulo dropped the bottle as his right arm encircled the guard's neck and face. He spun him around so that the man's back was to Chulo's front. I heard him making muffled sounds against Chulo's arm just as Chulo wrapped his left arm around the man's head and twisted it. I heard the man's neck snap.

Behind me I heard a sort of horrified gasp. I looked back. Romando was standing there looking horrified. I couldn't believe he'd lived so long in Mexico without seeing a man killed violently. I hissed at him. I said, "Get the hell back to your boat."

He began to move away, reluctantly. I turned back to the ship. By now Chulo had the guard under the arms and was walking him up the gangway like a man helping a drunk friend home. The guard's head wobbled loosely on his shoulders, as well it might.

We got quietly on deck. I had Chulo lay the man down just behind the railing, which was solid. In the shadows someone would have to walk right up to him to see him. I drew my revolver. Chulo did likewise. I could see lights in the cabin at the end of the ship where Romando had said the captain—and I had to figure that would be Sharp—stayed. There were no lights on the other side, the side he had said was where they ate. If we were lucky, we'd find Mr. Sharp just behind that door. I hoped he was going to be glad to see me. I knew for damn sure he was going to be surprised.

But first we had to make a quick tour around the ship to see if anyone else was prowling about the deck. We walked as quietly as we could in our high-heeled boots. We'd taken our spurs off when we left the horses behind.

We stepped along quiet and nice, but quick. All we were doing was making sure there wasn't anybody else on deck. The boat was pretty much as Romando had described it. There was a little low shack built up next to the rearmost mast. There was a light in one of its tiny windows, but it was so dim I figured somebody had left some coals alive to start the next fire. Besides, I wasn't paying much attention to anything. My main intent was to get at the door leading into that back cabin and see if Santa Claus had left a Philip Sharp in my Christmas stocking.

We came up on the door one from each side. I leaned against it and listened. I could hear a low murmur of voices but nothing I could make out. I'd tried looking through the little window, but it was up high and there were some kind of curtains over it so a man couldn't get a clear view of the room. All I could see was one small corner and the edge of the brim of a man's hat. I thought that Sharp might have some *rancheros* in there, negotiating for the sale of some cattle. If he did, I didn't know what I was going to do with them. I had no quarrel with them, but I couldn't just let them go so they could summon the *federales* and play bloody hell with my plans for Sharp.

Well, I was just going to have to play it by ear. I reached out for the door handle and gave it just the tiniest of turns. It wasn't locked. But one problem was that the door wasn't very big. In fact it was downright narrow. That meant Chulo and I couldn't go in together. I got his attention and pointed at the door. Then I pointed at myself and held up one finger.

He nodded. I held up two fingers and pointed at him. He nodded again. Using both hands, as carefully as I could so that it would not make a sound, I cocked the hammer of my revolver. Chulo did the same. Around us, in the stillness of the night, there was the gentle wash of the water and the creaking of the ropes and the rigging. The deck was making a slight motion under our feet, but it was so gentle and slow as to be unnoticeable. I thought, Surely to God Chulo won't get seasick on a boat that's moored in dock.

Then I opened the door and stepped into the well-lit room. I took it in in a single glance. Philip Sharp was sitting behind a fairly small desk. He was dressed like a man of means who could buy your cattle with a check you could depend on being good. His coat was thrown over the back of his chair, but he had on a vest and a long-sleeved shirt, with garters, and a four-in-hand tie. He glanced up as I stepped into the room and left the bottom of his jaw where it had been.

I said, "Hello, Phil. Remember me?"

He stared, his eyes getting nearly as big around as his open mouth. He said, "Oh, my gawd!"

Chulo had moved in to my left, right in front of a man leaning in the back corner. It must have been the brim of his hat that I'd seen, because he was dressed much as Chulo and I were, including the correctly hung gun rig. He didn't make a motion as he saw us come in, saw the drawn revolvers, other than to shift his weight to his left foot to make a right-handed draw easier. I didn't know where Sharp had got him, but he was a border gunman if I'd ever seen one. He was the one to shoot first if there was any trouble, and I knew I didn't have to tell Chulo.

Besides Sharp, who still hadn't come to his senses, and the gunslinger, there were four other men in the room. All of them were dressed in rough clothes like you saw on sailors or men around the dock. One of them was sitting in a chair at the corner of Sharp's desk, one was leaning against the wall directly behind Sharp, and two others were sitting on a bunk that was against the wall to my right. They all had guns in their belts.

I could sense that the door was still open, and I took two steps backwards, never letting the barrel of my pistol waver from Sharp's head, and shut it with my boot heel.

Sharp had quit gagging and flinching and was getting his voice back. He said, "Wilson Young, my gawd."

I said, "You ain't surprised to see me are you, Phil?"

He opened and closed his mouth and then said, "No. No, no, no. In fact I'm glad. Glad to have the chance to explain."

"Explain what?"

Before he could answer, I noticed one of the men sitting on the bunk edging his hand toward the weapon in his waistband. I just let the barrel of my revolver stray ever so slightly in his direction. His hand stopped. He pulled it back and put it down beside him on the couch.

"Explain what, Phil?"

"About the . . . the misunderstanding. You remember, in my office in Galveston. That was all a mistake. You wasn't supposed to be involved. Some of my boys got mixed up. It was all a big mistake."

"Yes," I said, "it was a mistake, Phil. A real big mistake. And as I recall it wasn't one of your boys that shot me, it was you."

He said, "Now wait—"

At that instant the door behind me opened. I whirled, knowing Chulo would keep the rest of the room covered. In the door was a man with his left arm around Romando's neck and a pistol in his right hand pointed at the boy's head. He said, "Look here what I found sneaking around—"

Then he stopped, staring.

For just a split second it was like one of them frozen tableaux they sometimes put on in stage shows. Nobody moved; nobody said anything or so much as blinked.

It had been my experience that once a situation turned bad, it wasn't going to get no better unless you did something about it. If I let that man get into the cabin with a drawn gun, we'd very shortly be the prisoners. I didn't even hesitate. The man was nearly a head taller than Romando, and I had noticed that he had his finger just loosely inside the trigger guard of his revolver. But it was going to have to be a hip shot, and even though the range was only about five feet, it was going to be a near thing. I reckoned, later, that no more than a second had passed since he'd opened the door and dragged Romando in. I fired. The bullet caught him square in the middle of his face, jerking his arm loose from Romando, and knocking him back through the door. At the same instant I fired, I heard a *Boom* right beside me and I knew that Chulo had shot someone.

I whirled back into the room. The gunman had slid down in the corner and was sitting on the floor. He had his hand on the butt of his revolver, which had never quite cleared leather. There was blood in the middle of his chest. After a second he fell over sideways.

The room was hazy with gunsmoke, but I was fearful someone might have heard the shots. Behind me Romando was saying, "Señor Young, I didn't mean—"

I said, "Shut up." Then to Chulo I said, "You and Romando get these bodies and throw them over the side away from the dock. Don't forget the one by the railing. Make it snappy." I looked at Sharp. I said, "Where's an axe?"

He said, "Uh ... uh ... I don't know."

I shoved the barrel of my pistol right up to his nose. "Where's an axe?"

The man standing behind him, leaning against the wall, said, his voice trembling, "The galley."

Without a word from us, they had all, with the exception of Sharp, put their hands in the air.

I said, "Romando, as soon as you throw those bodies overboard, show Chulo how to cut those hawsers with that axe. Then you get on back to your boat and tie on to us, and you and Rodriquez get on board."

He said, "But Señor Young, we must—"

He didn't get any further. Chulo grabbed him and pulled him over to the dead gunman, and together they dragged him out of the cabin. I just stood there watching the little herd I'd been left to guard.

When they had the gunman tended to, they came back for the one that had had Romando, and then Chulo shut the door.

Romando had been off in his count. The watchman had been one, the man sitting at Sharp's desk had been two, the two on the bunk had been four, the man behind Sharp had been five, the gunman had been six, and the one with Romando in his grasp had been seven.

And seven had been what I had calculated because, I hadn't been able to see Sharp walking around Tampico by himself. That was probably what he'd hired the gunman for. He was probably local. Well, it had just been his bad luck to be in the wrong place at the wrong time. Of course he'd been a fool also. He'd expected Chulo to turn his head toward the disturbance, giving him time to draw. He didn't understand that Chulo and I didn't both turn our backs at the same time. Well, he'd learned a good lesson. It was a cinch he wouldn't repeat his mistake.

I said to Sharp, "Any more?"

He had turned nearly white. He had his hands before him on the desk. They were trembling. He shook his head, slowly. "No, no."

I said, "If I get another surprise, the next man I shoot will be you."

He stammered he said, "Tha-that's all on b-board."

I swept my pistol around the room. I said, "I think it's time you boys all got rid of those guns you are carrying. You have just seen what can happen if you get careless with one. You can get hurt. Now, one at a time, as I point at you with my pistol, take the weapons you have and put them on the desk in front of Mr. Sharp. But be real careful. I mean *real* careful."

One by one, beginning with the man leaning against the wall behind Sharp, they all laid their pistols on the desk. I said to Sharp, "Now what have you got to contribute?"

He shook his head. "Nothing," he said. "I'm not wearing a gun."

"Not even that little .32-caliber you shot me with?"

"No."

"Stand up."

He rose, carefully putting his hands up as he did. I looked him over critically but couldn't see where he could have a gun concealed, other than maybe a derringer. Actually, I didn't give a damn if he had one or not. I kind of halfway wished he did and that he'd make a try for it. That would at least make up my mind for me. I told him so, leaving out, though, the part about my indecision.

He said, "Wilson, there's no need for trouble between us over this misunderstanding. I'm certain I can make matters right between us."

I laughed. I said, "I'm certain you can too. I ain't certain *you're* going to like how matters get settled, but they'll suit me."

He went to trembling again.

The man sitting by the side of the desk was a little better dressed than the other three. He said, "Look here, I don't know what is going on, but it's nothing to do with me. I'm a businessman. I've come over from Cuba to meet with Mr. Sharp. I run a business importing cattle into Cuba. So I'd just like to step on along. You and I got no quarrel."

Outside I heard a *Thunk*. Then another *Thunk*. That, I figured, would be Chulo cutting the hawsers.

I didn't like all those revolvers laying so handy on top of Sharp's desk. There was a little chest up against the wall just to my right. I switched my revolver to my left hand and then, without looking, lifted the lid of the chest. One by one I pitched the pistols into the chest and then shut the lid. I said, "Boys, I hate to do this, but I'm going to need your clothes. One at a time, just like with the guns, start taking off your clothes. Boots first. Go on down to your underwear. If you ain't wearing underwear, why, don't be embarrassed. Ain't everybody can afford it. I don't wear it myself as a matter of convenience. Now, you back there against the wall. Get over here to the left so I can see you. And skin down. Any derringers fall out of your boot, don't make no grab for them."

I heard another *Thunk, Thunk,* only this one sounded more distant. I figured it was Chulo cutting the hawser up near the bow. I'd be glad to have him back because my herd was getting a little unruly, especially the little man sitting at Sharp's desk. He said, "I will not take off my clothes. I tell you I am a businessman from Cuba, and I have nothing to do with this except for some cattle."

I smiled at him. I said, "Would they be cattle with hoof-and-mouth disease?"

I didn't miss the startled expression on Sharp's face, but the little man from Cuba tried to brazen it out. He said, "I don't know what you're talking about, hoof-and-mouth disease. I own a cattle company out of Houston, and I ain't going to take my clothes off!"

I said, "Stand up."

He looked at me. "What?"

I motioned with my pistol. I said, "Stand up."

He reluctantly got to his feet. He faced me, his hands in the air.

I said, "Turn around."

"What?"

"Are you deaf? Turn the hell around!"

He slowly brought his back around to me. I raised my pistol and brought the barrel down hard on the top of his head. He fell in a heap on the floor. I moved over to the right and sat down on the chest I'd put the guns in. I said, "Now, Phil, take the man's clothes off. But do it from the upper end so I can see anything that might get stuck in your hand."

I was beginning to feel the boat rock just a little more. I supposed that we were drifting. More, I hoped that Romando and Rodriquez had got tied on and were able to get aboard. Me and Chulo would be in a hell of a mess out in the middle of the ocean in a boat we didn't know how to make work.

Chulo come in about the time Sharp got the cattle agent stripped down to his drawers. He'd had no hideout gun. I had Sharp throw his clothes over in the corner next to me.

Chulo said, "Thees boad ain't here no more."

By that I took him to mean we were drifting away from the dock.

I motioned at Sharp. I said, "Take a seat, Phil. I wouldn't want you getting all wore out standing around."

Then I said to the three that were left, "Now, y'all want to go ahead and take yore clothes off or you want the same treatment this here poor fellow got?"

Sharp said, "Does that include me?" He was still badly uneasy, but he was starting to get his feet back under him a little.

I said, "Why, hell no, Phil. A man of your dignity? Wouldn't think of it. Besides, I know you wouldn't have no hideout gun hid in your clothes. But I don't know these other gents like I know you."

I waited while the three men undressed one at a time. We came up with two knives that looked like they could do a body some harm, so Chulo took them in hand and I had him pitch them in the chest with the guns. Only one of the men wasn't wearing any underwear, and I let him put his pants back on once we'd checked to make sure he wasn't carrying anything he might hurt himself with.

Sharp said, "Look here, Wilson, I wish you'd tell me what you're planning. I know we can come to some sort of arrangement. Let's don't let this matter go too far before we talk it over."

I said, "Oh, we're going to have us a powwow, Phil. You can bet on that. But first I got to get matters all arranged. Chulo," I said, indicating the door to what Romando had said was the eating room, "step over there and see what's in that room."

I was beginning to feel the boat rock and sway just a little more with every passing moment. We were very obviously not there no more, as Chulo might have said.

He went into the room. I could see it was dark. Then I saw the flare of a match, and the room filled with light as he lit a lantern. He came out in a moment, shrugging. He said, "Es a table. Es sum chairs. *Nada mas.*"

"Any other doors out of there?"

He shook his head no.

"How about windows?"

"Choust leetle round ones."

I said, "All right, blow that lantern out. Then step back out here and help me escort these gents in to dinner."

I directed the two that were standing in front of the bunk in their underwear to get hold of the cattle exporter and drag him into the dining room. The one I'd let put his pants back on led the way. When they were all inside the room, I shut the door and locked it and put the key in my pocket. Then I walked back over to Sharp's desk, shoved my revolver back in its holster, and dragged around the chair that the cattle dealer had been sitting in, so that I was face-to-face with Sharp. With all that had been happening, I hadn't had a real good chance to study him closely. I looked at him across the desk. It was hard to believe that he was a man who'd robbed me, shot me, and then kept my life in a turmoil for going on close to two weeks. He looked like a chubby little businessman who gave to charity and went to church and who you could trust with your last dollar. His hair was a little thin on top, and his belly was straining the buttons of his vest, but his jolly little round face said you'd never want to meet a nicer person.

It made him nervous me staring at him like that. He took a handkerchief out of his coat pocket and wiped his hands. I guessed they were getting a little damp.

I said, "Got anything else in that coat, Phil?"

He shook his head. "No, not really. Not anything of interest. My wallet, but it hasn't much money in it."

I said, "I was thinking more about that little .32-caliber pistol of yours. Wonder where that is. I got just an over-powering curiosity about that gun."

He said, "I—"

There came a knock at the door. I got up quickly, drawing my revolver as I did. Chulo flattened himself against the wall. I put my ear to the door. The knock came again. Romando said, "Señor Wilson!"

I breathed a sigh of relief. They were on board. I said, to Chulo, "Watch our friend there. Let me step outside and talk to Romando for a moment."

Romando started to say something, but I cut him short. I said, "Damn you, boy, what did you mean sneaking back aboard this boat? You could have got us all killed!"

He said, "No, no, no. That was not the way of it. I watched from the dock while you and Señor Chulo searched the deck. I saw that you did not notice the galley. I could see from the dock that someone was cooking in it. I could see the smoke rising. I think you were too close. So I ran back to my boat and got my *pistole* and went to the galley to make a prisoner of the man that was cooking in there."

"What happened?"

He looked down at the floor. He said, "He took the *pistole* away from me. I had forgotten it was not double-action, and I tried to pull the trigger without cocking it. That was a mistake."

I tried not to laugh. I said, "Well, it worked out for the best. Did you and Rodriquez get aboard all right?"

He said, "Oh, yes, I threw a line over the stern before I

left the ship. We climbed up that and my boat is in tow."

I suddenly became aware of my surroundings. I was on deck, looking back toward the harbor. The lights seemed a long ways off. I said, "How are we doing?"

Romando said, "We are trying to get a little sail up. Soon we will be in the Gulf and I must get steerageway. Rodriquez and I can handle it for a little while, but when we are well out into the Gulf, I will have to have some help to get more sail up."

I said, "I'll have some help out right quick. Just as quick as Chulo and I get our business finished with Sharp so that one of us can come out and keep guard on whoever is helping you."

He said, "When do I have my chance at this Sharp?"

"Soon," I said. I patted him on the shoulder. "Soon."

I looked up at the masts. At the rear one I could see Rodriquez struggling with one of the big squares of canvas, trying to secure it. I could see it was a hard job for one man. I said, "What's that pole he's standing on?"

"The yardarm, señor. He is only going to drop those two bottom sails. That will be enough for now, but soon we will need more sail and we must have help."

"How come you ain't steering?"

"It is not necessary yet."

I said, "Did we make a clean getaway?"

He looked blank.

"Anybody chasing us?"

"Oh no," he said, shaking his head. "We are simply a ship drifting out on the tide. There are others."

I said, "I got to get back. I'll send you out some help quick as I can."

I went back into the cabin and sat down across from Sharp. I still had my revolver in my hand. He looked at it in some alarm. He said, "What are you planning, Wilson? Surely you are not going to shoot me in cold blood over some misunderstanding."

I said, "Oh, no. I ain't going to shoot you in cold blood. I'm mad as hell. My blood is about the same temperature as my temper, and it is way on up there."

He swallowed, visibly. He said, "You put the witnesses away so they couldn't see you do it."

I laughed. I said, "That bunch of crooks? Hell, I'm going to throw them overboard as soon as we get out to sea."

He was really starting to get nervous. He wiped his hands on the handkerchief several times. He said, "This is all so unnecessary."

I said, "Sharp, where is that little .32 pistol of yours?"

"I don't have it."

I motioned to Chulo. I said, "Look in his desk."

Chulo started forward, but Sharp stopped him with a trembling hand. "All right," he said. "All right." He opened a drawer, took the pistol, out and laid it in front of me. He said, "That's what you're going to shoot me with, isn't it? That's why you wanted it. Because I accidently shot you with it. You're going to shoot me with the gun I shot you with by accident."

I laughed. I said, "You mean the gun you accidently didn't kill me with. Wasn't nothing wrong with your intentions, Sharp, just your aim. You just didn't want to pay me that twenty thousand dollars you owed me because you was nearly broke. Ain't that about the size of it?"

He said, earnestly, leaning forward across his desk, "We can work something out. I have a business deal afoot that is going to make a lot of money. I'll give you half of my share. It will, in the goodness of time, make you a great deal more than what I owe you."

I laughed. I said, "You mean your hoof-and-mouth business in Cuba? I reckon you can forget that."

It was the second time I'd mentioned it, and it furrowed his brow. He said, "How . . . ?"

I was about halfway tempted to just let him keep on wondering, but I decided not to. Not out of kindness, you understand, but just to cut him down a little more. Of course I had decided not to kill him. I didn't know when I'd made the decision, but if I'd been going to kill him, I already would have done so. Or at least I wasn't going to kill him unless he made me.

But I sure as hell intended to torment the fire out of him. I didn't intend that he should have a single second when he could relax and not be in fear of his life.

I said, "Those other two ships you've been expecting

won't be coming, Phil. Mike Hull and the rest of your vigilante outlaws are in jail."

He started. "What?"

I told him the whole story and his face got longer and longer. When I told him the part about peeling the soles off Hull's feet, he looked over at Chulo and shuddered. Chulo gave him a big grin back.

I said, "Did you take note of that young Mexican that got brought to the door? Did you recognize him?"

He frowned. He said, "I'm not sure. Maybe I did."

I said, "That's the mayor of Bodega. I'm having a hell of a time with him because he seriously wants to skin you alive, and not just the soles of your feet."

He licked his lips. His hands trembled. He said, "I've done him no wrong. I was going to buy some cattle from him. I gave him five hundred dollars."

"Yes," I said, "for six hundred cattle at ten dollars a head. Which Mike Hull was supposed to come along and pick up with them two other ships you was going to steal from a company that ain't yours anymore. Six hundred head at ten dollars a head. That's six thousand dollars that them Mexicans would never have seen. And there wouldn't have been a damn thing they could do about it because by then the whole bunch of those cattle would have been sick."

Sharp said, "Mike would have paid them the difference. I told that to that young *alcalde.*"

I said, "Where would Mike Hull have got fifty-five hundred dollars even if I hadn't got on to him?"

He said, "Why . . . from the company."

I laughed. "Bullshit. I've had quite a talk with Mr. Patterson. He ain't as dumb as you think he is. He is piecing that company out to your creditors. By law you stole this very boat we're on. No, Hull wouldn't have had any fifty-five hundred dollars to give to that village. He'd have just taken those cattle. Probably, on account of them five sick head you drove into their pens first, the people would have been glad to get rid of the cattle. But if they'd put up a squawk, Hull and his hooligans had orders to shoot the place up and rob it as well. Oh, Mr. Hull done quite a bit of talking once he got started."

Sharp didn't say anything, just watched me.

I said, "Sharp, I ain't known as a deacon in the church or even one of the choir members, but I'm a son of a bitch if I could be mean enough to cheat and starve a whole village of poor peons. Them cattle and a few dried fish was all they had to live on."

He just licked his lips and said nothing.

I said, "Sharp, you are a circular son of a bitch. A son of a bitch from any angle."

There came a banging at the dining room door. I could hear someone yelling, and I figured it was the man from Cuba and Houston and all points crooked. I pitched Chulo the key and told him to quiet the man down.

Chulo opened the door and disappeared. There was a thump and then it all got quiet again. Chulo came back in and shut and locked the door. He put the key in his pocket and then leaned back and crossed his arms.

I stared at Sharp, deliberately letting an ominous atmosphere come into the room. After a moment Sharp felt it. He said, his voice shaking, "Are you going to kill me now?"

I give him a surprised look. I said, "Phil, how could you figure such a thing?" I unbuttoned the flap of my shirt pocket and took out the deck of cards and put them in front of me. I said, "Me and you is going to play some poker."

He looked startled. He said, "Poker?"

"Yeah." I took his .32-caliber pistol and emptied the cartridges out in my hand and counted them. "Six," I said. "Good. That means we'll both have the same stake."

I put his empty gun in front of him. Then I took my revolver and emptied the bullets out of my .42-.40. Of course there were only five, since I'd used one to shoot the man who'd had Romando. I dug in my pocket and came up with a sixth. I reached across the table and put my cartridges in front of Sharp. I said, "There, that's your stake. Of course they don't fit your gun. I got your cartridges, the ones that do fit. And you got mine. Understand?"

His face was a mix of worry and wonder. He said, "No."

I said, patiently, "We're going to play one hand of five-card stud. We bet the bullets. If you win your cartridges back, you shoot me. If I win back the ones you got, the ones that fit my revolver, then I'm going to shoot you."

His eyes got as big as the open end of a coffee cup. He said, "Whaaat?"

I said, "I think we'll call this Dead Man's Poker. That sounds like a good game, don't you reckon?"

I took up the cards and began to shuffle them. "Ante up," I said. I shoved one of his .32-caliber cartridges into the middle of his desk.

He didn't move.

I said, "Goddammit, ante up!"

He said, "I don't want to play."

I said, "You ain't got no choice. Now, goddammit, ante up!"

With a shaking hand he pushed one of my .42-.40 cartridges into the middle of the desk. He said, "Why—" He cleared his throat because he had started off with a squeak. He said, "Why are you doing this?"

I stopped shuffling. I said, "Because you ain't very much of a man. In fact you remind me of what comes out of the cow when the calf is born. And I got a rule that I don't go up against nobody that ain't got a chance against me, and you wouldn't have a chance if I put a loaded revolver in your hand, cocked it for you, and gave you to the count of three before I drew. So this is all I can figure. You can play poker. Not real good, but you can play. You win your cartridges, you load your gun and shoot me. I win mine, I shoot you. Understand? I am just nearly eat alive to kill you, but I got to give you a chance."

He mopped his brow with his handkerchief. He said, "But this doesn't make any sense. Even if I win, you're not going to sit still and let me shoot you." He nodded at Chulo, who was lounging by the dining room door. He said, "He'll shoot me first."

I shook my head. I said, "No. He is not going to shoot you. He's got orders to stay out of this, haven't you, Chulo?"

"Chure," he said.

Which was a damn lie since he didn't know any more about what I was up to than Sharp did. Besides, Sharp wasn't going to win. I'd stacked the deck and I wasn't going to offer him a cut. I was going to give him two pair, queens over tens, and I was going to deal myself three jacks, catching the third jack on the last card just when Sharp's hopes were the highest.

I said, "You ready? To play for your life?"

He swallowed. His eyes were riveted on the deck in my hand. He said, "Is there no other way?"

"Nope."

"Then deal."

I gave him a card facedown, a queen, a jack myself, and then dealt him a queen faceup and gave myself a four. I said, "You're high with the queen."

He mopped his forehead and said, "I check. No bet."

I smiled at the perspiration on his forehead. I said, "Phil, I've heard the saying, but I never thought I'd see it. You are actually sweating bullets."

He swallowed and said, "Deal."

I gave him a ten and myself a jack, pairing the jack I had in the hole. I said, "Queen, ten high. Your bet."

He cautiously pushed a bullet into the pot.

"I call," I said. I flipped a .32-caliber cartridge into the middle of the desk.

I turned his fourth card. It was another ten. Now he had two pair, the queens and the tens. I gave myself a seven. Something like hope was beginning to build in his face. Two pair is a mighty good hand in five-card stud.

"Pair of tens high," I said.

Even though hope was glimmering for him, his hand was trembling badly as he pushed two cartridges forward. "Bet two," he said.

I went through a big show of looking at my hole card and then looked at what I could see of his hand. I fidgeted and acted unsure. Finally I reluctantly called his bet. I said, "Last card."

He watched it as I turned it faceup in front of him. It was a five. No full house, but then he hadn't really expected one. He was expecting the two pair to stand up.

Then I turned the jack for my fifth card, matching the one showing and the one he didn't know about what I had in the hole.

He stared at the jack and licked his lips. The odds were still on his side. Two pair was much more likely for me than three jacks, and his two pair would beat mine, which would have to be jacks high since I didn't have another card higher than a jack showing.

I put the deck down on the top of the desk. I said, "Well, now I am high for a change with two jacks. I guess I'll just bet a bullet on each one."

He looked at my hand and then at his. Then he looked at my face. He said, "What happens if I don't call?"

I said, softly, "Then I take the pot. You know that, Phil. And there are four of my cartridges in it. Guess what I'm going to do with them? First I'm going to put them in my revolver, and then I'm going to put them in you."

He said, "Then I have no choice."

"No. I don't need but one cartridge anyway."

He heaved a breath and slowly pushed his last two cartridges into the pile. He said, "What have you got?" His voice was trembling.

I watched his face. I smiled. I slowly turned over the third jack.

He went dead white in the face, his eyes riveted on that hole card that beat him.

I raked the whole pot in and then picked up my revolver and slowly began picking out my cartridges and loading my gun. When I was finished I snapped the cylinder gate closed and cocked the hammer. I said, "I'm going to shoot you slowly on account of all the bother and trouble you caused me. One bullet here, one bullet there."

He suddenly jumped up and screamed. Screamed just like a girl. "*No!*" he shouted. "*Wait! No! No!*"

CHAPTER 14

He was still yelling, "*Wait, wait, wait!*" like I was going to shoot him that instant. He had his hands up as if by raising them he would stay the bullet.

I said, "Goddammit, Sharp, shut up! They can hear you in Dallas!"

He said, "Just don't shoot until I can say something."

"Then say it, dammit!"

He was so scared that he was babbling, but it came out that he had a safe, right there in the office, with a lot of money in it, and he'd give it to me if I wouldn't kill him. He said, "But it's a combination safe. The kind you have to know the numbers. The—"

"I know," I said.

He went on, stumbling around, to make the point that he was the only one who knew the combination and that if I killed him, I'd never be able to get it open.

Well, I didn't know about that, but I said, "I don't see no safe."

He half turned toward the rear of the cabin. He said, "It's in that bulkhead there. Right behind that louver. It's a fake louver."

I looked at the wall behind him. Sure enough, right low on the wall, almost to the floor, was a little slatted louver that I figured was for ventilation. It was made out of the same wood as the rest of the cabin, teak or mahogany or whatever they used on boats. I said, "Then open it."

He put his hand in his pocket. I raised my revolver level with his chest. I said, "Careful."

"It's just a penknife," he said. He dug it out and showed it to me. "I have to pry off the louver."

I watched while he knelt by the wall and sprung the latch on one side of the louver. It was hinged on the other side. He swung it back, and I could see that it had concealed a small safe. In the middle of the front of the safe there was a knob with numbers on it. He put his hand on the knob and started to fiddle with it. Then he looked back at me and said, in a kind of anguished voice, "Please don't point that gun at me. It makes me so nervous I can't think of the combination."

I lowered the gun to my side. I was about two feet on the door side of the desk; he was about eight feet further on, at the wall. I'd already reckoned the office to be about fourteen feet square. I figured if he came out of that safe with a derringer, he wasn't going to hit me, because a derringer, even in the hands of a good shot, is only accurate up to about six feet. And he wasn't going to be dumb enough to come out shooting against two men that could make him look like a sieve before he could even draw a breath.

He fiddled with the knob, turning it first this way and then that, and finally took hold of a handle and opened the door and swung it back. He put his hand inside and then turned toward me, still kneeling, and fired. He had, indeed, had a derringer in the safe.

I was so surprised that I didn't shoot him. For the rest of my life I would never understand why I hadn't instantly brought up my revolver and gunned him down.

For a second we just stared at each other. At first I thought he'd missed me completely, but then I felt a little burning sensation at the point of my shoulder. I saw that Chulo was about to draw, and I yelled, "No, Chulo!" His hand relaxed, but he took a step toward Sharp.

Sharp and I were just staring at each other. He was still holding the derringer, and he still had one shot left in the double-barreled weapon. But the trigger pull on a derringer, especially for the second barrel, is a hard business. Sharp's hand was starting to tremble. He said, "I forgot it was in there." His voice quavered. He said, "It went off by accident."

I leveled my revolver right between his eyes. It was still cocked. I said, "Why don't you try the other barrel? The minute I see your finger tighten, I'm going to shoot."

He swallowed hard. His hand was shaking so bad the small gun fell out of his grasp. Chulo stepped over and picked it up. Sharp slowly stood up. He put his hands in the air. He said, "I swear to God it went off by accident. I was going to hand it to you, that's all. There's money in the safe. Look for yourself. A lot of money. Cash."

His whole body was trembling. I turned and looked at my shoulder. The bullet had just nicked me, barely breaking the skin. But a little blood was oozing out, and it had made a hole in my shirt.

I said, "Goddammit, Sharp, enough is enough. That's the second time you've shot me and the second time you've ruined a shirt for me. You silly son of a bitch, I wasn't even going to kill you. I was going to take you back to Galveston and see you in jail."

"What!" he said. "Not kill me?"

I wasn't listening to him. I was sighting my pistol at the side of his head. I said, "If you value your life, you'll hold real still. Don't even breathe."

I fired. The slug took off the biggest part of his left ear. He let out a high-pitched scream, clamped both hands to the left side of his head, and pitched over sideways on the floor. Blood was spurting everywhere. Ears will bleed like that, but they won't bleed long.

Chulo laughed. He said, "Es that whot chou meen when chou say chou choot my ears off?"

"Yeah," I said. I went around the desk. Sharp was rolling back and forth on the floor, screaming his head off. I said, "Hold still, goddammit, or I will kill you."

But he just kept flopping around like a fish out of water. I finally had to get him by the hair of the head and hold him still while I shot away his right ear. If he hadn't been so wild and had listened to reason, he wouldn't have got the dose of powder burns he did on account of me having to be so close.

Now he really was screaming and flopping around on the floor like a chicken with his head cut off. He didn't know which side of his head to hold, so he finally just put one hand to the remains of each ear. Blood was flying everywhere, some on my pants.

I said, to Chulo, "Unlock that door and then throw him in there with them others. I never heard such a racket in all my life."

Chulo unlocked the door and then got Sharp under the arms and dragged him over to the door and heaved him in. He shut the door. It cut down on the screaming a little but not all that much.

About that time the door from the deck opened. It was Romando. He looked around, seeing the blood, hearing the screaming. He said, accusingly, "You have kill this Sharp. You said I could take my vengeance."

I said, "He ain't dead, just nicked a little. How are we doing?"

He said, "We are almost in the Gulf. We have the wind. Now is when I need the help."

I said, "Go on back out. I'll send you some right away."

He turned to go, and I saw that he was again wearing his gunbelt. I said, "Romando!"

He turned back to me. "Señor?"

I said, "Take that goddam gunbelt off before somebody takes that gun away from you again. And I'm getting tired of telling you. Take it off and pitch it in behind that chest there. You can wear it when you get home."

He did as he was told, looking a little guilty. I never could figure out why folks who didn't know how to use a gun wanted to wear one. To me that was just an easy way to get killed.

When he left, Chulo nodded at the room he'd just slung Sharp in and said, "Why you doan keel hem?"

I said, "You ought to understand that. You know me."

He said, "Two time he chout you. Two time."

I said, "Yes, and 'two time' I 'chout heem.' Now shut up and open that door. I need some sailors."

They crowded toward the light, all except Sharp, who was laying somewhere back in the dark moaning. Mr. Cattle Broker was in the forefront. I put my hand on his chest and shoved him back. He yelled, "I demand to be put off this ship!"

I said, to the three others, "I need some sailors to help work this boat to Galveston. If you help, you'll get food and water. If you don't, you'll stay in that room in the dark and you won't get nothing. No food, no water, nothing. What about it?"

They all began to surge forward, muttering various forms of yes. I said, "One thing you better understand. Either me or that man"—I pointed at Chulo—"will be on deck at all times. You try anything, you'll get yourself killed before you can even say you're sorry. You behave and do your work, and I'll set you free in Galveston with some money in your pockets. What do you say? Do you understand?"

They nodded and said yes. I let them get their clothes and told them that they were not to come into the cabin again. I said, "You use the cookshack, or galley, or whatever you call it, but don't even touch the door of this place again. Mr. Sharp is not going to need any help. Understand?"

Chulo took them out to report to Romando, to do whatever he told them. I shut the door behind them and then went over to the safe. Sharp was right; there was a bunch of money. Some of it was in gold, but most of it was in greenbacks. It counted out to a little over fifty-two thousand dollars, including the gold. I reckoned he'd gutted the company, and I was willing to bet that he'd had partners that didn't have their names on the sign out front and who were going to be awful angry at him. And I wasn't just talking about Patterson.

I put the money back in the safe and then pushed the door to. It wouldn't lock so long as the handle was down. Then I closed the louvered door and pushed it until the latch clicked.

I checked to make sure the door was still locked on Sharp and the cattleman from Houston and then rummaged around the cabin until I found the liquor cabinet. Amongst the other varieties, Sharp was good enough to have brandy. I got out a bottle and a glass and sat down in his chair at the desk and poured myself a drink. The damn foolishness was nearly over, and I was good and tired of it. Inside the dining room somebody was yelling for water. It was probably the important cattleman, but I didn't pay him no mind. I couldn't think of any place that I would rather not be more than on a boat, out on the high seas, going down to pick up a bunch of stinking cattle and then sail further out on the high sea and pitch them overboard. I wanted to be sitting at a poker table in Del Rio with a bunch of suckers who had plenty of money and no sense and Evita waiting for me later. "Shit!" I said. I knocked my glass of brandy back. I still wasn't sure I shouldn't have killed Sharp.

We sailed on through the night. I made Chulo drink some vinegar that I'd found in the cookshack, even though he didn't want to. But I'd explained, in terms as hard as I could make them, that I couldn't afford for him to get seasick, that one of us had to be on deck and one of us in the cabin at all times. The crew behaved pretty well. There was no belligerence, but they didn't seem to exactly enjoy their jobs. I think that was mainly because they weren't real sure about who I was or where we were going or what was going to happen. The dead cook, before he'd taken time off to let Romando give him his gun, had been making a pot of stew, and we all had a little of that from time to time. It was nice out on deck with the breeze blowing and the stars against the dark sky. We were sailing closer to shore than on the trip up, and far in the distance, I could see the dark mountains rising out of the real estate of Mexico. We were sailing faster; even I could see that. Romando had predicted that we would make the voyage to Bodega in not much more than thirty hours once we got sailing. Of course we'd wasted a lot of time drifting around, getting out of the harbor and being late in getting sail up, but now we were just flying.

Dawn came up, and I let Chulo sleep awhile while I watched my crew on deck. Romando and Rodriquez spelled each other at the helm. There wasn't much for the rest of the crew to do, so I let them rest in the shade of the cookshack, or the galley, as they called it. Though why a kitchen had to be one thing on the water and another on the land was the beat of me.

I called Chulo in the afternoon to relieve me. The Important Cattleman was making such a racket about water that I finally got a jug and filled it and unlocked the door and gave it to him. He tried to push past me, but I shoved him back. Then he demanded to be let off the boat. I told him he could jump overboard for all I cared, but that he'd better be a damn good swimmer. Then he wanted to know if I realized there was a wounded man suffering in the confines of that dining cabin. I gave it as my opinion that he wasn't suffering enough.

Me and Chulo took turns, after I'd had a sleep, standing guard duty. Then, about five in the morning, Romando had the crew drop the sails and let down the anchor. We had arrived in Bodega after a passage of about thirty-one hours. Or we had arrived close to Bodega. Romando didn't want to try and dock the ship in the dark. A little after six I went in the cabin and opened the safe and got out twenty-five hundred dollars. After I closed the safe and shut the louver, I went out on deck and hunted Romando up. I got him off where nobody could see us and gave him the money. He looked down at it and counted it and said, "What is this?"

I said, "Sharp gave you five hundred. Let's say you had three hundred cattle at ten dollars a head. That's the balance."

He said, "But I didn't have three hundred head."

I shrugged. I said, "Well, put the rest down for the use of your boat and that you're going to sail us on to Galveston and taking care of our horses and one thing and another. It's your money and your town's money. Put it away in a safe place."

By good light, around seven, the beach was just working alive with people from the village. They were shouting and waving and swinging their sombreros back and forth. Romando was coming home, the conquering hero.

I didn't know how he was going to get this big ship snug up against the cattle wharf, but he had the crew put a little sail on her, got up a little speed, dropped the sails, and then set that boat up to that wharf as neatly as you please. Of course there was no end of people to grab onto the lines that got thrown to them, to pull the ship up tight against the wharf so the cattle could be loaded. Now they were really cheering Romando. He was standing by the rail waving back. I went up to him and told him he'd better go get those *vaqueros* lined out to take the cattle on board just as quick as possible because I was afraid some of our crew might desert. But he turned stubborn on me. He said, "I want to bring this Sharp out here so the people can see I didn't let him cheat them."

I sighed. It was the kind of thing I didn't see no point to, but, in a lot of ways, he was just a kid and he had been a big help to me. I said, "All right. Have your day of glory. Chulo's in the cabin. Go tell him to let you have Sharp. But don't let that other fellow out. And tell Chulo to stay in the cabin. There's still some money belongs to me in there."

I was standing back away from the rail about ten or twelve feet, reminding myself to remind Romando not to forget our horses, or rather, Justa's horses. After a minute or two Romando passed me, leading Sharp by the left arm. Lord, Sharp was a sight. I had damn near shot his ears clean off, and the stubs that were left were just blood-caked. In fact he had blood all over him. I watched Romando lead him up to the rail, displaying his trophy. Something was wrong, but it wasn't until Romando raised his right arm to cheer the crowd that I realized what it was. While he was in the cabin the fool kid had put his gunbelt back on. I guess he'd felt that was the necessary touch for the conquering hero.

I started toward them. They were only about ten feet away. But I hadn't taken but one stride when Sharp suddenly jerked Romando's revolver out of the holster. He shoved the kid away and whirled to face me. Less than six feet separated us.

Sharp's voice was hoarse. The crowd had stilled. There was no noise except me and Sharp. He said, in that hoarse voice, "Now we'll see who gets the last shot, Mr. Wilson Young. I won't miss you this time. Not at this distance."

I said, "That's an old single-action revolver. It won't fire double-action and it ain't cocked."

I could see him try to make the gun fire by pulling the trigger.

I said, softly, "You got to cock it."

He put his thumb on the hammer to pull it back, and I drew and shot him. The slug took him at about his breastbone and knocked him back into the railing. My second shot took him in the head and flipped him over the railing. He disappeared. I walked over to the side and looked down. Sharp was floating facedown in the water. The little waves were washing him under the cattle chute. Romando came over to me with his head down. He said, "I am very sorry. You warn me and you warn me and still I don't listen."

I patted him on the shoulder. I said, "That's all right. It's over now. Let's get those cattle on board, and be sure and don't forget to bring our horses too.

I walked back toward the cabin, intending to get a drink. Chulo was standing in the door. I was sure he'd seen the second shot. He said, "Chou chure take chou time."

I said, "Aw, shut up." Then I jerked my hand at the remaining occupant of the dining saloon. I said, "Throw that son of a bitch overboard. And don't give him his clothes. I don't like him."

When they were loaded, we sailed the cattle out in the ocean and dumped them.

We sailed on to Galveston with no trouble. The minute we touched the dock, our three crewmen were over the side and gone. I'd figured to give them ten or twenty dollars apiece, but they wern't waiting for nothing.

We got in about ten of the morning, and I was a little anxious to get going myself. I planned for Chulo and I to be on that noon train through Blessing and then San Antonio and finally to Del Rio. But first I had a little business to attend to. I dragged Patterson out of his office, took him aboard the ship, and showed him the safe and the money. He looked like a man who'd just had a cow lifted off his shoulders. I said, "You was going to give me twenty thousand dollars for bringing the ship back, right?"

"Yes."

"That won't be necessary," I said. "I've taken twenty-one thousand. Sharp owed me a little over twenty thousand, and I took a little more for my expenses and trouble." Then I explained to him about the twenty-five hundred dollars I'd given Romando and why. He agreed to that. I said, "So that leaves you a balance of a little over twenty-eight thousand dollars. I want you to give me a receipt for turning this money over to you."

He said, "Oh, Mr. Young, I don't know how to thank you. You may have been the saving of this company."

I said, "I don't want no thanks. I don't want nothing else except to get the hell out of here. I am in a blistering hurry to get home."

He hesitantly asked me about Philip Sharp. I just said that Mr. Sharp had come to a fitting end and wouldn't be a bother to nobody no more.

Then I tore myself away from him. Romando and Rodriquez had finished provisioning their little boat for the trip back to Bodega. We shook hands all around. Romando started to say something about thanks, but I hushed him up. I said, "Let's just leave it square all around. We'll meet again. Now, adios."

Chulo and I mounted our horses and rode hard for the train depot. It felt mighty good to have a horse between my legs again.

We didn't make the train with a whole hell of a lot of change to spare. I was just barely able to get a stock car put on for us and the horses as far as Blessing. After that me and Chulo would ride the chair cars to San Antonio and then Del Rio. I managed to get off a telegram to Justa telling him we'd be leaving his horses at the railroad stockyards in Blessing. I apologized for not returning them to his ranch, but pleaded a desperate need to get home and do a little dancing. I ended by inviting him to get down to Del Rio and see me, or maybe I'd get back up and see him. And to bring the guitar player.

I knew the railroad in Blessing would take good care of Williams horses, so I didn't feel too bad about leaving them off there.

And then, finally, we were pulling out of Galveston and heading down the line. We were on another train, but at least this one was going in the right direction. For a long time me and Chulo just rode along, staring out the car door, and smoking and drinking. Finally Chulo said, "Et was bad. The cattle."

"Yes," I said.

It had been awful. When we'd got far enough out to sea, we'd opened the big gates of the railing and herded the frightened cattle overboard. Most of them were so sick

249

they would have been dead in a few days anyway, but it was still a mighty unpleasant job. Romando had gone to his store and brought back a number of boxes of carbine cartridges. Chulo and I had leaned against the rail and, with our carbines, tried to kill as many of the cattle as we could to keep them from drowning. And then the sharks had come. The water had just turned red in every direction you could see.

Chulo said, "That es what chou chould hav done with thees Charps. Put heem over with the cattle."

I didn't say anything. There was a whole lot of the last two weeks I'd just as soon let be forgotten. And I didn't think anybody was ever going to be able to get me on a boat again.

As if he could hear what I was thinking, Chulo said, "Boads. Boads es no good."

I gave him a little salute with my brandy bottle and took a drink. I said, "Me and you wasn't made for riding on no boats. Or anything else, for that matter, that moves and that you don't need boots and spurs to stay on."

We had a few more drinks, and then Chulo raked him up a pile of straw and lay down and went to sleep. I swear that Meskin could sleep at his own hanging.

For a while I just looked out the door, smoking and drinking and watching us get closer to Del Rio. I was fairly contented with the way matters had turned out, but I still felt a little resentment towards Sharp for putting me to all the trouble he had. Of course feeling bitter at a dead man is about as useful as exercising a mule by letting him kick you in the head. But, by and large, I ain't ever been one to look over my shoulder. Once a hand is played and the winner has raked in his chips, it's time to deal again. If you still got money, you still got hope. If you ain't, it's time to go home. I'd got the money I'd had coming, and maybe I'd done a good turn or so along the way. That was enough. Besides, a little time away from home just might make me appreciate Evita all that much more. Though I doubted that.

Patterson, in the hurried discussion we'd had, had said that Sheriff Mills had arrested Mike Hull and eight others the night we'd left. They'd been busy at the task of stealing the other two boats. Patterson said the sheriff had said to pass on his thanks to me if Patterson ever saw me again. I'd asked after Bennet, but Patterson had said, so far as he knew, the man was still clear of the law. But I didn't figure that would last much longer. Sooner or later Mike Hull or one of the others would tell the sheriff that the high-toned gentleman was the brains behind the thefts on the docks.

But, hell, it was no longer my affair. My business with that gang was over and done with. All I wanted to do was get home and fleece some cardplayers who had more money than sense and get hold of Evita and turn her every way but loose. I reached around and got Chulo by the leg and gave him a good shaking. I said, "Hey! Wake up, you dumb Meskin! You hear me? Wake up!"

He came to, yawning and rubbing at his eyes. He said, "Wha'?"

I got out the deck of cards. I said, "I'm going to give you five hundred dollars against your wages, and we'll play some acey-deucey."

He said, "Why come chou always call me dumb? Chou theenk I am dumb?"

"Hell, no," I said. "I ain't even sure you're ignorant. Now here's some money. Put on your thinking cap."

He rubbed his hands together. He said, "Boy, I am goin' to beat chou theese time. I win all chou monies."

I dealt the cards. "Chure," I said.